AFTERSHOCK

RITA GIORDANO

AFTERSHOCK

TATE PUBLISHING
AND ENTERPRISES, LLC

Published by Tate Publishing & Enterprises, LLC
127 E. Trade Center Terrace | Mustang, Oklahoma 73064 USA
1.888.361.9473 | www.tatepublishing.com

Tate Publishing is committed to excellence in the publishing industry. The company reflects the philosophy established by the founders, based on Psalm 68:11,
"The Lord gave the word and great was the company of those who published it."

Published in the United States of America

ISBN: 978-1-63185-354-8
Fiction / Religious
14.04.22

I must acknowledge the many hours of help and the support from my publisher, editors and family. Thank you all. You are wonderful!

CONTENTS

MY DISCLAIMER

Dear Friend,

I must insert this disclaimer for the sake of those wonderful men and women of God who are working hard to fight the good fight for Christ. Please do not assume I am drawing my characters from anyone I know or have heard of. They are strictly from my imagination.

Prophesies of the Bible are always dependable. Most have already come to pass. I believe we are now very near the return of Jesus Christ. His return could happen today. I pray you will be inspired to read and study the Word of God on your own. I hope what you read here will set your heart on fire and ignite your time with God.

I pray, as you prepare yourself for the soon coming of Jesus, you will evaluate your own relationship with Christ and take advantage of the opportunity to turn everything in your life over to him. It is my desire that you attend the great and wonderful catching away of the church where we will meet Jesus in the air! I look forward to seeing you there! I pray God's hand will be on you.

Much love in Christ,
Rita Giordano

PROLOGUE

The Rapture

Pastor Jentson looked at his reflection in the mirror. He absent-mindedly wrapped one end of his tie around the other, something that after years of practice took no thought at all. He considered the previous day's sermon, one he personally enjoyed delivering very much. After the usual worship music, they concluded the series of songs with "We Shall See the King" by John B. Vaughan. The words so dear to his heart exploded in a whirl of praise set to melody:

> We shall see the King, we shall see the King,
> We shall see the King when He comes;
> He is coming in pow'r, we'll hail the blessed hour,
> We shall see the King when he comes.

The church began to explode with every note of each word. The joyous melody rang through the congregation. Both young and old alike rejoiced at the thought of the rapture of the church.

Pastor Jentson loved the old hymns; but, out of consideration for the young people and those who saw them as too outdated, he felt compelled to usher in a more contemporary music program. However, this time the church seemed to be electrified by the song. Age and background were set aside as the moment grew charged with a supernatural electricity that rocked the congregation.

Suddenly, Pastor Jentson was shaken from his thoughts. At that moment, all over the world, time stopped. The sound of a trumpet pierced the air. The graves and the sea gave up their dead! They were transformed: their now glorified, perfectly beautiful bodies were not scarred by sickness, disease, or even death! They were celestial bodies that were renewed to be like Christ. They looked up. They could see him coming in the clouds! Unhindered by earth's weights they rose toward heaven in full view of those who, like them, were also transformed.

Pastor Jentson and multitudes of others all over the world were captivated by the beautiful blast of the trumpet. The sound was something right out of heaven! The blast pierced the vale between the heavens and those who followed Christ upon the earth. Changed in the twinkling of an eye, their bodies, once mortal, became immortal; they soared up. Up through the ceilings of their homes, businesses, cars, trains, buses and airplanes, up into the atmosphere of the heavens they ascended. They were no longer bound to this earth by the confines of humanity. In an instant they changed, fulfilling the Scriptures that say, "Behold, I shew you a mystery; We shall not all sleep, but we shall all be changed, In a moment, in the twinkling of an eye, at the last trump: for the trumpet shall sound, and the dead shall be raised incorruptible, and we shall be changed" (1 Corinthians 15:51–52).

In front of them standing on a cloud was the King of kings—Jesus—the Savior of mankind! A crown of gold rested on his head. Angels flanked the path into glory. They rejoiced singing praises to the Lord. As they ascended, the transformed heard the sound of rejoicing, clearly coming from those who were standing just inside the gates of the eternal kingdom. There a party of unequaled measure was about to take place.

The men, women, and children of the rapture looked up to see a sight of inexpressible beauty. Their eyes watched as the gates of pearl opened wide to receive them. The streets of gold glistened, reflecting the colors of heaven. In the distance they caught a glimpse of the crystal sea. People of heaven waved to them as they entered. They were greeted with hugs and kisses by their loved ones.

Pastor Jentson saw the King of kings, the Lord of lords, the Alpha and Omega, the Beginning and the Ending! There, in that split second of time, every dream he had ever dreamed came true! The reality of the greatest event of all time was taking place. He was being supernaturally transformed from life to eternal life! There was no death, no sorrow, and no sting; there was the almighty presence of our soul-saving Savior and our God of unmatchable beauty. There heaven welcomed him and all those Christians who had faithfully followed the Lord Jesus. For them eternity had begun!

THE DAY JESUS CAME

Carly was on her way to work. The sun beat brightly onto the windshield as she drove. She grabbed her sunglasses and placed them on her face. The day had started off as any other, except she was late. She had dashed into the local coffee shop, where she picked up her favorite coffee and a bagel.

She was maneuvering her way back onto the freeway when she noticed there was an excessive amount of traffic. A car nearly hit her as it careened out of control to the side of her. She quickly moved toward the shoulder. "What was that?" she asked dumbfounded as she looked and saw there was no driver in the car. Stunned but unharmed, she noticed the freeway was littered by wrecked, and in some cases, abandoned cars.

In front of her she could see a small airplane. It howled loudly. Falling from the sky it crashed into a building exploding into a fireball. Her heart pounded hard in her chest. "Dear God," she whispered.

Dragging her attention back to the freeway, she tried to focus. In the distance she could see smoke billowing up from one of the vehicles in front of her. She could hear the sound of horns as people everywhere blasted them in rage and confusion. She noticed many cars in front of her were wrecked. She gasped as she watched in her rearview mirror one vehicle after another hit each other forming a pileup. She couldn't believe the mess. The continuing honking only served to give her a headache. Softly she pleaded with the other drivers, "Please, everybody, just stop honking."

Completely stopped she assessed the situation. This was the worst pileup she had ever seen. She knew she was not going to be able to make her appointment. She quickly dialed the office to let Carolyn know she would be late, "Hi, Carolyn. Yes, I'm here stuck in traffic. I don't know what is happening. There are wrecks and pileups everywhere! It's horrible. No, I'm not injured, but I'm in the middle of a pileup. This is a nightmare. What?"

She listened as the girl on the other end of the phone spoke, "Haven't you heard? Girl, it just happened. The news says we have been attacked. I'll—"

Hummmmmm. The line went dead.

"Hello, Carolyn, are you there? What do you mean, 'we've been attacked'? Hello?" Much to her frustration there was no answer! *Attacked?* Her mind reeled, wanting more informa-tion. She turned on the radio. For some reason it was difficult to understand the broadcast. Carly was unnerved. "What is going on?" she asked herself as she studied her options.

Looking to her extreme left she noticed the traffic in the lanes going the opposite direction were also piled up in much the same way. Her mouth flew open as she watched accidents continue to happen everywhere, like falling dominoes.

She noticed some of the other drivers were using the shoulder of the freeway to exit. She looked ahead. From here she could see there were several wrecked cars. She slowly picked her way to the shoulder of the right lane. Eventually she was among the other vehicles trying to exit the freeway. Her left tires hit the cuts in the pavement edge causing them to bump as she moved along.

From below the exit ahead of her she could see the traffic lights flashing on and off. Her heart pounded as she maneuvered around the stopped traffic. Thank goodness she wasn't trapped in one of the inside lanes. "This is crazy," she commented to herself. She moved slowly using the shoulder of the road as much as possible. When necessary she moved off the pavement onto the gravel. It looked to her as if the pileups were unending.

Thinking back on her call to Carolyn, she raised her forehead into a frown. *What has happened?* Her heart pumped furiously as her mind raced for an answer. She drove up behind a parked car. She moved to the right of it, squeezing past the automobile. She stared at it, stunned; to her bewilderment there was no driver. She noticed the passenger in the car, an older woman who was still wearing her seatbelt. The woman watched her drive by with an expression of complete confusion on her face.

Finally off the freeway, she pulled into a local mini-mart. The place was packed with people. There were cars everywhere. She had to know what had happened. Unbuckling her seatbelt, she picked up her oversized lime-green designer bag. The contrast was beautiful with her outfit. Her shoes were strikingly elegant, more to her usual good taste. Reluctant to leave it, she grabbed her coffee. She opened the door of her car. The little bell rang softly as she moved to get out. She was the picture of sophistication. Her long dark hair fell straight and sleek down the middle of her back. Her large brown eyes were covered by her sunglasses. She was barely five feet four inches, but with her heels, she looked five foot six. She reached for the mini-mart door; it opened from the inside. "Thank you," she said as a man held the door open for her.

He smiled back. "It's a little crowded in here," he said, almost apologizing.

She removed her sunglasses, placing them on the top of her head. Her gold hooped earrings swung as she adjusted her glasses. The clerk inside had on the local news. Everyone in the mini-mart stopped to listen.

Charlie, the local news reporter, spoke as if he was traumatized. He mentioned mass disasters around the country. She caught her breath; the cup in her hand began to shake as she heard the report. "It's true; we have received confirmation. The aircraft simply plummeted to the ground." The reporter was clearly upset. The screams of the people in the general area of the plane could still be heard. She watched as the reporter made a sweeping motion with his hand, "There are reports coming in of vehicles suddenly being unmanned. No one has any answers." Charlie stopped to listen to a colleague. "That's right, Karen. There are also abandoned big rigs. Some of them have turned over and are blocking traffic. It's hard to comprehend what has happened. You just have to see it to believe it."

Karen continued to cover the breaking news. "We have been receiving reports of missing people. Many schools have reported children missing. Coworkers are saying that people they were sitting next to or standing beside just disappeared. The county jails and prison officials are saying they have inmates unaccounted for. They are asking people to be careful. They are unsure at this time if the prisoners have escaped or if they are also some of those who have disappeared. The most bizarre reports are that some graves have been disturbed. Eyewitness reports say that many of the graves have spontaneously erupted, leaving them opened. Their remains are also missing. It is unknown what has happened to the bodies at this time. The National Guard has been called in."

Carly couldn't breathe. The room started to spin. The man next to her looked at her. His face showed that he was worried, "Miss, are you all right?"

She raised her hand to her head, trying to get control of herself. "Yes, thank you. I'm just a little unnerved." Suddenly her coffee seemed sickening. She was definitely becoming ill. *Get a hold of yourself,* she thought. She dropped her coffee into a nearby trash and quickly dialed her mom. Nothing, not even a dial tone. She tried again—still nothing! "Mom, please answer!" she begged. This time she heard the phone ringing. No one answered. A very real pain struck her heart. She was quickly moving into a panic attack.

She dialed her auntie, "Hello, this is Sue Strom. Please leave a message at the sound of the beep. God bless." The words on the machine sang up the scale as she listened to the familiar sound of her auntie's voice. She was not in.

Carly dialed her boyfriend. He answered immediately, "Hi, Carly."

"John, what is going on? Are you all right?"

"I'm fine, babe; I've been trying to call Dad."

Remembering her dropped call to Carolyn, she asked, "Was he there?" She held her breath, praying that John had talked to his father, Pastor Jentson.

John answered, "No, I haven't been able to reach him or Mom."

"John," the desperate tone of her voice spoke volumes. "I can't reach Mom or Auntie Sue either!"

"That doesn't mean anything. There's a lot of confusion going on. Maybe they're all out trying to help people." John tried his best to sound calm.

"John, I'll try Nanna; she never goes anywhere but to church. I'll call you right back." She immediately dialed her grandmother. The machine picked up.

She dialed John, "She's not in either."

They both panicked. Fighting to remain calm, John asked, "Have you called anyone at work? Did Carolyn pick up?"

"Yes." She started to cry. "The news is on here; they say an entire school of children is missing. The teachers said the kids just disappeared!" Her voice was shrill as she finished her statement. "Oh, John, I think it happened. I think Jesus has raptured out his church!"

John choked back the tears. He didn't want to upset her more, so he tried to remain calm. "Where are you? I'm coming to get you or..." thinking it over, he asked, "Honey, can you make it to where I am? We'll go and look for them together."

Carly took in her location. "I think I can make it to the church from here. Can you?" she asked.

John agreed to meet her at the church. "Promise me you'll wait till I get there. I may be a while; if I arrive first I'll wait for you."

"I'll wait," she promised, sobbing into the phone. "John, what are we going to do?"

She sounded so desperate. He wanted to comfort her but didn't know what to say. "I'll be there soon, honey; don't worry. We're in this together."

She walked, shaken, back to her car. She did not notice the sun shining brightly, welcoming the day, nor the clear blue of the sky. She did not glance at the paint or the sleek shape of her vehicle. She opened the door and sank into the luxurious comfort of her beautiful Mercedes. This was her latest toy. She had worked hard always reaching for something new. She was never satisfied. She longed for more of everything. Now it only served to remind her of her foolishness. Her hand reached for a tissue as she started to cry again. Leaning her head back against the headrest, she waited, giving herself a moment to regain control.

She turned the key in the ignition, and the engine purred to life. Carefully she picked her way through the maze of confusion. The stoplights were all flashing. There were several cars that had been wrecked all along the streets. She noticed a burgundy car, with no one in it, just stopped in the middle of the road.

A young lady flagged her down. She was hysterical. "I don't know where my baby is! He was in his seat a few minutes before I hit the car in front of me. I looked back to check on him." Her body shook with sobs as she tried to speak. "He's gone!"

Carly tried to help her, but in her heart Carly knew Jesus had returned. She believed this mother would not find her child. Carly recalled Pastor Jentson once saying the youngest children would be gone. He stunned her when he explained to the church that the innocent children would not be left behind when Jesus returned. She took the young woman's phone number and asked if she could call to check with her later. She agreed.

Carly drove on toward the church, making her way down alleyways and through parking lots, avoiding the main roads as much as possible. Finally she saw the little building. She had attended Faith Fellowship all of her life. She and John had met there. They always knew they would be together. But they had chosen to take a different path than their parents had wanted for them.

John had avoided the ministry like the plague. Carly was thrilled. She did not want to be a pastor's wife. She wanted to climb the corporate ladder. John was far too talented to waste his time in some broken-down little church, tending to people who did not appreciate him. He was an artist. His music was far too important for him to be stuck here, in this city, with no real future. But now, as she considered their life's goals, it all seemed pretty empty. The things she had valued only moments ago now seemed so very insignificant.

She saw John's car parked near the church. He saw her coming and walked toward her. His normally handsome face was pale with fear. His beautiful dark hair curled out of control. Reaching down, he opened her door. She could see he had been crying. His blue eyes still held unshed tears.

The look on his face spoke volumes. Her heart sank. "John." His name entered the air and dropped. She knew they were in trouble.

He took her in his arms. "I'm sorry, babe. I can't find anyone. They're all gone." Dropping his head, he cried into her hair. She broke down, clinging to him as if he were her lifeline. They allowed themselves to grieve, not apologizing for their pain. At that moment they understood the depth of each other's regret. No words were necessary.

After a few minutes he pulled her toward the church. "We need to talk." He took her into his father's office and let her hear the many messages. Person after person had called the church looking for their loved ones. Carly noted that, coincidentally, all of the missing people were faithful followers of Christ. She sat with a tissue in her hand, wiping the tears that continued to flow. The message box was full of those messages. There were also calls from local associations trying to confirm that the church could still be used to care for people who needed help during a crisis.

John took down all of the messages and numbers. He called the local authorities first. "Hello, I am John Jentson. My father was the pastor of Faith Fellowship Church. Many of our own members are also missing, but we will do everything possible to help the community, as was arranged between you and my father."

Carly listened as John explained to the voice on the phone. "Jesus has returned. He has taken his church and we are left. I know it is hard to believe, but that is what happened. Why didn't I go? Well, honestly, sir, I wasn't ready. You see, only the people who actually had a real relationship with Christ are the ones who have been taken. That's right; I have not been living a Christian life. No, sir, just going to church does not count. If it did, I can assure you that I would not be here now. It seems to me I've spent my life here in this church. Unfortunately I have not been willing to live the life. When a person loves Jesus, they allow him to live through them." John tried to control his grief. Carly watched as his hand came up to wipe away tears. "Maybe I can make myself a little clearer. It is like a guy who is married. He may wear the ring and go home to his wife, but secretly he actually cheats on his spouse. That's not much of a marriage. God expects us to do more than simply show up. He expects Christians to love him without reservation. I was more like the cheating spouse. I just didn't commit my life fully to that relationship."

John turned to blow his nose on a piece of tissue Carly handed him before he continued. "If you want to come by, I can explain the rapture to you in more detail. You know, show you what the Bible says. Any time, just call me, I'll be happy to talk to you. Here, take down my cell number." John gave the man his number and continued to call everyone on the list, explaining to each person the same thing. He ended up agreeing to call an emergency meeting at the church to answer all of their questions.

Carly sat quietly. It had happened in no more than a couple of hours: John changed from being a young man determined not to follow in his father's footsteps to being exactly like his father.

He was the man his father had prayed he would be, and at this moment the man every one needed. She listened for a while and then started helping with the callbacks. She tried to explain as well as she could.

When they stopped calling, they just stared at each other. They both knew things had to change between them. They couldn't go on the way they were living.

"Carly," he started to say it out loud, but she didn't want to hear it.

"No, don't say it. I can't lose you too."

"Then we only have one choice. I can't ignore God any longer. I have to change my direction. If you want our relationship to work, you have to understand that. I can't live with myself if I don't make things right with God." The look on his face told her he was completely serious.

She nodded her head. "I know, me too. I keep thinking of all the times my mom tried to tell me." Tears filled her large brown eyes then started to run down her face. "I just want us to work it out together. I don't want to lose you because of this." An unthinkable question swam its way into her consciousness. "Do you hate me?"

"No, I don't hate you; I love you." he said.

"But I kept you from following the Lord. I was the one who held you back," she insisted, trying to apologize.

"No, you weren't. I held myself back. I have no one to blame but me. I knew better; I chose to follow you instead of God. You wanted so much, and I wanted to please you. I made the decision to put off God. It just caught up with me." He dropped his head as he choked on the words. "I knew better."

She persisted, "I was wrong to keep you from following the Lord. I feel so bad. If I hadn't interfered, you would be gone." She looked into his piercing blue eyes. For a second she could see he agreed with her.

Then he shook his head. "No, I did it to myself. Satan may have used you to influence me, but I let myself be led away from the Lord. You are not to blame. If I had been more committed I could have convinced you to live a Christian life, and we would both be gone. We can't allow ourselves to blame each other. We both knew what we were doing.

I think it is the Lord's mercy that neither of us died in one of the traffic accidents. I know I would not be in heaven. We have a lot between us and the Lord. I intend to straighten things out. From hereon, Carly, I'm going to do what is right. If you are willing to join me, wonderful; if not, I am never going to choose anyone over the Lord again. We have to change our lifestyles. I intend to obey the Lord."

She studied the young man she loved so deeply. He was right. Jesus had returned and nothing was going to change that. They had lost their way in life. They had no choice but to get back on track with God. His blue eyes told the story. He was not up for games. She noticed the stubborn set of his jaw. Yesterday he was pliable, but today he was different. In the last few hours he had been transformed into a leader. He looked at her with fire in his eyes. His determination was such that she knew if she did not choose every word very carefully, no matter how much he loved her, she would be out of his life for good. "I understand. I agree with you." She noticed the look of doubt on his face. "I'm not just saying it. I agree. All of the things I wanted yesterday are nothing to me today."

Then she said something she did not mean to say. "I want you to be happy. I would rather be out of your life and know you are doing the things you need to do, than be in your life hindering you." *Wow,* she thought. *I just said something completely unselfish. I am facing the worst day of my life and I mean it. I don't want him unhappy. I'll do whatever he needs me to do.* She continued out loud, "I want to marry you. But if you aren't sure about us, I'll move away and get completely out of your life. I don't think I can stay near you and not see you." She ended her statement. Their eyes locked as they studied each other. Carly turned her head; she did not want him to see her cry. She wanted to let him go with as much dignity as she could muster.

He knelt in front of her. She looked at him. He took her hands folded tightly on her lap and unfolded them. He watched the gold flecks in her brown eyes catch the light. "I just want you to be sure you want to serve the Lord."

She nodded. "Of course I'm sure. I may be stubborn, selfish, and a little self-absorbed, but I'm not stupid. I have no intention of going to hell if I can avoid it. I need God. When I realized Jesus had returned for his church and I was left behind, my heart started to ache. I don't know if I will ever feel normal again. For the first time in my life I understand I can't do it by myself. I can't be efficient enough, or good enough, or even smart enough to make it without Jesus!"

He shook his head up and down agreeing with her. "It's time to pray." She watched as he walked to the office door, opened it, and held it for her. They walked together to the altar of the little church. It wasn't like the benches the old timers used. It was just the steps up to the platform, but for Carly and John this was holy ground. She knelt beside him.

"Jesus," the words poured out of him from somewhere deep in his being. "We need deliverance from sin. We are both late in asking, but we need your forgiveness. We know we should have been ready. Please, Lord, forgive our rebelliousness. Wash away our sin and turn our lives around, change us. Show us how to be like you."

Carly started to pray with him. "Yes, Jesus, we need you to forgive us. Lord, I've made such a mess of my life. I thought we were on top of everything, that we were successful and doing well; but we weren't. We failed to be ready for you to come back. We lost out on your deliverance, but we don't want to lose out on your mercy. Please forgive our sins and cleanse us from all evil."

They prayed for a long time, each taking time confessing their own sin, asking God to intervene in their current situation and show them how to go on.

People had started to come into the church, but they were oblivious. John had left the front door open for anyone who needed refuge or just wanted to pray. The people heard their prayer and joined them. The house of God filled up. People kept coming even after all of the pews were filled. They were kneeling in the aisles and some were lying prostrate in front of the pulpit.

There was a group of teenagers who had congregated near one side of the sanctuary. Carly noticed the frightened looks on their faces. She felt tremendous compassion for the young people near her. One young man wore a black jacket with silver studs and dark makeup; his hair, died black, was jelled to stand up and out from his head. She looked into his tearstained face. Her heart melted. She ran to him and put her arms around him. He clung to her, sobbing big uncontrollable sobs. "My mom's gone." He kept saying it over and over again. She held him, offering comfort. As she did, she looked around; near him was a young girl, also dressed in black, with black makeup, a nose ring, and several other rings in various places. She looked lost and scared. Carly reached for her and embraced her too. Without thinking about it, she made her way to each of the young people she saw. They ranged in age from what looked to be about thirteen and up. She spoke words of comfort and love to all of them. As she did, John made his way to the pulpit. He raised his voice to speak.

One of his band members quickly moved to the sound board. He motioned to John to pick up a microphone, and immediately John's voice was coming through the speakers loud and clear.

"As many of you may already know, we have been left behind. The Lord Jesus"—he stopped to clear his throat and wipe the tears from his eyes—"has come, and we are the ones he did not take with him. I have been asked by the local authorities to leave this building open for the needs of the community. Many of the people here already understand what has happened. Many don't."

Carly watched him, mesmerized. Where had this man been all these years? As she listened, he spoke with such eloquence she was captivated. He didn't miss a beat. He showed no signs of stage fright. He was transformed into God's man for this time in the world. She couldn't say she had ever actually known this man at all. She felt embarrassed as she realized she had held him back. He was incredible. She had never been prouder of him than she was at this moment. A pang of guilt stirred her heart. *If only Mom and Dad Jentson could have seen him,* she thought.

The young people she had been comforting watched as he went through the Scriptures flawlessly. They barely moved. They listened to every word. His countenance was unusually intense as he explained their position.

"For those of you who have your Bibles, I am reading from 1 Thessalonians 4:16–18. I have the King James Version. I will have to cover a lot of Scripture in order to show you what the Bible says has happened and what that means to us who are still here. Please read with me."

> For the Lord himself shall descend from heaven with a shout, with the voice of the archangel, and with the trump of God: and the dead in Christ shall rise first: Then we which are alive and remain shall be caught up together with them in the clouds, to meet the Lord in the air: and so shall we ever be with the Lord. Wherefore comfort one another with these words.

John stopped to explain. "You see, the Lord foretold the coming of Christ many times in the Word. For example, turn with me to 1 Corinthians 15:51–53,"

> Behold, I shew you a mystery; We shall not all sleep, but we shall all be changed, In a moment, in the twinkling of an eye, at the last trump: for the trumpet shall sound,

and the dead shall be raised incorruptible, and we shall be changed. For this corruptible must put on incorruption, and this mortal must put on immortality.

John stopped and looked up. The intense expression on his face reflected his sincerity. "I think this passage is important. It explains that the dead in Christ rose first. This is why the graves were disturbed and abandoned."

John waited for the room to quiet. The stirring of people as he read the Word was both heart-wrenching and expected. Some were starting to moan, others sobbed quietly to themselves. Many of the people looked worried and confused. His heart went out to all of them as he started again. "These two texts speak of what is known in the church world as the rapture. It is referred to, in the Bible, as the catching away. God has removed his followers from the earth." The listeners shifted uncomfortably, looking around at their neighbors.

"The Bible interprets, backs up, and confirms itself. You may be wondering, "Has this happened before?" or "Is it an isolated incident?" Well, it has happened in the past but not to so many at once. The Old Testament records two such events. At that time the people who were taken were individuals. Let's take a look at them. Turn with me to Genesis 5:21–24. You will notice the terminology the Bible uses: the word *begat*. That simply means they fathered the person listed."

And Enoch lived sixty and five years, and begat Methuselah: And Enoch walked with God after he begat Methuselah three hundred years, and begat sons and daughters: And all the days of Enoch were three hundred sixty and five years: And Enoch walked with God: and he was not; for God took him.

The sound of understanding went through the congregation. Many gasped as he read the words "for God took him." It was hard for people to remain silent. Murmuring scattered through the room as many repeated these words.

John continued, "Now, let's examine Elijah. This dynamic prophet was a powerhouse in his day. He ministered to the children of Israel. The Lord used him to warn that nation of their sin. Great signs accompanied his ministry. He had a servant named Elisha. They are two different men. He trained Elisha to continue the work of the Lord after he was gone. Turn with me to 2 Kings 2:5, 6, and 11, and it says,"

> And the sons of the prophets that were at Jericho came to Elisha, and said unto him, Knowest thou that the LORD will take away thy master from thy head today? And he answered, Yea, I know it; hold ye your peace. And Elijah said unto him, Tarry, I pray thee, here; for the LORD hath sent me to Jordan. And he said, As the LORD liveth, and as thy soul liveth, I will not leave thee. And they two went on.

Please drop down to verse 11.

> And it came to pass, as they still went on, and talked, that, behold, there appeared a chariot of fire, and horses of fire, and parted them both asunder; and Elijah went up by a whirlwind into heaven.

John looked up from his Bible. His gaze was intense. He scanned the faces of the individuals he was speaking to. "You are probably asking yourselves, 'Why would God take these people now?' The Bible also tells us, through Bible prophesy, about this time that we are living in. The Word explains in Matthew 24:5–14. Jesus is speaking,"

> For many shall come in my name, saying, I am Christ; and shall deceive many. And ye shall hear of wars and rumours of wars: see that ye be not troubled: for all these things must come to pass, but the end is not yet. For nation shall rise against nation, and kingdom against kingdom: and

there shall be famines, and pestilences, and earthquakes, in divers places. All these are the beginning of sorrows.

Again, John stopped reading long enough to say, "I believe we can all pretty much agree that we are living in a time when all of these things have been happening. Now let's read on."

Then shall they deliver you up to be afflicted, and shall kill you: and ye shall be hated of all nations for my name's sake. And then shall many be offended, and shall betray one another, and shall hate one another. And many false prophets shall rise, and shall deceive many. And because iniquity shall abound, the love of many shall wax cold. But he that shall endure unto the end, the same shall be saved. And this gospel of the kingdom shall be preached in all the world for a witness unto all nations; and then shall the end come.

John stopped to explain more to the people. "My friends, I am sorry to have to tell you, the times ahead are going to be terrible. The Bible also speaks of those who will be martyred for the sake of the gospel."

"The Bible tells us of a man who will rise to world power. Mankind will look to him as the answer to all of the world problems. They will even worship him as god. This man is the Antichrist. He will impose a mark that people will be forced to accept before they can buy or sell. This mark is an abomination to God. Anyone who takes this mark will be condemning himself or herself to eternal damnation." A gasp of surprise went through the crowd. John waited for the crowd to come to order. "If we do not take this mark we will be beheaded for the cause of Christ. Turn with me to Revelation 20:4. Please read with me."

And I saw thrones, and they sat upon them, and judgment was given unto them: and I saw the souls of them that were beheaded for the witness of Jesus, and for the word of God, and which had not worshipped the beast, neither his image, neither had received his mark upon their foreheads, or in their hands; and they lived and reigned with Christ a thousand years.

The young preacher looked up from his Bible. His face showed the strength of his conviction. "They will try to starve us out. They will come against us by not allowing us to buy or sell. Finally they will be determined to kill us. But if we do not turn from the Lord, the Word says, 'We will live and reign with Christ.' I will go into this further tomorrow night; please come back then."

"The people who have gone on to be with the Lord were raptured out of the trials to come. They were as Noah and Lot—two men God saved from punishment. Those who have been raptured were delivered before judgment and before the terrible time when the Antichrist will set up his throne in Jerusalem, declaring that he is God. You see, the Word tells us in 1 Thessalonians 5:9–10: "For God hath not appointed us to wrath, but to obtain salvation by our Lord Jesus Christ, Who died for us, that, whether we wake or sleep, we should live together with him."

"People who were following God with all of their hearts were not destined for the wrath to come. If you are interested in studying about Noah and Lot, you can read about their experiences in Genesis 7 and 8. Noah was delivered from the flood by the mighty, awesome power of God. And there is also Genesis 19 where God delivers Lot, the nephew of Abraham, from the judgment of Sodom and Gomorrah. I urge you to read these scriptures for yourself. I will make a list of the scriptures you will want to study. I will try to have them for you tomorrow. If you like, you can come by the church and pick them up, or leave your e-mail and I will e-mail them to you. Also I want to add one more thing. I believe there is coming a day soon when we will not be allowed to have a Bible. I intend to hide mine. I think the last thing the Antichrist will want is for people to understand what is really going on."

Carly listened as John expounded the Word using these two men as an example. In the end he gave an altar call inviting everyone to come forward and pray with him. Carly watched as the altar filled up and spilled over into the aisles. The young man she had first comforted was one of the first to move to the altar. He bowed himself as tears ran down his face. John joined him and started praying for him. He seemed to open the path for others. Soon all of the young people were going to the front. One of the young girls asked her if she would go with her. "I'm afraid. I don't know what to say."

Carly walked with the girl to the front of the sanctuary. Carly looked at her new young friend. "It's simple; all you do is talk to him; he listens to you. He doesn't care how you say it. All you have to do is talk to him like he's your best friend. Sometimes words won't come. He can even hear your heart." After that, she stayed to help with anyone who wanted prayer.

That night the church did not close down. No one was in a hurry to get home. The only thing anyone was interested in was calling on the Lord.

A FAMILY TORN APART

Carly didn't know it, but in the back of the church was a man she had crossed paths with that morning. His name was Brad Holden. He had also been on the freeway at the same time as Carly.

Brad thought back on his day. He had rushed out of the house, barely saying good-bye to his wife. "Sarah, I've got to go," he said. She smiled at him; her belly was swollen with their second child. He quickly kissed her, patted her stomach and said, "I'll see you tonight." She watched as he left. He gave her the familiar wave good-bye and he was off.

He entered the freeway at precisely the same moment the woman in front of him had some kind of attack. Brad swerved his truck with the quickness of a man in his prime. Unfortunately his coffee spilled all over his lap, burning him, as he drove his truck to the shoulder. "What on earth?" he could not believe his eyes. There was one car after another piling up on the freeway. He watched as the disaster continued. "Dear God!" he cried as they kept crashing.

He jumped out of his truck and started running from vehicle to vehicle. Suddenly there were others; they were all working together to rescue the many victims. He rushed to a car where the passenger was trapped. "Someone help me!" Brad called out as he kept trying to open the door. He ran back to his truck where he found a bar. The car looked as if it might at any moment explode; he worked frantically. Finally he managed to pry it open. The lady was pinned. A young man, who identified himself as a rescue worker, showed up and started helping. Soon there were others. They all worked quickly going from one victim to another.

He finally had the opportunity to call his wife. "Honey, I just wanted to let you know I am fine." He was sure she would have heard the news report. He didn't want her worrying needlessly.

"Where have you been? I've been trying to reach you!" She was panicked. "I can't find Joey."

"What?" Brad was confused. "He's got to be in the house somewhere!"

"No, honey, I can't find him." She was crying pitifully into the receiver. "Brad, I've lost the baby."

Brad listened, but his mind could not process the information. "You what?"

"I've lost the baby!" She was crying so hard he could barely hear her.

"Honey, are you sure?"

"Of course I'm sure." She slid down the wall and sat on the floor of their kitchen. The pains had started almost as soon as he had left. Then she realized Joey wasn't there. She looked everywhere calling his name; he was gone. His pajamas were still lying in the bed. She was sure someone had kidnapped him. That's when she started calling Brad. "I called you," she cried, "but I couldn't get you!"

"I'm sorry, honey. I left my phone on the seat. I've just witnessed the most awful accidents. There are more injured people than you can imagine. I've been trying to help. I'm on my way now. I'll be there soon; don't worry, I'll take care of everything. We'll find Joey." He moved his truck into position to drive anywhere necessary to leave the freeway. The truck moved easily through the non-road terrain along the highway and along the side of the road to where he could make his way home.

"Sarah," he called as he entered the house. He found her in the kitchen. She was trembling with shock.

Her eyes were wide with fear. "I can't find him; I've looked everywhere!"

Bounder, the family's yellow Lab, was bouncing around them, looking concerned. "Down boy," Brad said as he tried to listen to Sarah. The dog whined pitifully. Leaving them alone, he went to his corner of the kitchen and lay down, placing his head on his paws. His sad eyes looked up, watching them as though he could almost speak.

The news was blasting; Brad heard loud and clear, "All of the children are missing!" He looked at his wife. Horror filled her eyes.

"We have to find him!" she said in a voice shrill from panic.

Brad looked everywhere; Joey was gone. He was concerned about his wife. How long could she go without medical attention? He couldn't locate Joey. He scooped up Sarah and carried her in a blanket out to his truck. "I have to get you to a doctor."

"No, we have to find Joey," she trembled as she insisted.

His eyes held hers steady. "Honey, he's gone. I don't know where he is, but he is one of the children missing. I have to get you some help. I'll come back; I promise. I'll look everywhere. I'll scour the neighborhood and report it to the police, but right now you need help. I can't look for him now. I have to get you to the hospital." She settled back in the seat in a shock-induced trance as he drove her to the emergency.

There was a cop near the entry door. As Brad carried her into the emergency room, he stopped long enough to ask, "Is it true? Are children really missing?"

The cop looked at Sarah. "Yes, sir, it is. We have received reports from preschools and elementary schools everywhere. All of the children are gone."

"Our son is missing. And my wife seems to have miscarried."

The cop looked at Sarah with compassion. "I'm really sorry to hear that. We're doing everything we can to find out what has happened to the children."

Sarah started to cry as understanding permeated her reason. She lifted her face away from Brad's chest. "Honey, I know where he is." Brad gasped at first; a wave of relief ran through him. He listened, hoping to hear her say she knew of a hiding place or somewhere she had forgotten to look. He was just beginning to laugh with relief when he heard her say, "Jesus has returned and he has taken all of the children with him."

His heart sank. "No, honey, that's something your grand-mother told you. It's just a story!"

"Is it?" She looked at him, challenging him to give her another answer. "Brad, Grandmother used to warn me. She was always talking about Jesus returning for his church. She said all of the innocent children would be with him at this time."

She looked at the cop. "Isn't it true, all of the younger children are missing? But the older children, say thirteen to eighteen, only some of them have disappeared?"

The man seemed surprised. "That's right, miss."

She looked him directly in the eyes. "It's because they have reached the age of accountability. That's the age when they are able to understand right from wrong. The older children, even some middle-school children, are not innocent; the younger children are. Jesus has raptured his church. He took the people who are closest to him and the young children." She thought of her baby and added, "And the babies."

The cop watched her as if she had lost her mind. "Many of the older children are safe at home with their moms and dads," he said, trying to encourage her.

Sarah spoke with total clarity. "That's right; the older children who were Christians are gone. The ones who were not are still here."

The cop looked at Brad with pity in his face. "Sir, I think your wife needs to rest." He escorted them to a nearby seat.

Brad sat Sarah down. "Honey, I'll be right back. I'm going for help; stay here." He walked up to the overflowing line extending from the emergency desk. The line was so long a young woman had been called in to assist the team of people on duty in admissions that day. She was going from person to person, trying to assess the need and help plug the people into the line according to the urgency of their emergency. She finally made it to Brad. He took her to where Sarah was sitting. Sarah was still trembling but seemed surprisingly calm.

All at once a hysterical young bride, still wearing her wedding dress, suddenly burst through the emergency room doors. Behind her following closely were what appeared to be her dad and several bridesmaids.

"Chelsea, you have to get a hold of yourself," the older man said.

"Get a hold of myself. Are you crazy?" she yelled back at him flailing her arms up and down as she talked. "Why are we here? Why isn't anyone helping me look for him?" She walked quickly pacing the floor; her bridal gown billowing out from her bounced whimsically as she moved around erratically. "No one just disappears like that. You have to help me find him."

The cop who had been watching the door was close behind her, coaxing her to calm down. "Listen, miss, everyone here has someone missing and there are several injuries. Please keep your voice down for the sake of the other patients."

"You don't understand." She grabbed the cop by the front of his jacket, holding on for dear life. She faced him with a look of panic nearing insanity. "He just disappeared! My groom was standing right directly in front of me. I was as close to him as I am now to you, and he disappeared right into thin air!" Her hand waved upward as she described the event. She sobbed and then coughed as if she were choking on the words. Her eyes lit up with renewed fire as she continued. "The preacher had just pronounced us husband and wife; then *poof*, he was gone! Even the man who was marrying us—Pastor Smith—they both, at the same time, just disappeared." She placed her hand up to her throat. "I can't breathe," she gasped. She reached for her abdomen bending herself in half; she continued gulping for air.

The officer was at a loss for what to do. Reaching, he said, "Maybe, miss, you need to loosen the back of your dress."

Her voice, now hoarse from the ordeal, rang higher than normal, as Chelsea denied his suggestion through clenched teeth. "No, I do not need to loosen my dress. It is a perfect fit. I dieted for three months to be able to wear this dress, and it is perfect." She held his arm for support, still trying to catch her breath.

The officer had been dealing with this kind of thing all day. The bride's story was a new take on the day though. "I am sorry to hear about your groom, but you have to try to calm down."

At that moment an elderly woman with an oxygen tank walked pass Chelsea. The poor woman seemed disoriented. She focused her attention on the nurse in front of her. She needed help with her oxygen. She had removed her mask, holding it in her hand while she spoke to the nurse. "Miss, can you help me?"

The bride reached out and grabbed the poor little lady's mask. Holding it up to her own face, she began to breathe deeply. Slowly she was able to stand up.

"Really, miss," the cop said. "You have to let go of the mask. It's not yours. Please give it back to this patient."

Reluctantly Chelsea released the mask, "I'm so sorry," she said to the lady who seemed fearful of her. "I just needed it for a minute. Here, let me help you put it back on." Chelsea began to laugh as hysteria bubbled up uncontrollably. "You see my fiancé, well, technically, he's my husband now, just disappeared." That's when Chelsea stopped laughing. The floor rose up to greet her as her legs turned into jelly and she blacked out.

～

"Miss, can you hear me?" Rebecca said from a long way off. Rebecca could not imagine the stress of a bride, well into her wedding day, suddenly seeing her groom vanish. "Everything's going to be fine. That's it, just breathe slowly, in now, out; that a girl. You just have to try to relax." While she continued in a calm business-like tone, she took Chelsea's pulse. "When was the last time you had something to eat?"

Chelsea barely managed to whisper, "Yesterday."

Rebecca turned to the girl standing closest to her. "Can you go get her something to eat and drink?" The girl nodded and took off to find a snack machine. "I want you to sit here and eat something. I'll be back as soon as possible to help you."

Back on track, Rebecca looked over at Sarah; she was still eerily calm. "Hello, I'm Rebecca. What seems to be the problem today?" She was taking Sarah's pulse and making notations.

"I've had a miscarriage. My baby is gone; I mean, she's missing," Sarah said.

"Did you actually give birth? Where is the child?"

"No, I just know the baby is gone. I started having contractions, but I don't have a baby. I have lost our little girl. She's gone, like all the other children." Sarah's eyes watered up as she finished her statement.

Compassion covered Rebecca's face. "Why don't we get you checked out? Then we'll know for sure what is happening." She motioned to someone nearby and gave the necessary instructions to have Sarah examined.

Since Sarah was now in the capable hands of the hospital staff, Brad felt desperate to return to look for Joey. "Honey, I think I need to go back to the house now. I'm sorry. I hate leaving you here but I have to find Joey."

"He's not there, Brad. You know he's gone. Otherwise you would never have left home to bring me here in the first place. He is with all the other children. Jesus took him to heaven when he came for all of his people."

Brad did not want to let on, but he was very worried about her mind. "Honey, you have to stop saying those things. You're just in shock. I know your grandmother was a superstitious old lady and you dearly loved her, but why would a loving God take our son?"

She answered his question with conviction. "Because he is a loving God. God loves Joey more than we do. Honey, I know you think Grandma was a little crazy, but she was right. The Bible says somewhere, I can't remember where it is, that the followers of Christ are not appointed to wrath" (1 Thessalonians 5:9).

Honey, God is going to allow many terrible things to happen on earth because of sin. But he promised to protect his followers by taking them away. That is what is known in the church as the rapture. Go home, look for Joey; you won't find him. When you don't know where else to look, go to church. You know the little church around the corner from the house? There will be other people there who have missing loved ones too. They will help you. Someone will be able to explain it. And when you come back, bring the Bible I leave on the desk near my computer. It's Granny's Bible. She'll have the verses marked I need to see. Bring it to me. I love you. I'll be fine. You go and see for yourself. I'll pray for you."

She was so calm it was eerie. He watched her. She looked at him as though he were a pitiful stray cat she felt sorry for. Something about the things she said made him want to choke. He wondered, *How can she lie there so calm? What is wrong with her?*

At home, Brad searched everywhere. He found a photo of Joey on his third birthday. It was new. They had taken it less than two weeks ago. He began to make copies on the copy machine. Brad decided he would show them all over the neighborhood. He also intended to post them in various places.

He walked miles searching all of the alleyways and backyards. He looked under boxes and in holes. He also hung the posters where he could. The bold print read, "Have you seen this boy? We are offering a $10,000.00 reward for any information leading to his return." Then, of course, his phone number followed.

He finally was at the church. He had actually been walking all around it for hours. He didn't want to go in. He could not bear to hear the words his wife had been spouting repeated. But there was nowhere else to go. He walked through the doors of the building. He could hear people crying. The sound of mourning was everywhere. A young man was speaking. Brad would have interrupted the meeting to ask for help but at that moment the young man said, "Many of us know what has happened. Many people don't. We will have to explain it to them. You see, Jesus has taken away his church. These missing people are the true followers of Christ. They are the men and women who were watching and waiting for his return, such as my mom and dad, and so many others. Jesus has also taken the children. The news has reported all the children are missing from all of the daycares and elementary schools. People were sitting next to others who just disappeared. This is foretold in the Bible. It says in Matthew 24:38–42, I am reading from the King James Version,

> For as in the days that were before the flood they were eating and drinking, marrying and giving in marriage, until the day that No-e entered into the ark, And knew not until the flood came, and took them all away; so shall also the coming of the Son of man be. Then shall two be in the field; the one shall be taken, and the other left. Two women shall be grinding at the mill; the one shall be taken, and the other left. Watch therefore: for ye know not what hour your Lord doth come.

"Two women shall be grinding at the mill; the one shall be taken, and the other left" (Matthew 24:41).

Brad's mind shot back to the passenger who was trapped in the car. She kept saying, "She just disappeared. My friend just disappeared. I was looking at her and *boom*, she was gone. She just disappeared."

At the time Brad had thought the lady was in shock, but all day long he had heard similar stories. It was as if the preacher had shown a spotlight on the day's events. Now he knew what his wife had been trying to explain. He understood how she must have felt as she started to realize for herself the truth. His mind tried to process it, but it seemed so unbelievable. *Dear God, could this actually be what happened?* he prayed silently. He tried to focus his attention on every word the speaker was saying.

"I urge you to read all of Matthew 24. I will make a list of the scriptures that deal with this topic, for any of you who would like to study this for yourselves. I'll try to have that ready tomorrow. If you want to stop by, you may pick it up, or you can leave us your e-mail address and I will e-mail you these passages."

Brad's heart was pounding ninety miles an hour. He could not believe what he was hearing. The young man continued with his sermon, "You see, in the days of Noah the people were spiritually asleep. They did not believe God would ever flood the earth. Noah preached for many years trying to convert his friends and neighbors, but no one would listen to him. They were going on with their lives as if nothing was any different."

"One day, when they did not expect it, the Lord did something he had never done before. He flooded the earth. They should have expected it. Noah had preached to them for years. He warned them of the coming events, just as we should have expected the rapture. But we, like them, did not listen to the message of the Lord."

"People have reported the flood of the whole earth from many different nations. There are ancient writings that tell the story. Many of the stories are so nearly alike that even modern science has to accept that there was some kind of worldwide catastrophic event. There are numerous artifacts that record this happening."

"Noah was a man who found grace in the eyes of the Lord. The Lord spoke to him and told him the flood was coming. He gave him the dimensions of the ark. That is a large boat. God gave him the size and shape. The Lord also explained to Noah how to build it and waterproof it. Then the Lord spoke to all of the animals, and they entered the ark—male and female, two at a time. He told Noah to go into the ark. So Noah, his wife, their three sons and daughters-in-law went into the ark. God shut the door so no one could get in or out. That's when it began to rain. At that time God flooded the whole earth because of the evil of mankind" (Genesis 6, 7, and 8).

"You see, we believe we are not so bad. We think no one is looking when we cheat a neighbor, sleep around, steal, kill, or lie. But someone is watching. God sees it all. What men don't understand is the extent of his goodness. He is holy, he is perfect in every way, and he is a God of justice. He will not tolerate sin. If we as people fail to be just, God will not fail. He promised Noah he would never flood the earth again, but he is still just. Mankind has become so evil; God can no longer allow the sin that is rampant to continue. He will punish the people of the earth. And just as he made a way of escape for Lot before he destroyed Sodom and Gomorrah, he has made a way of escape for the ones who were raptured."

"If you recall, Lot was a man living in a city God decided to destroy because of the sin. He sent in two angels to look the city over. When the men of the city saw these angels, they wanted to rape them. They began to break down the door of Lot's home, trying to capture these two angels. The angels blinded them and took Lot and his family out of harm's way. Then the Lord caused fire and brimstone to fall from the sky, destroying Sodom and Gomorrah. That is an example of the seriousness of our situation" (Genesis 19:1–29).

"You see, there will be seven years of trouble. This is a time of testing. Many will turn to the man of Satan. He is called the Antichrist, the beast and the man of sin. He is going to seem to be the answer to all of the world's problems, but he is the worst thing that could happen to the world."

"During this time, we will be expected to take what the Bible calls the mark of the beast. This is the mark of the Antichrist.

Anyone who takes this mark will be condemning his or her soul to hell. Do not take this mark. I believe it may be a chip in your hand or on your forehead. Whatever form it takes, do not make the mistake of taking this mark. The problem is anyone who doesn't take this mark will be killed—martyred for the cause of Christ. Also, anyone who does not take the mark will be unable to shop. They will not be allowed to buy or sell. It is a terrible thing, but that is better than going to hell for eternity."

"You are either on God's side in this thing or you are his enemy. There are no other options. I choose to be on the Lord's side. If you want to make that decision with me, then please come forward. The altar is open. I am willing to stay here and pray with you as long as you need me. Come, make Christ your King. It's too late to escape the tribulation, but it's not too late to choose Christ."

The altar filled up as literally every person in the church tried to go to the front. The whole church stood to their feet. There were so many. The preacher indicated he would pray with them now and continue to pray for them until he had prayed for and with everyone.

Brad was not aware of the tears. He just knew something in the man's words rang true. He remembered Granny announcing she would pray for them after one of her intense Bible lessons, one they had tried hard to ignore. She had been gone for almost two years now. He didn't consciously get up out of his seat but he was at the altar. His heart pounded as he beat his chest and pleaded with God for help. The loss of his children was more than he could take. The young preacher was there beside him praying for him. The young man seemed to understand the depth of his despair as he prayed a prayer of restoration even in this time of great sorrow.

The night passed much quicker than anyone in the little church could have anticipated. The people gathered there had no reason to leave. They stayed where they could make the biggest difference—the difference started in them.

A kid had been holding Carly's hand. The young boy was somewhere around twelve, maybe thirteen. He tightened his grip on her hand as John spoke of the time of tribulation. He stared at John with wide-eyed terror. As John described the many horrible times ahead of them, Carly asked him, "What is your name?"

"I'm Justin," he said.

Carly was concerned about the kid. "Where is your mom?"

"She's with Jesus." He looked at Carly with fear evident in his face.

"Where is your father?" she persisted.

"I don't have one," was all he said.

"Do you have anyone?" Carly was beginning to really be concerned.

"No, I don't. I came here to look for my mom. She was always here. About a year ago she just became a religious fanatic. She told me she was done with the drugs. Her whole life was different because of Jesus. Now she's gone and I'm here. As you may have guessed, I didn't believe her when she told me Jesus would forgive my sins and I could go away with him. I thought she was"—he stopped for a moment, searching for the words. He shrugged then continued—"you know, crazy. I mean, she's my mom and I love her, but I just thought she was high or something. But don't worry about me, I'll be okay. Most of the time I take care of myself anyway; I'm pretty good at it." His big blue eyes looked innocently into hers. The look of fear denied his heroic words.

Carly said, with as much confidence as possible, "Oh, I'm sure of that. It's just that there are so many people who will need help around here. I was thinking maybe you and some of the other young people your age could help us out by staying with some of the people who need help. You know, since you don't have anyone to go home to, maybe there is someone here who shouldn't be alone. There is also the law, you know. I have to let the proper authorities know when a kid is alone."

He started to look skittish. "I've been in foster care before. I think I'll just stay on my own."

"Well, I just thought perhaps some of the people here would need help, and maybe, if we ask, since there is so much confusion with so many missing, they would let you stay with one of us. You could be a big help to someone alone."

"Oh." The word slipped out of his mouth as he processed her point of view. "I guess you're right; I hadn't thought about that. I could try to help."

She pulled John aside and reminded him that they had children in the room who might not have parents or guardians to care for them. "We need to call the authorities," she said.

He asked her to do it. She went to the office. The police lines were all busy. She found the number for Child Protective Services. The lady told her they were so overwhelmed they could not get to the children in the church for at least a few days. They had no more homes to place the children in and their facilities were completely full.

"We will check with you as soon as possible," the woman on the other end said. Carly assured her she would try to find qualified temporary homes for the young people.

She explained the problem to John. He stopped ministering long enough to announce to the congregation the need for help. "Excuse me, folks, but it has been brought to my attention that with the disappearances, some minors have been left without supervision. Child Protective Services is overwhelmed by the need. If any of you has worked with CPS in the past, please talk to Carly." Two couples stood to their feet. They met with Carly and agreed to take three of the minors. She was careful to get their addresses and driver's licenses. She was uneasy not knowing exactly who they were, but she didn't know what else to do under the circumstances.

Brad heard the announcement. He knew it was a bad time to bring a child home after losing Joey and the baby, but his heart went out to the young teens he saw crying at the altar. They were too young to be on their own. He knew personally how much trouble that could lead to. He and Sarah were foster parents for his younger brother a few years back. He felt compelled to invite one of them to come home with him.

"You," the word slipped out of his mouth before he could catch it. He knew this kid.

Justin just looked at Brad. He felt a sickening feeling starting in his stomach. "No, Carly, I am sorry but I can't go home with this guy." He began to panic as he thought of the last time he saw the rather large contractor. He was sneaking around the guy's truck, looking for something worth stealing, when the guy grabbed him from behind and proceeded to scare the living daylights out of him. The red-flushed face of Brad was burned into his memory. This was not a guy he was going to be able to handle. In fact, he was convinced Brad might just kill him if provoked.

On the other hand, once Brad got over his initial shock, he relished the opportunity to educate this kid on the dos and don'ts of life, starting with the kid's mouth. "I'll take him home with me." Brad said with a smile forming at both edges of his mouth.

Carly was rattled. She could plainly see Justin was uncomfortable with the idea. "I really don't think you two are a match. I mean, he looks scared."

Brad turned on the charm. Justin watched horrified as Brad smoothed away all of Carly's concerns with, "I know the kid is a little gun shy. He's been bounced around a lot and the thought of a big guy playing dad is a little intimidating. But I believe I can really help the young man out. He's one of the kids who is into a lot of self-destructive behavior in the neighborhood. Personally, I welcome the challenge. I've observed his behavior over the past couple of years, and I think he is basically a good kid. He just needs the guidance of a man in his life."

Justin's jaw hit his chest as he watched the smooth-talking Brad brush away every fear Carly had with all the right answers.

Brad smiled charmingly. He looked totally sincere as he said, "I'm sure if you'll just go ahead and help some of these other young people and allow me to talk to the boy alone, I can make him understand. If not, then he can go with someone else."

"Well, all right then. That sounds reasonable. He has been through a lot today. Why don't you two take a minute to talk? I'll check back with you both in a few minutes." She smiled and continued down the line trying to place the other young people with responsible adults.

"Oh, no you don't," Justin was not having it!

"Come on, kid, this is going to be fun. Where else are you going to go? You could always spend some time with the police. After all, I'm sure there are some people you've recently visited who would be happy to see you locked up. We could start by announcing your escapades right here to all these fine people. I'm sure they would all be interested to find out who the guy is who has been breaking into all their homes." Brad raised his hand to get the attention of the church people.

Justin quickly stopped him with, "Come on, man, don't rat me out; I'll cooperate."

Carly approached them with a question on her face. "Well, what have you decided?"

"We are going to give it a trial run," Brad responded. "If it doesn't work out, Justin knows he has other options. I explained them to him as best I could."

"Is that right, Justin? Are you okay with going home with Mr. Holden?" she innocently inquired.

Brad turned and looked at Justin, his face echoing the words, "Don't mess with me, kid."

"Uh, yea, he's cool."

"Wonderful!" Relief flooded Carly's face as she took down all of Brad's pertinent information for her files.

Outside the church, Justin said, "I don't have to go with you. You can't make me. I'll report you to the police." Justin threw out all of his usual threats; he looked at Brad, but they seemed to do little more than bore Brad.

"Come on, kid, is that the best you can do? First of all, you and I both know I can make you do pretty much anything I want. You've gone around the neighborhood tormenting everyone, stealing and such. I think there's a chance that people, even the police, would celebrate knowing you were under my roof. One thing's for sure, if I catch you doing your usual stuff I'll make you sorry you ever crossed me. I don't play, and you can't trick me. I know who you are; I was just like you when I was your age."

"You might have been able to trick your single, drugged-out mommy into believing your lies, but you're not getting away with that stuff around me. Kid, I'll clean your clock for you and enjoy doing it. My advice to you is to do exactly what I tell you. That means while you're with me and my wife, you have a curfew, you go to school and do your homework. I intend to check with your teachers daily to make sure you're there and working; if you're not, I'll find you and wear your backside out!"

Justin's mouth dropped open as he listened to Brad's plans for him. "You can go to the police, but we both know by the time they get around to checking on your complaint I can have you dead and buried in the backyard. Who would even notice? You've got one chance, kid. You better not mess it up. If I catch you getting high, well, I think we understand each other—every rotten thing you can think of doing pretty much ends badly for you." Brad looked at the youth with his best poker face.

Justin was stunned. As he watched Brad, he could see there was a reason this guy hadn't gone away with Jesus. Justin swallowed hard, trying to rid himself of the lump in his throat. "You'd do that? You'd just kill me? I'm just a kid. That's criminal; you should be in jail or something."

"Yeah, kid, you're one to talk." Brad smiled a sinister little smile.

"There are laws; I'll call CPS," Justin promised.

"Go ahead, kid. I'll tell them you're lying as usual. Do you think they'll believe you—a known thief and liar—over me? You think you're good at playing people? Just wait till I talk to those people; they'll give you to me for good."

Justin decided to shut up and watch Brad for a while. As soon as he could, he'd find a way to fix him.

Brad knew he had gotten to the kid. Somehow he would turn him around. The idea of beating the living daylights out of him really appealed. However, Brad had meant it when he went to the altar. He wanted to change his own life. Maybe if he could teach this kid to respect other people he could help Justin change too. He watched the little delinquent trying to decide what he should do next.

Brad decided to tell Justin what was going on in his family. "My wife has gone through a lot today. Our son disappeared and she miscarried with our baby. I want you to promise to be on your best behavior with her. She doesn't need a brat like you giving her a bad time."

Justin was upset. "I don't have a chance. You hate me. Your wife hates me. What am I suppose to do?"

Brad shrugged his shoulder. "She doesn't know you're the one who tried to steal from me, and I won't tell her as long as you don't give me a reason to have to. As far as I'm concerned we can forget about last week. As long as you go to school and behave, we'll have no problem. But if I catch you cutting school, not doing your homework, or being impolite to my wife, all bets are off. She's special. She believes people are basically good. She'll be kind to you. You'll like her."

They walked into the hospital late that night. The night nurse told them where she was. Because of the overflow of patients, she was lying on a bed in the hall. It was past visiting hours but they went to see her anyway.

Sarah was asleep so they watched her. Justin noticed the way she seemed to cry at times in her sleep. Brad sat down on the bed and held her hand, watching her as if she were the most beautiful woman in the world. After a while they went downstairs for something to eat. There was nothing available so they took what they could get out of the vending machines.

"Did you mean it?" Justin asked Brad. "Would you really do all those things you said to me?"

"Kid, I would beat the thief out of you and enjoy myself. I don't really intend to kill you, but I intend to teach you to behave while you're around me. I'll do whatever I deem necessary to accomplish that. And, by the way, that includes chores and working for a living instead of stealing. The kind of thing your dad should have taught you. By the way where is he?"

"I don't know. I never knew him. My mom was always high. I'm not sure she even knew who he was."

"So where is she now?" Brad thought maybe she was injured or something.

"She's with Jesus." Justin noticed Brad's look of doubt. "Yeah, that's right. She became a Christian and now she's gone. So I guess you're stuck with me for the time being."

"Okay, kid, as long as we have an understanding." Brad searched the boy's face for some glimmer of compliance.

Justin was fed up with being called kid. "My name is Justin. We understand each other. I have to do whatever you expect, or you'll make my life miserable."

"I'm glad you've got it. Now let's go check on Sarah. She's going to want to meet you. Let's see if she's awake."

Sarah was still sleeping. The night nurse told them she had been given a sedative and would sleep through the night, so Brad took Justin home. Bounder met them at the door. While Brad opened a can of dog food, Justin played with him. "You're a good dog. Yes you are," he said, laughing at Bounder. Justin spotted a picture on the wall of a guy in an army uniform. "Who's this?" he asked, walking over to it and studying the friendly looking face in the picture frame.

"That's my brother, Owen," Brad answered without looking up.

"Where is he? Has he called you since the disappearances? Do you know if he's missing?" Justin asked, concerned.

"He was killed in action last year." Brad held his emotions tightly in check.

"Oh, I'm sorry," Justin said and dropped the conversation. Brad showed him to his room. "Can Bounder sleep with me?" Justin asked.

"Sure," Brad responded. "Now get some sleep." Justin went to bed; as soon as he lay down he was out. Bounder lay down at the foot of the bed. He watched over his new charge faithfully.

Brad walked into the living room. He missed his brother, but his heart really ached for Joey. As he thought about his son he started to cry. What was he doing, bringing this kid home? He wanted his own son. At that moment he started praying fervently. "God, help me. I don't know what to do." His heart ached as he spoke every word in his heart.

Justin was awakened by a sound he couldn't quite make out. He slipped out of bed and tiptoed down the hall to the living room. There, Brad was holding what looked like a picture and crying. For some unexplainable reason he felt really sorry for the guy. Brad looked like his world was falling apart.

Justin said, "My mom's gone. I know it doesn't mean much coming from me, but I'm sorry for you and Sarah. I noticed the picture when you first brought me here. He looks like a real good kid. I'll bet he would never have grown up like me. I mean, having a dad like you around. And Sarah seems real nice too. She's probably a really good mom."

Brad listened to Justin. Just a few hours before he thought he was doing the kid a favor by taking him in. He was hoping to teach the kid to care about the people he hurt. As he listened he realized Justin did care. He wasn't a bad kid, just a kid who needed love.

"I'm sorry about your mom, too, Justin. I think if she would have had more time to reason with you about Jesus and this whole rapture thing, you would have listened and you'd be with her now instead of with us."

Justin walked over to Brad and took the picture of Joey, holding it where he could study it. He suddenly looked happy as he said with conviction, "I'll bet they're together. I'll bet Joey and the baby are with her, and she's taking care of them the way you're taking care of me. She's fun too. You would have liked her. I mean, she had a problem with drugs, but she was clean for the last year; that's when she started going to church and praying all the time." Justin's face showed regret. "I didn't give her a chance. I was mad about the way she used to be, so I just acted like she didn't mean anything to me. But she did. She's my mom. I love her." Justin started to cry. He wiped his tears with his shirt sleeve, trying hard not to show his emotions.

"What do you say we start over, kid? From hereon out, with a clean slate, all of my rules still apply, but this time we start out as friends."

Justin shrugged. "I guess so. You won't tell Sarah, will you, about me stealing? I mean, it's kind of embarrassing."

"Not unless you go back to your old habits."

Justin had to ask. "Did you mean it when you said I have to get a job?"

"Of course I did. You can work for me weekends helping around the place with odds and ends that need doing. I might even teach you how to operate a tractor sometime."

"Are you serious? Me operate a tractor for real?" Justin was excited.

"Yeah, man, of course, for real. You might as well learn the business." Brad gauged Justin's response. "But you also have to go to school and do your chores."

They both said good night, and this time both of them went to sleep.

Early the next day they went to see Sarah. She was waiting for them to take her home. Brad introduced Justin to her and told her about his experience at church. "Babe, we have to go back tonight. You were right. We have to hear what is going to happen next."

Sarah listened to Brad, intrigued by his newfound interest in church. She was also taken by Justin's winning smile. He was such a gentleman. As she stepped out of the truck, the young man took her things and tried to help her down.

"Be careful," he said as he watched to see that she made it.

Sarah was aching, mostly from the pain in her heart. Physically she would be fine. She slowly walked up the path back into the house. When she entered the front door she started to cry. Brad put his arms around her and held her, shushing her and cooing into her ear, "It's all right, honey; we're going to be with them both soon."

Justin wanted to comfort her but he didn't know what to say. So he went into the kitchen and put on some water for tea, the way he used to do for his mom. A few minutes later he came walking into the family room carrying a cup of herbal tea.

Sarah was seated comfortably. Her face lit up as Justin entered the room announcing he had a cup of tea for her. She watched him through unshed tears. "You're spoiling me."

Justin looked embarrassed and said, "I used to take care of my mom. She was sick a lot." He watched her for a minute then said, "You'll be fine, you just need some time."

"How are you doing, Justin? Here you are waiting on me. What about you?"

Justin opened up to Sarah. He liked her. "I had a really bad time yesterday. And then that guy, John, started talking about all the things that had happened. My mom tried to tell me Jesus was coming back, but I didn't listen. I was really unhappy, but now I'm doing better. Brad and I talked last night and cleared up some things. I think we all need time to adjust to all of this. I'm sorry about your little boy and baby girl. I told Brad my mom will take real good care of them for you."

He looked a little concerned. "I know Brad said I could stay here, but I wanted to ask you too. You've been through a lot, and I understand if I'm in the way or something."

"No, not at all. I'm glad you're here. I won't lie to you. I wish things were different. But since they aren't"—she stopped, searching for the words—"I'd rather have you here than not. I think you are just what Brad and I need to keep us from feeling sorry for ourselves."

That evening they went to church. She hadn't been to church with Brad in a long time. She listened to what the pastor had to say. It was all familiar. She had forgotten the scripture references but remembered the content. The years she spent in Sunday school came rushing back with every word. When the pastor gave the altar call, she went forward, even though she had prayed from the time she had felt life leave her womb. She wanted to reaffirm her commitment to Jesus.

After she left the altar, she talked to Carly, who introduced herself. The music invited her to sit and reflect as she rested. In just a little over twenty-four hours her life had gone completely off track. The sorrow of unexpected loss, never far from her mind, had derailed her. But as she looked around the little church, filled to capacity with people, she felt she was back on track. All those prayers her grandmother had prayed for her were answered in one day. Sarah had gone from being a nice person who just never seemed to have time for God to being a woman of faith, the kind of faith the women of her family had always had. She was a woman of generational blessings passed down from the women closest to her who had lived it in the face of tremendous adversity.

Now that she thought about it, she couldn't remember them ever not trusting God. Her mom had been a rock. One day her dad was there, the next he was gone. That was it; he was killed in the line of duty, as were so many others in his profession. But her mom and her granny had faced life's blows with confidence and trust in God. They believed he would not fail them. They knew he would make a way. She looked around and wondered why she had taken that great heritage for granted. "Oh God," she breathed. "I didn't appreciate the blessings of being born into that kind of faith." She had always believed in God but felt there was plenty of time to follow him later. How wrong she had been!

The warm glow of the lights lit the little church and turned it into a place of refuge. *This is where I belong*, she thought. *Thank you, God.* Praise filled her up. The horror of the day before was bearable because God had forgiven her.

Justin watched over her as if she were a doll that might break. She sensed his protective nature. She looked over at Brad. As she watched the two of them, she was amazed by how much alike they were. The same tough-guy image softened when they were with her. They could in no way hide from her their gentleness. She was no one's fool. They were like two peas in a pod. They would be good for each other.

God, I don't know what you're doing bringing this young man into our lives, but thank you for the chance to be part of this child's future. As she sat there watching and praying, she found comfort in the familiar surroundings. She was finally home. The years ahead would be unspeakably difficult, but for now they were safe. And she found sweet comfort in the Lord.

REBECCA

The Day after the Rapture

The automatic doors slid open as Rebecca walked out of the hospital. The brisk morning air touched her skin. The sun felt warm and seemed to contrast with the previous day's disaster. *Life continues,* she thought, as she looked out into the beautiful day. She thought of the tragedies yesterday's events had thrown at the world. She had been asked to stay when the hospital started receiving the emergency calls. Her mind reeled as she remembered every case she had worked on. "I've never seen anything like it," she mumbled to herself. She dialed her best friend trying to reach her once again.

"Hello, this is Angela, leave a message, and remember the Lord is with you wherever you go."

The upbeat voice sounded out of place after the last day and night. She knew Angela would be trying to reach her if she could. But unfortunately, there were no messages from her. Tears started to prick her eyes as she tried not to imagine all of the horrible things that might have happened to Angie.

She decided to call a mutual friend she had lost contact with. She and Angie attended the same church. Angie had mentioned it to her in passing. Perhaps she would have heard if Angie was okay.

Angie had married a guy who was involved in the music department of his church. This guy convinced Angie to become a Christian. He was radical. Angie followed him right into the whole church thing. Rebecca began seeing her friend less and less after Angie married. It was weird how different she became.

Her mind raced to understand. In the confusion of the last twenty-four hours, she kept remembering the rambling of her patient Sarah. The poor woman kept saying she had lost her baby, that it went to live with Jesus. She would have marked it up as the unbearable grief of a mother, but the maternity ward made her think twice. The nurses on duty said the babies just disappeared all at once. *Gone,* her mind said over and over. *All of them just gone!* Her friend was on duty when the disappearances happened. She told her the maternity ward was just suddenly empty. The parents were beside themselves with grief. They were all threatening the hospital with lawsuits until the reports came out that this had happened everywhere—everywhere, all over the world; not only adults but also children and all babies were missing.

Her heart pounded as she thought of the story of Dr. Simons who had just delivered a baby boy. He said he cut the umbilical cord and the child in his hands was gone: one moment he was holding the child, the next moment nothing! She swallowed uncontrollably.

That wasn't all. The pediatric ward, where she went to help, was empty. The place was eerie: only a few of the older children remained. All of the younger children were gone. This was everywhere. The news reported children missing. Oddly, it was infants and young children who had been targeted by this phenomenon.

At the moment this happened she was helping an elderly woman out of bed. She turned to look at the equipment of the woman in the next bed, and her patient just disappeared. Panic shook her as she looked unsuccessfully for her patient. Rebecca walked up and down the hall looking for a woman who only moments earlier had been quite ill. "What on earth is going on?" she asked herself.

Bringing herself back into the present, she scanned the roads in front of the hospital looking around at the damage. Everywhere there were abandoned cars—either wrecked or, strange as it seemed, actually left by their owners for no apparent reason. The roads were still bogged down from the previous day's accidents. According to the morning news, police officers had spent a considerable amount of time just driving the vehicles they could move off the roads and out of the way. The streets were lined with abandoned cars. Tow-truck drivers were working around the clock to remove the abandoned vehicles. She decided to dial Carly immediately.

"Hello, this is Carly."

"Carly, thank God! I am so glad to hear your voice. It's Rebecca. I have been trying to reach Angie." A barely detectable catch caught in her throat as she continued, "I've left several messages but she hasn't called me back. Have you heard anything? I'm starting to really worry."

"Rebecca, I'm so glad you called me. I need to talk to you as soon as possible. I know what has happened to Angie, and I'm sure she would want me to tell you. Where are you? Can we meet?"

"Of course. I'm just leaving the hospital. I had to take a double shift. Where are you? Maybe I could come over."

"That would be great. I'll fix us some breakfast and we'll talk." Carly gave Rebecca the address to her apartment and started to fix eggs and toast. She dreaded having to explain this to Rebecca. She knew Rebecca would have a hard time understanding the situation. God had never been a topic Rebecca wanted to discuss. She somehow seemed threatened by the idea that God wanted control of a person's life. She had always wanted to be in charge, and giving up control was more than she was willing to do.

Rebecca rang the doorbell. Carly opened the door and immediately welcomed her with a warm hug. "I am so glad you're all right. Please come in." Carly invited Rebecca to sit down and have breakfast. She was certain Rebecca needed the meal. After a few bites, the girls started to talk candidly.

Carly started. "Rebecca, I know Angie is all right; in fact, she's better than all right, she is with Jesus. You know how close she has become to the Lord. Jesus has returned and taken his church with him. He has taken all of the babies, the children, and those adults who have been living a true Christian life—you know, people who love him more than anything else. This is spoken of in the Bible as the catching away of the church." She turned in her Bible to 1 Thessalonians 4:16–18. "It says here starting with verse 16,"

> For the Lord himself shall descend from heaven with a shout, with the voice of the archangel, and with the trump of God: and the dead in Christ shall rise first: Then we which are alive and remain shall be caught up together with them in the clouds, to meet the Lord in the air: and so shall we ever be with the Lord. Wherefore comfort one another with these words.

"There will be some horrible things that will happen. The Lord Jesus in his mercy came for the people who were ready to meet him. I was not one of those people. I put my career, pleasures, and things before God. When Jesus returned he was only able to take the people who were ready to go to heaven. You see, just going to church doesn't make a person ready to meet Jesus. I sure wasn't, and neither was John. This was a wakeup call for us. We have both recommitted our lives to Christ and are trying to help those who are coming to the church with the same questions as you have. I know it sounds unbelievable but it happened."

Rebecca heard the words coming out of Carly's mouth but her mind could not grasp them. She listened as Carly explained in some detail the reasons for her conclusions. Rebecca finally had to speak. "How can you think that? You're delusional. I think you should talk to someone at my work. I know a really wonderful doctor. He has done wonders for me. He can give you medicine that will help you deal with the trauma. I'm so sorry! I think I've added to your confusion by coming here." She started to leave.

Carly stood with her. "Just a minute. I can understand your being concerned about me, but I want you to listen. Don't run away; let's talk about it. If after we discuss this and you still think I'm crazy, I will talk to your doctor; but just hear me out. I want you to ask the questions that bother you most. I'm willing to talk to you and help you understand where I'm coming from."

Rebecca was suddenly angry. "Okay, you want to discuss this? Why would a loving God allow the world to go through all this horrible stuff you're talking about? And, to be quite honest, I don't see how he has done anyone a favor by stealing the people we love. If you could have seen the devastation I saw at the hospital you would understand. Parents lost their children and were grieving. There was nothing any of us could do for them. They were past comforting. What about all of the accidents? Are any of the terrible things coming going to equal the worldwide loss of life and mass hysteria that has already happened because of this?"

Carly took a deep breath. "I guess you're right, so much of what has happened is beyond comprehension. But the truth is God was extending his mercy, and yes, what is coming did warrant the terrible devastation we have just witnessed. You see there will be earthquakes and natural disasters which will leave people hurting, and many deaths will happen. The world economy will collapse. The Bible tells us one-third of all the trees and grass will die (Revelation 8:7). There will be worldwide hunger during these events. The world will welcome one individual to lead it. He will establish a one-world order.

This man, who comes to power, will appear to have the answers to all of the problems. People will see him as the messiah, you know, the deliverer. They will follow him. The Bible tells us he is the Antichrist. He will demand that everyone take a number. This number is called the mark of the beast. It is a mark that aligns an individual with Satan. Everyone who takes this mark will be condemned to hell. It's like telling God 'I don't want any part of you.' But if we don't take this mark we will not be allowed to buy or sell. In other words, how are we going to live?" She flipped through her Bible. "Here it is." She pointed to Revelation 13:16–18.

> And he causeth all, both small and great, rich and poor, free and bond, to receive a mark in their right hand, or in their foreheads; And that no man might buy or sell, save he that had the mark, or the name of the beast, or the number of his name. Here is wisdom. Let him that hath understanding count the number of the beast: for it is the number of a man; and his number is six hundred three-score and six" (666).

"We will also be forced to either deny God or we will be put to death. The Bible talks about those who will be martyred for the cause of Christ (Revelation 6:9–17, 15:2–4). I believe that this is for people like me who have accepted Christ after the catching away. I realize that taking the mark is wrong in the sight of God, so I will choose not to do that. If I am discovered by the authorities after this one-world order is set up, I will be condemned for being a Christian and killed. That is why Jesus took the believers out before this all started. You see, that's only part of what is expected. The Bible also tells us the sun, moon, and stars will not give light for a third of the day" (Revelation 8:12).

"But I don't understand why." Rebecca asked, "Why would God allow all of this?"

"The world has not followed God. Our own nation, as a society, has stopped asking him to be part of our lives. We've taken prayer out of school, and the Ten Commandments are no longer on the walls. We haven't taught our children about God. We haven't told them he holds people accountable for their actions. The darkness is an illustration of the darkness of hell. If God is not there, how can there be any light? The flames of hell still will not be able to light that place. God is illustrating to people what it will be like without him.

Also, the Bible tells us that the water will become blood. The fish in the sea will die. The Bible says one-third of the fish will die (Revelation 8:9). Rebecca, the hunger that will hit the world is going to be devastating. I believe that is one of the reasons that the one-world order will insist we either take the mark or not be able to buy and sell. If we don't do as they say, they will just decide we aren't worth feeding."

Carly stopped. She knew she was giving her friend a lot to digest, but she wanted to warn her. Carly swallowed nervously. "And there will be these really awful monsters: They're like scorpions that will come out of hell; they will sting the people who do not follow God. The Bible says men will want to die but they won't be able to" (Revelation 9:1–11).

As Rebecca listened, she sat back; a strange chill started to run down the length of her spine. Her eyes widened with horror as she listened to the Bible truths laid out. Something in the way Carly spoke of the future events left her with a sickening feeling; they had a ring of truth.

Carly moved her hands, a little self-conscious of her explanation. "I don't know the Bible the way John does. He is going to be at the church tonight explaining it to people. Do you want to come?" Rebecca wanted to run away but something held her.

"Think about it, Rebecca. Were the people you know who have disappeared all Christians? Why did God take only the babies and younger children? Why not all of the older children as well? If this had been a terrorist act, why would they have been concerned about age? Were the older children who are missing Christians?"

"What about the adults? Do you know of anyone disappearing who did not believe in God? Why weren't there any non-Christians taken? Why were only believers targeted? Whom among those you know who have disappeared are you sure did not know Christ?"

"How could anyone, other than God, arrange to take only Christians and not get caught in the act? If this had been a terrorist attack, why weren't some of them caught? Why would the

Bible predict such an event and it not happen? Everything the
Bible predicts comes to pass. For example, the nation of Israel,
God spoke to Abraham telling him he would become a great
nation, and he did. (Genesis 12:1–2 and Exodus 1:1–5; Jacob is
the grandson of Abraham.) Everything God foretold concerning
the nation of Israel has come to pass, with the exception of the
very last days.

"Jesus was foretold in the Scriptures and all of the events concerning his birth have happened just as was spoken by the prophets. God has promised us he would never leave us. He has also
promised that he will never forsake us (Hebrews 13:5). We must
believe he is taking care of us even now."

The pieces all added up. Rebecca remembered everyone she
was close to who had disappeared was a Christian. She could
not confirm all of her coworkers. Maybe some of her coworkers
weren't, and she just wasn't close enough to them to know for
certain. She decided to talk to everyone who knew these people
and confirm whether they were followers of Christ. She wanted
to know for herself. She didn't want to take the first explanation
handed to her and go with that. She was going to find out for
herself. "Carly, I appreciate everything you are telling me. And
I am starting to see why you would think this, but I need more
proof. I need to find out for myself if they were all Christians. If
what you say is true and they all were, then I am willing to listen.
In the meantime, I will go to church and at least hear the Bible
explanation from John. I don't understand why, if this is true,
Angie never told me about it. Why didn't she mention it to me,
at least once?"

"I think she was afraid to. She told me once; she didn't want
to push you too hard. She said she prayed for you, and she hoped
someday you would know Christ personally. I believe she just ran
out of time. She would have said something if she had felt you
were open to it. I know she prayed for both of us. She told me so."
Carly's eyes glistened with tears. "She was a good friend to us."

Rebecca started to get up and leave. Carly suggested that instead of driving back and forth with the roads so messed up, she could just take the guest bed. "I have an extra nighty; I just washed it so it's clean, and you can borrow my clothes. The guest bath even has a new toothbrush. You are welcome to stay."

Rebecca looked into the angelic face of her friend. She felt unbelievably tired. "That would be great. Thank you, Carly."

Carly showed Rebecca around the little apartment. "Here is a towel. I promised John I would be at the church early to help, but you can call me if you need to talk. There is food in the fridge and service starts at 7:00. You go ahead and just rest; I'll see you tonight." She hugged Rebecca good-bye and left.

Rebecca stepped into the warm shower. The water seemed to deny any of the sorrow of the past day. She spoke into the room. "God, if you're there, I need help understanding." She was spent. She no longer had the energy to cry. Her emotions that had been firmly held in check while she worked now seemed to be gone; all she felt was a wave of physical exhaustion. She was thankful for a good friend and a warm bed to crawl into. She spoke a prayer as she slipped off into the world of rest. Her body, unable to keep up any longer with the world's events, carried her into blissful peace as sleep overtook her.

She woke up to the sound of a little alarm going off. She had forgotten Carly had set it for her before leaving. She looked at the change of clothes her friend had left; they still had the price tags on them. Carly had great taste; the little jeans were a little tight but they were cute. She picked up the shirt; it was also new. She ripped the tags from the sleeve and slid it over her head. They weren't church clothes, but Carly had assured her they were fine. There was a cute little jacket hanging on the door.

Rebecca combed her hair and scooped it into her trademark ponytail. She reached into her purse and pulled out the lipstick. After applying some mascara and lipstick, she felt quite presentable. Her reflection caught the image of a girl next door with natural beauty. Her blond hair was long and straight. She had large brown eyes and tanned skin that glowed. She was the picture of health. She counted her calories and faithfully watched what she ate.

She smiled as she considered one good thing about all of this doom and gloom. If the world, as she knew it, was somehow coming to an end, she was going to eat chocolate as long as she could and as much as she could. Out loud, she said, "There will be no more dieting for me." She laughed, for the first time, as she joked to herself. Then her smile was replaced with the seriousness of her thoughts. She repeated to the Lord, "Oh God, if this is true, I am so going to eat chocolate." Her large eyes filled with tears as she considered the end-time prophesies.

She walked through the doors of the church. At first she was sure she was late. Carly came up to her and welcomed her with a warm hug. She led her to a seat she was saving for her. John was right in front of her. "I have to greet people," Carly explained. "I'll be back, to sit with you, when the service starts."

Rebecca watched as people prayed. Apparently they were there all day, some of them never leaving the night before. There was a steady buzz of voices. Something electric filled the air. She had never been to a church service like this before. She had visited this church many times with Angie, but this was different. There was an atmosphere of intensity she had never seen.

John stepped to the pulpit. "Thank you all for coming." His smiled reflected his gentle way. "I appreciate all of you so much. I want to thank those of you who continued the prayer vigil through the night and during the day. We need the Lord more now than ever before. Please turn with me to Nehemiah 1:2, 3, and 4."

> That Hanani, one of my brethren, came, he and certain men of Judah; and I asked them concerning the Jews that had escaped, which were left of the captivity, and concerning Jerusalem. And they said unto me, The remnant

that are left of the captivity there in the province are in great affliction and reproach: the wall of Jerusalem also is broken down, and the gates thereof are burned with fire. And it came to pass, when I heard these words, that I sat down and wept, and mourned certain days, and fasted, and prayed before the God of heaven.

John looked up from his Bible into the faces of the listeners. "In the days of Nehemiah, the city of Jerusalem had been overthrown. In fact the children of Israel had been turned over to their enemies because of their sin. Nehemiah had received word that the city walls were broken down. He became so full of grief it consumed him."

"Nehemiah was the cupbearer for the king and he had never before been unhappy in the presence of the king, and the Bible says Nehemiah was worried because he was sad as he tried to go about the task of serving the king and queen."

"The king asked him, 'What is wrong? What is making you so sad?' Nehemiah explained he couldn't be happy as long as the walls of the city of Jerusalem were torn down."

"I know I promised you I would explain more about the end-time prophesies, but first I want to speak to you for a moment about the walls of our lives being torn down. You see, when the city walls were torn down, the enemy could access the city. There was no protection. There was no way of defending the city from the enemy. I want to speak to you now about the walls of your heart."

"In his day Nehemiah was given permission by the king to go to Jerusalem and rebuild the walls. We are today faced with a similar situation. The walls have been torn down. All of our defenses are gone. We have no way of keeping the enemy out. The walls I refer to are the praying people of God, who have interceded for years on our behalf, and now they are gone. But I encourage you to become a wall builder. We must rebuild the walls by praying and fasting for all of us who are left behind. The years ahead will be trying, and that leads us to our text."

"Some of you were here last night, but for the sake of those who weren't, let me recap. The Word of God tells us about a man known as the Antichrist. This is a man who will captivate the hearts and minds of mankind. He will be inhabited by Satan himself. He's even going to be raised from the dead (Revelation 13:3). His purpose will be to lead as many people to hell as possible. He will have a number; the Bible tells us to mark this number, it is the number of a man. The number I am referring to is 666. The Bible talks about this number in Revelation 13:16–18 of KJV."

> And he causeth all, both small and great, rich and poor, free and bond, to receive a mark in their right hand, or in their foreheads: And that no man might buy or sell, save he that had the mark, or the name of the beast, or the number of his name. Here is wisdom. Let him that hath understanding count the number of the beast: for it is the number of a man; and his number is Six hundred three-score and six.

"Yes, everything you have heard about that number and more is probably true. The Antichrist will set himself up as the Messiah. He will abuse the holy temple in Jerusalem. Many will worship him thinking he is the Christ."

"He will form a treaty with Israel which he will break in three and a half years. Then look out, the events that will follow will be horrific! We are going to be tried by fire. We, the children of God who were not ready to leave when he came, will be forced to either denounce Christ our Lord and King, or face beheading."

"There will be a one-world order that everyone will be expected to follow. There won't be any exceptions." John stopped speaking and dropped his head. Words had ceased to come. His heart seemed to break in front of everyone. Finally he spoke, "You are my flock now. I am here to assist you and help, in any way possible, to guide you into and through the difficult days ahead of us."

Rebecca held her breath. She saw clearly the seriousness of the situation. Many of the people in the room, who obviously understood what John was trying to convey, started to weep. Actually, they began to mourn. Sorrow filled the little church.

A man who had been sitting in the back of the room stood to his feet. He was tall. His blond curly hair framed a picture-perfect face. He was dressed in a suit that far outshined anything the rest of the people were wearing. The dark-blue color caught the light and reflected the rich fabric. The man was lean and in his prime. He made his way to the pulpit.

John watched him as he approached. A little nod between them, and the stranger reached out to embrace John in front of the congregation. Rebecca overheard the mystery man say affectionately to John, "Good job, buddy. Your dad would be proud." John nodded his acknowledgement. To Rebecca, these two really seemed close, more like brothers than friends. The man then stepped to the microphone; his baritone voice resonated as he began to speak with the polish of someone who had done this many times before.

"I am Paul Stevens. I was the pastor of Redeeming Hope Church here in town." Murmurs immediately filled the room. "Yes, I was the senior pastor of our church. I also was left behind." A gasp went through the congregation. "John has asked me to come here tonight to help him, so I'm here. His father was my mentor, and a father to me in the Lord. He had been counseling me for the last few years. You see, two weeks ago I was dismissed from my church. I am guilty of adultery."

The crowd stirred as people took in the information. The pastor dropped his head, obviously hurting as he fought to go on. I want you to know how sorry I am for what I have done. I was not ready to go with the Lord Jesus. As Rebecca studied him, the expensive suit with its perfect tailoring faded away. She saw only a man standing in front of them all, admitting he had sinned. He humbly asked everyone there to pray with him. "I have asked God's forgiveness. My wife and I plan to serve the Lord, no matter what the future holds."

John also invited the people to come to the altar. He and this pastor friend of his were willing to pray for anyone who wanted or needed prayer. She listened to the music John's band members played. He was a gifted musician and singer. His band was there. They all grew up with him in the church. They were there to support him and help him in any way possible. They, like John, had chosen money and fame over their relationship with Christ.

She watched as the aisle and the front of the room filled with men and women seeking God. She noticed a woman working with the visiting pastor as if her hands were an extension of his arms. They stood side by side and worked flawlessly as person after person sought some kind of solace. Their offers of comfort, easy and practiced, made known the years of experience they had spent in ministry together.

Why is she here? How could she forgive him? Rebecca wondered. The woman must have noticed her staring. She made her way through the crowd and knelt directly in front of Rebecca.

"I hope you don't become offended with me, but I couldn't help noticing you sitting here all alone. Is there anything I can help you with? I am happy to answer any questions you may have, or just pray for you." The gentle voice of a woman approximately ten years her senior touched her. She had been so caught up in the evening's events she hadn't realized Carly never came back to sit with her. The woman continued to speak. "My name is Shelby. I am Pastor Stevens' wife."

"I am Rebecca. As a matter of fact, you can help me. I'm overwhelmed by the things I'm hearing. Will you pray with me?" Rebecca was stunned by her own response to the gentle, kind voice of Shelby. The look of I-care-for-you written in her expression seemed so real Rebecca responded without hesitation.

"Of course, I'll pray with you," Shelby answered. Rebecca broke and looked down at her hands. Her shoulders trembled like a small child's who had been caught out in the cold. Shelby took her in her arms.

Rebecca tried to explain. "My friend is gone. She knew Jesus."

Shelby started to speak. "Father, I bring Rebecca before you. She needs your comfort. Her heart is in shambles. You have to help her through this. She needs you now." That's when it happened—something Rebecca did not expect. She reached out, for the first time in many years, to the Lord. She was hungry for his comfort. A sweet, loving hope began to fill her. She remembered this feeling; she had experienced it before, a long time ago, when she was around ten, before all the horror of life had started. It was just before her mom remarried and her stepdad became her idea of what a father's love meant.

Now, wrapped in the arms of a stranger she knew she could trust, she felt this overwhelming love that scooped away the shame and hopelessness of the last several years and reintroduced her to a loving, caring Savior.

She did not know what had gone on between Shelby and Paul. She couldn't have guessed about the hours they had spent the day before, right after Jesus came, repenting and determining to change their lives. How could she have known the truth about this husband and wife team?

FALL FROM GRACE

Only recently, Paul Stevens was the hottest, coolest young pastor in the area. He had watched his church grow to staggering numbers. Everyone seemed to want something from him. He had formed a father-son relationship with Pastor Jentson. Pastor Jentson appreciated his talent and natural ability but sought to help Paul become a man of integrity. He often chided his young friend for counting too much on his good looks and natural charisma.

Paul saw his older friend as kind and well meaning, but he realized something that Pastor Jentson didn't. People wanted something new from church. People were no longer content to go to church and actually be preached to. The new culture wanted to be entertained, and entertain them he did. He brought in all of the latest young Christian artists. Then he cultivated an atmosphere of harmony while watching his own tendency to judge. He tried very hard not to do that. He preferred to get along with people. This was exactly why so many of the people were leaving Pastor Jentson's fellowship and moving over to his.

He was a forward thinker. He was not stuck in the past, doing everything the same. He was innovative. He liked to go fishing; and to fish you have to have bait. He brought in so many new programs—he had a program for everybody. The atmosphere was crucial. His church had to be a place of fellowship where men and women, regardless of their past or even present lifestyles, could come together and just worship God.

All of these ideas sounded good as he was choosing to adapt them to Redeeming Hope Church. But as Pastor soon learned, compromise can be very damaging. He had compromised himself right into the arms of another woman.

It had all started out so innocently. He just saw her one day. She was beautiful. Her long blond hair touched the middle of her back. He knew he was not supposed to notice, but the legs on this young woman were beautiful. She was younger, and she made him feel like he was single.

He looked over at his devoted wife, Shelby, with a little less interest. She had at one time been a true knockout, but the years of waiting for him to come home, while giving birth and raising their two children, had taken their toll. It wasn't as if he didn't still love her. They just didn't seem to like each other anymore. She had let herself go. She only seemed interested in the kids and the ministry. There was nothing left for him. The many nights of loneliness seemed to scream out to his humanity. He wanted a woman who needed him; Shelby needed no one, and that was a problem for both of them. She spent her days working and tending to the kids while he spent his working to help the unending stream of people who always needed and required something from him. Perhaps that was one of the things he loved about Shelby in the beginning—she was not needy. But now that particular personality trait seemed to be cold and aloof.

A few days passed by, and there in his office was the young woman who had taken his breath away. Deseraie Simms looked up at him as if he were a close friend. "Pastor, I was wondering if you could give me a few minutes of your time. I need to speak to someone."

"Of course," he replied. "Let's step into my office. How can I help you?" he asked with a warm smile.

She dropped her head slightly and began to tell him how difficult the last few years had been. She wanted out of a bad marriage but wasn't sure she actually had the right to give up on her marriage just yet. Pastor Stevens set up a schedule of counseling sessions. She looked relieved as she left his office saying, "I feel I can tell you anything. You are so wonderful. I really appreciate your taking time for me."

He really didn't mean for it to happen. It had slipped up on him. No one just decides to walk away from their principles of a lifetime in one moment. The deception had been a subtle movement in his heart. All the compromises he had made to get to the top had taken a toll on his relationship with God. He had learned to censor the word of God. He worked to better suit his sermons to his more forward-thinking congregation. Why had he left so much unsaid? Not one word about the consequences of sin. Instead he chose to put a more passive spin on it with trite sayings like, "God is love." He chose not to explain that hell is a literal place, a place for Satan and his demons. The Bible says, "Hell has enlarged itself" (Isaiah 5:14). It grows larger all the time to receive the people who disobey the laws of God. But being the young, cool pastor he was, he knew better than to teach that! He just sort of walked away from God slowly. It was almost as if he went to sleep, and when he woke up he was a married pastor having an affair.

Shelby watched as her husband made a fool of himself. He was always smiling and holding Deseraie's hand just a little too long as they greeted each other after church. She had warned him. She told him, in no uncertain terms, that he was risking their ministry and their marriage. But he just wouldn't listen to her. He had gotten too far, too fast.

He thought it was his innovative ideas that were producing growth in the church. He foolishly forgot it was the Lord. God had given him a gift some pastors long for throughout their ministries. He had supernatural favor with men. Her husband could have gotten up in front of his congregation and told them word for word what the Bible said and they would have loved him for it. It wasn't his training or his unique way of viewing the church;

it was the spirit of God on him that had moved people toward him as though they were following a movie star. Nothing he did displeased them. He was blessed beyond belief. She sat back and watched as in five years he grew a congregation larger than her father ever had. It wasn't his understanding of what the people wanted; in fact, it was the opposite—he was clueless. It was the precious anointing that had been poured out lavishly by a loving, giving God, who had chosen to bestow on him a gift with people.

She had stood beside him through all of the church stuff, the deaths, the marriages, the baby dedications, and the extra nights out several times a week. There were also the hospital visits, the emergency calls in the middle of the night. It was overwhelming. The only way she knew how to deal with it was one day at a time. But one day, she looked up and he was moving away from her. She didn't know when it had happened, but he wasn't hers anymore.

She sobbed as she remembered that horrible night. It was just like in the movies. The rain was coming down hard. He came home with the smell of that woman on him. He reeked of her. He ran to the bathroom to try to clean up, but his suit, set aside to go to the dry cleaner's, still carried her smell. Shelby lashed out at him. "You've been with her. Don't lie to me. Don't you realize I can see it in your face? I know you're lying. Get rid of her now!" she screamed.

He looked at her with those piercing blue eyes and said, "I can't. I can't let her go."

Shelby fired back. "I mean it, Paul. It's her or me!"

In that earth-shattering moment, he dropped his head and said, "I'm sorry." The two most horrible words she had ever heard. She had never dreamed he would choose another woman over her. It was as if he had run a knife through her soul. It pierced and somehow destroyed the very depth of her. Now, she was just a hollow empty shell. She could smile at her children, talk to her mom, and buy food. But she was just going through the motions. Her life ended that night. Her body just didn't know it.

The months that followed were now all a blur. Shelby remembered going to bed and not getting up. Her mother took over the duties of mom for her kids. Paul moved out that terrible night and Shelby started to become familiar with two emotions she had never really known before: jealousy and hatred.

Deseraie had taken over. She took her husband. She was planning to take her home and was now instructing the children to call her mom. Just like that, Shelby's world had fallen apart.

The church had recently taken action to remove Paul. He finally confessed to the church his sin and his intention to marry the homewrecker. Shelby found some comfort in the knowledge that the thing Paul wanted most in life he had lost. The church wasn't quite as forward thinking as he imagined. The board held a special meeting and asked for his resignation. He submitted it upon their request.

Shelby slid further down into the sofa. Now he knew what it was like to lose something you loved. He too had to give up his life's work. She smiled to herself as she relished the knowledge that Deseraie would never be able to make that up to him. He'll start to hate her now, she thought. Every time he looks at her, she'll remind him of what he gave up. She put another chocolate in her mouth, laying her head back, as she indulged the thought. She won't know what hit her.

Deseraie worked tirelessly trying to please Paul. She had taken his children to the park, made cookies with them and spent the afternoon working in the kitchen, trying to make his favorite dish, some chicken thing Shelby used to make. She watched him out of the corner of her eye. He didn't want to be happy. She had tried to convince him that leaving the church was a good thing. He could be a pastor anywhere, once people realized they were sorry for what they had done. After all, weren't Christians supposed to forgive? How could they sit back and judge them like this? The women in the church hadn't said a kind word to her in weeks. Paul asked everyone to forgive him; what did they expect? As she tried to reason with Paul he would just become more depressed and push her away. It was weird, how now that they were living together, he didn't seem to want to be with her. She wore her cutest jeans, the ones he liked, and he didn't even notice.

Two weeks after Paul had been asked to resign his position in the church, Jesus returned. Paul waited in the nearby cafe for his friend Pastor Jentson, but he never made it. In a flash, the people sitting in the chair directly across the path from him disappeared. Their items sat in the booth undisturbed; the woman's purse was abandoned. Paul rubbed his eyes and took a sip of his coffee. He had been under a lot of pressure recently. He must have missed their getting up and walking off. He looked around the room. The place had been full only a moment ago. Now it seemed less crowded. He watched as a young woman stood up, looking for her elderly mother. "Mom, where are you?" she asked in an alarmed tone.

An emergency banner came over the television. There was a stir and a hush among the customers as they turned up the news station. The broadcaster said, "It just happened only moments ago. We are receiving reports. People are missing all over the world! We are not sure what the cause is, but people are disappearing into thin air." Pastor Stevens dropped his cup of coffee as he realized the truth. He had been left behind!

Shelby had spent the morning plotting her next attack. She was going to make Paul sorry he had chosen that tramp over her. She intended to make Deseraie pay too. She would let them take the house. There was no way he could make payments on it with no more than Deseraie earned at that bookstore where she worked. He would have to take another job. Whatever it was he wouldn't like it. He liked being in charge. What kind of job offers do washed-up pastors get these days? She smirked to herself. She knew with his talent he could find something in advertising or just about anything he desired because people loved him, but he wouldn't be the pastor of Redeeming Hope Church, and that was really his love. She was on the phone with her mother when all at once there was no one on the other line.

Deseraie was frustrated. She didn't understand why she was expected to pay for all of the problems in Paul's life. It wasn't her fault he had lost his job. She had nothing to do with those closed-minded people. Anyway why didn't he let them know they were in love? She loved Paul so much more than she had ever loved anyone before. Wasn't that love from God? Paul still put her on a very strict budget and she was just expected to stay there. Well, he had another thing coming. She was making her own money and he couldn't tell her how to spend it. It happened to be her day off, so she was on the way to the mall. She had just turned into the parking lot when the car in front of her suddenly careened off in a weird direction. Her body ached as she fought to breathe. There was a funny smell in the car. Thank God a good Samaritan came along and helped her out of the seatbelt. She was freed from the car. Her neck hurt but she was fine. People everywhere were running. She hurriedly moved her car out of the way. She stepped out of the car to study the confusion. "What happened?" she asked as no one in particular stopped to answer her.

Devastation was everywhere. She managed to catch her breath and look around. From here she could see the main roadway—cars were crashing as though they were dominos lined up. She watched as a plane seemed to be falling from the sky. Her heart was in her throat. "God, oh God!" she screamed. Smoke was everywhere. She watched as the airplane continued to fall in the distance. *Boom!* She heard it hit. The sound was something she couldn't describe. She heard the explosion; it seemed to carry the wind with it. The people standing near her watching were crying. She was unable to catch her breath.

"Oh, my God," she heard the man next to her say. "Oh, my God," he repeated.

She sank to her knees, unable to stand. She watched, horrified, as cars burned, people screamed, and sounds of fire engines whirled by. She tried to pray. The words just didn't come out.

Shelby tried to call her mom again. "What is going on?" she asked herself.

The phone rang. It was Paul. "Hello," Shelby heard his all-too-familiar voice.

"I told you not to call me. I don't want to speak to you."

"Shelby, you've got to listen to me," he sounded upset.

"Okay, but make it quick, I was talking to Mom."

"Shelby, turn on the news."

"Why, what's going on?"

"Please, honey, just turn on the TV."

"Don't call me, honey you, oh"—she screamed—"I don't even have a word mean enough to describe you!"

"Okay, I get it, just turn on the TV."

"I am," she said as she hit the power button. She could see a plane falling from the sky. The cars along the roadways were wrecked. The site was devastating. She sank onto the cushions of the couch. "What is it?" she asked, still not remembering the end-time prophecies she had so often heard.

His words shattered what was left of her life, "I think Jesus came. I think we were left."

The phone dropped out of her hand as she fought with her mind to gain reason. "No," she said. "No! Jesus wouldn't just leave me like this."

Paul was already on his way to her when he called. He knew it was going to take a while with the roads torn up like this, but he had to get to Shelby. He tried to get her attention. He wanted to know if the kids were all right. Shelby left the phone as it was. She ran to Chelsea's room; there was no sign of her. The outfit she had chosen for the day was in a rumpled pile on the floor. Joshua's room was also empty. They were gone!

She ran back to the phone. "Paul! Paul, are you there?"

"Yeah," he replied.

"Paul, they're gone. The children are gone."

"I'm coming over, Shelby. Stay there; I'll be there soon."

She sank back down on the sofa and listened to the news. She was in shock when he walked through the door. He stepped over to her and pulled her up off the couch and into his arms. At that moment she didn't care if he was the most horrible person on earth; she held onto him as though her life depended on his support. They held each other crying long, hard sobs. "Maybe it wasn't Jesus," she tried to reason. "Maybe we're wrong."

He looked at her as he picked up the phone. "All right, we'll see." He dialed Pastor Jentson; his message box announced that it was too full to take another message. So he called John Jentson.

The young voice was soft. "Hello, this is John."

"John, its Paul Stevens. Is your father there?"

"No, Paul, he isn't; in fact no one but you of the old gang has called me." John sounded as though he was crying. "They've all disappeared," he said with obvious pain. "Paul, they're all gone. It's just me and a few others."

"I'm sorry, John," Paul said. "Can I do anything? I'll be glad to help you in any way I can."

John thought about it. "What about your congregation?"

"They don't really want to hear from me," Paul said, struggling to speak. "I was voted out, you know."

"No, I didn't," John said. "I'm really sorry to hear that. Listen, I would like to see you; if you get a chance, come by. I am going to be holding special services to try to explain what has happened."

"I will," Paul promised. "But right now I have some unfinished business. I have to clear some things up with the Lord and with my wife." His deep blue eyes watched Shelby. As he hung up the phone, he said, "We can't go on like this, Shelby. We have to make up and we have to make things right with God."

She folded in half, crying, "I don't get it. Why did God leave me? I didn't do anything. I didn't cheat. Why would God just forget me?" She was like a child.

He felt more compassion for her than ever before. "Shelby, you weren't ready. You've allowed yourself to become bitter. This bitterness has been eating you up. I know it's entirely my fault, and I'm so sorry I hurt you. But this bitterness, honey, is what has been destroying you."

She listened for the first time in months to her husband. "What will we do?" her simple childlike question broke his heart.

"Honey, we are going to straighten things out and then we are going to live the best lives we can for God. We aren't going to allow ourselves to give up on God. No matter what the future holds, we are going to serve him with all we have, and if necessary, die serving him with our last breath." He shrugged, adding, "It's all we can do."

She walked into his arms. "Are you coming home?" she sobbed.

He pushed her away from him and looked into her face. "Do you want me to?"

She nodded. "Yes, but only if that's what you want." She looked as though the thought brought her pain. "I won't share you with anyone else." The look of determination on her face affirmed her resolution.

"I understand. Shelby, I don't know what I was thinking. It's as if I lost my mind. One moment I was fine, life was good, and the next thing I knew I was caught up in something that was stronger than I was. I wanted to come back weeks ago. I just thought you would never forgive me. You have to forgive me or we won't make it."

"I know," she said. Sobs shook her body. He held her trying to comfort her until they stopped. At that moment all that mattered was they were in this together. The sorrow of knowing Jesus had come was eased by their recommitment to each other.

He held her and whispered into her ear, "We won't give up. We won't stop serving the Lord. We will look to him. We missed God's deliverance but we will not turn away from him."

"Yes," she looked up into the face of the only man she had ever loved, with renewed strength. "We will continue to work for him together. And when we leave this earth, we will be leaving here to join him for all eternity." They smiled. The greatest test of their lives had almost cost them their relationship with Christ and their marriage. They had been derailed. Satan had taken them out of the game for a season, but he would never keep them out of eternity. God wins, Satan loses!

～

Deseraie was worried. She had been trying for hours to reach Paul. She finally decided to call Shelby and see if he was there. "Hi, Shelby, this is Deseraie, is Paul there?"

Shelby's hazel eyes stared questioningly at Paul. "Yes, Deseraie, he is here." She handed the phone to Paul, who took it as though he were picking up the tail of a rattlesnake.

"Deseraie, I know I should have called sooner. But…" His words just trailed off. He listened as the woman on the other end went into a tirade of considerable proportion.

"How dare you go over there? I thought you loved me. I was in an accident and I have been trying to reach you for hours."

"Didn't it occur to you that in the event of a worldwide disaster, I would, of course, go home to check on my wife and kids? By the way, Deseraie, the kids are missing!"

She was heartbroken, "Oh, Paul, I'm so sorry."

"I know you are. Deseraie, please listen to me. Shelby and I have been talking. I wanted to tell you this in person, but since you called, I'll tell you now. What happened today was a wakeup call to Shelby and me. I hope you take it seriously also. You see, we believe Jesus has come back for his church, and you, Shelby, and I were left behind."

"What are you talking about, Paul? You are a pastor, for heaven's sake. Why would God leave you behind?"

He took a deep breath. "We both know I am no longer a pastor. In fact, I have been behaving as anything but a Christian. Being a pastor is no guarantee I will go to heaven. I still have to maintain a relationship with Christ, and he expects me, or anyone who is professing to be his, to behave as though we do belong to him. Adultery is not allowed. I failed to make things right with God and with Shelby. That is why I am here now."

Deseraie started to cry for real. "I don't understand; I thought we were Christians."

"We are. But we weren't behaving like Christians. You can't do the things we did and have a relationship with God. He is serious. God expects more than lip service. Unfortunately, that's all you and I have given him for quite some time."

"I don't blame you, Deseraie, even though you tempted me the way you did. If I had been walking the walk and not just talking the talk, you would never have been able to get to me. I want you to know I am sorry. I was the one who should have stopped this whole thing before it got out of hand. You were a baby in the Lord. I should never have seen you alone. I take full responsibility for failing you as your pastor. Please forgive me. That is why I have to stop this thing now before it destroys all of us. God is real and he loves you. You are very special to him. But I can't see you or even be in the same room with you alone ever again. Shelby and I have straightened things out and we are getting back together. We intend to live for Christ. And we intend to do it as husband and wife. Please don't call me again."

And with that the line went dead. Deseraie was speechless. No one had ever broken up with her before. The tears had stopped and all she felt was numb. *He used me,* she thought. *I was just a play thing. He didn't even love me.* She was sick. She looked around; she would have to find the way back to her apartment. She started walking.

She had been walking for miles. She rounded the corner; there was a little church. She looked at the name on the sign. She knew the pastor. What was his name? Oh yeah, Pastor Jentson. She had met him once. He was one of Paul's best friends. The look he gave her sent shivers down her spine. He turned to Paul and said, "Her feet go down to death; her steps take hold on hell" (Proverbs 5:5). She later asked Paul what he meant, but Paul just said it wasn't important.

She could hear the sounds of people praying. How long had it been since she had prayed? She really hadn't talked to God in months. She timidly walked up to the double doors. Slowly, she pushed one door open and walked in.

There was a young man speaking. He introduced himself as John Jentson, Pastor Jentson's son. She took a seat in the back. His sermon was not familiar to her. She had heard stories but nothing recently. She sat there, helpless, as John explained the catching away of the bride. The sick feeling that had started when she was on the phone with Paul began to surface. She quickly made her way to the ladies room. Tears rolled down her face; her nose was running. She started to cough. Then she became really sick.

A young woman came into the restroom. Her hair was black and her skin was sickly white. Her eyes searched Deseraie. "Um, excuse me, but are you okay?" She was clearly concerned.

Deseraie was spread out on the floor in the middle of a complete breakdown. "No, I'm not. I think I am really sick. I mean, I have heard of the rapture, but I didn't know all this stuff that guy, John, is talking about. And on top of everything else, my boyfriend broke up with me today. I think I'm losing my mind or something. I don't seem to be able to get up off this floor."

The young woman looked at her with pity. She sat down next to Deseraie and put her arm around the stranger. "It's okay; I didn't know any of that stuff either. You'll be all right. You just need time, that's all. You'll see, things will look better after you have yourself a good cry."

Deseraie sat quietly listening to the soft, sweet voice of the young woman, grateful for a friend, even if she was a stranger. The girl introduced herself as April. She told Deseraie her story. Deseraie was glad not to have to speak.

"I didn't even believe in God. I came here with my boyfriend. His mom is one of the ones missing. Anyway, he is convinced this stuff is real. He's the guy in black at the front of the church. He's still praying." She looked at Deseraie as if the idea was unbelievable. "His mom, she was a Christian, you know, always going to church. She used to sing in the choir. We came and heard her sing one time. She had a real pretty voice. She was..." April dropped her head and stared at her hands picking at the cuticles of her fingers. When she looked up she was crying. "She was special. She loved me, really loved me, you know? I mean all my life no one really cared about me before. I was in all these foster homes. My dad was bad; he used to hurt me and my sister. My mom didn't care what he did, as long as she got her drugs. When I was fifteen I ran away. It was awful."

"But then I met David. He and I really got along. He introduced me to his mom and she kind of became my best friend. She was more of a mother to me than my real mom ever was. She used to tell me, 'Someday, child, you'll understand. God has his hand on you whether you like it or not. He will always be there, no matter how low you go.' I guess she forgot about this rapture thing because, the way it sounds, he came, took her and a bunch of other people, and left me here wondering what on earth I'm going to do now."

"She's right you know." Deseraie found her voice for the first time in several minutes. "He does love you. I mean, I messed up bad, but I used to go to church. I was really serious once. I know—because I found Christ then—that he is real and he loves you and me. It really doesn't matter what my boyfriend or your mom and dad think of us; I know God is for real and he cares about us even when no one else cares."

"I went to the altar," April offered. "I just didn't know what to do."

"I know. Would you like for me to go with you? I need Jesus myself. I don't really know why I ever stopped serving him. I know I have to get back to where I was."

"All right," April agreed, her dark eyes tearing up. "I'd like that."

The two girls got up off the floor and walked out of the bathroom. For the first time that day, Deseraie knew what to do. They walked as far into the sanctuary as they could. People were everywhere. Many were lying face down, praying for God to forgive them and give them strength to face the devastating future. The two young women knelt. Deseraie started, "God, I know I have done everything wrong. Please forgive me."

She looked at her new friend and said, "Just talk to him, April, just like he is your best friend. The way you've been talking to me. And if you can't say the words, he listens to the cries of your heart. You just have to think to him and he is there."

Tears welled up and spilled over as April talked to God. "I'm sorry." As her heart started to speak, the words she couldn't find came pouring out. All she could do was ask him to love her. That's all she had ever wanted in her whole life; it was real, unconditional love, the kind her father and mother could not give her. The bottomless pit she had never been able to satisfy was crying out for that love that would never die.

The young man, John, placed a hand on her forehead and said, "Father, she needs you. She needs to know you, personally. Even now, Lord, please reveal yourself to her through your mighty, awesome power."

The load April had carried all of her life was lifted from her. It was funny, really. She didn't even realize how huge the weight had been until, somehow miraculously, she felt it lift and it was no longer there. She was free. The feeling of being released from something that had held her bound for years came over her. Her heart seemed to sing. She felt as if she were the lightest person on earth. She opened her eyes just to see if she was still on the floor. She was, but she was free—free from the sorrow of a soul without God, free from the pain of abuse, free from drugs, and free from witchcraft! She was a new creature: "Therefore if any man be in Christ, he is a new creature: old things are passed away; behold, all things are become new" (2 Corinthians 5:17).

Deseraie was also set free! The need to be desired was gone! She was talking to Jesus for the first time in a long time, really talking, not just going through the motions. Her heart seemed to beat, "I love you," with every beat. God's love was better than the love of a man. He was what she had wanted, even when she was walking away from him. She craved his love. Strangely, all the years of looking everywhere else had brought her back to God. He unconditionally loved her, not because she was beautiful, not because of what he could get from her or how he could use her. His love didn't demean her and turn her into less of a person. His love made her more than she had ever been. It made her valuable beyond measure.

She remembered the story of Mary Magdalene. Mary was a woman who had given away her self-respect for the love of men. Mary had also been used by men, that is, until Mary met Jesus. Now she understood; she finally got it. She had found what Mary Magdalene had found—unconditional love without measure. The love of Christ, who loved her enough to leave heaven knowing she would fail him, knowing she would not be ready when he came back for his church; he came to earth and stretched out his hands on a cruel cross giving his life for her (John 12:2–7).

Amazing grace!
how sweet the sound,
That saved a wretch like me!
I once was lost, but now am found,
Was blind; but now I see

—John Newton

A NEW DIRECTION

The Day of the Rapture

Damien Connors was a thief. He was known to his friends as DC. He had blown into town the night before, just a guy looking for a new location where he could continue his occupation without being noticed. Unfortunately, he had become too well known in the last place. He barely managed to escape with his life. The people he had angered weren't concerned about where he got his information; they just wanted him dead. They did not like guys who knew too much. He had just robbed the wrong guy. That, of course, was his mistake. He barely got out of Chicago.

He hitchhiked for a while then eventually took a bus. He just bought a ticket to the farthest place he could travel. The bus pulled into the terminal. It was late and Damien was tired. He stretched his tall, thin frame as he pulled himself up. He waited as the people in front of him unloaded. They were slow moving. He watched as a little old lady struggled to remove her luggage. He was just reaching to help her when she spoke. "Damien, could you please help me? I am afraid my old bones don't move like they used to."

He smiled his most gentlemanly smile and said, "Of course."

She reminded him of his grandmother. Grandma Grace was a fragile woman who had worked all of her life caring for people who had used her then moved on, starting with Damien's own father. Damien had grown up to become the same kind of man he swore he would never be. Damien loved her but didn't want to be around her. She reminded him of all the promises he had made and not kept. "Someday, Grandma, you wait and see; someday

I'm gonna make you proud. I'll never be a thug like my old man. I'm gonna make something of myself." But he had failed to do any of the things he had dreamed of doing. In the end he was just exactly like his dad. The thought haunted him and caused a small contraction in the pit of his stomach.

Grandma Grace had passed a few years back, and with her, every decent thing that was left in him had also passed. He hated God for taking her. He blamed God for who he had turned out to be. If God had been fair at all, she would never have spent her life doing good just to end up alone.

The little old lady thanked him for his help and moved on. Unnoticed by most of the passersby she was just a lonely figure that disappeared into the cold night air. Damien made his way into the bus terminal. He decided to pretend he was going to catch a bus that left in the morning. That would allow him to hang out in the terminal all night. He made himself comfortable on one of the chairs and stooped down allowing his head to rest against the wall as he slept.

The sun was starting to peak through the sky. The warmth of the morning light hit his cold frame, warming him. He tried to sleep a little longer, not wanting to face the day just yet, but the sun on his face would not let him rest. He was hungry. He loved coffee and decided it was a good time to make his way across the street to the local coffee house.

The smell hit his nostrils even before he opened the door. He quickly checked out the merchandise. DC was not here to actually drink coffee; it was more of a stop off before hitting one of the fast-food restaurants for breakfast. He noticed a guy in the corner working on his laptop. The guy was a little too attentive. He watched DC come in with a look of disapproval. DC knew better than to try that guy.

He scanned the room. He noticed a young woman talking to a friend on the phone. She had her laptop close by but her attention was directed to her friend. The laptop was still tucked neatly away in its carrying case. *Perfect,* he said to himself as he let the door fall closed behind him. The young woman looked up and gave him a smile. He sat a seat over watching her without appearing obvious. The guy on the laptop had gone back to work and was no longer watching him.

She said, "Oops, Cathy, just a minute. I've spilled my coffee." She held her phone in one hand. The other hand burned and was dripping with coffee. As she reached for more napkins she stopped watching her case just long enough for DC to grab it and walk out the door.

He smiled to himself. The moment of conscience he had experienced the night before was gone as he quickly made his way down the alley out of sight. He was opening up the case when he heard several cars crashing. "What?" he stopped what he was doing, picking up the case; he took a look at the busy street he had just left. The lights were working fine but for some reason cars were crashing. He looked a little closer. That's when he noticed some of the cars were without drivers.

DC was never one to worry much as to the whys; he just instinctively went into the now-is-the-time-to-strike mode. He loved opportunity. He ran to the car closest to him. It was empty. A quick move he was used to making, and he was in the car, no problem. He grabbed a wallet and noticed another case with, no doubt, another laptop. He took them and ran. He could hear the sirens of the police cars coming toward the scene of the accident.

He decided to make a quick exit back down the alleyway he had just come out of. He found a nice little nook he could tuck himself into and just wait it out. Unfortunately, the cops seemed to be overinquisitive. He did not want to get caught holding onto the merchandise. He would find somewhere to unload the stuff. He was used to finding people who would take his peculiar treasures off his hands. He was good at getting rid of the things he stole.

He moved down the alley and around the corner. He almost didn't see it, but out of nowhere was the cutest little yellow house. Imagine that, right here in the middle of the big city was this house just waiting for him. Things were looking up already. He walked up to the door. He didn't like hurting people, so he conjured up a story that he could give if the owner happened to be home. He rang the doorbell. *Ding, ding, ding.* No response. After a minute he tried the door. He gave a quick look in each direction and slipped a hand over the doorknob. It was locked. He tugged and pushed a little harder. The old lock gave way under his practiced hands.

He walked in and looked around. There was nothing to speak of in the little house that a thief would really want, but he was hungry. He surveyed the house. A familiar-looking suitcase lay across the room on a chair. He looked around and found several pictures. It was her house. He looked at the recent picture of the old lady he had helped the night before. She was smiling, looking at the person taking the picture as if she were laughing at some private joke.

He picked up another frame, touching it as though it were very precious. He stroked it gently. It contained the picture of the lady with a man. They were smiling for the camera. His arm protectively draped over the woman's shoulder. She looked all lit up inside. She had a joy that seemed to be lacking the night before. As he studied the couple, he realized the man must be dead. He stared at the elderly face with affection.

At first she said little on their journey, but when she spoke she sounded as if she valued his opinion. He had slowly let down his guard to allow the woman some companionship. She had introduced herself as Millie Mayfield, or Miss Millie to her friends. His smile formed easily as he remembered the way she had opened up to him on the bus. She was a Bible teacher. She told him she was writing her stories. She continued for hours talking easily of her husband as if he were still with her. He felt a pain of sorrow as he realized she had been reliving the days when life had been less lonely.

He walked down the hall checking to see if she was around. He didn't want to surprise her. He wanted her to remember him the way he had been on the bus, just a guy taking a trip.

The house was empty. He was hungry. He opened the fridge. There was very little food. "Miss Millie," he said out loud to himself. "I am going to have to buy you something to eat." He scoured the cabinets and managed to find some peanut butter and jelly. He poured himself a nice cup of coffee. She had obviously made coffee that morning and forgotten to turn off the pot before going out.

He was about halfway through the sandwich when he turned on the TV. "It's true, folks, the reports continue to come in, the whole world is experiencing the same phenomenon." The broadcaster continued to talk about the accidents, "Airplanes have just been falling out of the sky for no apparent reason. Some drivers have reported cars just becoming unmanned right in front of their eyes." DC panicked. His mind began to pick up the sounds still going on outside the house. People were running and screaming. He hadn't even noticed. He had tuned out the cries of humanity. The broadcaster continued, "It seems to be some kind of act of terrorism. People have just disappeared into thin air. No one has any idea how something like this could happen."

He looked around. He noticed the unmade bed, the coffeepot still on and the purse he had left untouched sitting by itself across the room. Was Miss Millie one of the people missing? He suddenly felt sick. His heart was pounding as he thought of how terrifying this must have been for her. He wanted to hit someone. If he ever caught the guys who did this, he would make them sorry. That was when he decided to stay. He knew Miss Millie wouldn't mind, as long as he didn't mess up her place. In the meantime he could stay out of sight and maybe find out who took her. It was then that the phone rang. A young lady on the phone sounded upset. "Uh, Miss Millie, are you there? Please call me. I'm worried about you. It's Anne, my number is…" She called off the numbers quickly and hung up.

He was really getting worried. Who would just take an old lady like that? She hadn't done anything to anyone. He thought back to the scene the night before. Why had he allowed her to walk home alone? He could have at least carried her suitcase for her.

He decided to do some investigating on his own, just as soon as he had some money to fund himself. He opened the laptop and erased the personal data he found on it. He slipped out the door unseen and down around the corner. Everywhere he looked there was havoc. He saw a guy coming his way. "Hey, Buddy, I've recently fallen on some hard times. I'm not looking for a handout or anything. I really need to sell my laptop. What do you say?"

The guy started to wave him off, then he noticed the laptop. "What do you want for it?"

"You know, man, this isn't a cheap piece of merchandise I have here. But I'll tell you what, since it's for you, $200.00. That's just enough to help me make my rent."

"Dude, I don't have $200.00. What about $50.00? That's all the money I have, man." He stopped, waiting for DC's reply.

"$50.00, you've got to be kidding." DC made a face as if he were being tortured. "All right, man, if you've got cash it's a deal." The young man reached in his pocket and pulled out $50.00, and they were done.

DC made his way through part of the city picking up odds and ends here and there. He was careful not to rob the stores. There were too many cameras; a guy could end up on *World's Stupidest Criminals*. He stayed more under the radar by checking out abandoned cars while pretending to be helping the local emergency workers. Man, it was like taking candy from a baby.

He finally had more than he could carry. He had even picked up a couple of bags of groceries from an empty car. There was a cart nearby so he "borrowed" it to help with moving his newly acquired merchandise. He covered his treasures with a blanket he had found in the dumpster and pretended to be homeless. He even mumbled to himself when a couple of cops almost caught him. Then he turned and walked away, pushing his cart while they watched him.

He didn't want Miss Millie's neighbors to become suspicious so he took the cart around to the back of the house near the kitchen door. A quick jerk and he was in easy as pie.

After a shower, a nap, and dinner, he settled in enough to start looking for information. He reasoned with himself noting the house seemed completely untouched. It looked to him as though Miss Millie must have known her abductors. There was no evidence of a struggle of any kind.

According to the news, everyone just disappeared into thin air. As far as he was concerned that dude was trippin'. No one just disappears. He started going through her notes to see if anyone had called her. Did she have an appointment? He turned on her computer and started going through her files. "Wow, Miss Millie, you sure have a lot of pictures." He read some of the mail she had left untouched on the table.

After a while of looking he still had no clues. He decided to read her book she had told him about. Near her computer was the whole thing, entitled, "A Sunday School Teacher Tells All." After pouring himself something to drink, he settled onto the sofa and made himself comfortable. He could almost hear her speaking as he began to read the manuscript. The stories she had shared with her students poured out onto the pages. He read till late into the night. The words reminded him of Grandma Grace's stories. Man, he used to love to hear her talk about the Bible. She would sit for hours, after working all day long, and tell him one story after another. It was funny but somehow he had forgotten many of these Bible stories.

He finally laid down the book and started to turn off the lamp when he saw it. It was lying there in plain sight right under the lamp.

To the person who finds this note,

I have decided to leave this letter to you because I am convinced you will need it. My name is Millie Mayfield and I give you permission to use my home when Jesus comes. I know there will be a lot of confusion at that time. People will disappear, causing cars to crash and planes to fall out of the sky. The disasters will be terrible. It will be a time of sorrow, but God has a plan. I am assuming if you find this that Jesus has returned and taken away his church. I believe that I will be in the rapture of the Lord's bride so that is why I am writing to you. That also means you were left behind. Feel free to read my books and, of course, the Bible. You are my guest now, even though I am not there. Take care of yourself and go to church. You will need to understand what has just happened. The little church around the corner, "Faith Fellowship," is the one I've always attended. I am sure someone will be there to help. I know everything is strange and you are probably confused by the stories of terrorism and such. I have not been kidnapped. I have gone to live with Jesus.

Sincerely,
Miss Millie Mayfield

It was worse than he had thought; the poor old lady was out of her mind. What was she thinking? As he wondered about her, his heart went out to the lonely old soul who had become so confused. There was one thing though. He should definitely check out that church. Maybe some of her friends would know where she was. He could say he was a friend who was just there to visit her. This was his first real lead. Tomorrow he would run by and see if anyone was around. Chances were someone had taken her to a place for people like her who need help. He settled into the guest bedroom as if he were used to sleeping there. She had, after all, invited him.

It was a surprise to DC when he opened the door of the church at 10:00 in the morning and found a crowd of people. Many of the people who had visited the church the night before were still praying. As he watched, he shifted uncomfortably. There was a presence that made him feel dirty. He remembered the shopping cart he had left in Miss Millie's kitchen. People were talking to God as though he were right here with them. One guy kneeling near the front pounded on his chest and looked to be in extreme pain. As DC listened, he heard the man say, "Oh God, forgive me!" DC knew one thing for sure—coming here was a bad idea.

He was on his way out the door when a young man with a big smile stopped him and asked him if he needed help. "Oh, by the way, my name is John. My dad was the pastor here, until yesterday morning, of course, when Jesus returned for his church." John was carrying a cup of coffee in one hand with a donut in the other. "This way," he said as he showed DC to a small office and indicated he should take a seat. Would you like a cup of coffee? Here, have a donut." He moved to hand DC a napkin.

DC answered, "Oh no, man, I'm good, but thank you."

"So how can I help you?" The young man looked as if he had been up all night. His face was unshaven, his clothes rumpled, and his hair was definitely uncombed.

DC watched as John devoured the donut, swigging down the coffee as though he were being sustained for an Apollo mission. "Yeah, man, I'm just here to check on Miss Millie. You know, she's a friend and I wanted to see if she was getting along okay. I'd appreciate any information you have about her. She mentioned this was her church."

"Well," John stopped, waiting for DC's name.

"Oh, I'm sorry man, my name is DC."

"Well, DC, it's like I said out front, she has gone away with Jesus, just like my dad and mom." Seeing the look on DC's face, he continued, "I assure you, she is fine. It's guys like us who are in trouble. She was sure a sweet old girl. We are really going to miss her." John seemed to tear up as he looked into DC's eyes. "I'm sorry, man. She's gone." You see, Jesus tells us about his return here in his word. 1 Thessalonians 4:16 and 17 says,"

> For the Lord himself shall descend from heaven with a shout, with the voice of the archangel, and with the trump of God: and the dead in Christ shall rise first: Then we which are alive and remain shall be caught up together with them in the clouds, to meet the Lord in the air: and so shall we ever be with the Lord.

John read the scripture slowly with his finger marking the spot. "See, they're all gone. It's not a hoax or a terrorist act. Jesus has returned and taken his church. The Bible refers to it as the catching away; that is, specifically, the people who were serving him with all their hearts. That's how all those people disappeared at once: the children, the babies, the unborn, and people like Miss Millie who loved him. There is going to be some pretty serious stuff hit the earth. God is going to pour out his wrath on the unbelievers. The book of Revelation talks about it. That's why he took Miss Millie and the others—to spare them the misery to come. Here are some scriptures you will want to study. Do you have a Bible?"

DC sat, stunned. All he could say was, "Yea, man, I have a Bible."

"Good. By the way, we're having special services nightly for the time being to help explain to people what has really gone down. You are welcome. Service starts tonight at 7:00. I hope to see you here."

DC walked out as though he had been hit with a club. His mind was reeling. Those people were as crazy as Miss Millie, but something had started to percolate deep inside him. He didn't know what it was but it bothered him. It bothered him a whole lot...

He told himself he would not be back as he walked out of the church that morning. But here he was walking into the church at 7:00 p.m. sharp, as though he did it daily. It wasn't so much what the young pastor had said, even though the hair at the back of his neck did stand up as John read the scripture. It was the thought that Miss Millie deserved to be heard out. She had left him that note and her home for sanctuary. He couldn't escape the feeling she would want him to go and really listen to what the pastor was saying.

The sermon was something like a futuristic horror film. The text was taken from Revelation and many others as the young man, John, flipped through the pages with the practice of years. He could hardly get the words out without stammering at times. He was so full of the Word, it was hard for him to slow down enough for people to follow him.

DC was beside himself as understanding collided with Grandma Grace's teachings. He had forgotten her warnings. "Be not deceived; God is not mocked: for whatsoever a man soweth, that shall he also reap" (Galatians 6:7).

The weight of many years of serving another master threatened to crush him. He was finding it hard to breathe. It felt as though an elephant had just decided to sit on his chest. His mind reeled as he listened to the message: "For all have sinned, and come short of the glory of God" (Romans 3:23).

The words of Pastor Paul hit their target as the pastor stood there and openly confessed his sin. That was it! He couldn't take anymore. He stood up intending to run away. But before he could, he crumbled to the floor, sobbing, as shame flooded him. "God," he screamed. "God, please forgive me!" The words ripping from his lips were a plea from the depths of his being. "God, I know I'm a sinner! Please help me!" Pastor Paul knelt beside him, placing an arm around him; Paul began to pray for him. Long, hard sobs shook his body as he confessed his sin to the Lord. Time passed as though it were minutes. When he got up from the floor, to his amazement, he had been there for hours. Something else amazed him. He felt clean from the inside out—the kind of clean you can't get from just taking a bath. The elephant that had been sitting on his chest was gone. He took a deep cleansing breath. His mind was free of pain. And the hidden thing—the thing only he and God knew about, that monkey he had carried around for years—was gone. He knew he was free!

HEARTBROKEN

For the gifts and calling of God are without repentance.

Romans 11:29

Two days after Jesus returned, Paul Stevens received a call. "Hello, this is Paul Stevens."

"Pastor, it's Ron Chambers, I think we should talk. Can we meet for coffee?"

"Sure, Ron. Where do you want to meet?"

"There's a diner near my job over on Second Street, Amelia's. Do you know it?"

"Yea, I do. When can you be there?"

"I have a meeting at 10:00 this morning. Can you meet me there at 9:00?"

"All right, I'll see you there." Paul hung up his cell.

Shelby was looking at him questioningly. "What's up?"

"Ron Chambers wants to talk to me. He didn't say why. I agreed to meet with him at 9:00."

She studied Paul. "Do you think he wants you to come back?"

"I don't know. I do think the church needs a pastor, especially now."

"They need you there, Paul. You were wonderful last night. I've never been prouder of you than I was when you asked the church to pray with you. God may be opening a door."

"There must be a lot of hurting people. I would like to help them through this. We could do a good work for the Lord. Would you be interested in going back?" He waited for her to confirm what he already knew.

"Yes, I think we belong there," she answered without hesitation.

"Me too, if they'll let me. I believe I can make a difference. I want to help people understand what is coming."

"By the way, John asked me to officiate over his and Carly's wedding last night." Paul laughed as he thought about John teasing him. "He said it was hard to find an ordained minister these days. It looks like they're stuck with me since they want to be married at Faith Fellowship and not at the justice of the peace."

"Have they set a date?" The look on her face reflected the wheels were beginning to turn.

"As soon as possible. They are staying in separate homes for now, but they want to be together."

"Oh, Paul," Shelby looked heartbroken. "They won't have their families. They are just trying to get married. It sounds like they've given up their dreams. I know Carly wanted a big wedding with all of their friends and families."

Paul looked at his wife, his blue eyes telling his thoughts. "I think that's us now, babe. I don't think they have any family left at all."

"That's so sad. We have to make this special for them." Shelby was giving him a look that meant she was kicking into a whole new gear.

"No, honey. John was clear about this. They want to be together as husband and wife as soon as possible. John said Carly no longer cares if she has the"—he raised his hands in the air to make parentheses—"'big day.' They just want to be married, no big fuss, something simple with some of their friends." He continued to make his point. "I mean, think about it, her mom is gone, her Auntie Sue, and her grandmother too—the whole family. All they have left is each other and their friends like you and me. I guess they don't feel much like throwing a big party. John and I agreed to meet today at 10:00 to discuss the need for food, clothing, and other basic essentials. When I asked him if they were going all out, his answer was, 'How can we? Soon it's going to be difficult to even buy food.'"

Shelby's big green eyes filled with tears. "We can't let them do this without a celebration. They can invite the church and their friends from work, etcetera. The wedding can be announced from the pulpit on Sunday. Their friends can be called. I'll start planning."

"Now, honey, they are the ones doing this. If they want to keep it simple we have to respect that."

"I do. I just know Carly. She wants more than a few friends. She has always planned on a big wedding. I remember on our wedding day she hung out with me watching me in my dress. I told her she was a beautiful flower girl. She giggled, twirled around, and told me, 'When I get big I'm going to wear a dress just like yours. I want to look like a princess.' Her eyes were as big as saucers. She said, 'I want a dress that goes all the way out to here.' She even held her arms out as wide as she could to show me. Oh, honey, she was so cute dreaming about her own wedding. We have to make it perfect for her."

Shelby made a mental note clicking off each item. "Now let me see, you're doing the ceremony. They can have the church whenever they want it. The ladies can cater the whole thing; we just need a menu, flowers, and music. I'll call the ladies. We can all work together. It'll be great. I'll keep it simple. Anyway, it's like you said, we're all they have now. It's my duty to step in and help her as if she were my own little sister."

Paul shook his head in disbelief. Jesus had come only two days ago, and already his wife was planning a wedding. He knew better than to argue with her about this so he just cautioned her again not to step on anybody's toes.

"Paul Stevens, how dare you? Of course I will get Carly's okay on everything. What do you think I am? But there is no way I'm going to let those two young people get married without a party."

Paul laughed as his wife ushered him off to his meeting. She was a force to be reckoned with and she had made up her mind. Carly was not going to be a wallflower at her own wedding. Shelby would see to that.

He arrived a little before Ron, so he took a booth, ordered some coffee, and waited for his friend. He hadn't seen the news that morning, so he was glad for the time to catch up. He pulled out his phone and brought up the headlines. He wanted to know the world's spin on everything. It was incredible. The article read, "Aliens Invade the World." The story went on to explain the many sightings of aliens at the time of the disappearances. It would have been funny if it wasn't so sad. He could not believe the eye-witness testimonies he was reading about. He also couldn't help but wonder what drugs the so-called witnesses had been taking when they had their "encounters."

He scanned more articles; his finger stopped as he noticed tucked neatly away was a blurb about the president of the United Community. This was originally a coalition of ten countries working together who, by forming an alliance, had gained world power. The story would have led the headlines if the rapture had not happened. As he viewed the story he was shaken by the report. It said, "The president of the United Community has been working with the Israelis; his dream for peace with Israel is his priority." The picture showed the president excitedly shaking hands with the prime minister of Israel. How had he missed this? Where had he been? Why hadn't he noticed how close Israel was to forming a Peace Treaty with this man? As he read on, the answer to his questions appeared on the page in front of him. The reporter wrote these peace talks have been held in secret. The president and the prime minister believed the talks would be more effective without outside interference. They had reached an agreement the day of the disappearances. Out of respect for the missing, they had decided not to make an announcement that day. He shook his head in disbelief. The seven-year countdown had started behind closed doors.

His thoughts were abruptly interrupted when Ron walked up to him, set his briefcase down, and took a seat opposite his. The waitress came by to get his order. "I'll just have coffee." She picked up their menus and walked away. Ron looked a little uncomfortable. "I called you because we want you to come back and I'm the guy they nominated to ask you."

Paul thought for a minute then asked, "They. How many?"

"Everyone on the board. The church is in chaos. People keep calling wondering what happened. People are scared, Paul. Their children just disappeared. Pastor Ken and almost the whole youth group are gone. We don't know what to say to people. We can't help them. We're desperate."

"Would this be a permanent position or do you just want someone to help until you can find another pastor?"

Ron looked frustrated. "We don't honestly know. None of us was thinking that far ahead. We just know we need someone now. You were the only guy we could think of."

"Don't you mean left?"

Ron smiled and acknowledged the question. "Yeah, I mean left."

"Okay, I'll do it." Paul knew he had to.

Ron looked a little surprised. "Just like that, no promises."

"No promises. Call the board and tell them to contact everyone they can. We will be holding special meetings starting tonight at 7:00. I want everyone they can reach by phone or e-mail to be notified. These meetings will be nightly until I say different. Paul stood and counted out his money, leaving it on the table for the waitress. Is that all?"

Ron looked at Paul with relief. "Yeah, that's it."

"Then I need to be going, I have a 10:00 as well." He should have asked sooner but he had not dreamed there would be so many. "By the way how many of the congregation was left behind?"

Ron looked at him and repeated his statement as if he was confused. "Left behind?"

"You know, how many didn't make the rapture?" Paul just assumed most of his congregation was gone.

Ron looked really uncomfortable. "Well, pretty much all of us. Are you trying to say you think Jesus has raptured out his church?"

"Yeah, that's what I'm saying." Paul was bewildered. His mouth suddenly felt dry. His legs seemed weak; he slid back down onto his seat.

"Well, I don't think he did. Listen, Paul, almost everyone from the church is fine. Whoever has dropped in and taken the children, it wasn't the Lord. If Jesus had returned we would all be with him. This is an act of terrorism. We have our children missing and some of the adults, but most of the adult congregation is still here." Ron moved in toward Paul as if to share some deep secret. "I've been thinking about it. You know; why would they take the kids? I think they intend to brainwash them and place them back into society. The adults they took to help take care of the kids, maybe even give them information, who knows?"

It seemed to Paul that he had just been given the news an atomic bomb had struck his congregation. As he listened to Ron's theory of the missing, an inexpressible sorrow came over him. "How many were left behind?"

Ron answered again, "Almost all of us."

Paul couldn't speak. How had he failed his congregation so completely? They didn't even realize Jesus had come back! "Ron, I'll see you tonight. I have a lot to explain to you and the others."

Paul arrived at Pastor Jentson's church at exactly 10:00. Shelby was already there going over her ideas for the wedding with Carly and John. He could hear Carly saying, "Oh, Shelby, thank you. That sounds so beautiful."

John looked very much like a deer caught in headlights. He seemed dazed and unable to respond. Carly, on the other hand, was glowing. The girls looked up at him as he walked in with tears shimmering in their eyes. Their smiles lit up the little office.

"I guess Shelby has been making plans." he smiled, not wanting to stifle the joy he saw on the girls' faces. Shelby looked like her old self for the first time in months. Carly looked radiant. He wanted them to have this time of joy. There was enough unhappiness to deal with.

"Shelby offered to let me use her wedding dress." Carly bubbled. "She's planning to invite all of our friends. It's going to be beautiful."

John noticed Paul looked unhappy. He asked, "How are you doing, Paul?"

Paul did not want to answer that. He had been driving around hoping he had misunderstood Ron in some way, but he couldn't see how. He looked at John, the joy of a minute ago already gone. Unable to pretend, he answered honestly, "I'm devastated. I just found out almost my whole congregation was left behind."

The four stared at each other, the others trying to accept what he had just said. "How," John inquired, "How can that be?"

Paul broke. "I failed them." He sniffed, trying to hold back the tears. "They've asked me to come back."

Shelby slipped over to Paul. "You aren't the only one who failed them. I was in this with you. And they have to take some responsibility for their own behavior. You can't carry this; you won't be able to help anyone if you fall under this load."

"I wasn't ready and that was my fault, not yours. I knew I couldn't have unforgiveness in my heart. No one had to single that sin out for me. I knew it. I am the one who messed up. I should have asked the Lord for forgiveness. I was just too stubborn to forgive you."

"I should have warned them. I should have made them understand that God is love, but he is also just. I was afraid of losing them. I wanted to make people happy and keep attendance up so I didn't preach the warnings."

"You're right," Shelby admitted. "You should have told them they were in need of God. That hell is real and that Jesus was coming back for his church. You should have made them understand that he was coming for the people who were watching and waiting for him. We should have anticipated his return. But you didn't. That doesn't change the fact that they all had Bibles. They could have and should have read those scriptures for themselves" (Luke 12:37 and 38).

"I'm not going to let you carry this whole thing yourself. You can't help them if you fall apart. You're here with them and we're going to help everyone we can. God has forgiven you and now you're going to do what is necessary to help them all survive the days ahead. You have to warn them and prepare them for what's coming. Your guilt won't help anyone. You have to give this guilt to God. You can't blame yourself. You have to be strong for them. And you have to be strong for me."

John understood his friend's pain. "I know just what you mean. I should have been ready. I should have been working to help make others ready; I wasn't. We have to pick up the pieces of our lives and make these last days count."

"I want to pray for God to strengthen you through this time as a man and as a pastor." The little room took on a new glow as the four prayed for strength to endure and bear the responsibility of ministry.

John was the first to mention it. The prayer time had died down and they were just beginning to come together as a group. "We have to have a plan. We know we are not going to be able to buy or sell. We also know the church will have to go underground just to survive. I think we need to plant gardens and grow as much food as possible. We will need to can it or preserve it in some way and find a place or places for storage."

Shelby agreed. "We also need to look into some of the houses people left behind. I know it sounds like stealing but over the years many of the ladies have been canning and preparing for a disaster. The people in the church who have been raptured would want us to use their food and supplies."

John nodded his head. "I've been thinking. My mom and dad's house is big. It's paid for and a few years ago Dad put it in my name. It has a full basement with plenty of storage for canned goods and other supplies. The backyard is large enough to grow a big garden.

There's also Miss Millie's place. She has given the church her home in her will. We need to talk to an attorney and find out what the legal specifics are under the circumstances. With so many missing, these homes are going to put a big responsibility on the city. They need to be maintained. We'll need new laws addressing the future of these vacant homes. And with houses like Miss Millie's just sitting there, break-ins will be a problem. She also has a big backyard with plenty of garden space and a huge basement. I helped her take some of her canned food down there once. Her basement was full. She said she was preparing for an emergency. She also said, 'It will feed people someday.'" He started to choke up as he thought of her on her income trying to prepare for them.

"I'm sure there are many more," Paul said. "My church has a good-size kitchen. Everything is state of the art. We can use it for canning and such, and as long as the authorities will let us we can feed people right there.

After everyone decided, they had a workable plan. Paul took out his phone. He scanned the news looking for the article, then handing it to John who was standing, he watched as John fell back into his seat as if someone had deflated him. Paul's steel-blue eyes studied his friend. "Israel has signed the Peace Treaty." The girls watched the men as they both began researching scriptures for the upcoming events. Everything was happening just as the Bible predicted. The countdown to Armageddon had started.

The news had shaken them all. Shelby and Carly decided to let the guys do their thing. The girls needed a break. They wanted to see how the wedding dress looked on Carly, so Shelby invited Carly to her home.

$$\sim\!\!\sim$$

"Oh, Shelby, it's perfect." Carly petted the little flower petals on the expensive lace. The flowers stood up from the fabric. Tiny hand-sewn pearls adorned the already-beautiful garment. Carly swung from side to side watching the skirt swish back and forth. The neckline was scooped off the shoulder with long sleeves that were also lined and covered with lace. The back dipped down slightly with a row of satin-covered buttons. The waist was fitted, but on Carly it was loose.

Shelby moved to inspect the garment. Taking out her straight pins, she began to pin the garment for alterations. "It's really not a bad fit," she said as she looked at Carly and the garment in the mirror. "We're about the same height so the length looks good. You could wear a little higher heel. I think it's beautiful on you. Are you sure, Carly? I love this dress and I would consider it an honor if you wear it. But if you want your own, I understand. I just want you to be happy."

Carly looked back at Shelby with tears shimmering in her eyes. "I think it's perfect. I didn't think I would have anything like this. We just stopped wanting. You know, nothing seems important except pleasing the Lord. I haven't been feeling much like a bride. This is something of a shotgun wedding. I mean, John is marrying me because we can't go on living this way anymore—"

Shelby interrupted her. "Okay, stop right there. Yeah, I know you guys need to be married. That goes without saying. God ordained marriage. He patterned our relationship with him after that covenant. It delights the Lord when his children make this commitment with him and each other. But if you think John doesn't want to marry you, you're wrong. I've known John almost all of his life. I know he loves you. It's just that he sees God has drawn a line in the sand, and he realizes he can't cross it. Not even for you. As much as he loves you he loves God more. And that's the way you want him to feel, believe me. He'll be a much better husband with his priorities straight. He won't be living with all the guilt. He will be able to show you affection without feeling ashamed. This is a good thing. I'm proud of both of you. You've stepped up to the plate."

Shelby smiled, tears surfacing in her large green eyes. "Carly, watching you with those young people last night blessed me. They love you. And John, when he stepped to the pulpit and started to speak, it was as if a young Dad Jentson had taken the platform. He would be so proud of both of you. You have both become such precious vessels pouring out God's love on the people. It's not just John's calling. I see now it's yours too.

Don't allow the circumstances that caused all of this to be rushed along to stop you from knowing John loves you. I know it isn't what you envisioned when you dreamed of your wedding day. I know you saw yourself with your family there. But that doesn't mean it won't be wonderful. And you both belong together, ministering. I saw that for myself last night."

Carly was touched. "I thought my mom would be helping me plan my wedding. It was going to be this really big thing with all of our family. When they disappeared it just didn't seem to matter anymore. I really appreciate your making it important again."

Shelby smiled at her friend. "Jesus said, 'For as in the days that were before the flood they were eating and drinking, marrying and giving in marriage, until the day that No-e entered into the ark,' (Matthew 24:38). Even in this time of sorrow and great challenge, life goes on. Maybe not how we planned but it still continues. You are going to have a beautiful wedding. You will be the most beautiful bride ever. And you'll be there with your new family—the people God is entrusting into your care as the bride of the new pastor of Faith Fellowship Church. We are all your family now, Carly, and we want to make your day as special as you are." Shelby reached out and hugged her young friend. "You'll see, sweetie. It's going to be wonderful. Now, more than ever, we all need a reason to be happy. We're going to throw you a beautiful wedding."

THE MESSAGE

Paul Stevens walked into the sanctuary a little after 7:00. He was purposely late, choosing to stay in prayer. He did not want to answer any questions about his affair or why he was back. He knew many people were hurting, wondering what had happened to the children. He wanted to address the church at one time rather than repeat himself to each individual. The music service was just getting underway. The last half hour he had spent on his knees. He dreaded the news he knew he would be giving his congregation. The music was charged with electricity. Something in the atmosphere of the church seemed different, or was it him? He knew he was definitely different. The worship concluded. As he walked up to the podium he was all business.

"Good evening, everyone. I have been asked to return here as pastor for the purpose of helping you through this difficult time. I have requested that you all be here tonight because I believe Jesus has returned for his church and we have been left behind." There was a stir among the people. "I understand many of you have missing children. Let me set your minds at ease. They are with Jesus. My wife and I are dealing with the catching away of our own two children. We are both convinced they are safe with the Lord."

He placed his hands on both sides of the pulpit, grasping it for support. He fought to maintain his composure as he struggled with the words to use. "I want to apologize to you personally for my own failure as your pastor. A couple of weeks ago I thought the biggest problem I had was infidelity. But now I realize that was just a symptom of my own lack of understanding, just how far I was getting away from God and how very quickly Jesus was going to return." Paul's voice echoed his heartbreak. "Tonight, I stand before you a broken man because of my sin as your pastor. I confess to you tonight. I allowed pride and the desire to succeed to keep me from warning you every time the Lord prompted me."

"The Lord in Isaiah 58:1, speaking to the prophet, says, 'Cry aloud, spare not, lift up thy voice like a trumpet, and shew my people their transgression, and the house of Jacob their sins."

"Again, God speaking to the prophet Ezekiel, in chapter 3, verses 16 to 21, says,"

> And it came to pass at the end of seven days, that the word of the Lord came unto me, saying, Son of man, I have made thee a watchman unto the house of Israel: therefore hear the word at my mouth, and give them warning from me. When I say unto the wicked, Thou shalt surely die; and thou givest him not warning, nor speakest to warn the wicked from his wicked way, to save his life; the same wicked man shall die in his iniquity; but his blood will I require at thine hand. Yet if thou warn the wicked, and he turn not from his wickedness, nor from his wicked way, he shall die in his iniquity; but thou hast delivered thy soul. Again, When a righteous man doth turn from his righteousness, and commit iniquity, and I lay a stumbling-block before him, he shall die: because thou hast not given him warning, he shall die in his sin, and his righteousness which he hath done shall not be remembered; but his blood will I require at thine hand. Nevertheless if thou warn the righteous man, that the righteous sin not, and he doth not sin, he shall surely live, because he is warned; also thou hast delivered thy soul.

Paul cleared his throat. Taking out his handkerchief, he wiped his eyes. "I have failed to warn you. I am truly sorry." The congregation stirred as they listened to their pastor bare his soul to them. "Turn with me to Matthew 25:1–13. Jesus is explaining the parable of the ten virgins. It says,"

THEN shall the kingdom of heaven be likened unto ten virgins, which took their lamps, and went forth to meet the bridegroom. And five of them were wise, and five were foolish. They that were foolish took their lamps, and took no oil with them: But the wise took oil in their vessels with their lamps. While the bridegroom tarried, they all slumbered and slept. And at midnight there was a cry made, Behold, the bridegroom cometh; go ye out to meet him. Then all those virgins arose, and trimmed their lamps. And the foolish said unto the wise, Give us of your oil; for our lamps are gone out. But the wise answered, saying, Not so; lest there be not enough for us and you: but go ye rather to them that sell, and buy for yourselves. And while they went to buy, the bridegroom came; and they that were ready went in with him to the marriage: and the door was shut. Afterward came also the other virgins, saying, Lord, Lord, open to us. But he answered and said, Verily I say unto you, I know you not. Watch therefore, for ye know neither the day nor the hour wherein the Son of man cometh.

Paul hesitated. Taking out his hankie, he wiped his mouth. "The bridegroom is Jesus. The ten virgins are the church. Five were ready; they were waiting and watching for their bridegroom. They kept their lamps trimmed and full of oil. They even had extra oil in case they needed it." Paul stopped and cleared his throat. Fighting back the tears, he continued, "Five were foolish. They did not have enough oil. The Bible tells us in verses 10–12 that while they were buying, the door was shut. Even though they pleaded with the bridegroom to let them in, he answered, 'I don't know you.'"

There had been an ongoing hum throughout the congregation—the sound of mourning mingled with disbelief. The crowd grew louder as some openly disagreed, while others could not contain their sorrow. One of the men in the congregation stood up waving his fist at Paul; he booed him. The atmosphere of the crowd was becoming hostile. Paul was not the shrinking-violet type. He did not care how the man threatened him. He stood straight as he reasoned with the man and the others. Looking at the crowd fearlessly, Paul pressed on. "We did not keep our lamps trimmed and full of the Holy Spirit. When Jesus came we were not watching. He warned us in verse 13, saying, 'Watch therefore, for ye know neither the day nor the hour wherein the Son of man cometh.' There are some here who think if Christ has returned, why didn't he take all of us? I believe this parable explains that to us."

Paul stood quietly, waiting for the people to come to order. After a few minutes people began to quiet one another; all over the room Paul heard them saying, "Quiet, let him speak."

Paul began again, "I used to believe that God was love and he loved all of us. I am convinced this is still the case. However, I now believe that he does not indulge us as if we were spoiled children. He expects us to be as the five who were wise—expecting him, waiting for his return, anticipating the trumpet blast."

"We no longer have the option of the rapture, but we do know he will return again. Revelation 1:7 tells us, 'Behold, he cometh with clouds; and every eye shall see him, and they also which pierced him: and all kindreds of the earth shall wail because of him. Even so, Amen.'"

"We still await his coming when he will stand on the Mount of Olives. At that time he will cause an earthquake. The mountain will be divided in half; the people of Israel will run into the canyon created by him into safety (Zechariah 14:4–5). He will make war against his enemies. Praise God, he is coming again. And he will set up his throne in Jerusalem. He will reign there for one thousand years. Please read Revelation 20:4 with me."

> And I saw thrones, and they sat upon them, and judgment was given unto them: and I saw the souls of them that

were beheaded for the witness of Jesus, and for the word of God, and which had not worshipped the beast, neither his image, neither had received his mark upon their foreheads, or in their hands; and they lived and reigned with Christ a thousand years.

"My friends, we are living in a time when the events of the next few years will be both exciting and terrifying. Exciting because we have a front-row seat to the fulfillment of Bible prophesies and terrifying because the world will reject us. They will even kill us! We have to decide whose side we are on. The line has been drawn in the sand and the question is, 'Who is on the Lord's side?'"

"Just as in the days of Joshua when he stood before the congregation of Israel and said, 'Me and my family, we will serve the Lord' (Joshua 24:15). I stand before you now asking you: Will you serve the Lord? The days ahead are perilous times. Matthew 24:9–14 says,"

Then shall they deliver you up to be afflicted, and shall kill you: and ye shall be hated of all nations for my name's sake. And then shall many be offended, and shall betray one another, and shall hate one another. And many false prophets shall rise, and shall deceive many. And because iniquity shall abound, the love of many shall wax cold. But he that shall endure unto the end, the same shall be saved. And this gospel of the kingdom shall be preached in all the world for a witness unto all nations; and then shall the end come.

The sorrow of a church that had come to terms with their own sins and shortcomings was rolling through the congregation much in the way the ocean rolls in and out. The waves of grief carried their own repentance as men and women understood: Jesus had returned for his bride and they were not ready.

Pastor Paul said, "Please join me at the altar." The crowd gathered at the front, some kneeling, trying to find comfort and forgiveness, others standing in the aisles anywhere they could find a space. Paul had spoken to them of the Lord's appearing but the hope of those words was stifled by the understanding of the time of sorrow they were facing. Many knew the Scriptures and, like Pastor Paul, had simply failed to stay awake. Others had simply not bothered to even learn for themselves the warnings that filled the Word of God. All grieved and sought the Lord in their own way.

After some time in prayer had passed, Pastor Paul asked, "Who is on the Lord's side? Who among you will say, 'Me and my family, we will serve the Lord' (Joshua 24:15)." Hands went up all over the sanctuary, even the one that belonged to a traitor. She had the face of an angel. Her long, thick hair hung softly down her back. She wore a blue dress with high heels; her nails were manicured to perfection. The smile on her face was one of indulgence. She had often played the part of someone who was completely sold out to Christ; but her many interests had kept her from a true relationship with the Lord. She was not the type to be manipulated like these weak-minded followers she was watching. She had a purpose for everything she did.

THE ANTICHRIST

The man of sin stood on a high pinnacle. The darkness of the night was lit by the many city lights below. Off in the distance he could see them, all the countries of the world. Beside him stood a dark presence, the hand of the dark being reached out and held him at his back. The being stretched out his hand, waving it across the sky as he spoke, "All of this you see is mine to give to whomever I desire. I will give it all to you if you will only worship me."

The moon cast an iridescent glow over the earth. The clouds moved slowly past the light it gave. There in the darkness of the night under the canopy of the stars the man bowed himself to his master. The dark hand of evil reached out and touched the head of his anointed one...

The man of sin electrified the nations. He held the attention of his followers. "We can change the world. Nothing like this has ever before been attempted. We now have the technology to feed everyone. No more will there be a difference in class determined only by wealth. The poor, as well as the rich, will be given every advantage. We will feed the world and put an end to the problems of society."

Cheers rang as this handsome, articulate man in his prime spoke of a brighter day. Near him were his disciples, those who had been handpicked by him. They smiled at him as he gave another great performance. He was on his way to the top and they were going with him. In the shadows of the stage stood another man, he was content to allow the speaker to have his day in the sun. All that mattered was that the man who was speaking be able to continue to fool his followers. An evil shiver ran through this man as he considered the master's plan. The smile that touched his lips reflected the sick manifestation of a demon. For those watching with eyes that could discern, the spirit was obvious. But to the person who did not know Jesus, the demon was well hidden. His host was a warlock. He practiced witchcraft passed down through the ages. The demon smiled as he thought of the trick he would soon be playing.

As the Antichrist spoke, a hush came over the enthralled crowd. A cloud moved behind him and stood over him. It reached high into the heavens, shaping itself into an angelic presence. The sun hit the silhouette, and the people gasped as they announced, "It's an angel. Look, it's an angel watching over him." The demonic being held his angelic pose, smiling at the gullibility of everyone. *Soon*, he thought. *Soon I will have your souls for meat.* As the Antichrist continued to speak, Satan kept his hand on the man's back; after all, that is the way a puppeteer handles his puppet.

The man of sin finished his speech. A smile touched the corners of his mouth, exposing perfectly straight, brilliant white teeth. Once again he had accomplished his mission. One day soon he would be appointed to rule the world. He felt goose bumps rise all over his body as he momentarily focused on the power that would accompany such a position. Then he could introduce his real plans. There would be no stopping him. The cheering crowd was intoxicating as he listened to them chant his name. His soul was a small price to pay for their adoration.

He did not consider the truth of the Bible. He had avoided the Scriptures, wanting only the fame and glory that accompanied his position. As Hitler and so many others before him who had become drunk with their thirst for power, his only thought was for this moment. He did not look ahead to hell, the place where the soul never dies. It is a place where there is a burning, literal fire that is never quenched. The Bible tells us when God created man he formed him out of the dust of the earth. Then God breathed into his nostrils the breath of life, and man became a living soul (Genesis 2:7). That is why the soul of man lives on forever, somewhere. It does not burn up and is not destroyed. It does not cease to exist. The Bible tells us their worm (speaking of the soul) never dies (Isaiah 66:24).

There is also separation from God. Hell was created for Satan and his angels, but it has enlarged itself for those who set God aside and exclude him from their very existence (Isaiah 5:14 and 15). There, the fire is not quenched and the soul never dies (Mark 9:43–48). The blackness of hell is like no other (Matthew 25:30). God is light and without him there is no light (John 1:4–5, Revelation 21:23–24). People who reject God in this life are doomed to hell without God to remain there forever. Man's rejection of God in this life becomes his sentence in the world to come.

The very beings that tempted and persuaded mankind to follow them while here on earth are revealed as they truly are. These filthy beasts hate every soul with a murderous passion. But there in hell the soul cannot die—there in the vast depth of darkness with only the flames of hell that give no light, because God is light and man is separated from God (Jude 1:13). The soul's only companions are the demons that have violated, followed, harassed, tormented, and dragged the soul of that person into hell. Their screams of anguish express the torment that never ends. The sounds heard are the screams of others as they are burning, tormented by the fire that is never quenched. The smell of sulfur steals breath and chokes the lost, leaving them fighting for air. This place was not meant for mankind. It is the punishment of fallen angels. But it has enlarged itself to accommodate the souls of people who have rejected the one and only Savior, God's Son, Jesus Christ (Isaiah 5:14).

Yes, only Jesus can save us from that pit. He is the Holy One of God, the one destined from the fall of man to bear the sin of man, in order to reconcile mankind to the Father. In the Garden of Eden God first spoke of Jesus as the Lord; he cursed the serpent, saying, "And I will put enmity between thee and the woman, and between thy seed and her seed; it shall bruise thy head, and thou shalt bruise his heel" (Genesis 3:15).

Later mankind offered up burnt offerings to God. They offered him perfect lambs. The blood of the lambs reminded Father God of his Son who would come one day. The Bible records, "The next day John seeth Jesus coming unto him, and saith, Behold the Lamb of God, which taketh away the sin of the world" (John 1:29).

The Bible also records Jesus talking to Thomas, "Jesus saith unto him, I am the way, the truth, and the life: no man cometh unto the Father, but by me" (John 14:6). We think we can find God on our own, we believe there are many ways to heaven, but Jesus said, "I am the way." He illustrates his point with this example, saying, "VERILY, verily, I say unto you, He that entereth not by the door into the sheepfold, but climbeth up some other way, the same is a thief and a robber. But he that entereth in by the door is the shepherd of the sheep" (John 10:1–2). "I am the door: by me if any man enter in, he shall be saved, and shall go in and out, and find pasture" (John 10:9).

In Ephesians 5:5, we read, "For this ye know, that no whoremonger, nor unclean person, nor covetous man, who is an idolater, hath any inheritance in the kingdom of Christ and of God." Also Isaiah 35:8 says, speaking of the New Jerusalem, "And an highway shall be there, and a way, and it shall be called The way of holiness; the unclean shall not pass over it; but it shall be for those: the wayfaring men, though fools, shall not err therein."

We can't earn our way into his kingdom by being good; because, the Word says, "For all have sinned, and come short of the glory of God" (Romans 3:23). We don't have the power to live a life that is righteous. So God had a plan. He never intended that mankind would die in their sin, lost and hopeless without

God. "For God so loved the world, that he gave his only begotten Son, that whosoever believeth in him should not perish, but have everlasting life" (John 3:16). "For God sent not his Son into the world to condemn the world; but that the world through him might be saved" (John 3:17).

By refusing God's plan, we accept the alternative. We actually make the decision that condemns our soul to hell. We are the ones who reject God; he simply honors our wishes.

THE STAGE IS SET

The Antichrist worked diligently for peace. His primary objective had been Israel. The peace talks were a success. *Israel will now cooperate*, he thought to himself. He studied the world map in his office. His plans were coming to life in front of his eyes.

He had taken full advantage of the missing by stepping to the forefront on the wings of the United Community. The nations of the world were stunned by the tragedy of the recently missing people. They mourned the loss of their loved ones. They sorrowed for those who had died in the many accidents as a consequence of the disappearances. The world watched in horror as reports flooded in of the many victims. Grief overwhelmed the nations as people had to admit their loved ones were gone without a trace.

The Antichrist sprang into action, elected to power by the nations. He had been waiting for such a time as this. His work for the United Community was very impressive. The World Federation, which included the UC, took notice of him. The WF had grown to include all of the major players. Under their directive he was asked to organize emergency relief for the world.

He ordered the military of the World Federation to move into each country with a promise of relief. His many philanthropic works were known; his kindness was publicized. Reporters announced, "He is a man of peace. His message to our shaken world is one of hope and direction. He has worked tirelessly for peaceful solutions to the world problems and uses his powerful military force to help support these very important programs."

After the rapture he won the hearts of people by moving his army in with the directive to clear the highways and assist with any local efforts. Their purpose was more of a mercy mission. They were to console the mourning, deal with the burial of the dead, and organize removal of abandoned vehicles. They also led the way in disbursement of food and necessities to the needy. Oh, how the people loved him. Their financial problems left them hungry and vulnerable. His tactic was one that proclaimed peace, but with it came total submission. His army, now massive, quickly fell into place to back up all of his desires.

The president of the United Community was elected to world leader almost overnight. His friends and followers quickly created a new position for him. Humbly he took the world stage announcing his sorrow for all the disappearances. His manner was kind and caring. His show of love melted the hearts of the people. "My beloved friends, it is with a heavy heart I accept this position as the world president. Thank you for your faith in me."

Immediately after his inauguration, he ordered his military forces to occupy the nations with the greatest needs. He imposed a tax on the rich to help those who were unable to support themselves. His military might—the armies of the World Federation—became more massive as it absorbed the military power of the nations he moved in to help. No nation was able to object. If they did, he would move his massive military force against them ultimately, bringing them under subjection to his authority. Checkmate!

Two men stepped out of heaven and onto the stage of planet Earth. Their clothing was of sackcloth. They walked into Jerusalem declaring the word of the Lord. Their dialects were old. Although they spoke in their ancient tongues everyone who heard them understood them perfectly (Revelation 11:3–13).

The news carried the reports of two homeless men who stood in the streets of Jerusalem preaching. "Hello, this is Barbara Lamb. I am on location in Jerusalem. I am standing in front of the Wailing Wall where two men are declaring the fall of the world."

Bob, the anchor, listened attentively to his associate. "I understand they have caused confusion by disrupting the celebration of the Peace Treaty between Israel and the world president today. Tell us what has been going on over there, Barbara."

"It is really incredible. As you know, Bob, this celebration has been put on hold for the last few weeks out of respect for the missing. Also, with the inauguration of the world president coming right on the wings of the signing of the Peace Treaty, there simply has not been enough time. But the atmosphere was one of jubilation, until about a half hour ago when two men just showed up. They say they are the two witnesses who have been sent from God to warn the world of the wrath to come. They have condemned the world president of unspeakable acts. They are boldly proclaiming that the world is coming under the judgment of God. I understand the world president has just ordered his military guards to remove them immediately."

Swoooooosh! An odd sound rang through the air. Barbara cried out as she watched an explosion of fire shoot from the two witnesses. It consumed the soldiers, burning them alive.

People ran, screaming as they tried to escape, "They're firing at us." Panic ripped through the crowd.

The police announced over a loud speaker, "Remain calm, everyone. Please leave the area in an orderly fashion."

"What was that, Barbara?" Bob asked, concerned.

Barbara was visibly shaken. "Bob, it's the most awful thing I've ever seen. The guards who were called in to control the situation just exploded into flames."

"Just a minute." She ran toward the crowd. "Sir, did you see what happened?" she asked, placing a microphone in front of an eyewitness.

The man, obviously upset, fought for composure. After a moment he began to speak. "Well, those two homeless guys came out here causing a disturbance. They were rambling on about the end of the world, saying they were witnesses from God. Those guys are really off the charts, if you know what I mean. After a while the guards showed up to calm them down. All the guards did was order those two witness guys to stop what they were doing and come with them. One of the witnesses just pointed at them and said no. I saw a flash of fire shoot from the guy to the guards, and the next thing I knew, the guards just burst into flames. It was horrible!"

A loud blast barreled through the air as a horn blew. The camera kept rolling in the background; a fire engine pulled up to the victims of the fire. Emergency workers were dealing with crowd control as the paramedics removed the bodies from the scene.

Barbara persisted, "Did you see the weapon they used?"

"No, ma'am, Like I just said the witness guy answered no, and the fire shot out of him. It looked like it came from his mouth. I know that sounds crazy, but that's what I saw. Excuse me, I have to find my wife." The eyewitness hurried away.

Barbara composed herself to sign off. Behind her the crowd was dwindling as people ran for their lives. She raised herself to her full height, drew the microphone up to her mouth and said, "You've seen it here folks. This is Barbara Lamb on location from Israel. Thank you and good-bye for now. Back to you, Bob."

Bob shook himself as he realized he was still on air. "Thank you, Barbara, for that amazing on-the-spot story. We will be hearing from Barbara later. Be sure to keep it here for the update. This is Bob Carson for *WNCB*; thank you and good night."

The Antichrist walked into his palace. He was not happy. The accusations of those two men repeated themselves in his mind on the long ride home.

His commander in the field had called him, concerned. "Everyone we have sent in there has been killed. Their weapons are undetectable. The only way to stop them is to try luring them out, away from the wall and the city. If we can lure them away from civilians we can call in fighter planes and take them out. We have to fire on them before they kill anyone else."

The Antichrist agreed, "Of course, do what is necessary to eliminate the problem. I want them destroyed. We can't allow them to terrorize the public. If you are unsuccessful in your attempts to lure them away from the people, then you should fire on them anyway."

"Excuse me, sir," the commander asked, needing confirmation. "Did you say fire into the crowd?"

"Yes, Commander, I did. As you say, we must stop them before they kill anyone else. Who knows who these terrorists intend to incinerate next. What if they open fire on the public? We are better off to stop them quickly."

"Yes, sir; I just wanted to confirm your last order?"

"Very well then." *Click.* The Antichrist hung up the phone. He took a deep breath and released it, forcing himself to relax. The only problem he saw was the two witnesses. These two men seemed to come from nowhere. They were obscure, but their tongues held fire. Vaguely he remembered a passage in the Bible referring to the two witnesses; he shook slightly as a tremble went down his back. He ignored it. They were still vulnerable. He simply had to discover their particular weaknesses. He thought back on the chaos that had disturbed the celebration. His men moved quickly, removing him from danger. Later he had watched the footage of the guards being incinerated. A strange fear ran through him. Again, he chose to ignore it, choosing rather to make light of them. *It's some kind of magic,* he mused. *Witnesses from God.* An evil fire leaped into his eyes.

Why was he fretting over the words of two old fools? Who in their right mind would listen to them? For the moment, he was content to bask in his accomplishments. He was, after all, the world president; for now that was enough.

THE WEDDING

Weeks flew by. The church was filled to overflowing every night. Church membership was up. New people were joining almost every day. Not long after the rapture the church held an election. John was voted in unanimously as the new pastor of Faith Fellowship. He was becoming well known in the community. Carly spent her days at work, while John continued to counsel people during the days and study for the nightly sermons. He was under a lot of pressure but seemed to be at home with the whole business. He felt useful. He was fulfilled in a way he could never have imagined before. Paul checked with him daily. They confided in one another while holding each other accountable for their actions.

Shelby worked her magic and managed to help plan a beautiful wedding. John and Carly understood from Bible prophesies that their time together was short. They didn't want to waste a moment of it. They chose to invite the congregation and set a date for one month later. Shelby was used to putting together events. She called some of the ladies from the church, and before Carly knew it, the wedding plans were in full swing.

Kerry Cassidy was a gifted baker; she willingly agreed to bake the cake. After some discussion, Carly and John decided on chocolate cake with raspberry filling. Kerry flushed with pride as Shelby bragged about her. "Kerry's cakes are not only beautiful, they are delicious." The pictures of her cakes were impressive by anyone's standards.

Kerry smiled as her hands brushed off the edge of the display counter in front of her. "I know this is a difficult time for everyone. I will be happy to keep my hands busy. I have been taking some orders from that Dennis Billings person. He gives a lot of parties. After the rapture, with all the people missing, there haven't been many people wanting to celebrate except for him and a few others. He makes sure my supplies are delivered. So I have no complaints." Looking at John, she added, "Your dad was always good to me. I loved that man. It would be an honor to bake your wedding cake."

John smiled. "Thank you, Kerry. You know I would be very happy if you ever decided to join us one night at the church."

"I know. Pastor Jentson was always asking me to visit. I never made it over there. I feel bad about that now. But I'll be there for your wedding, I promise."

"We want you to stay and celebrate with us too," Carly added.

"Thank you. I believe I would like that, dear. We might as well have some fun. Goodness knows we've had precious little of it these days."

Her business was slow. But, to her surprise, people were starting to get back to their old routines. She was barely hanging on, with people stopping in for a treat. She was still working hard but the joy was no longer there. She sighed to herself as she realized how barren life had become in such a short time.

Her son and daughter-in-law were among the ones who were missing. They attended Pastor Jentson's church faithfully. Her son had often invited her, but there was always too much to do to go to church. She just couldn't drop everything. A tear slipped down her cheek as she remembered her son's last plea for her to go to church with him. "Mom, I love you. Angie and I want you to spend more time with us. Please come to church with us. I'll pick you up. We want you to spend the day. Angie's been trying to learn how to make your meatloaf. You could show her after church." Oh, how much she had missed! Her shoulders shook as she succumbed to grief. "I'm sorry," she said to the little group.

"We understand completely. All of us have lost loved ones," Shelby said.

The church ladies were giving the reception. They decided to handle the table settings themselves. Several women all agreed to take responsibility for one table each. The ladies agreed to bring their own china and silverware as well as glasses. Bouquets of white flowers were used for centerpieces. The plan was to keep the flowers elegant with greenery and the dishes colorful. For the tables with white china, the same flower arrangements were used. They added bright colorful flowers for impact. Each lady took pride in her table setting—she chose the flowers for her table and went out of her way to showcase her own artistic touches.

Shelby decorated the head table. She and the other ladies used white napkins and tablecloths the church already owned. She brought in her wedding china. The soft yellow and gold accented the delicate pink flowers. Their green leaves and stems brought life to its pattern. For the glasses, she used her finest crystal. As a wedding gift, she had a couple of tall fluted crystal glasses rimmed in gold for the bride and groom. The silverware was laid out perfectly. Her table was long. For the centerpieces, she used three separate bouquets of flowers containing a variety of multicolored flowers arranged into crystal baskets she had been collecting. Then she added between the bouquets one lone white calla lily wrapped in a beautiful pink ribbon and placed on the table as though it just happened to be there between the bouquets of roses and other flowers. She scattered around tiny diamond-looking stones for bling and set a bucket of ice with sparkling cider within reach of the bride and groom. She stood back to survey her work.

"Oh, Shelby, it's beautiful," Carly whispered the words breathlessly. She looked around the room unsure where to look first. In her hand was the wedding dress. She was trying to keep it off the floor but the layers of lace and satin were fighting her.

Shelby reached up taking it from her. "Here, I'll put this in the changing room while you take a look around."

Carly was amazed at the beauty of each table, each showing the individual style and taste of its hostess. The reception didn't take place at a five-star hotel but it captivated the admiration of all its guests. The church also prepared a beautiful lunch for the bride and groom. The chance to lavish this young couple with their appreciation for all they had done as their new pastors was a challenge they gladly accepted.

The ladies had worked at the church all morning decorating the sanctuary and the reception hall. The sanctuary was a beautiful room already with its high beams that formed an arch in the center. The wide center aisle was flanked with bouquets of flowers. The beautiful room was accented with white and pink ribbons.

They could not believe how quickly the wedding day had arrived. John and Carly had spoken on the phone; both of them promised to be on time—something John suspected would be a challenge for Carly.

Rebecca and Carly had become quite close after renewing their old friendship. Rebecca had agreed to be her bridesmaid. Shelby was, of course, the matron of honor. The two girls giggled like schoolgirls as they helped Carly get dressed. Carly was beautiful. The three musketeers had indulged themselves with a morning at the beauty salon. Their hair, nails, and makeup was done to perfection.

Shelby went on to the church to do her last-minute things while Carly and Rebecca finished up at the salon.

John watched as Carly walked toward him. Tears welled up and spilled over onto her cheeks. The pride he felt for her that moment was something he would never be able to put into words. He smiled that crooked little smile of his and whispered, "I love you." When she was almost to him, he moved toward her;

reaching for her hand he squeezed it slightly. He looked down into the cherished face of the woman he had loved all his life. Without thinking, he reached up and wiped the tears from her eyes. She smiled and his world lit up. So this, he thought, is how the Lord sees his bride. The observation made the moment even more important.

Pastor Paul greeted the congregation. "Who gives this woman to be married to this man?" Carly's mouth fell open as she heard Paul ask the question. It had been difficult planning the wedding. Her dad had passed away a few years ago but she did think her mom would be here to walk her down the aisle and respond to this question. As though everyone in the room could read her mind, the whole congregation said, "We do." They had already been coached by the ushers. Shelby had given them specific instructions. The words were simple but the crowd was happy, and it reminded Carly and John they still had family, even now.

Paul continued, "Dearly beloved, we are gathered here today in the sight of God to join this man and this woman in holy matrimony. This is a covenant between them and God and should not be entered into lightly." He watched the two as he continued, "The Bible gives us many references comparing the relationship we have as man and wife to the relationship we have with the Lord. We are to keep ourselves only for him. He instructs the wife to submit herself to her own husband showing him the respect due him. This has often been misinterpreted to mean women should be subjected to a tyrant, which is of course not true. But as we, the church, willingly submit ourselves to the Lord, so should the wife submit herself willingly to her husband."

"The Lord has given man the position of leadership in the home. But the woman was created by God to be a helpmate, not a slave. God took a rib from Adam and created Eve. God has created the woman to be the supporting pillar in the life of her husband. And, as many of us know, our wives are the glue that holds the family together. That is where the saying, 'Behind every great man is a woman,' came from. Your wife, John, is not to walk in front of you or behind you; she was taken from your side, therefore she should walk beside you. From this day forward, you will no longer be independent people. From now on you are one flesh in God's eyes. He does not see two people. God sees both of you as one."

"God's word instructs the wife, Carly, to respect her husband. There is at the core of every man a need for respect, as great as your need to be loved" (1 Corinthians 7:3).

"Likewise, John, you are admonished to love Carly, even as Christ loved the church and gave his life for it. You are to be willing to do whatever is necessary to keep her safe, loving her and showing her affection, providing for her needs. A man loves his wife and takes on the responsibility of providing for her emotionally and physically. He does not shirk or run from his responsibilities but is quick to work, and finds fulfillment in that.

"Do you, John Phillip Jentson, take this woman, Carly Jessica Edwards, to be your lawfully wedded wife? Do you promise to love her, to honor her, and keep yourself only for her?"

John smiled and said, "I do."

"Do you, Carly Jessica Edwards, take this man, John Phillip Jentson, to be your lawfully wedded husband? Do you promise to love him, honor him, and keep yourself only for him?"

Carly glowed. "I do."

They exchanged rings. John lovingly kissed her hand after placing the ring on her finger.

"Then, by the authority of Jesus Christ and the power vested in me, I now pronounce that you are husband and wife. You may kiss your bride." John dropped his head and kissed his beautiful wife.

Paul motioned for them to face the people. "Ladies and gentlemen, may I introduce to you for the first time, Pastor and Mrs. John Jentson.

The church clapped and cheered as the newlyweds walked back down the aisle as husband and wife.

Pastor Paul said, "Carly and John would like for you to join them in the fellowship hall for the reception."

Pictures were taken of the bride and groom. Pastor Paul and Shelby joked with them as DC snapped several shots. "Just one more, that's it, now hold it. Thank you very much. Rebecca, step forward and join them. Where's Brad? Hey, man, get over here. All right, that does it." Thirty minutes later, John and Carly entered the reception hall. They greeted their guests and thanked them for the love they felt from them.

Miriam Tenny watched the couple as they went from table to table welcoming and hugging their friends. She was not a friend. She had attended only to observe. She had, for a long time, wanted to take John from Carly. She did not consider his rejection of her okay. She did not want to just be friends, but she smiled and kissed each of them as if they meant the world to her. "Carly, you're so beautiful. John, you hit the jackpot with her."

John agreed, "Thank you, I think so too."

Miriam was polished to perfection. She would never allow her poise to slip. Her long blond tresses were highlighted and straightened to sleek sophistication. She smiled through full beautiful lips exposing her perfect white teeth. The dress she wore was expensive. Everything she wore was couture. No one had ever rejected her. No one, that is, except John. She promised herself she would make him regret that day.

John watched the she-vamp as she lavished his bride with compliments. He was uncomfortable with the obvious display of hypocrisy. He knew that was just Miriam's way, but something in her eyes looked downright evil. He nudged Carly away from her, whispering into her ear, "I don't trust her. Believe me, Carly, she is not a friend."

Carly looked up at John; a worried frown crossed her face. "Who is she, John?"

"We'll discuss it later," was all he would say.

Carly turned back to look at the woman John so obviously disliked; she was watching them walk away. Something in her smile made Carly feel like John might be right. Carly looked at her husband. He was already back to greeting his guests as if nothing had happened, so Carly decided to forget about the woman for now.

DC made small talk at his table. Everyone introduced themselves. He watched as the newlyweds left Miriam. He was used to reading people, and he did not trust Barracuda Lady. He knew her type. He was pleased to see John excuse himself and move on.

DC made the rounds taking pictures of the wedding guests. Pulling his camera up and focusing, he took a picture of Miriam. He had a feeling about this lady. "Smile for the camera," he said, clicking her picture more for his own curiosity than for the wedding. He liked John and Carly a lot ever since he first attended the church that fateful day he was faithful to come back. He made friends with Pastor John; and so far, everything Pastor taught seemed to bring Granny's words back to life. He spent time studying the Scriptures John used when teaching. He also continued to read the stories of Miss Millie.

He decided to do what he could to get the stories out to the people. After all, isn't that why she had spent so much time writing them? As he watched John, he made the decision to speak to him. Maybe they could use those stories to help teach the new converts the Bible. He thought about it for a moment. Miss Millie spent her life teaching the Bible to people and now that she was gone, she was still teaching. He shook his head. *God,* he thought to his new best friend. *She was a special lady. Thank you for bringing her into my life. I would not be here if I hadn't met her on the bus that night.*

John shook DC's hand. Carly greeted DC with a kiss on the cheek. He boldly proclaimed, "If I had met you first this guy would be out." She laughed, seeing Sarah waving at her. She excused herself to join her friend. John sat, comfortably talking to DC. "I'd love to read those stories. Miss Millie was one of my Sunday school teachers. I think you're right. Her stories could really help people learn about Jesus and what it means to have a personal relationship with him."

"Good," DC nodded. "I'll bring her manuscript by so you can read it for yourself. I want to reproduce it as quickly as possible, while we still have the chance to do something for Christ. Once the Antichrist shuts us down, it will be hard to teach people personally. Material like the Bible and study books will be hard to get."

John studied DC. "You know, I think you should consider teaching them."

DC looked skeptical. "Me?" he questioned, pointing to himself.

"Why not?" John said. "You're not the shy type. I think you could do it. Your Grandma Grace taught you all those Bible stories; with the Bible and Miss Millie's manuscript you would have plenty of study material. We could have a regular Sunday school program. Will you think about it?"

DC was amazed by John's confidence in him. "Man, you know my background."

"Yes, I do." John nodded. "And you know mine. We both messed up. You're a changed man, DC, I see it. That's what God does—he changes people."

Carly made her way to her new friends, Brad and Sarah. They had proved to be constant dependable churchgoers. Carly had learned to go to them when she needed help. They were always willing to lend a hand. Justin seemed to adore them both. He walked toward them carrying two cups of punch. He carefully sat them down between Sarah and Brad.

Carly reached out and hugged him. "Oh, what a gentleman," she laughingly bragged as she continued to talk to Sarah. "What a guy. Does he help out like this all the time? He needs to come and spend some time with John and me. We could use this kind of attention."

Justin beamed. "Do you want some punch? I can get it for you."

Carly smiled and said, "I have to wait until I sit down. I don't want to take a chance of spilling it on my dress. Thank you. You're so sweet." She hugged him again.

Justin was all smiles. He was thriving. He looked at Brad. "Brad's teaching me how to work, Carly. He let me operate a bulldozer the other day. He said I'm a natural. Didn't you, Brad?"

"I said it because it's true. You have an instinct for it. No one can teach that." Brad looked completely serious, as though it was just a fact of life. "Once you get really good on the tractor I'll start teaching you to operate the backhoe."

Carly smiled as the two exchanged words. Justin was elated. He continued to spill over with conversation about Brad and Sarah. "They want to adopt me, so we're going to be a real family. I mean, I miss my Mom, but I've never had a Dad before and been in a real family."

"I'm so happy for you." Carly beamed at her young friend. "That's great. I wondered about you guys at first."

"I know," Justin admitted. "I was a little afraid at first." Justin dropped his head and confessed. "You see, Brad knew me because I tried to steal from him and he caught me. I thought he was going to kill me. You wouldn't believe how mad he was. He told me if he ever caught me stealing again, even if I was stealing from someone else, he would haul me down to the police station and make sure they locked me up and threw away the key." Brad laughed at the young man as he told the story. "That night, when you put us together, I was sure he was going to kill me the moment he got me alone, but he didn't. He said that dads teach kids how to act and he was going to teach me. That's when he gave me a job. He said I was going to learn to be a man. I've been working ever since, cleaning up around the jobsites and learning how to take care of the equipment." Carly watched as the young man beamed from the attention of a positive male role model.

One of the women at the table, Jenny Parks, was appalled by the story. "You don't think he went too far, threatening to turn you over to the police?"

"Naw, he was just making sure I got my act together."

She continued to speak her mind. "I don't believe children should be subjected to that kind of brutality. It is mental abuse." She was obviously disturbed.

Sarah spoke up. "I know we girls think men are too hard on children. We are mommies and our heartstrings are tugged on by these big beautiful eyes and precious little arms that reach out to us with total trust. The truth is that is how God created us; to nurture. But God also created men to take a stand against the evil that is around them, such as children who are out of control. If more children, like Justin, had a strong-willed father type in their lives, our children would not get caught up in the traps this world has set for them. Justin is a wonderful young man who needed someone like my husband to take an interest in him and teach him there are consequences for our decisions."

"He had a mommy who was addicted to drugs. She fed her habit while doing her best to raise him. In spite of all her problems, she was his mother and much like me, wanted to love him and reassure him everything would be fine. But everything wasn't fine. He had started down a wrong path. He was left behind—not because he did not hear about Jesus. He was left behind because he was rebelling against God. He needed someone to draw a line in the sand and make sure he lived on the right side of that line. Brad is doing that. He's going to school too, Carly. He's making really good grades. We are so proud of him. He's been working hard to catch up. He is really a good student. He has tremendous potential," Sarah added.

"Congratulations," Carly gushed.

"I didn't have any choice." Justin said. "I was either going to go to school or Brad was going to take me and sit through all of my classes until I learned to be responsible. He actually called Harry, his foreman, and told him he wouldn't be coming to work because he had to go to school with me." The whole table laughed. Justin blushed as he confessed Brad took him to school and was taking a seat in his homeroom. Then they reached an agreement that he would attend school without any argument. Everyone at the table roared as Justin recounted the day in painful detail. "I'm making good grades now. I can't believe it, but I actually like school. Sarah has been teaching me at home. She's real smart. I just have to do my best."

Carly was deeply touched by the scene. This was a family. Each person had a choice not to be a part of the other lives; but they had all chosen to pull together and make each other's lives richer because of their love. Justin sat down near Sarah who hugged him publicly and mentioned how handsome he was. Unlike most young men his age, he didn't pull away or act embarrassed. All of the years of wanting to be loved were now over. He was loved without hesitation. Instead of being ashamed, he enjoyed it.

This is what gives people the will to go on, Carly thought. *They could have locked themselves away in some private hell because of the horrible loss of their children; but somehow, Sarah and Brad had found a way to set aside their sorrow and use this opportunity to change the life of this wonderful young man. They were heroes.*

John showed up to greet everyone at the table. He placed his arm around Carly's waist, looking down at her with pride. She glowed as she looked up at him. Sarah became emotional watching them. She remembered vividly her own wedding. Brad had been so handsome. She loved him more than she had thought possible. Looking up at him, now she realized their love had grown beyond measure. Brad was everything she had prayed for her husband to be, and more. "God," she prayed silently. "Make

Carly and John's time together sweet and wonderful. Thank you again for Brad and Justin."

Carly wanted to talk to everyone so she and John moved on to greet David. He had shown up the first night after his mom disappeared. He had also begun to thrive. His died black hair had been replaced with a soft brown. His eyes danced as he greeted her, kissing her cheek. His girlfriend, April, sang out her name. "Carly, you look beautiful!" She reached over and hugged Carly. Carly looked at her young friends; both of them were thriving. April had also exchanged the black hair and makeup for a subtle red. Her dancing brown eyes reflected pure happiness. They were the cutest couple. "Look," she said as she held up her hand displaying the new engagement ring.

"Oh, how beautiful." Carly was all lit up with the story of young love. The two girls talked as John and David discussed the worship songs they wanted to do. David had recently started leading worship and was completely happy doing it. His sweet spirit was a blessing to people as he led them into the presence of the Lord. He remembered some of the music from the times his mom had dragged him to church, but he had also been writing new music. John, who had majored in music, had several songs he had passed on to him. Much of this was music the church did before the rapture. Together they were quite a team. John was thankful for the help. It was great to be able to focus on the sermon while someone else led worship.

"When are you guys getting married? Have you set a date?" Carly asked. They had a date in mind but also wanted to have a church wedding, so they needed to talk to John when he could look at the church schedule. "We are willing to change the date if necessary, but we really want to get married here. We'll call you after your honeymoon," they promised. Carly hugged David and April one more time.

"By the way," David added. "Can you marry us? I mean, I know you are our pastor, but would it be legal?"

John nodded affirmatively, "Yes, I can. I am an ordained minister. My dad wanted me to go to Bible college just in case. They had a great music program so it seemed like a good compromise. I agreed just to make him happy."

Shelby came up to them. "They're ready to serve dinner." With John and Carly seated at the head table, the dinner began. They toasted with punch and laughed, telling stories of their first meetings. Paul, who was always good for a laugh, told stories he remembered John's dad telling to him as John was growing up. The overall mood was happy-go-lucky. It was a time for joy, something they had wondered if they would ever really feel again. For a few hours people allowed themselves to laugh. Life was good today. Tomorrow would be here soon enough.

As King Solomon said in Ecclesiastes 3:1–8:

> TO everything there is a season, and a time to every purpose under the heaven: A time to be born, and a time to die; a time to plant, and a time to pluck up that which is planted; A time to kill, and a time to heal; a time to break down, and a time to build up; A time to weep, and a time to laugh; a time to mourn, and a time to dance; A time to cast away stones, and a time to gather stones together; a time to embrace, and a time to refrain from embracing; A time to get, and a time to lose; a time to keep, and a time to cast away; A time to rend, and a time to sew; a time to keep silence, and a time to speak; A time to love, and a time to hate; a time of war, and a time of peace.

Today they would rejoice. They would love. They would be happy. Tomorrow was not promised to anyone.

REBECCA'S DREAM

"Aah!" Rebecca woke from a deep sleep. Her body was trembling and she was fighting to breathe. The covers were pulled tightly around her. She sat straight up. The memory of her dream was something out of a horror film. She threw the blankets off of her and swung her legs around placing her feet on the cool floor. "Calm down," she whispered to herself. She walked to the bathroom, switched on the light, and reached for a glass of water. She drank it down without stopping. Still trembling, she sat the glass down and wiped her mouth on the towel hanging next to the sink.

The dream would not go away. She could still see it. She was being dragged from a room with bars. Her abusers were pulling her by her hair; a handful came out. The angry hand of her tormentor reached out and grabbed her arm. She felt as if it were being pulled out of its socket. She screamed with fear as she was pulled toward the town square. Her heart pounded so fast she felt as though it would pound right out of her chest. There was a man wearing a hood. He held an ax with a long wooden handle. It was like something out of a medieval movie. Her hands were tied behind her back and she was forced to place her head on a block with a notch just large enough for her neck. The ax came down; her dream ended. But the fear stayed with her.

She remembered a man in her dream. He stood in the shadows, never coming into the light. He was dressed in a pinstripe suit. She couldn't make out his features. The only thing she could see clearly were his hands. On one of his hands he wore a distinctive ring. She remembered this man had betrayed her. She just couldn't remember who he was or how he had done it. She wanted to pass the whole thing off as something she ate, but that feeling of doom would not leave her. Rebecca couldn't help but feel she was in serious danger.

She recalled, in the Bible Daniel had dreamed of the last days. Did God give other people dreams? Could this be a warning? She reached for her Bible and spent the next couple of hours chasing down the word "dream." By 6:00 am she was sure God had given her a warning.

She went to work with a greater awareness of the people around her. That day she watched everyone she knew. Trying not to be obvious, she kept an eye on all of her coworkers. She was very careful to notice their hands. She did not remember where, but she was certain she had seen that ring before.

"Hello, John, it's Rebecca. I know you two are still on your honeymoon, but do you think you could give me a call? Thanks. It's really important." Last week John had just spoken about the dangers of being a Christian in the world today. He said Christians would be betrayed by people they trusted and turned over to the authorities to be martyred. That feeling of panic rose up again. She walked quickly toward the doors of the hospital and out into the courtyard; she had to get some air.

John called back immediately. "Hello, Rebecca, what's up?"

"John, I know I might be overreacting, but I had to talk to someone. I dreamed I was going to be beheaded. I mean, someone I trusted turned me in for being a Christian, and I was being killed for it."

John held his breath. He was reluctant to respond. Finally he said, "Rebecca, I think that is going to happen to a lot of people. God seems to have given you a warning. Do you know who the person was who betrayed you?"

"No, John, that's the thing. I'm looking over my shoulder and suspecting everybody. I've been so upset I can barely work. It's like this guy is looming over my head; he could be anyone."

John agreed. "That is exactly the point. He could be anyone. You have to be prepared. Don't trust anybody, not even your closest friends. Everyone is suspect. You know it was a guy. Do you remember anything else—his height, the color of his hair? What about his walk or distinguishing marks?"

Rebecca bit her lip. "He was mostly in the shadows. I couldn't see him. But he wore a suit; I think he had dark hair and there was this ring."

"Keep thinking about it." John thought for a moment then said, "He stayed in the shadows. I think that means he is hiding from you. He won't be obvious. He will be lurking and watching. Please be careful. When you get a chance to leave the job without causing suspicion, call me. I think we should meet."

"But what about your honeymoon, I don't want to be a bother?"

"Don't be silly. You could never be a bother. Carly and I want to help you. We're here for you anytime, just call."

Rebecca walked back into the hospital with a little more confidence. That's when she saw them. "Becky, darling." Her mom and stepdad were coming toward her. Her mother's arms swung wide open to embrace her.

"Mom, Dad, I didn't know you were coming."

"We wanted to surprise you, darling." Sharon and Dennis Billings were a striking couple, always the most attractive people in the room. Sharon was a breathtaking beauty. Her long, well-kept hair was pulled back and up. Her style was expensive. Her suit fit her like a glove. Dennis was handsome. Rebecca remembered how her friends used to admire him. The girls were all starstruck. They looked like they were the perfect couple; to them appearances were everything. Rebecca had rebelled against their hypocrisy when she was a teenager. But, in spite of everything, she loved them; eventually she settled into playing their game.

"Well, this is a surprise." Without saying it out loud, she whispered, "Thank you, God," as she hugged her mother again. "I'm so happy to see you two. I thought, from our last call, you wouldn't be coming this way for some time."

"I know, honey, but I was so happy you were all right after all those disappearances; I told your father we just had to come and see you in person."

"Oh, Mom, thank you for coming; I really needed to see you." Up to this point her stepfather had remained quiet. She had never had a good relationship with him; he was the kind of daddy girls try to forget. His usual cold manner seemed familiar to her. In the back of her brain she remembered the way he used to be. A chill hit her as she felt his eyes on her. She shoved the thought completely away as she hugged her mother. He stayed back and let her mom talk.

They all agreed to meet after her shift. She gave them the key to her apartment and went back to work. "I'll see you two later." She was happy they were there. She had a lot to share with them. She wanted them to know all about her newfound faith. She also wanted to share with them the Scriptures John had given the church describing the end-time prophecies. For the moment she forgot the dream.

When Rebecca walked through the entry door of her apartment, the smell of her mother's pot roast filled her nostrils. "Oh, Mom, that smells great," she called out from the entry hall. She threw her car keys in her purse and set it down. She slipped out of her jacket, hanging it on the hook near the door. Without thinking, she removed her shoes, leaving them tucked under a little table nearby. She walked into the kitchen to talk to her mother. "Where's Daddy?" she asked.

"Your father is taking a nap. We stayed at a motel last night; but you know your father, he didn't sleep well. We ended up leaving early this morning. He drove right on through without stopping again. He had a meeting today at noon. Then we went straight to the hospital."

"What kind of meeting?"

"Oh, I don't know, just business. You know your father; he doesn't waste his words." Her mother laughed.

"Mom, I have some incredible things to tell you. Remember I told you I was going to church?"

"Yes, dear. I am so proud of you. Your grandfather would be delighted." Her mother smiled that smile Rebecca loved; Rebecca thought she looked like an angel when she smiled.

"Well, I think I understand things now that I never understood before."

Her stepfather walked into the room looking refreshed. "Do I smell coffee?"

Her mother poured him a cup and asked, "Well, Rebecca, what were you saying?"

Rebecca started to continue, but as she opened her mouth, she saw it. "Father, what is this?" She pointed to the ring on his finger.

"Oh, it's just a gift from my new employer."

Her mother interrupted. "You've seen it, dear. Remember when we came to visit last fall? Rebecca gulped, trying not to show fear. She did remember her father had just been employed by the state. He received the ring for his many acts of service. Her heart pounded as she remembered she had asked her father at the time, "What acts of service?" He had never answered her, responding with, "There are things, my dear, only a few are actually privy to. And you are not one of those few."

Her mother's rambling brought her back to the moment. "Your father has been given a wonderful position. Best of all, we will be moving back. Rebecca, we'll be right across town from you; isn't this wonderful news? I wanted to tell you on the phone but he wouldn't allow it. He wanted to tell you in person."

Rebecca sank into the kitchen chair closest to her, feeling deflated, much like a balloon with no air. "Tell me what?"

Her stepfather outlined his new position, "There are a lot of changes that are just around the corner. I have been asked to head up a new task force, enforcing any"—he hesitated, adding the last few words with emphasis—"shall we say lack of loyalty to the new regime?"

"Excuse me, regime? What are you talking about, Father? What regime?" As he explained, Rebecca couldn't believe her ears. It sounded like her stepfather was the guy hired to hunt down, persecute, and kill her and her friends. "But Father, what about freedom of religion? You used to go to church yourself. You were a deacon. What happened to your faith?"

He just looked at her as if all her arguments were really unimportant. "What has freedom of religion gotten us up to now? People kill in the name of the cross. Look at the crusades. We need to put an end to the mindless following of just one God and allow people true freedom of religion. That is to say freedom to believe in whatever they personally find valuable. I know this isn't popular with you and your church friends, but I believe it is a better way to live. We are not subjected to the close-minded teaching of the Bible. We can move forward with a new outlook. If you think about it, this makes so much more sense."

"But," she had to ask, "what about the truth, Father? What if people know the truth, and, as the Bible says, 'There is only one way to God, through Jesus Christ.' The Bible says in John 14:6: "Jesus saith unto him, I am the way, the truth, and the life: no man cometh unto the father, but by me."

"Well, listen to that, Momma. She's finally got religion. The way you're talking, girl, a person would think you've changed your mind about God. What other things have you been doing?"

Rebecca didn't want to deny Christ. She also didn't want to be her father's first offender. So she dodged the question and changed the subject. "Oh, Daddy, you are so silly. Tell me more about your new position." She sat there for over an hour listening to plans for a new order.

"This is the vision for the future." Her stepfather sat back in his chair opposite her and looked at her, studying her.

He really believed everything he was saying. No wonder he was such a hypocrite when she was little. She turned from God because of this man. As she listened to him spew the words of the new world president, she understood why he had been her nightmare as a child. He had no real faith. He must never have believed, not really. "Rebecca, your mother and I want you to be a part of this new vision. We want you to join us as we serve this dynamic young man." He reached out taking her hand in his. "You are our child, and we love you." Beseechingly, he added, "I love you."

Something deep inside Rebecca went cold. She smiled a trembling little smile. "I love you guys too," she added. Then pulling her hand out of his grasp, she dropped her head in a childlike manner; not knowing what to say she said nothing.

She tried, but she could not enjoy her mother's pot roast. She promised them she would think about their offer. Her stepfather had mentioned he had contacts that would see to it she would be placed into a position worthy of her talents. Then she went to bed. That night she did not sleep. Her heart raced as she contemplated eternity for her parents. She had wanted to talk to her stepfather about God. She had hoped he would change and become the man her mother believed him to be. But he was lost to her. He was a robot for the new regime. Her conscience fought with her fear as she thought, *They will go to hell if I don't talk to them.* She was sick with grief.

The next day she spoke to her mother. "Mom, I know Daddy means everything to you. But you know better. Grandpa always talked to you about God. This new-world order is a road to hell. You know Grandpa would not agree with this. If he were alive today, Daddy would have to report him for being a Christian. You grew up with a Christian father; how can you allow Daddy to lead you away from God like this?"

Her mother, true to form, simply dismissed her plea. "Your father is right. Daddy was too close-minded. Rebecca, I know you are having trouble understanding, but I really believe your father is doing the Lord's work. God is love. He is not this being in heaven, sitting in judgment over everyone. He wants us to come to him. For some people it is easy, they just believe. But for others, there are many ways to heaven and I believe they are also very valid."

Rebecca drew back. She had lost her. Her mother was not able to believe the truth. "I'm sorry for you, Mom. I'm sorry you can't believe what you have known your whole life to be true: That Jesus is the one mediator between God and man" (1 Timothy 2:5).

Her stepfather emerged from the guest bedroom with his suitcase. He was wearing a uniform. He looked elegant. He was a handsome man. His dark hair waved slightly and was combed to perfection. "Father, you look so handsome," she said honestly.

"Thank you, my dear. Have you thought about our conversation?"

"Yes, I have; I am sorry, I love you both very much, but I can't take the path you have chosen."

His brown eyes darkened. "I see." Only the stiffness of his posture gave away his anger.

Her mother opened the door to the coat closet and removed her coat, pulling it on. She added, "He is supposed to report for duty today."

Rebecca kissed them both good-bye; in her heart she knew it was forever. They were lost to her. Even if she saw them daily she could never trust her stepfather. She closed the door and dead bolted it behind them. A river of tears started to fall. She was alone. She had never before felt such deep loneliness.

The outside of the letter was embossed with gold. Paul studied the odd-looking envelope. The return address read, "Governor

Ross Howard." He picked up the letter opener on his desk and slid it across the top.

"Governor Howard requests the pleasure of your company."

What would he want with me? Paul asked himself. The invitation was just a little unnerving. Things had been falling into place according to Bible prophesies at an alarming rate. Already the Antichrist was in power. Paul had kept a constant eye on the news and the way things were going, the world president assuming his new position had just been a matter of formality. He was in power almost as soon as the Lord had returned.

The two witnesses preached daily, warning people of the sins of the world. They proclaimed the world president to be a demoniac. They announced the pastor of the One World All Faiths Church was nothing more than a warlock. Their words were harsh with no concern for political correctness. Secretly, Paul had been enjoying all their sermons. He listened to them daily via the Internet and watched, captivated, as those who tried to stop them from speaking were incinerated. These guys were not to be messed with; God had appointed them their time of ministry and they were taking full advantage of every minute.

Paul looked around the private office of the governor of the state. "As you can see, Pastor, we are in need of ministers to help quiet the hearts of the people. You were chosen to represent our state based on your past history as a man of the people." Paul felt sick. He was here because he was a minister who had compromised. As he listened to the plans the governor laid out, his heart sank. "You see, sir, we are on the threshold of a new day. We will be pioneers forging a new frontier where no one is left out. The whole world—every nation—will be an integral part of the world order. I, and others like myself, have been asked to seek out men of distinction who are capable of seeing a better way. We need men, as yourself, to introduce to your congregation the ideas we now hold dear.

We are no longer interested in the old, more conservative plat-
forms that have been considered the foundations of liberty. We
are opening our hearts—and literally the doors of our country—
to the whole world where no one is excluded for race, religion, or
gender. Men and women of all backgrounds and creeds are considered religious leaders and worthy of respect. Men of all faiths
are at this very moment being considered for leadership in the
new One World All Faiths Ministry. You have an opportunity
to be one of the first in this life-changing work. We are forging
a new world with a new understanding of God, one that will no
longer tolerate discrimination. Christians, Muslims, atheists, and
satanists—everyone is welcome."

Paul sat stone still as he listened to this man's plan. "Sir, may I
ask what in particular caused you to single me out for this honor?"
Paul asked in the calmest voice possible. Inside he was panick-
ing; on the outside he was as cool as a cucumber. He flashed his
famous smile exposing those million-dollar teeth.

"Of course, Pastor. We actually have had an eye on you for
some time. A member of your congregation has distinguished
you as a leader, a man capable of making people believe anything
you want. You are just the kind of person we need." Paul felt
another wave of nausea; every time this blustering fool reminded
him of his sin he became a little more annoyed.

"May I ask who this person was?"

The governor answered. "Of course. You were referred to our
office by Miriam Tenny. I assume you know Ms. Tenny. She has
been most helpful in the move to organize and develop our state.
She is a beacon for all of us who are working so diligently to make
this One World All Faiths Religion a success. You will extend to
her my greeting when you see her on Sunday."

Paul was flabbergasted. He knew Miriam was something of
a socialite, but he did not realize her influence extended to the
governor's office. "Of course, I will be happy to say hello for you."

Unsure how to answer, Paul decided to be as diplomatic as possible. "Well, sir, you have given me a lot to think about. I will need a few days to mull it over and, of course, talk to my wife. I can't commit to something like this without her input. If I were to agree to this, I would want to be available to give this program my undivided attention. I value her opinion, and if she isn't completely on board, I would have to decline."

"Yes, of course." The rather crafty older man studied him curiously. "You know, Paul, only those who are smart enough to give their support will be welcome into the new era."

"Yes, I completely understand." Paul looked at the governor with curiosity. "I just have one more question. How is it that a politician like you is involved in the course of setting up an all-denominational church? Don't politicians preach separation of church and state?"

"As I explained before"—the governor coughed as if to clear his throat—"this is a new era. There will be no need for boundaries. In the new world, men and women will live in harmony with each other and religion. I myself am an atheist, but I would very much enjoy attending a church where I was not judged for my lack of faith. I personally believe churches can evolve into community meeting places where anyone can benefit from the friendships formed there while taking an active part in leading their community with good works. Your church has, for many years, distinguished itself as a church that cares for its community. I find that very inspiring."

Paul was speechless. After a moment, he choked out, "Thank you, sir." He shook the governor's hand and walked out of the office, shutting the door behind him. *This is it*, he thought. *The Scriptures are being fulfilled on a minute-to-minute basis. The book of Revelation is happening.* He left the capital with a purpose, driving each step. This is war. Satan is defeated. Jesus is the King!

JOHN THE EVANGELIST

"Help me! Someone, please help me!" the scream came from down the hall. John ran toward the sound coming from the emergency room. "I'm dying." A young man, who looked to be in his teens, was screaming and crying. "I'm dying. Please, somebody help me!" The sound of his plea touched John to the bottom of his soul. Doctors and nurses were working with the young man, trying with all of their might to stop the bleeding. His screams of agony continued. "I'm dying! Please don't let me die." One last plea, and he was gone.

A group of teens stood helplessly nearby. They were crying. The doctor came out to speak with them. They stood there just watching the doctor in disbelief. "He's not dead!" one of the young men said. "He can't be; he's only seventeen." He looked at the emergency room doctor as though he needed someone to explain it to him.

"I'm sorry, son," was all the man said, shaking his head as he walked away, in obvious pain himself.

John had been thinking about Rebecca. Their phone conversation had stayed on his mind. He decided to stop by to see her. Instead, he had followed the screams of the young man. He wanted to speak to him, but it was too late. Filled with grief, he looked over and noticed the teens.

Rebecca had been assisting the doctor. She looked relieved as their eyes met. She immediately introduced him to the group. "This is Pastor John Jentson; perhaps he can help." She escorted

John and the grieving friends into a nearby lounge. "You can talk here," she said as she closed the door to give them privacy.

John asked, "What was your friend's name?"

One girl with shocking red hair and blue eyes was crying so hard she could barely speak. She took a deep breath and said, "Ryan"—she cleared her throat—"his name was Ryan."

"Did Ryan know the Lord?" John asked. His voice sounded kind, his expression echoed his genuine concern.

They looked at him, confused, "What do you mean?"

"Was Ryan a Christian?"

"No," one of the boys said. "He never went to church, if that's what you mean."

John felt sick. "Yeah, that's kind of what I mean. But you see, when someone is a Christian they do more than go to church. They ask Jesus into their heart. That is what I mean by 'was he a Christian?'"

A young man stood leaning with his back to the wall. He had dark-brown hair with a black shirt rolled up to just below his elbows. He wore black jeans, black boots, and a silver-studded belt. He looked up. He had been silent until now. "No, man, he didn't know Jesus."

The girl with the red hair introduced herself as Candy then asked, "Do you think he went to hell?" Her big, sad eyes shimmered with tears. "That's what you're asking us, isn't it?" She looked up at John, questioning him. "Did he go to hell?"

"I don't know," John replied. "None of us know his heart. After the disappearances, a lot of people have turned to Jesus. Perhaps he was one of them. But we should always be ready to meet the Lord. We really don't know when we might step out for a moment and just never come home again. We all need Jesus to save us, or we can't go to heaven. The Bible says, 'For there is one God, and one mediator between God and men, the man Christ Jesus' (1 Timothy 2:5). Ryan may have known Jesus. He may have asked him into his heart. We have to leave him in the

hands of the merciful Savior. We won't know for sure until we go
to heaven ourselves."

John watched their reactions and then asked, "How about all
of you? Do you know Jesus as your Lord and Savior? If you were
to die the way Ryan did, are you ready to meet the Lord, or would
your soul be lost?"

Josh, the tall, lanky young man dressed in black leaning against
the wall asked, "What do you mean by *lost?*"

John smiled, encouraging his new young friends. "The world
has fallen out of fellowship with God because of sin. We—you
and I—are the world. Mankind was originally created without
sin to live with and worship God, the creator. But man sinned
by choosing to disobey God's law. Sin is anything that separates
us from God. God is holy and without sin. God hates sin, but he
loves mankind."

"He gave man freedom of choice, to choose to love him or to
love sin. Because mankind is born into sin, God knew we would
need his help. He knew, even those of us who want desperately
to have a personal relationship with Him, would fail because our
nature is sinful. The Bible says, 'The heart is deceitful above all
things, and desperately wicked: who can know it?' The Bible also
says, 'I the LORD search the heart, I try the reins, even to give
every man according to his ways, and according to the fruit of his
doings'" (Jeremiah 17:9–10).

"God, who is sinless, could not have fellowship with us because
of our evil hearts. He sent his Son, Jesus, who was without sin, to
pay the price for all humanity. He took it upon himself to come
to us as a baby. He chose to live among mankind and die in our
place for our sins."

"In the beginning, after man sinned in the garden, they would
sacrifice a lamb for their sins. They would choose out the most
beautiful, flawless creature they could find. They would kill it and
burn it on an altar to God. God designed that form of repentance as a picture of his Son, Jesus—his lamb—who would die

for the sin of mankind. Because of sin, we were worthy of death. When we ask him to forgive us, he comes into our hearts and lives through us."

"We cannot go to heaven without Jesus, because nothing evil can enter the kingdom of God (Ephesians 5:5). The Bible tells us in Romans 3:23, 'For all have sinned, and come short of the glory of God.' John 1:12 says, 'But as many as received him, to them gave he power to become the sons of God, even to them that believe on his name.' Jesus took our sins. He paid our price for those sins by dying in our place so that we could escape the penalty of death."

"It's like this: Jesus came into the world born of a virgin. The angel Gabriel appeared to his mother, Mary, and told her she would have a son—the son of God. She asked the angel how that was possible since she had not been with a man. He explained that she would become pregnant by the Holy Ghost. He told her the child's name would be Jesus, which means 'Savior.' He also told her he would be called 'the Son of the Highest' (Luke 1:26–35). She was at that time engaged to a man by the name of Joseph."

"When Joseph found out she was pregnant, he made plans to put her away secretly. He loved her and did not want to embarrass her publicly. But the same angel appeared to him and told him not to be afraid, but to take Mary as his wife, for the child inside of her was of the Holy Ghost" (Matthew 1:18–20).

"You have all heard the Christmas story. Jesus is the son of God. The Bible tells us in John 1:32–36 that John the Baptist saw him and witnessed, as the Holy Spirit landed on Jesus in the shape of a dove. God the Father had already told John the man on whom the Spirit settles was his son. Also Luke 3:22 says, 'And the Holy Ghost descended in a bodily shape like a dove upon him, and a voice came from heaven, which said, "Thou art my beloved son; in thee I am well pleased."'The Scripture also tells us in John 1:36 that John the Baptist identified him: "And looking upon Jesus as he walked, he saith, 'Behold the Lamb of God!' You see, Jesus came into the world for a purpose. John 3:16–17 says, 'For God so loved the world, that he gave his only begotten Son, that whosoever believeth in him should not perish, but have everlasting life. For God sent not his Son into the world to condemn world; but that the world through him might be saved.'"

"I don't know what your friend believed. I am asking you: What do you believe? These disappearances weren't accidents. The truth is Jesus has returned for his church, that is, the people who loved and served him. Think about this: How many of the people who disappeared were Christians? How many did you know personally?"

Josh was crying. His hand came up to wipe his whole face; all at once he sniffed, then, placing both hands folded under his arms, he started shaking his head. "I knew someone—my brother. He was always going to church. He tried to get me to go but I wouldn't. We didn't get along very well. When everyone disappeared, he was one of the people. I just never put it together." Slowly they all began to tell of someone they knew who had talked about Jesus: family members, coworkers, other students— all missing.

Candy looked at John as if he had two heads. "I've heard this stuff before, but I didn't believe it. I just thought it was a nice story. I always knew Christmas and Easter were holy, but I didn't believe Jesus was the Savior of the world. I thought there were many ways to heaven. Why didn't anyone tell me the truth?" She looked around the room at her friends. "Why didn't you guys explain this? I thought all you had to do to go to heaven was be a good person."

Josh spoke up. "It's just that if you don't know Jesus personally yourself, how can you tell other people about him? I thought he was some mythical character out of the Bible who was going to come down and punish me if I didn't obey. The only person who ever talked about God was my brother; Mom and Dad sure never talked about God or Jesus." They all had questions. Patiently, John sat answering them.

Amongst the tears and grief of sudden loss, they all, one by one began to acknowledge they did not know Jesus. Each one asked John to pray with him or her to become a Christian.

John said, "All it takes is a simple prayer. I will say the words. All you have to do is repeat them after me." John bowed his head and said, "Lord Jesus, I acknowledge that I am a sinner." John stopped, waiting for the others. "I realize I am out of fellowship with God because of sin. I want to have a personal relationship with you and with the Father. Please forgive me. Change my heart and make me into a new person. I want to go to heaven. Please, Lord, make me clean. Wash away my sin with your blood so I can know you as my Savior."

"Father God, I come before you through the blood of your son, Jesus. I ask you to bring me into fellowship with you. Give me the strength to endure to the end, in the precious name of your Son, Jesus Christ."

He finished praying and looked at his friends. They were still crying, but a new light was in each of their faces. He invited them to church. He wrote down all of their names and phone numbers. Candy was brokenhearted over the loss of Ryan. She self-consciously asked John if he was sure she could go to his church. John assured her she would be welcome.

John's heart sorrowed for their friend. He promised to visit the parents of Ryan. John felt mixed emotions. He felt joy for their salvations, but because of the loss of Ryan, somberly he said good-bye to them. His heart ached as he remembered the young man's desperate call for help. He had failed him. He was too late. John's heart broke.

The church had grown till it was bursting at the seams. John had obtained permission from the local school to hold some of the church services in the gymnasium. After the disappearances, the community was happy to have anyone who was willing come and speak to people in an effort to offer comfort. He was pleasantly surprised when the principal of the local high school had asked him to talk to the students.

John, of course, was still not allowed to speak to the student body about Jesus during school hours, but they did cooperate with the use of the facility. During his day visit they allowed him to invite the students for an after-school meeting. Those who desired spiritual counseling were told they could attend. The first afternoon, almost the whole student body showed up, including some of the faculty. He told them about the missing. He asked, "How many of you would like to know Jesus as your Savior?" Hundreds raised their hands. Since then, the young people had become a huge part of his church. He loved and enjoyed them.

Carly seemed to thrive on their fellowship. She was amazing with all of them. He decided to push her out of her comfort zone and appointed her the new youth leader. John was thankful for the open door at the high school. He knew it was a temporary situation and soon the doors would start to close. The crowds grew with every meeting. The gym would not be large enough for long. What had started out with the question, "Why are so many missing?" had turned into a full-blown revival.

Paul had also reported record-breaking numbers and had made the move to rent the local arena. This was going on everywhere. Men and women of God were speaking out. Some, like John, who were not pastors prior to the disappearances, found themselves teaching and preaching that Jesus is the Christ. They were on street corners, in abandoned churches, and making use of every venue they found.

Salvations were occurring at a rate of speed that was mindblowing; but still, people who did not know Jesus were dying and going to hell. John thought of Ryan and gasped, trying to breathe, as he considered the place of eternal damnation. "God, please help me to reach the lost." Somehow, in the middle of his deep sorrow, he regained composure enough to walk to the podium.

"My friends, I come to you today with a heavy heart. As I look out over this crowd, I am reminded of the many who still do not know Christ. Today, as I was visiting a friend at the hospital, a young man came into the emergency room." John stopped and cleared his throat trying to breathe, tears pouring down his face. He wiped them away and continued. "This young man had been in a terrible accident. He died." His voice strained to croak out the words. "The doctors were unable to save his life. When I asked his friends if he knew the Lord, they said they did not know. They were upset; their friend had died. I was asked to speak to them to try to offer them some kind of comfort. At that moment I talked to them about their own souls and told them they had the opportunity to meet Jesus. Those young people are here tonight." The crowd started to clap as John added, "They have all accepted Jesus as their Savior." A roar of congratulations swept through the auditorium. John raised his hands to quiet the crowd.

"I do not know if this young man went to heaven or hell. I did not know him. There may have been a moment when he asked Jesus to forgive him. I do know he is in the hands of a merciful God. But this young man's death hurts me, because I can't be sure he knew Jesus. His death reminds me of why Jesus came to the earth. The Bible tells us, 'For the Son of man is come to seek and to save that which was lost' (Luke 19:10). He came here for you and me. He came here for the world, for all the people outside these walls who still don't know Christ."

"The world is trying to understand what has happened. They ponder, asking themselves and each other, 'Why have so many disappeared?' They have come up with some interesting theories, but their theories are wrong because they don't consider the truth. They do not think about the rapture of the church of the Lord Jesus. There have been a few news commentators who have touched on it. But instead of searching it thoroughly, they pass over it; they take the easiest answer. They say it was an alien invasion. And the world goes on in darkness, never accepting the truth."

"But there is a truth that must be accepted! It must dominate our thoughts and become our mission on earth! The world is lost, and every day people are still dying! They are still going to hell! The rapture does not change the heart of the Lord Jesus. We are commanded to go, "And he said unto them, Go ye into all the world, and preach the gospel to every creature" (Mark 16:15). The great commission has not changed. It may be more inconvenient. It may mean we will suffer for our convictions. But 'that no one should be lost' is still the cry of the heart of God. God waited to rapture out his church. He waited, sharing his glorious salvation with the whole world. He wanted people to come to know Jesus as their Savior (2 Peter 3:9). Read with me in Revelation 7:9–10 and 13–17."

> After this I beheld, and, lo, a great multitude, which no man could number, of all nations, and kindreds, and people, and tongues, stood before the throne, and before the Lamb, clothed with white robes, and palms in their hands; And cried with a loud voice, saying, Salvation to our God which sitteth upon the throne, and unto the Lamb.

John stopped, instructing them, "Drop down to verse 13."

> And one of the elders answered, saying unto me, What are these which are arrayed in white robes? and whence came they? And I said unto him, Sir, thou knowest. And he said to me, These are they which came out of great tribulation, and have washed their robes, and made them white in the blood of the Lamb. Therefore are they before the throne of God, and serve him day and night in his temple: and he that sitteth on the throne shall dwell among them. They shall hunger no more, neither thirst any more; neither shall the sun light on them, nor any heat. For the Lamb which is in the midst of the throne shall feed them, and

shall lead them unto living fountains of waters: and God shall wipe away all tears from their eyes.

The crowd broke into spontaneous rejoicing as John finished reading the Word of God to them. Raising his Bible high in the air, he added, "This is us. It is to our Jewish brothers and sisters, to all who come to know Christ during this time of great tribulation. We are the great multitude from every nation and language. We are the ones who have washed our robes in the blood of Jesus Christ, the precious Lamb of God!"

Men and women stood to their feet clapping their hands with joy. Cheers rang throughout the room. Finally the crowd began to quiet. "No matter what happens to us now, we must preach the gospel. We can't be safe in our homes avoiding the truth of eternity. God is real. People can't wish him away. We cannot receive the truth in portions; if part of the Bible is true, it is all true."

"There is a heaven, which means there is also a hell. We know there is a hell; men and women have been searching for it all of their lives. They look at the stars to tell them their futures. They speak to mediums to give them insight into their souls. They are reaching out to evil for understanding and enlightenment. And the lessons they are being taught will take them to hell (see Galatians 5:19–21)—hell, where the fire is not put out and the worm, which is the soul, never dies (see Isaiah 66:24)."

"Jesus told us he would not return until the whole world had heard the gospel. We heard it; but we did not listen. There are many more also. They, like us, have put God off. You see, even in this time of great danger, there are still those who must hear the word of God." His eyes blazed with fire as he added, "And we are in danger! The Bible tells us that we will be handed over to the authorities. In Luke 21:12, Jesus is telling his disciples what would be the signs of the end, 'But before all these, they shall lay their hands on you, and persecute you, delivering you up to the synagogues, and into prisons, being brought before kings and rulers for my name's sake.'"

"We will be martyred for the cause of Christ. Follow me to Revelation 20:4."

> And I saw thrones, and they sat upon them, and judgment was given unto them: and I saw the souls of them that were beheaded for the witness of Jesus, and for the word of God, and which had not worshipped the beast, neither his image, neither had received his mark upon their foreheads, or in their hands; and they lived and reigned with Christ a thousand years.

"We must not take the mark of the beast!"

John looked at the congregation and began to quote from memory. "But I also have good news. Paul the apostle says, 'We are confident, I say, and willing rather to be absent from the body, and to be present with the Lord' (2 Corinthians 5:8). Also Paul says in Philippians 1:21, 'For to me to live is Christ, and to die is gain.'"

"There is a land where the water is so clear it looks like glass. It is completely translucent. The throne of God has a rainbow above it. The colors are the most beautiful colors our eyes will ever behold. John, the revelator, spoke of jewels that adorn it. The streets of heaven are paved with gold so pure you can see through it. The gates of that city are enormous pearls (Revelation 21). Can you imagine a city paved with gold having gates made of pearls? There is no need for light because the lamb, Christ Jesus, is the light! (Revelation 21:23) There is a land of such supreme beauty, the half has never been told. That land cannot be described by mortal tongue; we don't have the ability to completely tell about this place."

"There, near the throne of God, are beings who continue day and night, as the Word says, 'And the four beasts had each of them six wings about him; and they were full of eyes within: and they rest not day and night, saying, Holy, holy, holy, Lord God Almighty, which was, and is, and is to come' (Revelation 4:8). He was God, he is God, and he will always be God. He is the beginning and he is the ending (Revelation 1:8). His mercy is from everlasting to everlasting on those who fear him (Psalm 103:17). He is 'King of Kings and Lord of Lords' (Revelation 19:16)! There is no being that can compare to him! He is the light of glory! The sun is not needed; he outshines the sun! (Revelation 21:23) He spoke and the earth was formed (Genesis 1). The earth is his footstool (Isaiah 66:1)."

"You ask me to prove there is a God. Look out at the night sky and consider the planets. They were all placed into orbit by him. The astronomical gyrations of the universe are so precise that they are obviously governed and controlled perpetually by a supreme, supernatural force! When he speaks, things happen! Worlds are spoken into existence!"

"I can't see the wind but I can see the effects of it. The wind blows and the trees sway. Sometimes the wind blows and the ocean overflows. The tide swells and a hurricane comes. God walks on the wind (Psalm 104:3). He created it. That is why the Scriptures tell us that Jesus spoke to the wind, rebuking it, and the wind obeyed (Mark 4:39–41). He speaks to it and it moves or quiets. God is real! Heaven is real! Hell is a real place!"

"We are living in a time of tremendous happenings. The people of the earth still need the Lord. They need us—you and me—people who are willing to lay our lives down for the cause of Christ. Jesus said, 'He that finds his life will lose it, and he that loses his life for me will find it' (Matthew 10:39). Jesus is speaking of giving God your life. My translation is 'to be sold out to God.' And the benefits are so awesome. Because we give him our lives, then we become his children! Just think, we are the children of God! We are no longer slaves to sin; we are now heirs with Christ.

The day is quickly approaching when the only way we will be able to avoid the sentence of death is to deny Christ. Soon the Antichrist will demand that every one of us take a mark. The Bible refers to it as the mark of the beast (Revelation 13:16). All we have to do to stop the persecution is to deny that Jesus is the Lord. That is all that is required of us. But for all who deny him, there is nothing left but eternal damnation! Hell is where the fire is not stopped and the worm never dies (Isaiah 66:24)."

"I am not willing to deny him! I will breathe my last breath calling his name! He is the greatest love of my life! How could I reject him? I will not give up. I will not shut up. I will not stop proclaiming Jesus Christ is my Savior. They can burn me, stone me, or even behead me. I stand with the apostle Paul, 'For to me to live is Christ, and to die is gain'" (Philippians 1:21).

The crowd of believers again rose to their feet clapping as John boldly proclaimed the gospel. The cheers from the crowd signaled their own commitment to spread the Word of God. The thunderous applause continued, as each one settled in his or her heart their own commitment to never turn back from following the Lord.

John and the people of the earth did not know they could not see that in the distant skies the sound of hoofs was heard. A rumbling of thunder announced their arrival as the four horses of the apocalypse pranced across the sky. Their riders glanced arrogantly at each other. The atmosphere changed as the world prepared for the wrath to come. They stopped looking down on the earth waiting at the threshold of time.

The white horse snorted, his nostrils flaring as he dug his right hoof into the clouds. His rider, the Antichrist, wore a crown and held a bow with no arrows. He rode out to win many battles and gain the victory.

Behind him was the red horse of war. Blood mingled with sweat dripped from his body. The stench of death was on him. His rider had been given a mighty sword and the authority to take peace from the earth. There would be death and slaughter everywhere. He was there to make war. The horse whinnied and reared back as if to throw off his rider. Standing on his hind legs, he pawed viciously at the air with his hoofs. His nostrils flared as he snorted into the sky.

The black horse of famine followed the others. The bones of his skeleton showed plainly through his flesh. His rider carried a scale. It was weighted down on one side with gold. The other side held a meager amount of bread. "And I heard a voice in the midst of the four beasts say, 'A measure of wheat for a penny, and three measures of barley for a penny; and see thou hurt not the oil and the wine'" (Revelation 6:6). His brown-black eyes cast a haunting look in the direction of earth.

Behind him came the pale horse of death. His color was pale green as a corpse. He also looked out toward the earth. The look of disease was on him. His bloodshot eyes sunk deep into his head casting an eerie glance toward his victims, and Death was the name of its rider, who was followed around by the grave.

They were given authority over one-fourth of the earth to kill with sword and famine and disease and wild animals. Their day was near; the four horsemen were prepared for their destiny. The earth was doomed. They looked down on the earth watching it. The people of the earth were their prey, their lives promised to them from the Scriptures of long ago. They waited. They could only move when the creator gave them the okay. The wrath of God has come (Revelation 6).

CHANGES

With the passing of the months, change in the lives of John and Carly came quickly. The little church grew daily with newcomers. They listened to the Word of God. No one could deny its authenticity. When faced with the ongoing daily headlines that had been predicted from the pages of the Bible, the new Christians watched in horror as the Bible's truth came to pass in their world.

The Antichrist had formed a league with Israel soon after the rapture. Every day it grew more dangerous for Christians and Jews all over the world. They were hated by everyone. It was as if the very knowledge of their existence tormented the people around them. Christians were unable to speak of Jesus in public. John did, and he was taken away by the police and beaten. Later they released him, ordering him not to ever speak that name again.

In Israel, the two witnesses ministered daily, winning thousands of souls to Christ. They were also hated. The world tolerated every religion, and evil multiplied. The only thing the world found intolerable were the people of God.

Mass confusion began to surface as all of the young people were being gathered together and taken away to camps. They were told that they should feel honored they were so loved by their leader, the world president; he considered them his own children and would be overseeing their training from now on. Parents who had escaped the loss of their children during the disappearances were willingly giving them into the hands of a tyrant who saw them only as tools. The parents who rebelled were punished for their hateful attitudes. These broken people wandered into the church daily seeking answers from God. The answers they received were heartbreaking. Their children were now under the total influence of the Antichrist. Grief mingled with fear as they began to understand what this meant.

Justin was among the children being forced into the camps. The military police showed up and held them all at gunpoint. Brad had been planning to move his family somewhere else, but somehow they found him out. Sarah was forced to pack Justin's things. She cried softly as she loaded his suitcase with as many of his personal belongings as it would hold.

Justin sat quietly, watching the armed guards hold Brad at bay. "It's okay, Dad. I really don't mind. You have to take care of Sarah. It's not like we'll never see each other again." Bounder sat close to Justin. His golden head was wrinkled at the brow line. His ears perked as he listened. He watched his family with a question on his face. He whimpered softly. Justin wrapped his arms around Bounder's neck protectively. He stroked the dog, trying to comfort him.

Brad asked the armed escort if he and Sarah could accompany Justin to the train. "We would like to say good-bye."

The young soldier looked a little embarrassed, then nodded yes.

Sarah called Carly and John for prayer. "We'll meet you there, Sarah." John hung up the phone. "Carly, we have to go. They are taking Justin. Sarah just called; they are holding Brad at gun point. Apparently they thought he would cause trouble."

Carly looked at John. "Oh, John, they must all be so scared."

"I told Sarah we would meet them at the train." Carly and John arrived a little after their friends. They watched as the little family fought to maintain control. Brad was obviously frustrated but kept his anger in check for the sake of Sarah and Justin. John and Carly ached for them; quietly, they prayed, "God, help us say the right things." They wanted to offer as much support to their friends as possible.

The young man threw himself into his new mom's arms. She put on a brave face as she reminded him to write and remember she would always love him. He obediently agreed.

Brad reached out to shake the hand of the young man then pulled him into his arms. "Listen, kid, we still love you, and if they will let you come home you are always welcome back. It doesn't end here. You're part of our family; we will be praying for you. Remember, you're a man now and you are an anointed servant of Jesus Christ. It could be he is sending you into this den of the lions for the souls of the young people you will be living among. One soul is worth the whole world to Jesus. The time is short; fight the good fight." As he pulled him closer, he whispered into Justin's ear. "I will try to get you out of there, son. Be brave and don't let them brainwash you. You are bought with the blood of Jesus Christ. The blood of Jesus is on your very soul. The anointing of Jesus Christ rests on your shoulders. He is sending you out as a sheep among wolves. But you are victorious through Jesus Christ."

Justin beamed back. "Thanks, Dad. I'll remember."

He hugged John and Carly good-bye, thanking them for coming to see him off. "Check in on Mom, Carly; I don't know how much more she can take."

"I promise. She is stronger than you think. You just worry about yourself. We love you and we'll all be praying for your safety."

"Thanks, Carly," Justin's face lit up with the light of Jesus. "I know the Lord is going to be with me. Remember when Pastor John told us the Bible story about Daniel. He and his friends were taken against their will too, but God was with them. He'll take care of me."

And with that, he boarded the train with his bag thrown carelessly over his shoulder. He turned to wave good-bye. Inside the train he took a seat. He watched as his new family faded out of sight. Brad was holding Sarah as though he was protecting her from being pulled away from him. Justin whispered to the only friend he had left. "I need you. I want to be brave, but Lord, I'm afraid."

All over the world all of the young people were being rounded up and taken to these camps to become a massive army for the use of the Man of Sin.

⌒

Alone in his office, the Antichrist sat, thinking about his newest project. He touched the power on his clicker and turned off the news report. He would mold his young people into true worshippers. They would be the ones who would follow him with no questions asked. Their parents, while easily controlled, still asked too many questions. He wanted men and women who would follow him without hesitation. He wanted total control.

⌒

John and Carly watched their friends say good-bye to Justin. Carly's heart broke as she considered the love the little family had for each other. The two couples looked around. All over the train station were men and women waving bye to their children for the last time. John felt sick. He knew they would try to brainwash these innocent children. The ones who rebelled would be destroyed or put into work camps. The ones who obeyed would become soldiers in the new regime.

All the Bible predictions were coming to pass. There had been some horrific natural disasters as was predicted in the Bible. Food was in short supply; many plagues had claimed crops all over the world. Men and women were hungry. Some mysterious plagues continued to bombard the farmers. Their crops were failing. Even soil that was known for production delivered unusually meager crops.

The president of the world just stepped right up to the platform. He promised food enough for everyone. There was just one catch—they all had to take the mark of the beast. It was an amazing little chip placed under the skin of the hand or the forehead. It could tell the person scanning it who you are and all your life history. No one seemed to care that it was a total and complete invasion of their privacy. It seemed the world had lost its mind. This technology was accepted as the latest security system. The whole world ran to do this with no understanding of the consequences to their own souls.

John and Paul preached every day. They held revival meetings and kept their churches open as much as possible. There were so many who needed answers. The time was short. They had to make the biggest impact possible in the limited amount of time they had.

John had discussed at length with Carly their being caught and martyred for Christ. They prayed daily for the personal strength it would take to stand up under the impending torture that would certainly come. John didn't worry so much for himself; it was Carly he cared about. He prayed their time of torment would end swiftly.

Paul had been on the move preaching daily. He and John both had online sites where they posted their sermons. They also taught in the streets, their pulpits, or any arena they could rent. Preaching in the streets was something they were not supposed to do without a license, which, of course, no one would issue. So they just went ahead talking to anyone anywhere who would listen. When they were questioned by the police, they preached to them too. They were unstoppable, with some unknown force surrounding them. The police were not inclined to challenge them. They did not want to encounter that hedge of protection that surrounded the men of God. Something unexplainable kept them safe. A shiver ran down the arresting officer's back as he thought of that presence.

God's hedge of protection followed Paul daily, but he was finding it more and more difficult to preach in the larger stadiums. He was unwanted. The more they discouraged him, the harder he preached. He had, of course, turned down the generous offer of the governor to be a One World All Faiths Religion (or OWAFR) church leader. That had gone over like a lead balloon. The governor reminded him that he had been warned.

Paul saw the whole end-time prophesies thing being fulfilled as a catalyst for a more dynamic work. He used every opportunity he had to preach. He was having the time of his life. He knew it was one of the worst times for Christians to be alive on planet Earth, but he found it all invigorating. If the Antichrist was going to take him out, he was going to go preaching all the way. He had no intention of stepping down, turning aside, or turning around. He had set his course and was headed full speed ahead—no looking back, no wondering about his options. He intended to die preaching to his last breath.

Shelby had made a similar commitment. She had started preaching on street corners, in back alleys, and was presently leading a women's group in the basement of one of their homes. She wasn't going to just ride along on her husband's shirttails any longer. She intended to win the lost. The fire he saw in her eyes left him breathless. She was an anointed force.

Before the rapture she had worked with him as the ever-present wife. Now she worked even harder fulfilling her own calling with a vengeance. He smiled as he thought it over; she could preach. She had proven to be a fire-and-brimstone speaker who left no one near her wondering what she thought of the signs of the times. Paul had never been more proud of her.

He looked out over the large crowd of people gathering in the marketplace and said, "Ladies and gentlemen, I ask you who your provider is. Who has given you this day? Who has caused the sun to shine? Who has allowed your lungs to take in air? Who has created all the beauty your eyes behold? Is he this new leader? Has he hung the stars in the sky? When did he create the trees that provide for shade? Did he speak this world into existence? I say no! A resounding no! He is not God! He has not ordained the spinning of the earth. He does not hold it in its course. He cannot calm the storm. He does not have the power to stop the suffering of this world. He could not stop the disappearances. He can't keep the earth from quaking. He cannot combat the plagues or the pestilence that will hit us all with the force that destroyed ancient Egypt. He is neither the Creator nor the King of this earth. That position belongs only to Jesus Christ, the Son of the Living God! He it is who formed the world, the heavens, and all that is in them. John the apostle spoke of him as the Creator when he said,"

> All things were made by him; and without him was not any thing made that was made. In him was life; and the life was the light of men (John 1:3–4). He was in the world, and the world was made by him, and the world knew him not. He came unto his own, and his own received him not. But as many as received him, to them gave he power to become the sons God, even to them that believe on his name (John 1:10–12). For there is one God, and one mediator between God and men, the man Christ Jesus (1 Timothy 2:5).

The crowd gathered, mesmerized by the words of this dynamic preacher. He, as Paul of old, held them captivated by the truth. The anointing on Paul could be felt. It had a substance that was like thick honey, but it was unseen oil. It dripped from his head, ran down his face, dropped to his shoulders and clung to his garments, unseen by mankind but very much felt. His voice rang out with power as he challenged men and women right there to make a decision for Christ, warning them of the consequences of taking the mark of the beast. People wanted to jeer at him but were held speechless by some unknown force they were powerless to fight.

The young preacher pounded out the words of Christ as the Scripture flowed out of him like water from a brook. He gave an altar call inviting anyone who wanted to know Jesus to come.

The answer from the crowd was in a plea for help. "What can we do to be saved?" they cried out!

Paul answered, "Confess you are a sinner. Ask Jesus to forgive you for your sins. The Bible says, 'If we confess our sins, he is faithful and just to forgive us our sins, and to cleanse us from all unrighteousness' (1 John 1:9).

"The days ahead will be difficult. We were left behind, but we are not forgotten. God has turned his back on this world. But God's will is that none should perish; 2 Peter 3:9 says, 'The Lord is not slack concerning his promise, as some men count slackness; but is longsuffering to us-ward, not willing that any should perish, but that all should come to repentance.' And in Ezekiel 33:11, God says, 'Say unto them, As I live, saith the Lord GOD, I have no pleasure in the death of the wicked; but that the wicked turn from his way and live: turn ye, turn ye from your evil ways; for why will ye die, O house of Israel?' It is not too late for God to forgive you. Isaiah 59:1 says, 'BEHOLD, the LORD's hand is not shortened, that it cannot save; neither his ear heavy, that it cannot hear.' There is nothing you have ever done that can keep you from the love of God. The only thing that can condemn you to hell is your unwillingness to accept him as your Lord and Savior." The crowd that had gathered bowed their heads as men and women dedicated their lives to God.

Meanwhile, Justin was making waves of his own. He had arrived at the compound only to realize it was more like a jail than a camp. He looked around at the other young people. No one there was any happier than he. The boys were placed on strict schedules. They looked across the yard. Behind a tall fence they could see the compound for the girls. The young ladies were not visible.

As the days went by, the young man grew more rebellious. Justin spoke daily to anyone who would listen about Jesus. His teacher was exasperated. "I have asked you not to speak specifically of any one religion. We are all important in the eyes of deity. You know very well, Justin, the world has chosen a religion of supreme understanding. Tolerance of others is our greatest achievement. We are not so antiquated as to look to one God. We are open-minded enough to see the beauty of all gods, of all faiths. Don't you see, young man, God is as close as this tree? This tree sustains us. Its shade protects us. We are better because of its existence. There are those of supreme enlightenment who believe it is God."

Justin tried not to be obstinate, but this was just too much. "Excuse me, teacher, but that's just a tree. It can't hear, it can't see, it can't speak; and while its existence is beneficial, it exists because of a loving God." Justin threw his hands up and made parentheses in the air as he said, "The one and only God." Bringing his hands down, he continued, "He realized people would need shelter. We need its shade. We also need the wood for building, and it supplies us with warmth if we burn it. Also God, the one who created it, knew the world would need the oxygen it provides. It was created for the use of man. We are all here because God created us. He created you and me—even this tree." Spreading his hands out in frustration, he said, "It didn't create itself. God put it here. That tree is not God. Why should I pretend to believe something I know is not true?"

His bold question only gave his teacher the right to punish him. Justin was miserable and grew more miserable daily. Time was also running out. They had been told they would be receiving their implants soon. Somehow he had avoided receiving the mark when he arrived. Oddly enough there had been a malfunction of some sort. The all-too-somber doctor had tried to administer the chip several times, but the implant device would not function. Consequently no one who had arrived with Justin had received the mark. However, his jailors had ordered new supplies, and they were planning to administer the new technology the following week.

He made friends with some of the other young men. They had a plan to break out. Three boys had sisters who were being held in the other building. They had to find them and somehow manage to get them out without being caught.

They had worked out a plan to escape: one of them, a volunteer, would go first creating a diversion. He would lead their jailers on a wild goose chase in the opposite direction, giving the others time. The others would simply slip away in the confusion. Once the coast was clear, all the decoy had to do was get away.

It was just past midnight when Justin slipped out of his bed. The trick was to get their attention, convince them he was acting alone, and somehow keep them running in circles. He covered his pillow with his blankets, pretending to not want to get caught. Then he made sure he was heard as he left the compound. The others acted quickly. They made a run for the grove of trees; once they cleared the open, they might have a chance.

The boys who had sisters had been watching the girls for days, catching glimpses of where they were most likely kept. They worked their way into the other compound. Slipping past the guard, they quietly moved along the side of the building, then in through a window. They breathed a sigh of relief as they were undiscovered. They crept along the hallway easing their way up the steps. There was some interest from the guards as to the disturbance next door, but they seemed content to believe it was the problem of the boys' compound. Slowly they made their way through the rooms, quietly checking for their family members. They opened a door and found the quarters where the girls were sleeping.

Some of the girls were up and watching out their windows to see what was happening. They looked at the faces of the young men who had just opened their door. One boy placed a finger to his mouth. "Don't make a sound," he whispered. "We aren't going to hurt anyone. I'm looking for my sister, Mackenzie. Do you know her?"

One of the girls nodded. She quickly ran to Mac's bed and shook her. The sleepy-eyed Mac looked up at her brother. "Simon, you're here!"

"Get dressed," he ordered. "We don't have much time."

The other girls were waking up as well. "Where are you going?"

"Shush," he said quietly. "We're escaping; we don't want to be here anymore."

"Can I come too?" one of the girls asked.

"We're coming with you," another girl added.

She was used to being obeyed. Simon studied her. She was trouble. "We didn't invite you," he said, intending to intimidate her.

"You either let us come with you or we'll scream. And you won't be going anywhere either."

"Okay, but you better do what you're told. I don't plan on getting caught because of some stupid girl."

Karen would have argued but now wasn't the time. "I can help. I know a shortcut out of here." The boys were ordered to turn around while the girls dressed.

Simon followed her begrudgingly. Quietly they made their way out of the building, down the back stairs, out into the courtyard, then off into the forest. The boys had set a place to meet. They had learned the woods from combat training. They worked their way through the forest to the set destination. They were all safe.

"This has to be a miracle," one of the girls said as they realized they had escaped completely undetected. Her long dark hair bounced wildly down her back. Her hazel eyes looked up at Simon, questioning, "What about the boy?" Anna asked, "Do you think he was able to escape?"

"I don't know. We will give him a few more minutes; that's all we can afford. Then we have to leave even if he doesn't make it. That was the deal. We stick to the plan. He will try to meet up with us later."

Justin veered off to the side. Years of being a delinquent had given him certain skills, one of which was not being caught. He had learned to avoid capture every time, that is, every time with the exception of when Brad got a hold of him.

"Over there," one of the guards had spotted him.

He ducked back behind a thicket. He had mapped his trail out when he was playing war games. He tried to be visible enough to keep them coming, but he was going to need a foolproof way of losing these guys. He doubled back; they were looking for him where he had just been. He climbed a tree and hunkered down into the cover it provided. He was going to be late getting back to the others. It hadn't been easy keeping these guys going in the wrong direction. He snickered to himself. In the movies they always get out the dogs for a chase like this. Thank God, these guys didn't have any dogs. The hunting party of guards had taken his false trail. He rested a few minutes. He couldn't wait any longer. It would be getting light soon. He had to escape while he still had the cover of night. He scooted down the tree. Once he was on the ground again, he ran toward his friends.

"Where were you?" Cole, one of the older boys, asked. His mop of wavy curls showed streaks of blond and brown. His brown eyes scanned the distance in front of them. "We have a long ways to go."

Justin had taken a shortcut through the woods. "I had trouble losing those guys. I ended up waiting it out. After a while they got tired and gave up the chase. Since it was so late I bypassed the original destination; instead, I came straight here."

"We have to go. The train will be here soon." Cole was already hiking up the hill. "We don't want to be caught out in the open. They'll see us."

"Why don't we steal a car?" Karen asked. "Why should we walk?"

"Because they will be searching all the roads. We can go through the woods and be at my Dad's cabin in two days." Cole was a kid who had grown up in the woods. His father had been taken in the rapture. Cole, a typical rebellious teenager, had not been ready. He and Justin had spent many hours bemoaning their mutual if only this and if only thats. They were not uninformed when Jesus returned; they were just rebels.

"My dad warned me," Cole had sighed.

They walked along staying close to the tree line. Cole made sure they kept under the canopy of trees. A couple of times a helicopter circled the area then continued on.

Cole was from a place that was only a couple of long days' walk from the compound. He had hunted and fished all over these back woods. Thinking of his dad's cabin, he smiled. "No one will know where we are. It's abandoned most of the year. Just maybe a hunter might find it. You'll see. We will be fine there. We can hunt and fish for food. My dad taught me to set traps. We'll know if any one comes on our mountain. There's plenty of room for all of us. If we want to, we can find our parents, but only after they stop looking for us." They had all agreed. Somehow the last few weeks had turned these teenagers into young adults. They swore to protect each other and never tell the location of the hideout. Justin was convinced a cabin in the woods with hunting, fishing, and freedom was a hundred times better than being kept against his will in a compound by the Antichrist.

The only problem he saw was the girls. It wasn't that he didn't like girls; he just hadn't thought about them being there too. One, in particular, stood out to him. She was bossy, too tall, and the most beautiful girl he had ever seen. Her long blond hair, big blue eyes, and smile turned him to putty. She knew it and she used it against him. One look and he was hopelessly in love.

"What if we don't want to live in your silly old cabin?" Karen asked. "I think we girls should be allowed to go wherever we want. I want to go home to my parents."

Simon seemed unaffected by her obvious charms. He snarled. Looking annoyed, he said, "I agree with you; but you are the one who insisted on coming with us. We are not going to let you go off, get yourself caught, and then sell all of us out for your own benefit. You are coming with us and you're doing it without complaint. We will help you get word to them when the coast is clear. In the meantime, we stick together."

Justin and Cole looked at each other, both thinking the same thing. Cole said to Karen, "You realize they will look for you at your parents' first, don't you? It isn't safe for them or you."

"My parents would never turn me in. They love me." She tossed her hair, crossed her arms, and glared at their stupidity.

"Sure they do. But it still isn't safe." Justin added softly, "It just isn't worth all of us being caught to let you take that chance. Things are different now. People are different. That's why we all had to leave that place before they turned us into robots for the regime."

Food and water was in short supply due to the unexpected girls. Each guy had been saving back his rations for the last couple of days. Cole had advised them to take more than they thought they would need. Everyone had also set aside a container of water. They had packed the extra rations into their backpacks before leaving. Each guy was assigned a girl with whom to share his water and food. The boys who had helped their sisters escape shared with them, leaving Justin and some others to take care of the interlopers. Justin shared his rations with Karen who picked at her food and acted like he may have contaminated it at some point. She sipped his water taking just a little more than she should. "We're going to need that on the trip, be careful," he cautioned.

Whenever they took short rest breaks, they watched for vehicles or planes that were suspicious. After a while they were convinced their captors had lost interest. Just to be safe, Simon doubled back after a couple of hours; he returned with the news that nobody was following them.

Justin was concerned about Sarah and Brad. He wondered what would happen to them. He had to get word to them soon. He just wasn't sure how he could do it.

The cabin turned out to be more fun than any of the boys could have dreamed. Cole's dad had left it stocked with extra guns and ammunition he had hidden away. There was also canned food, all hidden in a secret room behind the wall. "It looks like your dad was prepared for a war."

Cole looked at his new family. "Yea, he was prepared for anything."

THE YOUNG FUGITIVES

Brad received a visit from the police; they were looking for Justin. "Are you sure you haven't heard from him?" The officer looked at Brad skeptically.

"I'm sure, sir. He is just one of those kids who is always in trouble. His mom was one of the ones who disappeared. My wife and I tried to help him, but then he was taken to a military training compound. We haven't received any word from him. I sure hope he's okay."

The officer left his card. "If you hear from him, give me a call."

"No problem, officer. You have a good day." Brad closed the front door.

"What's going on, Brad?" Sarah watched him with a concerned look on her face. The two little lines above her brow furrowed together as she bit her lip. "Is Justin all right?"

Brad grabbed his wife, swinging her around in a circle as he celebrated. Finally he let her feet touch the ground long enough to talk to her. Brad smiled at Sarah. "If I know Justin, he's just fine." A mental picture of the police description of Justin's escape raced through his mind. Brad started to laugh. "He ran away. They just wanted to know if we had heard from him."

"What if he's hungry or cold?" Sarah wasn't so sure he was all right.

Brad's smile widened. "Sarah, that's one kid they won't catch. And he is definitely all right. It seems he broke out of the compound along with some other kids. The officer said he was a decoy so the others could escape. Don't worry, he's a survivor."

Weeks went by. Then, one fall day Brad heard from Justin: a postcard in Justin's handwriting arrived. It said, "Thinking of you, wish you were here." Justin signed the note *Will Granger*, using his granddad's name.

It was addressed general delivery. Brad wrote back, "We will see you soon." He addressed it general delivery. He knew the authorities might still be looking for Justin, so he drove around for a week, stopping in out-of-the-way, unimportant places, just in case he and Sarah were being watched. Finally they stopped at a little bed and breakfast in the same small town the postcard had come from.

"Brad, what do we do now?" Sarah asked.

"We wait. He'll let us know when it's safe. Meanwhile, we just behave as if we are tourists with no set destination."

It didn't happen for a few days, but one day they saw Justin. He was taller, leaner, and carried himself a little differently. He wore a large cowboy hat, sunglasses, cowboy boots, and a jean jacket that made him appear older than he was. The kid walked into the only cafe in town, talked to the lady at the register, and then left.

Sarah started to jump up and run to him, but Brad stopped her by holding her hand and saying softly to her, "Wait."

She was frustrated by this game. "Why didn't he just come up to us and say hi?"

"He can't." Brad took Sarah by the hand, looked deep into her eyes, and in a voice only loud enough for her to hear, he said, "I think he wants us to follow him. Let's just leave as though we're going for a romantic walk." They stopped at their car putting a leash on Bounder who was waiting patiently. They began to follow Justin. They meandered down the street. Justin stayed just close enough for them to see him. When they reached a secluded little alley they heard a whistle, turned into it, and there he was. Brad let go of the leash. Bounder ran full force toward Justin, jumping on him, almost knocking him down. Justin bent down throwing his arms around the dog's neck. He rubbed him happily. "You're a good boy. Yes, you are. That's right."

Sarah ran up to him. He raised himself to his feet. She threw her arms around his neck. Brad also hugged him. "We have been worried about you."

"I know. It's just that I couldn't take the chance of putting both of you in danger."

"You did well," Brad beamed.

Sarah studied Justin. He looked good. He was taller, leaner, and tanned. Wherever he had been, he had been spending time outside.

As they talked they walked out of town. There was a thicket of trees with tall brush that served as camouflage for an old pickup truck. Justin climbed in behind the wheel. They looked at him a little skeptically. "You're only fourteen. What are you doing driving?" Sarah asked concerned.

"It's a good thing I'm big for my age, huh." Sarah did not find it funny. She lingered trying to think. "Come on, get in. We have to go where we won't be seen." Justin looked concerned. "It's really not safe here."

"Scoot over." Brad got into the driver's seat beside Justin, then Sarah joined them. Bounder jumped in, landing on Justin's lap, and refused to move.

Justin showed them a way out of town. They drove down a deserted road, away from any signs of civilization. Slowly they made their way to the cabin. "We have a good setup; everybody says you can stay if you want. It's just up ahead, turn right here." He motioned to a road that looked washed out. The old pickup rocked and swayed as they headed into the forest. After driving a distance they stopped. "This is good." Justin smiled as he looked at Sarah. "We walk the rest of the way in." He dug around in the brush then grabbed a large net already strung with branches and twigs. We use this to hide our truck. Brad helped him swing it into place. "It's just through here." Justin picked his way through the brush. The side of the mountain exposed a small trail.

Soon they were at the cabin. Brad and Sarah were surprised. They had not thought about the other young people that morning. They looked up to see several teenagers, some about the age of Justin, some a little older.

Justin followed their eyes then added, "None of us liked it there. We didn't want to be zombies for the regime, so we all escaped. These are my friends."

Brad, Sarah, and Bounder were introduced to the group. They ranged in age from fourteen to seventeen. The oldest boy stood guard near the cabin. Apparently they always had a guard on duty. They were shown around the cabin and warned of traps. "We have to have ample warning should someone come to the cabin without an invitation. You are the first to see our setup. We are hoping to reunite with our parents at some point; but most of our families have already been marked. If we bring them here they'll lead the authorities to all of us. So we are going to visit them one at a time as we feel it is safe."

Cole spoke up with confidence. "The reason we have brought you here is we feel we should help others. We believe this is an ideal hideout for refugees from the regime. We have been preparing to move into the cave as soon as possible. We know we could be seen easily here. When winter hits we will have to have a fire; if we do we could be caught. Right now we have a stove in the cabin that works with propane; once that is gone we will even have to cook with fire. We have been drying most of our meat. We are also growing some food. We've been bartering for animals. Over there's the chicken coop. We have a milk goat. We plan on getting a milk cow soon.

But we will need access to the outside world, kind of an underground system, to get what we need from time to time: clothes, medicine, and other essentials. Would you be willing to help us?"

Brad didn't hesitate. "Of course, I'll do what I can."

"We realize there are Christians who need a place to hide from the authorities. We are willing to evaluate them one at a time. If they do not have the tracking device they will be welcomed. That's another thing; is there any way to deactivate the device once it has been activated?"

Brad shook his head. "As far as I understand, it is permanent." Some of the young people shuffled, looking uncomfortable.

"Did they mark any of you?" Brad was sick with the thought.

"No, we all escaped before they could do it. But we have friends, even family, who may have taken the mark. We were hoping to help them."

"I'm sorry. I don't believe there is anything that can be done for them, but I will check into it. Perhaps a doctor could remove the device. There are a lot of Christians who will need your help. You've all done a good thing here. Do you think I could see the cave you've been telling me about?"

They walked through the forest. The trail was barely distinguishable. One of the boys was careful to hide their tracks. Karen was a talkative teenager who seemed to mother all of the younger girls. Sarah noticed the unsettling friendship between Justin and the older girl. "What about sleeping arrangements? How do you manage with so many boys and girls?"

Justin looked embarrassed. "Mom, what are you asking us?"

Sarah decided not to mince words. "Where do you sleep?"

Cole interrupted. "I understand your concern, Mrs. Holden. But we are all Christians. None of us wants to bring children into our circumstance. As soon as we could we boys moved into the cave, But we are still concerned for the safety of the girls. That's another reason why we need to move them into the cave with us." He looked over at Brad. "We have been doing some remodeling. I'm anxious for you to see our setup; perhaps you can help us with some of the building."

Sarah still wasn't convinced. "You mean you have been living here unsupervised and there hasn't been anything going on between the boys and the girls?"

Karen spoke up. "That's exactly what he means. They all know we would kill them if they tried anything. These are unusual circumstances. We are dependent on each other for our lives. We have all missed the rapture and are studying the Bible for anything that will help us. We have a short time left to live or die. We will probably die, but we don't want to miss Jesus again. We don't want him to come back and find us living the kind of life that brought this judgment on the world. It's important to us to stay pure." She dropped her head. A tear ran down her face. She wiped it away and stiffened her back straight as a board.

Sarah melted with compassion. She opened her arms and wrapped the young girl in them. That was all it took. Karen broke and the waterworks started. She hadn't been aware of how tired she was of pretending to be strong. The truth was she wanted to go back in time. She wanted to relive the last couple of years. She wanted to talk to her mom and dad. She wanted them to know she was working hard and doing her best to make them proud. She wanted to be back in high school. She wanted to go to her prom. She wanted her life back. She wanted to be like a regular teenage girl. But that wasn't going to happen for her. She was now hiding from the Antichrist. Her responsibilities were to help these younger girls grow up and hopefully keep them all from dying just because they had chosen to follow Christ.

Sarah talked to her softly. "It's all right, honey. We're here now. Brad and I will help you, all of you."

Sarah looked up and almost jumped. She could see a tall, slender middle-aged man watching them from across the ravine. His German shepherd dog stood faithfully at his side. In one hand he held a walking stick, even though it appeared he did not need it. What frightened Sarah the most was the rifle in his other hand. He was standing on the mountain as if he owned it and they were trespassers. Karen followed Sarah's eyes and raised her hand to wave at the man. "Who is he?" Sarah asked.

"He's our friend." Mac piped up waving her arm back and forth excitedly. "He is the nicest man I know. He saved my life when I fell off the trail one day. I was pretty banged up so he took me to his cave on the other side of the mountain. He took care of me. When I was better he brought me back here."

Karen laughed. "He keeps to himself mostly. When we first arrived here he knew it. The next morning when we woke up there was a string of trout waiting for us on the front porch. No introduction, just the fish. Every day there was fish for the first week. Then one day he left us some deer meat."

Mac piped in. "He doesn't talk much, but he takes care of us. Cole says he and King, that's his dog, are better guards than a whole troop of soldiers. No one comes up this mountain without his knowing it."

"Where did he come from? Does he have a name?" Sarah asked.

Mackenzie was happy to explain. "His name is Ron Barton. He used to be a timber faller. He knows these mountains better than anybody, even Cole. He came here when the Antichrist took office."

The guys had ignored the conversation of the girls. After waving at their friend, they simply moved on, leaving the women folk to do whatever it is they do. They moved Brad along showing him their setup. Brad was intrigued. They had been busy. There was a garden with tomatoes, lettuce, and other plants. The garden was hidden from view of planes. They simply built a lean-to with a series of windows of screen on the top. They covered them with a drop cloth of greenery when they needed to be invisible, then opened the windows when it was safe to catch the sun.

Ron watched as his friends showed the couple around. He didn't feel comfortable with newcomers. He had gotten acquainted with his neighbors slowly. They were kindhearted young men and women who had been forced to grow up too fast. King growled softly at the other dog. Ron's hand touched King's head. "Shush. Don't you bother that dog. That's their dog. You behave."

Mackenzie was his favorite. He loved the young freckle-faced teen with all the questions. His mind shot back to the day he found her unconscious after taking a nasty fall. It was close to dark. She had wandered too far from her camp for him to return her to her companions that day, so he brought her to his cave. He had all the comforts of home. Living on the mountain agreed with him. He liked being in the country. He enjoyed the freedom he had here on his mountain. The girl had awakened a little sore from the fall. She was a little shaky on her feet so she stayed that night. The next morning he showed her a shortcut back to her home.

During that visit she was captivated by his collection of instruments. When he left for the mountain he had brought all of his favorite things. His guitars, his banjo, fiddle, and harmonica were just part of them.

"I've heard you play." She said, stroking the instruments affectionately. "The sound carries over to our side of the mountain. Do you mind?" she asked him as she picked up the fiddle.

"Not at all. Do you play?" he asked

"Oh yeah, Simon and I were properly trained: seven years of violin, the serious stuff." She raised the instrument to her chin, stroked it with the bow, and magic happened.

When she finished, he said, "It's yours."

Mac jumped with excitement. "Are you sure? How can I ever thank you?"

"Just play it for me some time." It felt good to do something nice for the girl. He hadn't seen that carefree happiness for a very long time. The new-world order had sapped all of the joy out of people. They bonded as friends. Ever since that night, she would play it after dark before bed. He waited to hear the serenade before going to sleep.

He had more guitars than he needed, so after talking with Mac, he shared two of his instruments with the group. They would get together from time to time and play. Mac and Simon were quick to pick up the country sound he and Cole enjoyed playing most. He had been invited to come and meet Justin's parents but had politely refused. "You need time with them yourselves; we'll get together another time." As he watched the newcomers, he decided he liked them. He was a good judge of character. His instincts told him they would be good for his young neighbors.

The cave was sectioned off with walls. Some were built with scraps of wood; others with rocks. The girls caught up with the guys. They listened as the guys continued to show Brad around. "The rocks were heavy and difficult to manage, so we brought in building supplies. That made the building easier. We have set up a kitchen in here. This is basically the living quarters for all of us, but behind these walls are the bedrooms. The girls' rooms are on the opposite side of the cave." Cole blushed slightly as he added, "None of us want to be parents." He looked over at Karen as he said, "We already have enough to do looking after ourselves and each other."

Outside Simon was busy tending to the daily chores. He stopped just long enough to be introduced to Brad. He held out his hand, taking Brad's; he shook it firmly. "It's a pleasure to meet you, sir. Justin has told us all about you. Ma'am." He tipped his head at Sarah. Brad and Sarah were amazed at the ingenuity of these young people. They had grown up overnight and were living up to the challenge.

Cole continued to speak. "We figure we can protect others as they need our help. No one is ever to come here without being blindfolded. That way they will be able to leave if they want to, but if they're caught they won't be able to tell anyone our location. We would be happy to listen to any suggestions you have that would help us with our living conditions."

Brad stood dumbfounded. "You guys amaze me. This is incredible. I see you have a fresh water source."

"Yes, sir. We are going to use it for drinking," Simon said as though he had been working on it. "We think by piping it we can also use it for washing. The only thing is heating it. There must be a way to heat it with solar energy."

Brad walked around. After studying the problem, he had an idea. "But I will need some supplies."

"That's not a problem." One of the boys pointed to the necessary pipe. "We have been collecting it."

Brad looked suspiciously at Justin. Justin looked a little sheepish. "I guess I'm not quite reformed." He flashed his most charming smile; the cute one his mom could never resist.

Brad glared at him. "Am I going to have to deal with you, boy?"

The smile disappeared. "No, sir."

"I better not hear of you going around like a thug stealing, ever again. Do you hear me?" "Yes, sir."

The other boys looked stricken. "It's not his fault, sir. We had to have supplies."

"Yes, and if you get caught, all of you pay the price. I don't want you stealing. I will find a way to help you without you disobeying the commandments. We have to develop some form of bartering system for the supplies we need. Nobody steals. You're Christians, not thieves."

"Yes, sir." The boys watched Brad.

All of a sudden Cole remembered what it felt like to have a dad around. He affectionately slapped Brad's shoulder; laughing, he said, "It's good to have you around, man."

The other boys looked at him, confused. They were not used to the whole dad-runs-the-house thing. But before long, Brad was teasing them and playing with them as though he were a kid too. It didn't take long for him to become their friend. The guys decided it was important that they put food on the table, so they all went fishing.

The girls rolled their eyes when Sarah asked if that was something they did a lot. Candy, a pretty, short little girl with freckles piped up. "They think they are men." She snickered as she told Sarah of one of her own fishing trips where she caught the largest fish in the group. "I'm a better fisherman than any of them, but they act like it's an accident if I catch the most fish. I've been teaching Justin though. We're friends. He's getting a lot better." She looked down self-consciously as she finished her sentence.

Brad enjoyed the boys behaving like boys. A lighthearted spirit came over them while they fished. They teased, played, and eventually gave up fishing for swimming. He sat contemplating the setup. He knew there were many Christians who would benefit from this place. He shook his head. How was it the Bible said, "A little child will lead them" (Isaiah 11:6)? A sad look overshadowed his face. But these aren't teenagers, not really. They are fugitives from the regime. The Antichrist wanted them. He would hunt them down, and if they did not surrender to his will he would ultimately kill them. His heart pounded. "God, don't let him get these young people. Help me to help them. We need your wisdom."

Brad and Sarah said good-bye to Justin and their new friends. "Take care of Bounder. We'll be back soon." Bounder stared up at Justin, watching him with pure love and trust.

The trip home from their visit with Justin left Brad and Sarah deep in thought. They knew they had to find a way to help. They wanted to be a part of Justin's life, not just his past. As they thought of the many plans the young men and women were making, they saw the hiding place as a dwelling of peace. It would give sanctuary to those battle-weary souls in need of a retreat without the demands of the modern-day regime. They realized this could be an awesome way of escape for the many who would be persecuted because of their love for Jesus.

They had watched with wide-eyed wonder as Justin and his friends held their own church service. They pored over the Word of God as though each word was a vital source of life to them: after all, wasn't it? These young people were more than just fugitives. They were studying the Word with such fervor they were quickly becoming magnificent examples of Christ. Brad and Sarah were taken aback by the thirst for learning they witnessed. Neither of them felt they were capable of expounding the word to these young militant preachers. They spoke the Bible with such passion; it was as if they were expecting Christ to walk through the door and instruct them personally in his desire for their lives.

Sarah was relieved to hear they were not involved with each other, but she didn't really believe them until she listened to their open discussions on the Word of God. Never in her life had she experienced that kind of passion. She felt just a little left out when her own puny understanding fell short in the face of these young Bible students. They read the Bible as though they were drinking in every word.

They also believed there would come a day when they would be found out and only the Bible Scriptures they had memorized would be left for them. So they studied as though today was all they had.

Brad and Sarah felt ashamed of themselves. All of the new Christian growth they had experienced had not prepared them for the possibility of being in the company of these young Bible scholars. Each one of them took Scriptures they were personally responsible for learning. Between them they had covered the entire book of John and were working on some others for their own studies. Mackenzie smiled as she read their daily Psalm. She later told Sarah the book of Psalms was her favorite. "I love poetry," she said, her eyes wide with wonder. "I have been memorizing as many of the Psalms as I can." The young man Cole was studying the end-time prophesies. He was memorizing them and trying to prepare himself and the others for the coming events.

After their Bible study time, the group began to pray. They prayed for their own safety, for wisdom, and for all those who were serving the Lord Jesus. They lingered, talking to God about their brothers and sisters who were in danger. They prayed for Israel. They prayed for their brothers and sisters in Israel who were being persecuted. They cried out to God. Their personal relationships with Christ showed on their faces as they did. Sarah and Brad wept tears of joy. These were young Daniels and Esthers, serving God and crying out in love for protection for people they didn't even know.

Then the music started. Mac and Simon could play just about anything with strings. Cole picked up the banjo and they were off; Cole began to sing "I've Got Jesus" by Linda McAbee:

> I've got Jesus in my heart
> And the Holy Spirit in my soul.
> Now my Jesus makes me happy.
> His Holy Spirit makes me whole.

After they decided to stop, Mac walked outside to make sure he would hear her. She started to play "Rock of Ages," the hymn by Augustus M. Toplady, for her friend across the ravine. It was a sweet, tender wailing sound that wafted over the mountain.

Karen explained, "That's his favorite. She tries to play something for him every night, but he absolutely loves it when she plays 'Rock of Ages.'"

"We have to find a way to help them learn," Brad mused out loud. "There must be a way to at least help them with their studies."

"They don't act like teenagers, do they?" Sarah commented. "What teenager studies the Bible all day long and then spends the rest of their time working and making plans for the many people they believe will need their help? They're my heroes," she said softly.

Brad reached over, squeezed her hand, and said, "Mine too, honey. We'll find a way to help them; I promise."

They knew they had to make some contacts. They were going to need supplies for the hideout. Sarah and Carly had already been collecting and storing food they knew would be needed as the Antichrist became more powerful. Miss Millie's basement was filled to the brim with all kinds of canned food. This was just one source. They had discovered food, clothing, and all kinds of useable items in all of the homes of the church people who had disappeared. They were waiting for the mark of the beast to be enforced. The plan was to feed and clothe as many as possible for as long as they could. The rest was up to God.

They needed carpentry supplies. Brad had a friend who would do some trading. He had to have a pass to haul anything like that though. Brad wondered if DC could help him out. DC was one guy who seemed to be able to get anything. And when it came to technology, no one was better.

The churches were talking about meeting in secret. But still, John, and even Paul, were holding church meetings in public. They were still keeping the doors to their churches open right on schedule. Brad and Sarah decided to go by the church and try to make some connections tonight. As far as they knew, it was still the best place to talk to some of their friends they believed would be willing to help. Brad and Sarah did not know what had taken place in their absence.

IT HAPPENED AT THE CROSS

Only a few days earlier, Carly sat on the front pew of the church listening to the old hymns playing softly:

> At the cross, at the cross where I first saw the light,
> And the burden of my heart rolled away.
> It was there by faith I received my sight,
> And now I am happy all the day.
>
> —Isaac Watts

Before the rapture she had not enjoyed these songs; but somehow, hearing them now brought comfort to her troubled spirit.

"Pass Me Not, O Gentle Savior" (Frances J. Crosby). The soft melodies of the old hymns played as John gave the altar call. Finally, "There Is Power in the Blood" (Lewis E. Jones) and "Nothing but the Blood of Jesus" (Robert Lowry). One after the other, the notes floated through the air as John continued to speak. "People ask me about the cross of Jesus. They want to know, 'Why did he willingly give his life? Why did he have to make that sacrifice? He is God. Why didn't he find another way?' The answer is he knew what we needed. He knew any other way would not be sufficient. That is why the old covenant of Moses wasn't enough. We cannot earn our way into God's kingdom. We are not holy. We do not have the ability to fulfill our commitment to God. The Bible says, 'And God saw that the wickedness of man was great in the earth, and that every imagination of the thoughts of his heart was only evil continually'" (Genesis 6:5).

"We had to have a Savior. We are doomed without Christ. Only his blood can save us. Isaiah 64:6 says, 'But we are all as an unclean thing, and all our righteousnesses are as filthy rags; and we all do fade as a leaf; and our iniquities, like the wind, have taken us away.'"

"Without Christ, on our best day we are on our way to hell. The covenant of Moses only went so far. But when Jesus came, he completed the promise of the old covenant. God the Father sent his own Son, Jesus, to be the sacrificial lamb. The Bible records, 'The next day John seeth Jesus coming unto him, and saith, Behold the Lamb of God, which taketh away the sin of the world'" (John 1:29).

"Under the old covenant, a perfect lamb was chosen. That beautiful, innocent little creature was then killed for the sin of man. The blood of that precious innocent animal was symbolic of the blood that would be spilled by Christ. It was an Old Testament picture of what was to come. But there's more. You see, God didn't stop there; Jesus didn't just come to die on the cross. He was beaten for our healing."

> Surely he hath borne our griefs, and carried our sorrows: yet we did esteem him stricken, smitten of God, and afflicted. But he was wounded for our transgressions, he was bruised for our iniquities: the chastisement of our peace was upon him; and with his stripes we are healed.
>
> Isaiah 53:4–5

"Remember when man sinned in the garden of Eden? There was a twofold curse that came onto humanity that day. The first is found in Genesis 2:15–17."

> And the LORD God took the man, and put him into the garden of Eden to dress it and to keep it. And the LORD God commanded the man, saying, Of every tree of the garden thou mayest freely eat: But of the tree of the

knowledge of good and evil, thou shalt not eat of it: for in
the day that thou eatest thereof thou shalt surely die.

"Eve ate and she gave it to Adam. He also ate, and they became
aware of their sin. That was the knowledge of good and evil. But
to God one day is as a thousand years (2 Peter 3:8). Disease that
day entered into their bodies and they started to die. That is when
sickness came into the world."

"Jesus was beaten for our healing. He was crucified for our sin.
He delivered us from the curse of sin and death. The Bible says in
Isaiah chapter 53, please read with me,"

> Who hath believed our report? and to whom is the arm of
> the LORD revealed? For he shall grow up before him as a
> tender plant, and as a root out of a dry ground: he hath no
> form nor comeliness; and when we shall see him, there is
> no beauty that we should desire him. He is despised and
> rejected of men; a man of sorrows, and acquainted with
> grief: and we hid as it were our faces from him; he was
> despised, and we esteemed him not. Surely he hath borne
> our griefs, and carried our sorrows: yet we did esteem
> him stricken, smitten of God, and afflicted. But he was
> wounded for our transgressions, he was bruised for our
> iniquities: the chastisement of our peace was upon him;
> and with his stripes we are healed. All we like sheep have
> gone astray; we have turned every one to his own way;
> and the LORD hath laid on him the iniquity of us all. He
> was oppressed, and he was afflicted, yet he opened not his
> mouth: he is brought as a lamb to the slaughter, and as a
> sheep before her shearers is dumb, so he openeth not his
> mouth. He was taken from prison and from judgment: and
> who shall declare his generation? for he was cut off out of
> the land of the living: for the transgression of my people
> was he stricken. And he made his grave with the wicked,
> and with the rich in his death; because he had done no vio-
> lence, neither was any deceit in his mouth. Yet it pleased
> the LORD to bruise him; he hath put him to grief: when

thou shalt make his soul an offering for sin, he shall see his seed, he shall prolong his days, and the pleasure of the LORD shall prosper in his hand. He shall see of the travail of his soul, and shall be satisfied: by his knowledge shall my righteous servant justify many; for he shall bear their iniquities. Therefore will I divide him a portion with the great, and he shall divide the spoil with the strong; because he hath poured out his soul unto death: and he was numbered with the transgressors; and he bare the sin of many, and made intercession for the transgressors.

John finished the chapter in Isaiah. He looked out into the crowd; his piercing blue eyes searched the faces in front of him. Extending his arms, he said, "He was innocent; we are guilty. We are the ones who have sinned. We read in Romans 6:23, 'For the wages of sin is death; but the gift of God is eternal life through Jesus Christ our Lord.' He was sinless yet he chose to die." The young preacher spoke with passion; his heart ripped open as he described the abuse of Christ. Tears ran down his face as he spoke. "He was beaten with a whip called a cat of nine tails. It was made of glass, bones, and knives; it was designed to tear and rip into the flesh of the victim. The whip ripped his body for our healing."

"If you need healing in your body, come. If you want to know him as your Savior, come. Christ paid the price with his suffering; it happened at the cross. Come, let him make you new. There is room at the cross for you. You don't have to worry, the work has already been done; Jesus is waiting to heal your body and soul. Receive his gift of love. John 15:13 says, 'Greater love hath no man than this, that a man lay down his life for his friends.'"

The altar filled up as many souls came to Jesus. Demons were cast out. Some were delivered from drug addiction or pornography. Many were healed of different illnesses all because of Jesus. It was all done at the cross.

Word of the meetings continued to spread. It was reported to the authorities by several informants. Rebecca's stepfather,

Dennis Billings, watched from the back of the room. He pur-posely showed up when Rebecca was at work. He did not want her telling her friends who he was. She didn't know it, but he kept her under surveillance. He knew when she was working and when she was here.

Today he was gathering evidence. He had brought some of his own men and women. They were all incognito. They dis-persed themselves into the crowd. There was the couple who were dressed nicely with a well-to-do air. Sitting in the third row was Dan, dressed as a homeless man. He hadn't showered or shaved in days. He slept outside staying near the church. A sinister smirk rose to Dennis's lips. The guy was committed. He snickered to himself. The unsuspecting ladies of the church had even been bringing him food. There was also Hostettler, one of his friends, who watched the crowd from a safe place near the door. They were gathering names. They watched the gullible, weak-minded people fill the front of the church as well as the aisles. They were breaking the law. Each of them was guilty.

Dennis reported to the head of domestic security. "I tell you these people are continuing to meet. They grow more power-ful every day. They have all been warned. It is time to make an example of this Pastor John. My people have also been following Pastor Paul. He is even more radical than his young friend. If you don't stop this thing now, they will turn the hearts of the people from the world president. They keep talking about Jesus. They call him the King of kings. They say he is the Savior and the only way to God. Their exclusive close-minded thinking is like cancer. It has to be cut out before it spreads. How can we ever be in unity with all religions as long as there are those who stand against everything we stand for?"

The report was disappointing to Preston Johnson, the head of domestic security. He had been placed in this position when his predecessor unexplainably disappeared. His office had been undergoing some radical changes. They were no longer concerned with terrorism as in the past. He found himself in the unhappy position of squashing independent thinking. Now that the world president was in office, the world was changing at warp speed. They simply could not encourage free thinking. This philosophy had proven difficult, especially to cultures that had not lived under a king or a dictatorship. He was plagued by the need for submission. It was for the greater good of mankind. He had spoken with Governor Howard explaining the radical ideas of these Christians. Governor Howard was very disturbed to hear that Paul Stevens was one of the ones leading this revolt.

The report explained that these men were taken downtown and warned many times. Still they continued to speak in the name of Jesus, proclaiming him to be the Son of God. They were repeatedly asked to not single out Jesus as the only way to heaven. They have to be stopped. This one-God concept is poisoning the people.

There was a new law that had been passed without anyone actually noticing it. With the many disappearances and disasters going on all over the world, people had missed it. It was slipped past them subtly. People had even found some peace because of it. It simply stated, "That the world was one people and one nation with many ideas and beliefs. No one person's belief system was more important than another's." The world's current value system was that this great world awakening was for the good of all mankind.

Also there was a new way of worshipping ushered in by the Church of One World All Faiths Religion or OWAFR. Its pastor, also known as The Sorcerer, was a man of renown. His many acts of philanthropy were well known. He held the hearts of the people in his hands. Everyone was loved and respected. Best of all, there was no right or wrong way to follow the many gods of earth. It was believed the earth had evolved into a society capable of governing and worshipping itself. OWAFR held firmly that the belief in one true God was an assault on all those who believed otherwise. Only their more radical, overzealous friends were accepted, and even loved, in spite of their exclusive teachings.

How sad, unfortunately, the world did not remember the commandments. No one thought about the first commandment found in Exodus 20:3–6.

> Thou shalt have no other gods before me. Thou shalt not make unto thee any graven image, or any likeness of any thing that is in heaven above, or that is in the earth beneath, or that is in the water under the earth: Thou shalt not bow down thyself to them, nor serve them: for I the LORD thy God am a jealous God, visiting the iniquity of the fathers upon the children unto the third and fourth generation of them that hate me; And shewing mercy unto thousands of them that love me, and keep my commandments.

OWAFR's only problem with their new belief system was the ongoing radicals of Christianity. These close-minded people insisted on right and wrong. They insisted that only through Jesus could a soul find salvation. These followers of Christ would not be tolerated. They planned to start with a sweep that encompassed the cities. They called it their grassroots plan to eliminate Christianity from the hearts and minds of the people.

Carly and John were startled as a military force came crashing through their door in the middle of the night. John was immediately seized and dragged out of their home. The men who took him said he was under arrest for speaking blasphemy against the One World All Faiths Religion.

At the same time they took Paul. He had already said his good-byes to Shelby. She knew he loved her. She also knew it was just a matter of time before they arrested everyone who loved Jesus. Carly was beside herself with fear. She trembled uncontrollably. She fumbled around but managed to dial Shelby.

Shelby tried to stay calm. "I know, honey. They just took Paul too. Listen, we can't fall apart. We know the Scriptures. We have to be strong for them. And I don't know about you, Carly, but if

Paul can't continue to preach, I will go in his place. I have committed myself to follow the call of Christ. They're going to try to kill us for loving Jesus anyway. We might as well continue to serve him, regardless of their threats."

Shelby took the bull by the horns and started to pray. First they prayed for their husbands' safe return, then for the souls of the men who had arrested them. She and Carly stayed on the phone for hours praising God. They thanked him for his hand of mercy since the rapture. They praised the Lord for his unending love. Prayer time started to slow down; then Shelby started to tell Carly what she thought of the new regime.

Carly couldn't believe it; she was laughing. Somehow Shelby had found a way to put a whole new spin on persecution. She was joking about the whole thing. "We have to laugh, honey," she said on a serious note. They hung up their phones and both ladies continued praying alone.

The next day both churches held a prayer vigil for those who were being persecuted for the cause of Christ. Carly and Shelby both took their husbands' places. They both fasted and both of them preached.

Carly didn't actually intend to preach. She just stood up to tell the church what had happened, but something she did not know she possessed rose up in her. "I will not be silenced. I will not go along to get along. I will serve Jesus with every breath I have in me. Who is on the Lord's side? Who is willing to say again, 'Me and my family, we will serve the Lord'?" (Joshua 24:15).

She spoke with authority. Every word was aimed at the enemy. "We are soldiers of the cross (Ephesians 6:10–18). And a soldier is willing to die for the cause. Jesus is my cause. He is the rock of my salvation (Psalm 89:26). I will not back down. I am convinced that he is able to keep me until the day he comes in his glorious appearing or he calls me home!" (Zechariah 14:4).

The people rose to their feet. Cheers rang through the old building. Men and women stood to confirm their resolve to recommit their lives to Christ. They had to be determined; the days ahead were going to be perilous. God promised, "He that overcometh shall inherit all things; and I will be his God, and he shall be my son" (Revelation 21:7).

Brad and Sarah had come in late. They had driven straight to the church from Justin's safe camp. They stood with the rest of the congregation as Carly proclaimed the gospel of Jesus Christ. They were swept away by the militant stance of the kindhearted, easygoing Carly. She cried out to the Lord for his protection. She prayed for her husband, Pastor Paul, and the many others who were being rounded up and hauled off to jail for speaking in the name of Jesus.

Brad looked around, his normal quick temper rising to a fire as he realized his friends were in mortal danger. "No, God," he prayed. "Not John, not Pastor Paul! They are working for you. Not yet! Please, God, give them more time to reach those who are lost. Don't allow the enemy to stop these men." As he prayed, an idea began to germinate in the back of his mind. Maybe he could help God along.

JAIL TIME

Paul and John had been abused. Their wives were told they could not receive visitors. The truth was they had been beaten. Their faces were swollen, their hands and bodies were sore. It was a relief to know their wives could not see them in this condition.

John and Paul continued to preach, even while they were being reprimanded. The guards did not want the other prisoners to hear them. They were causing people to actually receive Christ while they were incarcerated. They would speak openly to anyone with whom they were locked up. The guards decided to put them in a cell together.

They laughed as they tried to help each other; grimacing from pain, they regretted laughing. Both of them were too tired to stand, so they just sat on the ground. They had been given dinner which was decent enough. Unfortunately, neither of them felt up to eating.

They surveyed their injuries. John held his side. It hurt to breathe. He placed a hand on his broken ribs. His eyes were black and blue. Paul also nursed a couple of ribs. He put a finger on his mouth, feeling a space between his teeth. John reached over, taking his friend by the chin, he inspected Paul's mouth. "You're lucky," he smiled. "Your front teeth are fine. It's far enough back; I don't think it will show." The men were battered, but in time they would heal.

They knew Paul and Silas of old had sung hymns in jail, but they were so tired they just wanted to sleep. They each took a bunk and the two ministers went to sleep allowing rest to restore them.

The next day they were left alone. Their captors seemed to be trying to decide what to do with them. They were talking of a trial. The problem was in the new-world order no one was allowed an attorney. They were told they were guilty of preaching in the name of Jesus, a name that was strictly prohibited by the law.

The following day Paul and John were hauled into court. They stood before the judge. He was a thin, older man who seemed burdened down by the process. There were several others who were waiting to be prosecuted for their crime—the crime, that is, of serving Christ.

The prosecutor wore a rumpled suit. He shuffled through his files. He picked up the papers he was looking for. Standing to his feet he pulled off his reading glasses, dropping them on the desk. With a look of exasperation and contempt, he began to explain in great detail. "These young men, your honor, have been documented repeatedly preaching in marketplaces or on sidewalks. Sir, they have preached on street corners even to the prostitutes. They have openly and unapologetically held services in their own churches where they claim Jesus is the only way to heaven. Their crimes against the state are all listed here for you to see."

The judge looked over their many offenses. He raised his rather thick eyebrows and whistled as he let out a breath. After a moment of reviewing the paperwork before him, he looked up. "I have heard many things about you two gentlemen. Pastor Paul, your church has been very active in the community. And you, young John, your father was a well-known and beloved man. I want to extend mercy to both of you. I believe the disappearances of your family members have left you both with a feeling of loss, and therefore, I believe you have gone off on a tangent to do what you think is necessary. But you are wrong. The men and women who disappeared were vaporized into the atmosphere by the nuclear energy that has built up in the air. Each of you should read about it for yourself. The world president ordered an in-depth study of the effects this toxic buildup has had on the earth over the years."

"Now this is what I want to do. I would like for both of you to set all of this crazy, radical talk aside and acknowledge that Jesus is not the only way to heaven. After all, we know that God is in all of us. I am speaking to you as a father would speak to his own sons; listen to me." He continued to try to reason with them. In the end, they were asked to recant their rebellious statements publicly. If they did so, all would be forgiven and they could start over with a clean slate.

The two men looked at each other, then Paul said, "While we appreciate your gracious offer to forgive us if we deny Christ, we cannot accept it. We have already been forgiven by the Lord Jesus Christ who died in our place and has ascended up to the Father. He is the one who has returned, taking his bride—that is to say, those who loved and served him. We now serve him with all of our hearts. He is worthy of all of our praise and adoration."

The judge was incensed. He sniffed as if he smelled something foul. His nose wrinkled as he spoke. Paul, who was profoundly aware of his current lack of hygiene, sniffed also and shifted uncomfortably under the judge's inspection. The judge's bushy eyebrows rose as he spoke. "Put them back in jail. Perhaps a few more days will help them change their minds. Next," his voice rang through the air.

Another man was brought before him. This man complained of mistreatment and promised he would never talk of Jesus again to anyone. He was given the mark and told he would be allowed to buy from hereon out. Paul and John watched as the man looked down, obviously ashamed of his decision. They went back to their cell and prayed for strength for the next poor person who was asked to deny Christ.

In the cell next to them was a wild man. The day before, he was arrested; according to the guards it took ten men to restrain him. He was tall; his massive shoulders seemed to fill up the air.

He looked at them with hatred in his eyes and growled, "What are you looking at?"

Paul, no longer afraid to say what was on his mind, answered, "I see a soul that is lost. Your eyes are full of hatred."

The muscled, oversized man promised to meet with them personally when they were all allowed to exercise. His fist slapped into the other hand as he spoke.

Paul was not deterred. "We are all here against our will. What did you do?"

The giant of a man looked embarrassed. "I was caught stealing food. I didn't want that chip in me, so they have put me here to soften me up."

"I'm sorry to hear that," John said. "If you come by one of our churches when they let you out we will see to it you get something to eat. My name is Pastor John. This is my friend, Pastor Paul Stevens. What is your name?"

"I'm Harry," the big man replied. For the first time he seemed to relax. "I'm sorry, guys. I'm just a little on edge. I don't like the way they expect us to just give up our freedom and follow anything they dictate. I don't know why people don't stand up to them. I don't believe they have the right to just decide how I should run my life. They call the shots, and the next thing you know, people just go along with everything they are doing. Well, not me! I'm not going to give up my freedom that easily. I'm a soldier. I bled for this country. I have no intention of giving up my rights. What about you, guys? Why would two preachers be in here?"

"Well, I guess you could say we are here for something like your reason. We want to preach and tell people about Jesus; but, with the new-world order, we are hated for exercising our freedom of religion. The only religion that is not welcome in the new-world order is the truth. This government-imposed religion, OWAFR, is pointless. It is a delusion of the truth, all tied up into a pretty little package of hot air with no substance. We are here for refusing to go along with their One World All Faiths Religion."

Harry let his eyes scan the beaten men. "Tell me, what is it you believe that is important enough to let them beat you and throw you in jail?" His tall, muscled frame leaned toward them as he offered them the perfect opportunity to witness for Christ.

Paul started, "It's like this: we believe Jesus has returned for his church. He has taken all of the people who were following him and doing his will when he returned. He also took the babies and small children. The children who were older, the ones who were able to know right from wrong, were left behind like all of us. If they were faithful Christians, they also vanished."

Harry looked at them as though they had completely lost their minds. "You mean to tell me you think Jesus returned for his church and you two guys got left? You're preachers. Why would you be left behind?" His large muscular frame started to shake as he began to openly laugh at them.

John blushed uncomfortably. Paul plunged on, "We were both living lives that did not edify the Lord. Even though we were going along with our lives as if everything was fine, God saw through us. He knew we weren't ready to go to heaven. You see, no one unclean can enter into heaven. Ephesians 5:5 says it this way, 'For this ye know, that no whoremonger, nor unclean person, nor covetous man, who is an idolater, hath any inheritance in the kingdom of Christ and of God.' We know firsthand God doesn't play games. He is holy. People have to know Jesus as their Lord and Savior to enter into his kingdom."

"I personally was living a double life that, even before Jesus returned for his church, had caught up with me. I was so blinded by my sin, I failed to identify how far I had fallen away from God until the moment I realized Jesus had left me behind. We aren't going to whitewash it and pretend that there are many ways to heaven. There aren't. Jesus is the only way. It is by his blood that we are saved."

"John and I forgot for a while how important it was to have a personal relationship with Christ. That is why we were left. You see, we have always been believers, but for a short crucial time we forgot to put him first. I let fame and success cloud my judgment. I began to believe I was God's man for the hour, that I was somehow exempt from judgment. That was wrong. I am like anyone else who fails to follow the Lord. In fact, I am more responsible because I am a preacher (Ezekiel 3:17–21). I won't ever compromise the gospel of Jesus Christ to keep from hurting someone's feelings again. I intend to use every minute I have left on this earth to tell people the kingdom of God is coming."

Harry listened, captivated by the speaker. He watched each man as Paul spoke, noticing their individual expressions. Paul was enjoying himself. He added comically, "The Lord will deliver us from the world president and all of his merry men." Paul grinned, then on a serious, almost reverent note, he added, "We will see Jesus coming in the clouds riding on a white horse with his heavenly army! There will be a great battle. Jesus himself will overcome the wicked one with the Word of God!"

Harry couldn't keep quiet any longer. "The Word of God, are you kidding me? You had me going for a minute, preacher. But I know something about battle. It is going to take a lot more than speeches to overthrow the world president. Jesus better come with some weapons. And flying horses, are you serious? You two guys need to rethink this heavenly army thing. The world president has planes that fly themselves. They'll take out the army of flying horses before anyone gets a chance to speak."

Paul smiled, "I guess it does sound kind of funny at first but let me remind you: It was God who spoke the world into existence. Because of his word, this planet and our whole solar system exist. He holds the planets in space. It is by his will the rain falls. Because of his mighty power the winds blow, the earth shakes, and the seas roll."

"He is the one who orchestrates the rise and fall of a king. The Bible speaks of numerous battles fought by the Lord for his people. For instance, in the Bible we read in the book of Joshua, in chapter 10, that there were five kings, the enemies of Israel. They became angry with the men of Gibeon because they had formed an alliance with God's people. These five kings went out to fight against the Gibeonites. Then the men of Gibeon sent word to the men of Israel, 'Come and help us; your servants are under attack'" (Joshua 10:6).

"Joshua, the general of the Lord's army, prayed. God told him not to fear. He would fight with him. The Lord rained hailstones down on the enemy army, destroying them. More men were killed that day from the hailstones than from the sword of Joshua's warriors" (Joshua 10:11).

"No way," Harry sat straight up, listening to Paul's story. "You say that is in the Bible? I have heard some interesting stories about battles my friends fought. I've even seen some things for myself."

Paul was excited as he continued. Not only was Harry listening, but everyone in earshot was listening to the stories. "You can also find in Judges, chapter 7, the battle of Gideon."

"Wait a minute." Harry put up his hand to stop Paul. "I thought we were talking about these guys from Gibeon." Harry looked confused.

"I'm sorry, I should explain." Paul started again, "The men of Gibeon were people who lived in a certain area. The guy I'm going to tell you about next is Gideon; he just had a similar name. He, with the leading of the Lord, took three hundred men with him and went by night to fight against the Midianites, who were enemies of God. They were gathering themselves together to fight Israel, the people of the Lord. The Bible says the Midianites were as the sands of the seaside in number."

Harry let out a whistle. "Three hundred men against an army like that; they must have been massacred."

Paul shook his head up and down, "They should have been, but God was fighting for them. Gideon divided his men into three companies. He made his move on the other army at night. He and his men carried pitchers, trumpets and lanterns. At his signal the men broke their pitchers, blew the trumpets and stood holding their lanterns crying out, 'The sword of the LORD, and of Gideon' (Judges 7:20). This terrified the enemy. They started running away, and in total confusion, actually began to kill each other."

And 2 Kings 18 and 19 records the arrogance of the king of Assyria who came to fight with Judah. He insulted the Lord God and King Hezekiah. The king prayed and God sent an angel to destroy the army of Assyria, killing 185,000 enemies of God's people in one night. One angel did that. The world president serves a purpose and God will tolerate him for a total of seven years. Then Jesus will return."

Harry sat quietly musing over the conversation. He had forgotten that God had created the earth by speaking. He wasn't an atheist. He had always believed in God, mostly because of things he had seen in battle that he could not explain. He had witnessed some impossible battles. But this was a whole new take on what he knew and understood. After a moment Harry concluded, "There is no wonder they don't want you two talking in public. You make anything sound possible. All this stuff must blow their minds."

He lay back on his bunk remembering their story of a Great King with a flying horse. He shook his head. *No, it can't be possible.* After a few more minutes of thoughtfulness, he regained his usual attitude. With a laugh he began to state his conclusion. "You guys actually go around telling people what you just told me? Do you really say that the world president is going to be overthrown by a King on a white horse that flies? I'm sorry, guys, I have a hard time believing that." His previous anger that had turned into laughter was now just pity for the poor ignorant guys in the cell next to him. He felt somehow responsible to protect them from themselves. "Why don't we all get some rest?"

Paul and John were disappointed as they listened to Harry repeat their words back to them. From his perspective it did sound as though they were touched in the head. But they had hopes for Harry. Without a word between them, they both knew they would be praying for their new friend. They said good night. They lay down resting their heads on their pillows and slept as though they had no problems at all. God was taking care of them. If they died tomorrow, they would just be going home.

Harry watched them sleep as though they hadn't a care in the world. Poor boys, they were still hurt from the beatings they had endured. They were odd men, but the way they spoke about Jesus left something that tugged at his heart. He would see to it that no one would hurt them while he was around.

The guys woke up to armed guards dragging them from their cell. Harry tried to stop the guards the best he could by threatening them. "When I get out of here, you pigs better watch your backs."

He made such a racket they opened the door to his cell. One of the men used his club. "Shut up!" He shouted as he hit Harry hard from behind. Harry dropped to the floor not moving.

"Bulldog!" Willy shouted, trying to stop his partner. He bent down to check Harry. "Man, what did you do?" Willy asked.

"He's fine," responded the big guard called Bulldog. He was large. His frame filled the door to the cell. He smiled a sinister little smile. "He'll have a headache but he won't try that again."

They spent the early hours of the morning being told to recant their notions about Jesus. They were not allowed to sleep. They were guarded at gunpoint and told to run around the grounds without stopping. When they finally collapsed from exhaustion, they were dragged unceremoniously to a room with no windows. "You boys can stay here and rest up," the big man told them as he pushed them inside. They were thankful for the chance to pray.

The judge looked as tired today as he had looked before. His bushy eyebrows lifted and fell as he spoke. John and Paul waited their turn as the long line ahead of them slowly dwindled down to them.

"Well? Have you considered my offer?" He was growing tired of these two. "I assure you I will not be as kind the next time I see you."

John and Paul weren't looking forward to being punished; but they did have to take advantage of every opportunity to testify of Christ. "Sir, we are here for practicing our rights to freedom of religion and freedom of speech. We don't want to be difficult, but in order to serve the Lord according to our consciences we must speak out and warn people of the trouble that is coming." The judge leaned over, resting his arm on the desk with his head resting in his hand. He listened, looking bored. "I ask you to consider the fairness of a law that allows every religion to practice their beliefs without bias but refuses freedom of religion to Christians and Jews. This should not be."

The judge slammed his gavel. "Silence. You are not being asked to defend yourselves. You are being asked to recant your positions. Since it is evident you are not willing to do so, you will be punished. Take them away. They are to receive no rations for today. We will see if skipping a few meals changes your minds."

On their way back to their cell, Paul and John started praying. They asked God to take care of their wives and help them to withstand this time of testing.

"I've had it with you two." The guard who had abused Harry used his fist furiously swinging it at Paul and John. Both of the guys already injured from the previous beating fell to the ground, hurt and bleeding. "You shut up. Do you hear me? You stupid fools."

Willy grabbed him, pulling him away from the guys. "Man, you better stop this stuff. You will be reprimanded for sure if they see these guys."

Brad had spent the day waiting for the opportunity to speak to Paul and John. He was told they could not receive visitors. But after getting the run around, he finally slipped the guy at the front desk his pocket-size computer. Their eyes held each other captive. "This is illegal," the guard said to Brad. Brad expected to be thrown into jail at any moment with the preachers but all at once the guard reached out, grabbed the computer, and said, "This way, sir."

Paul and John looked awful. Brad felt physically ill as he looked into their beaten faces.

"Brad." They both lit up as they welcomed their friend. "Man, how'd you get past the guards?"

"Don't ask," Brad said, looking around as though the walls were listening.

He looked over at Harry.

John said, "Brad, this is Harry. Harry this is Brad."

"Hey, man." Both men nodded acknowledgement of the other.

Brad asked them how they were doing. "Are you guys eating okay?"

Paul looked a little regretful, "No. As a matter of fact, they just canceled our rations this morning. The judge said maybe we will be more cooperative if we did without for a while."

A guard showed up. "You're out of here, Harry. You must have friends in high places." Harry was released. The guard led him out and down the corridor for processing.

"What do you know about that guy?" Brad asked.

"He's a soldier," Paul said.

They all watched him as he walked the long walk down the hall to freedom. "They put him in here because he doesn't want the mark," John added.

"So he's a Christian," Brad said.

"No"—Paul shook his head from side to side—"he's not. He is objecting to the loss of freedom. He is really a nice guy once you get to know him. But he needs the Lord."

"A soldier, huh? Is he still active?" Brad was getting one of his ideas.

"He seems to be retired. You know, they didn't give anyone a choice about the mark when it was implemented. They just took all of the military and government employees and ordered them to cooperate." John studied Brad, confused by his friend's questions.

"Excuse me," Brad said, leaving his friends abruptly. He had to catch up with Harry. He might be just the guy Brad was looking for. "I'll try to visit you again soon."

Brad followed Harry's release with his eyes. Harry was held up in processing. He was handed a form; Brad watched him sign it.

Brad continued to walk toward the door. He wanted to intercept Harry as he came out of the building. He waited behind a pillar. Finally Harry emerged. "Harry," Brad said as he walked up to the stranger. "Man, I know this is crazy, but do you think we could go somewhere to talk?"

Harry wasn't sure he trusted this guy, but the preachers seemed to, so he decided to hear him out. "Okay, I think it's best if we're not seen leaving together. There's a park a couple of blocks from here. I'll meet you on the north side near the hotdog stand in half an hour. Don't be late. I won't wait for you."

"Thanks, Harry," Brad smiled. "I'll be there."

Brad went directly there. He wanted to be sure he was on time. In exactly half an hour Harry showed up. He walked up to Brad. "Well, I'm here. Let's talk."

Brad looked around, scanning the people in the park. "I have some friends who have a place safe from the current regime. They are willing to allow people who need protection to stay with them. I thought perhaps, with your background, you might know some people who could quietly slip refugees out of harm's way. Of course no one could ever go there without being blindfolded and no one who already has the mark. The person would have to be willing to give up their cell phones, computers, or anything that could be used to trace them to the safe house." Brad's dark, unreadable eyes locked on Harry. He studied Harry's every move. What if Harry was a spy? What if he was not the person Brad had hoped he would be? Brad prayed fervently. "God, you have to help me." I may have just made one of the worse decisions of my life. The thought of endangering Justin and his young friends made Brad physically ill.

Harry shifted nervously but the look on his face was all business, "How many can they accommodate?"

"We haven't worked it out that far. They, of course, need enough food as well as space for the people they take in. But the place can hold a large group. As long as they meet the requirements of the safe house they will be welcome."

"How do you expect to feed them?"

"We have an underground system for food in place. We just have to access it."

Harry thought for a moment then said, "I'm in. I'll contact you. Don't call me or try to find me. I'll show up when I have things worked out. And before I send anyone your way I have to see the place. I won't risk the lives of my men or the people who need help without seeing it for myself."

"I guess that's fair." Brad responded. "But I can't go back there without causing suspicion. My wife and I were just there a few days ago. I need some kind of reason to go back and forth that won't arouse curiosity."

"No problem. I have a friend who can take care of that. I'll see you soon," Harry promised. Then he quickly walked away, disappearing into the crowd in front of Brad.

THE SETUP

Two days later Brad woke to a sound he did not like. He looked over at Sarah. In the darkness he could hear her steady breathing. She was still asleep. He slipped out from under the covers and moved slowly and quietly down the hall to the living room. On his way he picked up Justin's bat from the corner of his bedroom. It stood silently in the place where he had been keeping it recently just for moments like this.

"Don't hit me, Brad," Harry said. "I have some friends with me. We're ready to see this hideout of yours." He stood in the shadows with the darkness covering him like a blanket. He stepped forward into the moonlight. Brad could see his face. It had been blackened. He was carrying a weapon and dressed in black. Two young men stood near him. They watched Brad. Their weapons were pointed at the ceiling. They were dressed head to toe in camouflage. Frightening thoughts flooded Brad's mind. At that moment he became terrified of his new associates.

Harry relaxed his position. "My friends were able to get assigned to make a delivery for the government. The town you mentioned where your friends have their safe house is on the way. We have a truck; we're ready to leave now. Get dressed."

Brad tried to sound as though he wasn't worried. Casually he asked the question, "Why the guns?"

Harry explained, "I thought you were interested in some protection. After all, you and your friends will need someone to watch your backs if things get hot."

"I appreciate the thought, guys, but the only guns I've seen lately are yours." The two guys who had shown up with Harry looked at each other then holstered their guns.

Harry chuckled, "Perhaps my friends and I are being just a little more careful than necessary." He stepped forward and slapped Brad on the back. "Man, you should see your face. We weren't sure what we would find here after seeing the way your friends—the preachers—were being treated. We staked this place out watching for any sign of you being followed. We waited until now to make sure you were alone. As for the guns, we've learned to be prepared for anything." He stood smiling at Brad.

"I guess you guys do have to be prepared." Brad responded, still a little unnerved. Brad quickly returned to his bedroom. He woke Sarah and told her he was leaving.

"But Brad, what if they're not who they say they are?"

"Sarah, we have to try, no matter what could happen. And we're going to have to trust somebody along the way, or it's all for nothing." She bit her lip then reached out to him. He held her just a little longer than normal. He whispered, "I'll be back."

She smiled. "I'll be praying."

Harry watched the scene from the doorway. Brad's wife was beautiful. He nodded at one of his buddies. The man went to the window and flashed a light at a tree in the distance. A flash returned; they were ready.

Brad was handed a matching jacket and told to wear it. They all stepped into the truck and took a seat. "So, where is this compound?" the driver asked. Brad began to tremble inside. He hadn't expected Harry to show up with a military escort. This seemed too much like a raid on the safe house for his comfort.

He decided to take them to a house he knew in the country. He had worked a few months for the owner before the disappearances. He and Sarah had talked to Justin and his friends about using it as a stop off for the pipeline. The house was empty the yard looked deserted. The soldiers searched the barn and found nothing.

"What is this? There's no one here."

"I didn't say there was."

"Who are these friends you mentioned?" Harry was becoming annoyed.

"Why me, of course. I thought you would be able to help me set this place up. I think with a little work it would be perfect." Brad looked out over the place with as much pride as he could muster. "The house has a large adequate kitchen for food preparation. The barn can be restored for rooms for our guests. All it needs is the refugees."

Harry was suspicious. He didn't think Brad was talking about an abandoned place. When they first spoke of this safe house he had gotten the impression the place was close to being up and running. "What about the address. We're nowhere near that post office or the town you told me about."

"Yea, I know. It's just a place I keep for messages. I don't want to accidentally lead someone to this location. I thought it wise to stay far away from here."

Harry studied the location. It didn't make sense. The sun was hot over their heads. This was going to be a long day. For some reason Brad was wasting his time. Harry didn't like that very much.

Brad watched the men. They seemed disappointed by the news there was no one to beat up or perhaps kill. He was thankful he had led them away from Justin and his friends. He didn't care what happened to himself. He just had to protect the camp.

Thankfully, the rest of the day was blissfully uneventful. The men made their delivery. Then they took Brad home. He looked around for Sarah. She was fine, but Brad was still concerned. He retraced everything that had gone on throughout the day. He took a deep breath. Relief flowed through him for the first time that day. They were all safe, at least for now.

Sarah was chomping at the bit for information. Brad was still suspicious. He didn't want to talk to her in the house so he took her arm and moved her toward the door. "Let's walk." As Brad told her of his change of mind he watched her closely. He knew all of her expressions. He watched as she absorbed the information.

She looked as relieved as he felt. "I'm so glad you didn't take them there. I don't know for sure but all day long I've felt as though someone was watching me." She focused on the scene in front of her, watching the sunset. After a moment she looked at him with a strange expression on her face. "I know it sounds crazy, but it's as if someone was following me. I took a walk downtown just to get my mind off all this stuff and I kept seeing this guy. Finally I turned a corner and slipped into the ladies room. When I came out he was all the way across the street. He was sitting on a bench waiting for the bus, reading. I thought, *Well, there you go imagining things.* So I just forgot about him. I decided to go into a store and didn't come out for at least half an hour. By then the bus should have come and gone. But later on I saw him again. I rounded the corner walking back home and there he was. He turned around and looked into a store window. I know it was the same guy. I got this eerie feeling he didn't want me to know he was there."

Brad wasn't surprised. "I think we are both going to be watched. We better be careful. From now on we don't discuss anything in the house. It may be bugged. We need to stay away from our friends. We can't risk placing them in danger. We have to disappear as soon as we can. But first I have to find a way to set up an underground railroad for the refugees. There has to be an answer."

Brad spent the next few nights sleepless. During the day he went about his job as normally as possible. There was a lot of work for a contractor after the disappearances. The roads were still something of a mess. Clearing away the abandoned and wrecked vehicles had been a nightmare. He could stay busy for now, but the pressure to take the mark of the beast was a daily frustration. He wouldn't be able to continue for long. He was quickly sifting through the rubble of the many cleanup jobs.

He spoke with the engineers on various sites. All of them had approved of his plans to recycle as much of the lumber and metal, etcetera, as he could. One of the demolition jobs included an old claw-foot tub. He made a deal with the project superintendent to remove it. He had a large truck that he was using for debris removal. He loaded the tub, some pipe, and lumber onto the truck. He knew Justin and his friends would be able to use all of his newly acquired treasures. He even found some old brick they were tearing out of a job site. The superintendent was more than happy to let Brad haul that off too. Last, but not least, he located a series of solar panels.

It hadn't been easy, but he found on the Internet a demolition job nearby with solar parts. When he drove up to the building he almost cried for joy. There was more than enough for their project. "Yes, thank you, God!" he exclaimed. The building had been abandoned by the county. There was no use for it at this time. The new regime had a policy of updating the buildings for disasters. The building was just old enough to need a makeover. Brad decided to try to trade some work for the panels. The superintendent took a liking to Brad and told him to come back for the rest as soon as possible. Brad loaded the truck several times then hauled them to his yard. He agreed to haul off some of the debris in exchange for the panels. He promised he would recycle everything he could. The superintendent was thrilled to eliminate that responsibility from his job.

Harry was interested in the activities of a certain contractor. He had assigned a man to watch Brad for the last week. Brad seemed to be busy working and indifferent to the politics of the day, but he decided to follow up on him just in case he made a move for the safe house.

Harry hated his meetings with Billings. The guy was something of a by-the-book nut case. He sat listening to Dennis blowing about the great dream of the future. He just couldn't understand how the guy had gotten appointed to such a position of importance. He was quite sure the guy was missing a few screws.

It had taken some fast talking but he convinced Dennis that the pastors were not international terrorists. "Maybe they're a little misguided, but those guys are just trying to help people. The only thing they know is what they've read in some old book. I know they worry you, but they're harmless."

Dennis looked out the window of his office then back at Harry. "I realize you like those two; they are likeable, but don't underestimate them. They are on a mission from God himself. Maybe you haven't seen it firsthand, but if God is helping them, and I know he is, they are dangerous to everything we stand for."

Harry listened, finding the fact that Dennis was so unnerved by Pastor John and Pastor Paul interesting. "They're just preachers, Dennis. They don't have any special powers; they're just flesh-and-blood men."

Dennis sighed deeply. "Say what you will, but I know personally—if they keep talking they can change the world with their message."

Harry started laughing. "Have you listened to their message? They think a king with a flying white horse is going to come down from heaven to fight against the world army. Who's going to believe that? They are delusional. It's sad, really. I tell you they are harmless."

Dennis realized he was not getting through to Harry. "All right. Forget the preachers for now and concentrate on their friend. Follow this Brad fellow, and get him to trust you. I want you on the inside where you can keep an eye on him. Report back to me daily. And Harry, if these preachers are somehow involved, I want to know about it."

Harry nodded his understanding and left.

That was almost a week ago. Now he watched through binoculars as Brad stacked another four-by-four onto the truck. "He's getting ready for something," he said to himself.

Brad decided to make the haul under cover of darkness. He and Sarah left at midnight. They didn't know it but Harry was watching them. They took all back roads. Brad avoided any known check points. He didn't want to be questioned, but if he was, the story was simple. He had located a buyer for the stuff northeast of here. All he was doing was delivering it.

Harry followed them up and down all over the map. They were definitely up to something. Finally they arrived in the little town Brad had originally mentioned. He watched as they stopped for a soda. They walked along, moving casually through the town. They seemed to be waiting for something.

Brad didn't want to go directly into the camp. He decided to spend some time sniffing the wind. He was sure they had been followed but thought he managed to lose the car. After a while he drove to town, but he wanted to wait and see if that car showed up again. It was not the best time to think about it, but suddenly he wondered if there was a tracking device somewhere on his truck.

After remembering his excuse to Harry, he decided to pass off the stop in town as only a mail stop. He went by the post office just in case he was being followed. He went in to make it look as though he had business there. Then out he came smiling at Sarah. "Let's go," he said. They left town and drove to a campsite. Sarah walked over to a table where she started laying out a picnic lunch. They ate, laughing and talking, as if they hadn't a care in the world.

After lunch Brad opened the hood of the truck, took out his tool box and began puttering around with the engine. Sarah picked up their groceries. Then she sat in the sun reading a book. Brad checked his load. As he did he went around the truck inspecting the tires with an air gauge. They seemed to have all day. Harry watched from a comfortable distance with his binoculars. To anyone watching they were just a couple out having a little fun together.

Brad found the device after about twenty minutes of looking. He pulled it out, a sick feeling in the pit of his stomach made him look up and around the surrounding hills. "Where is this guy?" he asked, wondering if it was Harry or one of Harry's friends. He felt sick thinking how he had led those guys right to the town. And now they were just minutes from Justin and the others.

Brad noticed a car off in the distance. It could be the same guy. He walked over to Sarah, "Let's camp here." He pulled out their sleeping bags. As he did, he thanked God for reminding him to grab their tent just in case they needed it. After a little while they were in business. The tent was up and their sleeping bags were in place. Sarah located the small camp stove and started dinner. She was happily moving around the camp, chattering with Brad about all the things they had seen and the book she was reading. Harry was stumped. They seemed to be just a couple in love with no evil plans against the regime. He sat back in the seat of the car eventually falling asleep.

Brad and Sarah talked quietly in their camp. Brad explained he had found a tracking device. Sarah shivered partly from the cold night air and partly from fear. "What are we going to do?" she asked.

Brad had the answer. "We wait. We'll slip out in the middle of the night again. I didn't destroy it. I just sat it aside on the grass. So it should be working all night as if we are still around. As soon as it's too dark to be seen from a distance, we'll take off. In the meantime, we're just a couple spending time together." He had the truck ready to go at any moment. "We might as well try to get some rest." Sarah nodded. They went to their tent and lay down, but sleep was not going to happen.

Again, around midnight, they rose quietly, removing their sleeping bags. Brad took the tent down quickly. They slipped over to the truck, quietly opening and closing the doors. Brad let the truck roll downhill with no lights. He started the engine and drove off, leaving their camp and Harry behind.

They drove around for a while until Brad was sure they weren't being followed. Then they headed for the safe camp. It was barely daylight when they arrived at the parking site. Brad pulled out his pruning shears and cut branches to cover the truck as much as possible. Sarah helped. She worked quickly placing the branches. They would have to walk the rest of the way in. Brad was careful to cover their tracks into the camp. He watched the mountainside for any sign of Harry or his friends.

Justin was all smiles. One look at his face reminded Brad it was worth everything to be with him and his friends. Sarah grabbed Justin and showered him with kisses. She went from person to person hugging each of them.

Sarah felt tired and dirty. She and the girls slipped away from the boys for some private time. Brad and the guys headed back down the trail to the truck.

"We can drive it in the back way," Cole assured Brad as the boys walked back down the trail to the truck. They looked over the treasure their friends brought to them. "Thanks, man! Wow, look at that." Their eyes took in the bath tub.

"A surprise for the girls," Brad said, grinning.

Cole backed the truck out of the hiding place. He rolled down his window. "We'll meet you guys back at the camp." He had assigned Hank as lookout. They posted him at the rock on the other side of the road. He was supposed to watch the road for unfamiliar vehicles or anything suspicious and meet them back at the camp with a report. Carl and Richard cleaned up the area where the truck had been. It took only a moment to erase all the tire tracks. Richard kicked at some dirt to cover an oil spot left behind by the truck. Then he brushed it off with a branch. The

boys looked around and waved at Hank then quickly took off
through the woods.

Cole and Brad drove down the road a couple of miles; then he
made a turn onto a dirt road that seemed to appear from out of
nowhere. It was still early enough to have the truck back at camp
before someone came looking for it. Out here dust could be seen
from a distance even with the thick cover of the trees. Cole held
firmly onto the steering wheel as the truck rocked back and forth.
"This road hasn't been used much lately. It was originally used
for logging. The hunters and fishermen used to come up here,
but since the regime outlawed hunting and fishing we're the only
ones who use it."

"My dad and I came in this way when we hauled in big things,
but none of us takes this road into the cabin unless we really have
to. It's a little further; we try to save gas. Since it goes right to
the cabin, we figure it's safer for the camp if people don't know
it exists." He turned this way then that. Brad was amazed at the
directions the maze of roads took. They picked their way through
the forest up the side of the mountain and around it. After turning right then making a left, Cole stopped the truck at what
appeared to be a dead end. Brush covered the terrain in front of
them flanked by oversized oaks. Cole stepped out of the truck
and began removing the debris.

To Brad's amazement there was another road hidden from view.
Brad began helping him. "You sure play it safe," he commented.

"Not just me, my old man," Cole smiled. He used to hide this
road from hunters and such. He didn't want anyone to find the
cabin. Cole moved the truck up the road. They covered up the
secret entrance by using the same pile of brush, piling it high
enough to block the road from view. "It's not far now," Cole
told him.

Brad was getting tired of eating dust. The long night caught
up with him. Rocking along he fell asleep. It took at least an hour

from start to finish, barely moving, before they finally stopped outside the cabin.

The girls were still gone when Brad and Cole arrived at the cabin. Brad worked with the guys unloading and stockpiling the lumber. They worked, lifting the tub out of the truck; it took some time to get it into the cave. The boys pointed to the area they had intended to use for bathing. It was to the side of the cave in a room to itself. Brad was tired. "We'll set it up later." The guys laughed and teased him. He smiled. For the first time that day since they had arrived, the guys were laughing and acting carefree. He marveled at the way they switched back and forth from young men to boys. A moment ago they were working hard; now they joked and laughed, teasing each other mercilessly. Brad smiled to himself. This felt right. He and Sarah belonged here with these young people.

The girls didn't see Brad and the guys at the cabin, so they walked to the cave. There in plain sight was the tub. Tears immediately moistened Karen's eyes. "A tub. You brought us a tub." The girls were smiling from ear to ear. Mackenzie ran over to it; her beautiful brown eyes danced as she sat in it trying it out for size.

Brad answered, laughing, "We did, and it's just for you girls. We also have the makings for a couple of showers, but this is for you ladies. No guys allowed. When we're through with lunch we'll start setting it up."

Karen went over to Brad. Reaching up on her tip toes, she gave him a kiss on the cheek. "Thank you." She hugged him.

That morning had been a bitter disappointment to Harry. He woke just as the sun was coming up. Looking over at his equipment he could see the truck hadn't moved. The icon on the screen indicated the truck was still in the same place. He stretched and yawned then looked confused. He could see from here, even without his binoculars, the truck was gone. He grabbed his binoculars for confirmation. The camp was vacant, even the tent was gone. He drove down to the campsite, got out of the car and began turning over rocks and moving things. He found his tracking device lying in an inconspicuous place still activated but not on the truck. He kicked the ground, annoyed with the turn of events. Brad was far too careful and much too suspicious. He wasn't making this easy.

He looked at the road ahead of him as if he could still see where the truck was heading. He drove slowly down the road looking for driveways or roads where they might have gone. In the distance he could see dust swirling. He took the trail to the side of the road and worked slowly trying to follow the path. After a while he could no longer see where it led. Reluctantly he turned the car around. He would come back here by helicopter. There was something about these woods. Harry wasn't used to being outsmarted. It galled him.

From a secluded vantage point Ron watched the stranger. The man got out of his vehicle and walked around looking for something. He seemed suspicious. King growled quietly at his side. "I know boy; I don't like him either." Ron agreed. Lifting his rifle he watched Harry through the scope. Something wasn't right about this guy. Ron looked out toward the direction of the kids. He had seen the truck coming up the mountain early that morning. The boys had assured him their friend was trustworthy, but this new guy looked anything but. He considered how easy it would be to shoot the guy, bury him and pass the shot off to the kids as a missed hunting opportunity. But in the end he let the stranger drive away.

After lunch, true to his promise, Brad helped the guys set up the tub. He had brought enough pipes to pipe in a water system to the bath as well as the kitchen. He worked with the guys using the water from the cave itself. They directed it from the room above them; using gravity flow, they were able to actually install a water system that was able to feed the entire cave. With the use of the sun they could even set up the system to heat the water. They had already been working on a solar heating system. It was supplying them with some hot water, but they needed to work the kinks out of it. Brad was impressed with the intelligence of his young friends. Simon smiled happily as he looked over the solar panels. Thanks Brad. Now we'll be able to supply power everywhere we need it.

The girls were told they still couldn't use the tub. Brad had more work to do on it first. So the girls went to sleep dreaming of a hot bath. The next day Brad woke the boys who were sleeping in the cave by pounding nails as he worked. Before breakfast he had framed out a wall and doorway for the bathroom part of the cave. They ate breakfast and he went back to work, building the room so the girls could get some privacy. After dinner, he started in where he was told the girls would be sleeping, building them a bedroom they could close off from the guys.

Before they turned in for the night, Cole called them all together for their daily Bible study. They read from Hebrews chapter 11, the faith chapter. "We have to be like they were: faithful to the end. They are our witnesses. They endured hardships. Some things they endured were unthinkable. They never failed to serve the Lord. We won't either." Brad looked over at Sarah; her eyes were filled with tears. She loved all of these courageous young people. They were her heroes. She would die to protect them. Brad took her hand; he would not let any of them down. God would make a way.

It seemed a week passed by like a couple of days. Brad's help had made their camp much more workable. The pipe he had brought them was like gold. They looked around their cave. It was taking on the look of a comfortable, workable living space. They smiled as they looked with pride at their accomplishment.

They had heard a helicopter circling the woods the first day of Brad and Sarah's return. So they stayed in; no one went out for hours. Eventually it went away without returning. Hank reported seeing a car head up their way, but eventually the car drove back to the main road. Hank concluded that the driver was confused by the maze of hunting and logging roads leading to nowhere and given up.

Brad knew they were still being watched. He had argued with Sarah, but eventually convinced her to stay at the camp until he could return with more supplies. Justin begged him to let him go back with him. "I'm sorry, son, you're only fourteen. If anyone sees you they will force you back into military camp. We can't risk your being returned to the Antichrist's compound."

"But I'm big for my age." Justin looked at Brad, pleading.

"I'm sorry, you look too young. Anyone looking at you in the face will know you should be at the compound. I'm telling you, Justin, it is just too dangerous."

Simon was the oldest. He was eighteen. He had his eighteenth birthday hiding out from the regime. "I'll go with you. I'm older than the others and I look older than I am. I could pass for at least twenty. Justin's right, you need help. I can help you load the truck and even drive for you." Simon reasoned with Brad. "You can say I'm a new employee. Didn't you say there were new guys being assigned to your jobs by the government? What if we say I'm one of those guys? With me helping you drive we can go and come faster. And you could use some help loading the truck." Brad had to admit it was a good idea.

As before, they would only travel at night. They planned to return in a couple of days. "If we aren't back in three days, something is wrong. We'll try to get word to you. Check the post office." Brad kissed Sarah bye and left with Simon.

Justin was heartbroken. He missed Brad and wanted to spend some time with him. What if Brad got caught and he never saw him again? Sarah noticed the look on Justin's face. She moved to comfort him but Justin walked away. She would talk to him later when he felt more like listening.

Someone pulled into the driveway of Sarah and Brad's house. Harry smiled to himself. This guy was slick. Brad got out of the pickup with a stranger. "Where's the misses? And what happened to the truck?" Harry whispered to himself. They went into the house, so Harry leaned back in the seat of his car to settle in for the night.

Brad motioned for Simon to be quiet. They had discussed the possibility of the house being bugged. They ate dinner, aware of their conversation, talking only of unimportant miscellaneous things. After they had both showered, Brad moved toward the backyard. Turning, he motioned for Simon to join him. They walked out into the night, looking up at the beauty of the stars. "We might as well take the pickup back too. We can load it with the couch and a couple of chairs. We could use some furniture at the cabin and definitely the mattress and springs."

Simon nodded his agreement, and then covered his mouth to yawn. He was tired. Brad was a hard worker. After driving all night they rested a couple of hours in the morning, and then off to the yard where Brad had more supplies. He and Brad loaded more lumber, pipe, and miscellaneous supplies for the camp. All Simon could think of was getting some sleep.

Brad felt as tired as Simon looked. "Why don't we turn in? You can take the bed in the other room."

"No, man, this is fine." Simon stretched out on the sofa. Brad looked down to see he was already asleep. He placed a blanket where Simon could reach it then decided to get some sleep himself.

Brad woke around midnight. He took a shower to wake himself up. Then he decided to scout the neighborhood for anyone who might be watching him and Simon. Outside, hidden behind an overgrown oleander, was a black car. It was backed into the Johnson's drive. The Johnson's were one of the families that had disappeared. He slipped up even with the car. He had taken a lesson from Harry. He stayed in the shadows. Quietly he sneaked over to the car. It was Harry in the front seat sleeping. The windows were rolled down. An empty bottle lay discarded on the seat beside him. Brad decided Harry had been drinking. He watched him for a minute; convinced Harry was drunk, he sneaked back to the house.

They loaded the truck inside the garage. Quietly they moved in and out of the house. One thing Brad knew he wanted was the mattress. Slowly they piled all they could into the pickup bed securing it with ropes. Brad opened the garage doors holding his breath. Again he let the truck roll back without the engine running. Simon pushed it down the road away from Harry. When Brad thought they were far enough out of earshot, he started the engine and Simon jumped in; they were on their way. They arrived at the yard around 2:00 a.m. Brad jumped into the old truck and they left as quickly as they could.

It was late morning when they approached the safe camp. Brad instructed Simon to take the lead into the back road. They intended to drive directly to the camp. Simon moved into position to guide Brad to the cabin. They were back, and this time without that watchdog, Harry, on their backs.

Sarah looked beautiful. Her smile lit up her face. As she greeted them she realized Brad and Simon must have driven nonstop, loaded, and came right back. The two men decided to get some rest. While they did, Justin and the others took it upon themselves to unload the two trucks. The furniture was a welcome sight to all of them. It wasn't much but slowly the cave was beginning to feel like home. The boys set up the bed while Brad lay sleeping on the cave floor.

After the hard work, everyone was hot, so the guys went swimming. The girls decided to give them their privacy and stayed at the camp.

Harry was becoming truly annoyed with Brad. He must have slept like a dead man. He was angry with himself: if his superiors found out he was drinking on the job again... Well, he didn't have time to think about that now. He decided to go visit the preachers in jail; perhaps they could shine some light on this whole business of Brad's.

"I'm sorry, Harry. I don't know where Brad is and as for this place you mentioned I've never heard of it." John looked a little concerned. What was Brad up to and why did Harry care what he did? Paul and John glanced at each other. Harry seemed so sincere but the way he was released had been a mystery to both of them. After all, when they thought about it, with the exception of that out-of-control guard whom everyone called Bulldog, no one had touched him. He hadn't even been summoned to go before the judge. Something wasn't right about the whole situation. Paul and John knew from the Scriptures that men would betray men. It was looking more and more like Harry was working for the regime. He continued to spill his annoyance with the current world president; but after his questions and interest in Brad, they were finding his rhetoric hard to swallow.

"Harry, why do you think Brad is dodging you?" Paul had been listening to John and Harry talk. Now he wanted some answers.

"I'm not sure. Some guys are just suspicious, especially now. I thought he wanted my help but after all this, I'm baffled. If it weren't for the fact that he's you two guys' friend, I would have given up on him from the beginning."

Harry was not working out; Dennis Billings was not satisfied with his report. How had he let this Brad guy slip away from him again? Dennis knew of Harry's weakness for the bottle. *I better not catch him drinking on the job again,* he thought.

Rebecca contacted Dennis after he ordered the raid on the two preachers. She had tried to use her influence with him to get them out of jail. He tested her by asking her who this Brad Holden was; she simply said, "I know him from church. Why do you ask, Daddy?"

"How well do you know him and his wife?"

"She looked concerned and immediately started hedging, "Oh, not very well. I've seen them around."

That was all Dennis needed to know she was lying. He had received reports on her known associates. He had a list of all of her friends. They were on that list. The way he understood his informants, she and Sarah seemed quite close. What was wrong with her? When he was promoted he had offered Rebecca the option of becoming someone of importance. Instead, she continued to associate with the very people who were out to destroy the present system. She was becoming a liability. What if the higher-ups realized she was his stepdaughter? What if they understood she was dedicated to the enemy? That would be the end of the promotions. He would not be allowed to advance any further. He had plans, and that meant he had to continue to move up. He couldn't allow anyone to stop him. Well, she was making her own bed. He wasn't responsible for the consequences.

~~~

Carly was waiting for John to come home. She worked tirelessly to make him proud. Sarah showed up asking her for a hand with food supplies up north. The black market for food was a daily challenge. So many people were afraid of starving. Slowly their congregation was dwindling to smaller and smaller numbers as people became more afraid of not being able to buy or sell. Some of the people had decided that John was wrong. God would understand; they were just doing what they had to do in order to survive. They quoted Jesus saying, "Give to Caesar the things that are his and to God what is God's" (Matthew 22:21). Their fear was heartbreaking.

Carly warned them as they reasoned away taking the mark of the beast. "The Word of God is clear—we must not take the mark. Revelation 21:7–8 tells us,"

> He that overcometh shall inherit all things; and I will be
> his God, and he shall be my son. But the fearful, and unbe-

lieving, and the abominable, and murderers, and whore-
mongers, and sorcerers, and idolaters, and all liars, shall
have their part in the lake which burneth with fire and
brimstone: which is the second death.

She was having trouble without John there to confide in. For
the moment the black market was still in full swing, but for how
long? They were bound to run low on supplies. Famine was now a
worldwide problem. She looked around at the inventory, praying,
"Oh God, help us to endure to the end" (Matthew 24:10–13).
Her heart sank as she wondered if John and Paul were eating.

PAUL AND HIS BROTHER

The crowd was quickly growing out of control. Bulldog and Willy worked trying to guide Paul and John through the courtyard of the courthouse. One of the people spat on Paul. "So you think you're too good for us. You think you don't have to obey our laws. You Christians think you're special. Well, we'll see how high and mighty you feel when Bulldog here is done with you." His smile was ugly. The perverted glee of a demon danced in his expression. These people resented the very existence of Christians and Jews. They claimed to be open to all faiths; but inwardly they were ravening wolves. They rushed the guards. Forcing John and Paul to the ground, the crowd screamed with joy as they attacked the two preachers.

Bulldog used his club forcing the crowd back while Willie pulled them to safety. Bulldog faced the mob. "They will be punished but not by any of you! Let us do our jobs." The crowd listened but watched Paul and John with bloodthirsty expressions.

Again they found themselves in front of the judge. As he had promised, he was not as patient as he was with them in the past. He was overworked. His mood was foul and he was beyond listening to their unrepentant ramblings. "You men have tried my patience long enough. I have extended to you the hand of friendship and you have thrown it back in my face. I have given you every opportunity to change your minds. But you are stubborn and beyond repentance. I must therefore make an example of you. You will be taken into the town square and beaten for your rebelliousness. I warned you. You leave me no choice but to have you punished." It had, in the past, been considered inhumane to fight or mistreat prisoners, but the new regime considered it sporting. The people seemed to agree with their new leader: the bloodier the better.

The bailiff turned to Bulldog. "You heard the judge, the people want a show! Give them a good one."

Bulldog took his fist to Paul, then John. He had been told by his superiors, since he liked to fight so much, he could do it publicly for the crowd. "Why don't you guys get up and fight back? At least it would be sporting." He jeered.

Paul wiped the blood from his mouth with his sleeve. He was out of breath from the last blow to his stomach. His speech was broken as he spoke through gasps of air. "Jesus said, 'If someone hits you to turn the other cheek'" (Matthew 5:39).

Bulldog laughed, then said, "Why would anyone serve a God who asks them to allow another person to beat them?"

John added, "Jesus said, 'Love your enemies, and pray for those who mistreat you'" (Matthew 5:44).

Bulldog reached out and grabbed John by the shirt. Holding him in place, he hit him, knocking him off his feet. "Are you going to pray for me, preacher? Tell me, do you love me yet?"

Paul and John looked at each other; they were both beaten. It was hard for them to stand up; but in unison they answered, "Yes, Bulldog, we love you."

Bulldog stopped to the disappointment of the crowd. He couldn't hurt these guys anymore. The truth was the anger he had held deep inside of him was gone. He had watched these two serve God with all of their hearts. He had listened to their stories about the Lord. His stomach turned as he thought of hurting them. He no longer wanted to beat anyone, least of all these two.

"They've had enough," he said to Willy. "Let's take them back to their cell."

Willy nodded. He did not like this business of hurting people. He just wanted to get the preachers away from the jeering crowd without someone getting hurt more seriously. The crowd booed and demanded more, but the guards refused to listen.

John and Paul sat in a common room of the jail, badly bruised. This time the guards didn't try to separate them from the other prisoners. They had endured the public humiliation of the many onlookers. The jeers and screams of the crowd were something they were getting used to. Their bodies were bruised and sore but their spirits were full. They began to speak to all those who were being held in jail with them. The broken spirits of their Christian comrades rose as they listened to the two young preachers.

"We aren't the first to be beaten for our faith. The great heroes of the early church were persecuted, hunted down, jailed, and condemned to death. We are no better than they were."

"I am reminded of the story of Paul and Silas. They were a dynamic team. They went around preaching and teaching of Christ to the gentile people. One day they were on their way to pray. A young slave girl approached them. She had been following them for days proclaiming they were servants of God who had come to tell people how to be saved. Now, she was a fortune-teller who was possessed with a demon, and her owners used her to make money. Paul was so tired of hearing her; he ordered the demon to come out of her in the name of Jesus. The demon obeyed, but that meant her owners would not be profiting from her in the future. Their income was gone, just like that. So they took Paul and Silas and dragged them before the authorities in the marketplace. They accused Paul and Silas. 'They are disturbing the whole city!' they shouted. 'They are teaching the people to violate our customs'. A crowd rose up against them. They were ordered to be beaten and thrown into prison. The jailer was ordered to make sure they could not escape, so he bound them in stocks, placing them in the dungeon. He was afraid that if they escaped he would be killed in their place."

> And at midnight Paul and Silas prayed, and sang praises unto God: and the prisoners heard them. And suddenly

there was a great earthquake, so that the foundations of the prison were shaken: and immediately all the doors were opened, and every one's bands were loosed. And the keeper of the prison awaking out of his sleep, and seeing the prison doors open, he drew out his sword, and would have killed himself, supposing that the prisoners had been fled. But Paul cried with a loud voice, saying, Do thyself no harm: for we are all here. Then he called for a light, and sprang in, and came trembling, and fell down before Paul and Silas, And brought them out, and said, Sirs, what must I do to be saved? And they said, Believe on the Lord Jesus Christ, and thou shalt be saved, and thy house.

Acts 16:25–32

John spoke with fire in his young face. "God did not abandon them, and he has not forgotten us. We are here because of our love for him." The young man in the front row smiled and tried to hide his tears. His back ached and he was bruised from his last encounter with the demands of the world order. He sat, shaking his head affirmatively, making his curly brown hair bounce up and down. John continued, "We will not turn from the Lord no matter what they do to us. The apostle Paul teaches, 'For to me to live is Christ, and to die is gain'" (Philippians 1:21).

Paul raised his hands toward heaven. "Praise you, Lord! You alone are worthy of glory, the honor, and the praise! You are exalted high above the heavens. You remember the sparrow that falls. I know you remember us! You are glorious beyond compare! You are the friend to the outcast. You stick closer than a brother." Paul began to sing; his worship filled the cell, bathing the place of sorrow with light.

Holy, holy, holy!
Lord God Almighty!
Early in the morning our song shall rise to thee.

—Reginald Heber

John piped in with,

Amazing grace! How sweet the sound,
That saved a wretch like me!
I once was lost, but now am found
Was blind but now I see

—John Newton

The room filled with a beautiful presence as the two preachers lifted their voices in song. The sound, so simple but filled with deep emotion, moved the hardened jailers as they, too, listened finally. "What a Friend We Have in Jesus," (Joseph Scriven) one of the sweet hymns of the church, came to John's lips. His beautiful tenor voice rang out, piercing the darkness of the room with a spirit unlike any other on earth. The melody wafted toward heaven. The darkness of the jail seemed far away as the men and women listened to the angelic voice of a soul who loved Jesus.

Bulldog watched in stunned silence as the preachers raised their hands toward heaven. Paul and the others joined John singing, "What a privilege to carry everything to God in prayer." *How can they sing this song with such joy?* Bulldog asked himself. He had been trying for weeks to beat the sermons out of them. It hurt him to hear them speak of Jesus, the lover of all mankind. When had God cared for him? Bulldog remembered hearing this song many years ago. Once upon a time he, too, had attended church. His neighbor lady, Miss Millie, had sung this song to him. She was always filling her car with children and taking them to church. The only good memories he had of his childhood were of her and her husband. The rest were blurs of hunger and neglect; finally, he and his little brother were taken from their mother. His brother was adopted out, but Bulldog had stayed in the system. He went from foster home to foster home.

The memory shook him. It had been so long ago. Then Miss Millie's kindness, smile, and songs disappeared from his life and from his memory until now. He reached up and wiped his face with his hand. The track of tears washed his eyes. He was embarrassed. He didn't want anyone to see how deeply moved he was. These men reminded him of something else too. They reminded him of the peace he had always felt when Miss Millie was around. He looked into the battered faces of these two preachers, worshipping God uninhibited, and saw Miss Millie. They were like her. They were full of something not of this world.

He stumbled forward unintentionally; his feet carried him to John and Paul. "Where did you learn that song?" he asked. His look was that of a child. The wonder in his face transformed his features into a little boy. "Who taught you that song?" he asked, searching their faces for answers.

John and Paul looked up. Paul answered, "I learned it in Sunday school. My teacher loved to sing it."

"My dad taught me," John said. "We used to sing that song all the time. Do you know it?"

John and Paul were seated on the ground. Bulldog knelt down in front of them. He looked directly into their faces. "Yeah, I do," he said. His voice was soft and thoughtful. "A long time ago there was this neighbor lady. She used to sing it to me and my brother all the time. Sometimes, when she was watering her garden, we used to go over and listen to her tell us stories. She was kind." He sniffed and looked down. "Then we got taken away. I never saw her again."

Paul studied the man. The hair on the back of his neck began to stand up. "Miss Millie? Are you talking about Miss Millie?"

"Yeah, how'd you know?" the rough jailer asked.

"Maxwell?" the name slipped out of Paul's mouth, barely above a whisper. "Is it you?" Even as he asked, he was reaching out to embrace the man in front of him.

"Yeah," Bulldog looked confused. "But no one calls me that. How'd you know my name?"

"I'm Paully. I'm your little brother." The two men embraced. Max looked stricken as he realized he had just beaten his own brother. A sharp pain hit him from deep inside. His heart broke. He began to mourn. "Oh God," he cried out! "Oh my God." His pain was profound as he understood the depth of his offense.

"No, don't!" Paul held Max by the arms, forcing him to look into his face. He wanted him to understand. "This is a happy day. God has answered my prayers. I'm so glad to see you, brother." His warm embrace tossed aside the sorrow, insisting that the joy of finding his only brother far outweighed the pain. "What happened to you? I've been looking for you for years."

After Max regained his composure, he explained, "I was never adopted. I stayed in the system till I was grown. I ran away a lot. It never seemed to work out between me and the moms and dads in foster care. There was a man who tried to help me. He gave me food and a place to stay. By then I was headed down a really wrong road. He got me off the streets. I was sixteen when I went to live with him. He was more of a father to me than I'd ever known. After two years with him he died. I was eighteen so I took his name, joined the military, and kept moving. I just returned recently. I can't believe it. You, a preacher! Miss Millie would be proud of you."

"I was adopted by David and Jessica Stevens. They were great." Paul looked at Max with compassion. "I'm sorry you never really had a home."

The man in front of Paul looked very different from the brother he remembered. Of course, he was only six the last time he saw his older brother. "When we get out of here, I want you to come home with me and meet my wife. We have two kids, but they were raptured out with the believers when Jesus came back for his church."

After a moment Paul said, "You know, those stories Miss Millie used to tell us were true. They were stories from the Bible. That's why I became a Christian. After they took us away, I was so scared, I used to pray. I would ask God to teach me to be courageous like Daniel and the three Hebrew children, or King

David when he fought Goliath. After I was adopted, my mom gave me a Bible. Eventually I was able to read all those stories for myself. That's when I learned how real God is. He loves you. He has arranged for us to find each other."

Max was stone still. "Look, Paul, I know you believe all this stuff; but I've chosen a different path." The hardened expression of an hour ago slipped back into his face, cloaking the look of youth and wonder. "I am not like you. You should forget we ever met."

Paul held his gaze. "I don't care what you've done. The past is the past. All I care about is that I have finally found my brother. There is nothing in your life, past or present, which could make me not want to know you." The kind, gentle words of Paul began to melt the tough, hurt, and battle-worn heart of the brother in front of him. "I love you. I always will."

There was that peace again—the peace Max had not felt since Miss Millie. Max didn't know what to say. He wanted to really know the brother he had lost, but so much had happened. For now he just nodded; it was a small gesture but one that pleased Paul. The look of joy that passed over Paul's face made him happy. There was something of the boy he remembered. The expression brought with it memories of pleasing Paul. He would have done anything when they were kids to see that look. Bulldog smiled. Something warm started to melt the life-hardened soul inside of him.

John watched in stunned silence as the reunion of brothers took place in front of him. The small congregation in the common room began to praise God. Tears rolled big and sloppy down John's face. He was amazed. In the middle of this nightmare something very heavenly was happening. Paul had finally found his brother.

One of the guards on duty with Bulldog was also watching. This relationship could prove to be useful. A sinister smile crossed his face. *Very useful,* he thought to himself.

Bulldog looked up, catching the eye of his longtime rival. He moved away from Paul. He was placing Paul in danger just by acknowledging their relationship. Bulldog knew the walls had eyes. He knew it was too late to deny his relationship with Paul. He would have to use the information he had been collecting to get Paul and John out of here before his enemies used Paul to force him into submission. Bulldog had learned the hard way; the only way to survive was to always keep the upper hand. He stared purposefully back at his enemy, daring him to try anything.

Ralph read the warning from Bulldog loud and clear. He straightened up, swallowed, and unconsciously tugged on his tie, fixing it. He did not want Bulldog coming after him. He knew the guy. Bulldog was crazy. Fear replaced his look of triumph. He backed down for now.

Bulldog wasn't taking no for an answer. He walked into the office of Dennis Billings right on time. The chief looked at him questioningly. "What is so important, Maxwell, that it couldn't wait until tomorrow? Why did you have to speak to me at this time?"

"I have some important information. I was hoping to trade this information for the release of the two preachers."

The chief looked bored. "What could you possibly have to tell me that could make me consider giving up those two criminals?"

"I know who has been selling you out. This guy is good. He has been sitting here right under your nose, watching you. He reports back to your superiors everything that happens in this place."

Dennis cleared his throat. He tried not to give himself away, but Bulldog had pricked his interest. "I understood that you have no love for the preachers. Why are you interested in helping them now?"

Bulldog knew he couldn't lie out of his reason to the chief. There were spies everywhere and too many witnesses. He tried to act nonchalantly, "Well, it turns out Paul is my long lost brother. We haven't seen each other since we were kids. We were adopted and our last names were changed. I just thought, after the way I've treated him and his friend, this was the least I could do."

"How touching for you," the chief spoke; sarcasm laced every word. "Who is the spy?"

Their eyes locked in challenge. "Release the preachers and take your dogs off them. As soon as the guys are home and safe with their wives and I am satisfied they are not being harassed I'll give you the guy's name."

"I want the name first," Dennis demanded.

"I'm sorry, chief. I want the two preachers home and safe, them and their wives." For now Bulldog had the upper hand and he knew it.

"I should kill you right now!" the chief spat out. "How dare you try blackmailing me?" His calm demeanor changed. His face flushed red. "I could beat it out of you."

"You could try." Bulldog said calmly. "I think you should know I also have files on you, which could prove damaging if they were to end up in the wrong hands. In case of my untimely death that information will go directly to your superiors. You see, I'm not just here to locate one spy. I was also sent here to watch you." Bulldog let his words sink into the heart of the man listening.

Dennis was stunned. He began to sputter, "But I don't understand. Why would I be under suspicion? You know I am faithful to the regime. Why would anyone doubt my loyalty?"

"Let's just say there have been some inquiries." Bulldog leaned back, placing his foot over the knee of the opposite leg. He began to reason. "Listen, Dennis, I don't have any particular reason to crucify you. It would frankly do me no good. I don't want to file an unfavorable report. You and I have known each other for years. We may not be friends but we understand each other. I prefer to work with you. You scratch my back and I'll scratch yours."

"So, just like that, I just let them go as if they were cooperating. You expect me to ignore the fact that they have never recanted their religious bigotry." Dennis was annoyed, but the look on his face began to reflect his compliance. Dennis had a policy. He believed in using everyone he could. Bulldog could prove to be helpful. He reigned in his temper for the moment.

"That's right; you can call it a loving act of kindness by the regime. The press will eat it up. I know you, Dennis; you're smooth. By the time you put your spin on how the regime is working toward better relations with those who are resistant to our cause, you'll end up looking like some kind of hero. This could work out much better for you than continuing to persecute them." Bulldog's cold blue eyes, the only physical resemblance to Paul, stared unwaveringly at Dennis. His look of calculating intelligence was in direct odds to his reputation for being a hot-head. *No*, Dennis thought. *Whatever game he has been playing here—pretending to be all brawn and no brains—that was not the man he saw before him or the man he had known in the past.* He made a mental note to not underestimate Bulldog. Many did, and they paid the price for that mistake.

Paul and John couldn't believe it. There was no fanfare, no going before the judge, no reason given to them; they were just told by the guard, "You boys are out of here." Just like that. They went through processing with no demands that they take the mark. Both men were praising God for his mercy when they noticed Bulldog was waiting for them at the end of the hall. Paul was all smiles. Pride danced all over his face as if he were greeting the greatest man on earth.

John remembered the angel releasing the apostle Peter from his jail bonds (Acts 12:3–16). What a strange angel Bulldog had turned out to be. John liked him. He liked seeing Paul so happy. He decided not to weigh all of the pros and cons of Paul having a brother so completely involved with the correctional side of the new-world order. He wanted to bask in Paul's happiness for now. How long had it been since he had seen Paul completely happy? Not since before the rapture. His mind rushed back to a warm summer evening at his mom and dad's. Paul and Shelby had come by for something. Dad Jenkins was barbequing; he insisted they stay. John recalled the carefree hours they spent laughing and talking about their lives and ambitions. John shook himself back to the present.

Bulldog was smiling back at Paul. His face was lit up with joy. He grabbed Paul around the neck, catching his head in the crook of his arm, "Let's go, brother. I'm anxious to meet my sister-in-law." The men laughed. All the beatings were dismissed from their minds. As far as they were concerned, they had just met Bulldog. Everything changed the moment they realized who he was. John and Paul were still bruised, but their hearts were laughing.

Shelby wouldn't let go of Paul even if he was trying to tell her something about his friend. She just couldn't seem to unwind her arms from his neck or stop showering his face with kisses. Finally she calmed down enough to listen to her husband's story. She walked over to Bulldog. "I am so happy to meet you, Maxwell. I have prayed this day would come for so long."

Bulldog leaned toward his sister-in-law, giving her a kiss on the cheek. "The pleasure is all mine," he replied. His cobalt blue eyes danced as he looked into her face. "You are far too pretty for Paul. How did he ever talk you into settling for a guy like him?"

She laughed shyly. "I want to know everything. Tell me what you have been up to. How did you two meet?"

Bulldog took a breath. This was what he had been dreading, but he might as well get it over with. He didn't want to have lies between himself and family. "Well, I'm not the kind of man my brother is. We have taken very different paths. I'm not a Christian." His eyes held a haunting gaze. "I'm a guard for the regime. I am the man who has been beating Paul and John. I'm part of the world system. For me there is no going back." He dropped his face, looking at the ground. He had heard the sermons from the preachers encouraging the believers not to take the mark. He knew from their warnings just how far down he had sunk. He was now aligned with the Antichrist. He was condemned to the same fate as all who became the enemies of God. When he looked up, he had an expression of resolve. "But I promise I will do everything I can to help you and Paul. I know now how wrong I've been. I'm not a good man, Shelby. But I do have certain skills and contacts that could prove useful to you and your friends. I will do what I can to help. That is until they stop me."

Shelby held her breath. How could she thank him for his offer? Her mind warred with the knowledge that he was the man who had beaten the guys, and the understanding that he was obviously sorry. She suddenly felt a shiver go down her spine. This would put Maxwell in great danger. "Oh, Maxwell, you mustn't take any unnecessary chances. We will get by. God has been sustaining us. Please, don't do anything that will bring you harm."

Max looked at her; a haunted expression marred his face, "I have lived a hard life. Many of my friends are dead. Each of them died in one war or another. We were soldiers. I gave myself for my country. I was a man of purpose. In the beginning I was like so many men or women who love their country and are willing to die for it. The military was my family. But I didn't die; I lived. When the one-world order began, I should have gotten out. But this is the only life I know. The world has changed. The more perverted our cause became, the deeper I sank into this mire." He dropped his head. "I'm not proud of what I have become. For years I thought I would never see Paul again. Now that I have found you guys, I have a purpose"—he cleared his throat— "a family. That means something to me."

Shelby could see a spark of Paul in the man speaking to her. There was this nobility about him, especially in his moment of deep understanding. Something struck her and pulled at her heart. She wanted desperately to comfort him. "You should never believe there is no hope for you. 'With God all things are possible' (Mark 10:27). We are all together now. That's all that matters." She squeezed his hand. "Come with me; I have pictures

of your niece and nephew." Her chatter was a welcome change
from the heartbreaking thoughts that had been running through
Bulldog's mind.

John said good-bye. He was anxious to get home to Carly.
Paul and Shelby walked him to the door. Shelby handed him her
car keys. "You can borrow my car." He thanked her. She reached
up and hugged him good-bye, kissing his cheek. "I'm so glad your
home." They made plans to meet the next day.

Carly was beside herself with joy. "John," she squealed out
three octaves higher than normal. She jumped into his arms.

He swung her around happily. Letting her feet touch the
ground, he buried his head in her long dark hair, "Hi, babe."

"When did you get out? How did you get them to release
you?" Her questions ran into each other.

He kissed her, smiling indulgently. He said, "You'll never
believe this."

Carly sat, mesmerized by John's detailed account of his and
Paul's time in jail. He left nothing out. He was so amazed by
the story. He wanted to tell it. Hearing the events that led up to
their release repeated made it no less true. God had reunited Paul
with his brother, changed the heart of a bitter, angry man and
used that same man to arrange their release. It gave John chills
to think of God's deliverance, and from one of the last people he
would have ever depended on.

"John," the name slipped out of her lips barely above a whisper. "God's ways are past finding out" (Romans 11:33).

He nodded his agreement and then said, "I need a shower."

For the first time, she stopped being happy long enough to
assess the damage. Tears filled her eyes as she took in the bruises.
New ones had formed from the beating that day. John was sore; he
held himself differently as if he were protecting himself. "Where
are you hurt?" she asked, reaching out to touch his ribs.

He grabbed her hand. "I'll be fine, honey. Don't worry about
me. A few days with you nursing me, and I'll be good as new."

She watched him with concern written in her expression. He turned to her. "Carly, can you make me something to eat?" She agreed and left the room.

John only wanted to get her away from him long enough to check himself out. Bulldog had broken a couple of his ribs; he could barely breathe for the pain. He eased himself into the shower, washing carefully. Once out, he toweled himself dry quickly. He didn't want Carly to see the damage. He pulled on a shirt, trying to hide his injuries. He heard her call out to him, "Dinner."

He moved slowly to the kitchen, wincing as he did. She caught his expression. He confessed sheepishly. "Bulldog can really pack a punch."

She grabbed a cold compress from the freezer; placing a towel around it, she handed it to him. "This should help. Your face looks a little worse for the wear too."

He reached up, delicately touching his cheek. "I'm sure glad he stopped when he did. You have to meet this guy; he's nothing like Paul."

She poured a cup of tea and handed it to John. He dived into dinner like he was starving. When he noticed her horrified expression, he laughed, "It's not so bad, honey. They fed us most of the time. It's just that nothing they had tasted like this."

Her mind focused on four little words. She repeated them back to him. "Most of the time?"

"Well, for a few days there, the judge thought we would be more cooperative if we fasted. We didn't change our position; so the next time we saw him, he lifted the fast and told them to feed us."

John decided to change the subject. "You haven't told me yet; how have things been around here? What's been going on at the church?"

She filled him in on everything from Shelby and her praying to their preaching, and finally how the church people had been slowly giving up. "They're frightened, John. They want to do what is right, but they're afraid of the consequences."

John felt sick. But he had known all along that many would fall away from the truth. The Scriptures he had learned from childhood came back reminding him of the challenges that lay ahead.

PARTING OF FRIENDS

Sarah had to do a lot of talking, but eventually Brad agreed to let her return home from camp with him. She wanted to meet with Carly. There was still so much for her to do before she could stay at the safe house.

They drove into the drive late in the afternoon. Brad did a search by foot for Harry. He didn't see Harry or anyone who looked suspicious. So he decided, maybe, Harry had grown tired of waiting around for them and left.

Sarah dropped her bags on the floor. She was exhausted. All she could think of was jumping into the shower to soak for about an hour.

She turned on the television to listen to the news. She and Brad hadn't been able to keep up with things while they were at the camp. Brad walked through the door. "Honey," she said to get his attention. "It's John and Paul!" They both sat glued to their television listening to the report.

"Yes, Charlie," the reporter said to her colleague. "The two preachers were released just this afternoon in an unusual turn of events. These two were jailed for their radical Christian beliefs." The lady reporter announced, "The kindness of the world president has once again proved to be magnanimous. These two men are known to be guilty of their crimes; but today they were pardoned as an act of love by our leader. Our own Captain Dennis Billings, head of operations in this region, spoke to us on behalf of the regime." The camera rested on Dennis as the newswoman questioned his decision. "Why, sir, did you decide to free the two preachers?"

Dennis sat calmly, looking elegant. "We have pleaded with these pastors to work with us. We have no desire to harm them. The world president is a man devoted to all of us. His determination to unite our world is an inspiration to us. We believe if he were here, he would be the first to extend the branch of friendship. We hope this act of forgiveness will help bridge the gap between us and our Christian brothers and sisters."

"As the world president's regional representative in these matters, were you operating on your own, or did you receive instructions to do this? What exactly prompted your decision?"

"As you know, Karen, the world president is a man dedicated to peace; this is his policy. I simply put it into action. I repeat, we hope to bridge the gap between ourselves and our Christian brothers and sisters. None of us wants the bickering to go on. We want to concentrate on the important matters of state."

Brad and Sarah called John; his phone was understandably busy. They then dialed Paul. He picked up. "Hello, this is Paul," his warm baritone voice rang through the receiver.

"Paul, it's Brad; I can't believe it! What happened?"

Paul laughed. "Brad, it's good to hear your voice. John and I have been wondering where you went. We never heard back from you after that day in the jail."

"Paul, I'm sorry, I need to talk to you and John. But now isn't the time. Tell me about your release."

"Brad, it's a miracle. Do you remember Bulldog the guard?"

"Are you talking about the big guard with the temper?"

"Yea, that's right. Brad, we started talking to him and he and I realized he is my brother."

"Your brother?" Brad echoed, shocked by the thought.

"That's right; we were both taken away from our parents when I was just a little guy. I was adopted by the Stevens. But Maxwell, I mean Bulldog, remained in the system. He was kicked around a lot and really got messed up. We both changed our names. That's why we couldn't find each other. When he found out who I was, he talked to his boss and somehow talked him into releasing us."

Brad was concerned. "Are you sure you can trust him?"

"Yes, of course," Paul said with no doubt. "He's my big brother. He always took care of me when we were kids."

Brad had another one of his ideas. "Do you think you could arrange for me to meet with him?"

"Sure, I'll have him give you a call."

"Thanks, Paul," Brad said as they hung up.

The time passed quickly. Sarah hardly took a breath. She and Brad had made plans on the way back from Justin's camp. The days flew by as they plotted and planned to help the young people. She had taken over establishing a black market delivery service. Carly had it up and running in this area, but they needed to be able to get supplies to the camp. She also planned to return the favor by sending as much fish and game as possible to Carly to help meet the needs of the hungry still living in town.

Brad received a call from Bulldog. "I hear we should meet."

"That's right. I want to talk to you, Pastor Paul and Shelby, as well as Pastor John and Carly. My wife and I will be meeting with Pastor John and Carly in a couple of hours. Is there any way you can join us? Paul and Shelby will be there. We are meeting at Pastor John's church."

"I suppose I can make it," Maxwell said.

"Good. Thanks, Max. Paul and Shelby know the way to the church. I look forward to speaking with you."

Bulldog held the phone to his ear even after Brad had hung up. He was worried about his brother and Shelby. John and Carly were also on his mind. If something happened to one of them Paul wouldn't be happy, and he wanted to keep Paul happy. But who was this Brad? He was concerned; he could only take care of the two pastors. Whatever Brad was up to could prove to be too much for him to deal with.

He arrived at Shelby and Paul's a little after lunch. Shelby had tried earlier to convince him to meet them for lunch but he begged off, telling her he had to work.

He told Willy he would be back as soon as he could. Willy was not happy, "I'm tired of covering for you man. You know what I mean. You've got to start pulling your own weight around here. I'm doing things that aren't my job, all because my partner just decides he needs to leave."

"I promise I'll make it up to you," Bulldog said.

"You better man. I mean it, no more," Willy warned.

The little group of friends gathered under a shade tree at the church. Paul introduced Bulldog to everyone, then turned to Brad, "Okay, what is the big emergency?"

"We've heard from Justin," Brad announced.

"How is he?" Everyone began to ask about him, bombarding Sarah and Brad with questions.

"Who is Justin?" Bulldog asked, looking completely out of the loop.

Sarah piped in. "He's our adopted son. He was taken away with all the other young people to the youth camps. We were worried about him. The police stopped in one evening to ask us if we had heard from him. We hadn't. They told Brad that he and his friends had escaped from their protection and they were looking for them."

"A few weeks later he got in contact with us," Brad said. Then he began to explain the unusual events of the past weeks. "We had just come back from his safe camp when we discovered you guys were in jail."

"They want to help others," Sarah explained.

Brad leaned forward. "Max, that's where you come in. We need to set up an underground railroad of sorts. You're on the inside; and with your contacts, I think we could reach a lot of people and do some good. I spoke with Harry, but he didn't work out."

Max looked concerned. "You told Harry what you're telling me?"

"That's why I rushed off the day I came to see you guys. I spoke with Harry, but there was something wrong. I told him I had a friend who had a safe house and asked him to work with me to set up the railroad. He agreed, but a couple of days later he showed up with some guys that seemed suspicious. I didn't trust him, or them, so I took everyone to an abandoned house in the country instead. I think he followed us for a few days, but lately I haven't seen him."

Max nodded affirmatively. "He's a snake. You can't trust him. Don't let him near you or your wife. I'm certain, if he knows what you are trying to do, he won't stop until he catches you with your son." Sarah gasped. She had been thinking the same thing; but hearing Bulldog say it frightened her.

"What was he doing there in the jail next to us?" Paul asked

Maxwell answered, "Honestly, he was a plant sent in by Dennis Billings, the biggest snake of them all. Dennis would sell out his own mother to advance his position."

"I don't understand how you talked him into releasing the guys," Carly stated.

"I blackmailed him." Maxwell answered bluntly.

"Of course," Paul said, looking at Max as the light began to dawn. "You must have all kinds of dirt on those guys."

Max nodded, "I do, and I am continuing to collect more information daily."

Paul looked at Maxwell. "I thought Billings was a friend of yours."

"He's the kind of friend I like to keep my eye on. He can't be trusted; and that slimeball, Harry, is just like him."

"I thought Harry was interested in what we were telling him. I really thought he was listening," John said unhappily

"He probably was. But you have to understand Harry, Dennis, and I all sold out a long time ago. He's not like you, Preacher. He's been twisted by life. After a while you stop feeling; something in you closes down. He's not such a bad guy. He's just learned how to stay alive; Dennis owns him. He does whatever Billings says, like his puppy."

Brad began to tell everyone about the safe house and the young people who live there. Pastor John and Carly sat listening with bated breath to the report they gave. "It sounds unbelievable," Carly exclaimed.

John looked at them wistfully as they explained the camp and the boy's love for fishing. "That sounds great! Boy, I would love to be fishing right now. I used to go whenever I could before this whole Antichrist thing started. We went water rafting, camping, and boating, the whole nine yards. But that's all behind us now. Most of the waterways are shut down. The new-world order watches everything people do."

Brad was on board. "Let's do it. Let's plan to go fishing when we go up to see the kids. The boys would love to show you around."

John looked sad. "I can't; just the fact that you are here with me now makes you suspicious. They have been watching me ever since they released me from jail. I can't take the chance of placing those young people in danger."

Paul agreed. "I am sure Shelby and I have been followed as well."

Maxwell knew who was behind their being followed. He grew angry as he realized Dennis had not called off his dogs.

Brad continued to reason with them. "But you're the reason they are doing this. They want to help people who are in danger to escape the regime and avoid being killed. You are the perfect candidate for the safe camp."

Bulldog liked the idea of the preachers going somewhere safe. "I think you should listen to him. It's only a matter of time before they bring you in again. I can't guarantee your safety. I know some guys who will help. You would be surprised how many of us there are who are not happy with the present regime; but because it is all we've ever known, we've just stuck around. I have friends."

John looked at his friends. The sadness that showed on his face broke their hearts. "I can't leave my church. This is my call. I forsook it once to do what was easy for me. But I have promised the Lord I won't do it again. I belong here, preaching the Word of God. Thank you so much for thinking of me. I would appreciate it if you helped Carly escape."

Before he could speak another word, Carly interrupted him, "My place is here with you. You are my husband; I'll stay with you as long as God gives us life." The look that passed between them was an unspoken confirmation. They were resolved to serve the Lord wherever his path led them.

Pastor Paul and Shelby shook their heads in agreement with John and Carly. "We must stay too. Our work here is not done."

Brad said sadly, "We may not see you again after today. We will try to visit when we can, but we are going to the safe camp to help the young people there. We want them to realize their dreams."

"Then our paths are taking a different direction," John said somberly. They looked at each other with love and respect.

Brad and Sarah stood up to leave. "I wish you would change your minds." Brad tried one last time to persuade them; but deep down inside he knew all along—this would be their decision.

"We will miss you all," Sarah said somberly.

Carly and Shelby hugged her good-bye. Brad shook hands with Paul, then hugged John. "You're like a brother to me," Brad said, wishing he could protect John from the cruelty of a God-hating society.

Sarah added, "Please, if you change your minds, remember you are always welcome."

Brad continued, "If you ever need anything. If you want some-one slipped out or change your mind, anything, just let me know." He left them with the same information about the general delivery mail. If we find a way to contact you we will.

Maxwell agreed to work out some of the logistics for Brad. "I'll talk to my friends. I'm sure we can find a way to help you with the refugees. You and Sarah, go on back, take care of your son and his friends. I'll take care of things from here." They agreed to meet in the little town in three days. Maxwell promised he would have a plan by then. "We'll talk soon." he assured them.

Paul, Shelby, John, and Carly watched as their friends drove away. Maxwell tried to reason with them but his comments fell on deaf ears. They all knew life for them was this path. They had chosen to stand up and speak out as long as God gave them breath.

Maxwell feared he would lose them all sooner rather than later.

Sunday morning both churches were filled to capacity. Many of the believers who had wandered away showed up to see their pastors in person. Simultaneously the preachers addressed their congregations.

John stood smiling, trying to quiet the crowd; their over-whelming welcome rang out as they clapped, whistled, and roared for their pastor's safe return. "Thank you. Thank you my friends, please be seated. It is a blessed day. And it is with great joy that I stand here before you." Again the crowd roared with enthusiasm. "I have no words to thank you for your prayers. I can tell you God carried us through our time of incarceration, and our release was nothing less than a miracle."

"After days of enduring the hospitality of the regime"—the crowd laughed as John made a face—"God provided a way of escape. Even in the middle of our worst storm, God has a divine plan. I am reminded of the three Hebrew children who were com-manded to bow before the golden statue King Nebuchadnezzar had erected. They refused, saying, 'If it be so, our God whom we serve is able to deliver us from the burning fiery furnace, and he will deliver us out of thine hand, O king. But if not, be it known unto thee, O king, that we will not serve thy gods, nor worship the golden image which thou hast set up'" (Daniel 3:17–18).

"Our God is a deliverer. He delivered them from the fiery
furnace. But he didn't just deliver them; he actually got into the
furnace with them. You see, we were never alone. Jesus, who lives
inside of us, was in there with us! He never left us!"

"Our God is a deliverer! He delivered Daniel out of the Lion's
den. The evil men of his day became angry because he prayed to
God daily. They tricked the king, who loved Daniel, into signing
a decree that stated, 'If any man worshipped any other god other
than the king, they would be thrown into a lion's den.' The king,
desiring to be worshipped, forgot about his friend Daniel, and
agreed to their plan. But Daniel was not touched by the lions.
The Bible tells us the king rose early in the morning and ran to
the cave, "And when he came to the den, he cried with a lamen-
table voice unto Daniel: and the king spake and said to Daniel, O
Daniel, servant of the living God, is thy God, whom thou servest
continually, able to deliver thee from the lions?" (Daniel 6:20).
Daniel answered the king, 'Oh king, live forever, my God has sent
his angels. They have stopped the mouths of the lions'" (Daniel 6).

John raised his right hand to the sky. "Our God is a deliverer.
When Paul and Silas were in jail they began to sing. As they
were singing praises to God, the earth began to shake. The bars
flew open; the bonds that held them fell off them. The jailer came
running; thinking they have all escaped, he took out his sword to
kill himself, but they stopped him, saying, 'We are all here, don't
hurt yourself.' When he realized they were still there, he asked
them, 'How can I be saved?' (Acts 16:23–36) God saved him and
his family."

"Our God is a deliverer. He is able to deliver us from the
Antichrist. But if he chooses not to, I will still not bow down and
worship the Antichrist." Cheers rang through the little church as
the young militant preacher spoke with renewed enthusiasm. His
heart was full of the magnificence of God. "Our God delivered
the three Hebrew children from the fiery furnace. He delivered
Daniel from the lion's den. He delivered Paul and Silas from jail.

He has delivered Paul and me from jail. He is God! There is none like him!"

Across town, Pastor Paul spoke with fire. Passion dominated every word as he told his congregation of the deliverance God had given him. Maxwell was there anonymously. He had already asked Paul and John not to point him out or talk about his relationship to Paul in hopes of keeping it all under the radar. "I just don't want anyone thinking they can get to me through any of you. It's bad enough Dennis and some of the guards know. If we don't make a big thing out of it, maybe it will just be a bleep on the radar screen. I intend to play it as just a fact of my life. With any luck at all and maybe some of your prayers, they'll let it go."

Paul understood his relationship with Max weakened Max's position with his enemies. He understood Max was making a magnanimous statement just associating with them. "Whatever you want, brother. We'll do this your way."

As Max listened to Paul speak, all the love they had shared as boys came flooding back to him with flashes of memories. He was so proud of Paul. "God, help me find a way to protect them." He prayed fervently. "Somehow, God, I have to help them."

Dennis had also shown up. He sat in the back watching Maxwell. A smile lit his devious face. He could put this relationship to work.

THE TWO WITNESSES

The world president was annoyed beyond belief. His secretary of state rushed into his office once again whining about the two witnesses. "Sir, we must do something. The people are ready to revolt."

He mulled over the situation in spite of the Scripture (Revelation 11:3). He had tried numerous times to blow up those old windbags—the two witnesses—but it was impossible. Even his attempts to fire on them by jet had met with defeat. They simply prophesied and fire shot from them to the planes, blowing the planes up before they could reach them. His missiles had failed also. Every time they fired one off, the missile would change course and return back to explode on his military. These two men were a thorn in the flesh of the whole regime! They were virtually impossible to kill. Every time they were approached by the world president's police or military they literally breathed fire. No one could get near them for fear of being incinerated. It was most distracting.

They preached, speaking openly in condemnation of the president of the world. They also condemned his most distinguished servant and pastor of the world church, the pomp and plush Medium of Excellent Supernatural Service, fondly known by Christians as "The Mess." They complained about the regime, the loss of freedom, and declared the Peace Treaty with Israel to be nothing more than a hoax. The problem was they had gained a large following of mostly Jews who had at last found their

Messiah. He sniffed the air and made a face, revealing his disgust at the thought.

They even criticized the existence of the world church OWAFR and all it stood for, calling it a road to hell. They were completely disagreeable. They were obstinate. They continued to speak of Jesus, the Lamb of God. They were unbearable. They didn't like anyone!

The citizens of the world were persecuted by them. They preached daily, declaring, "Nothing but the blood of the Lamb can cleanse the souls of men." Saying, "Jesus died for the sins of all mankind. It is only through the blood of Jesus that men can be saved." They knew they were in direct conflict with the religions of the world but they didn't care. They stood condemning the world, saying, "God's judgment is here." It was unnerving to so many who were forced to listen to them constantly, spouting out that ridiculous dribble! They continued to tell people, "You must turn your hearts over to Christ. Jesus will return to destroy his enemies and take out the present world system." The Antichrist snarled. It was appalling. No one who was anyone listened to them. The only problem was they wouldn't shut up. They controlled all of the satellite systems, forcing people to hear their messages of hate.

The troubled hearts of men and women were scalded by their words, demanding repentance. The angry mobs began to cry out for them to be punished. People appealed to their beloved leader demanding he remove them from the air waves. "They speak lies against the regime. We are being forced to hear them against our will." The outcry grew louder as they protested against their oppressors, "Kill them!" one man yelled. The crowd joined him, chanting, "Kill them! Kill them! Kill them!" Signs waved as the men and women rallied to have the two men murdered.

They were an enormous source of annoyance for the Antichrist and his cabinet. His press secretary tried to answer the outcry of the people. "This is obviously some kind of hocus-pocus." He laughed, trying desperately to make a joke. "I assure you we are making every effort to stop them. They are simply more intelligent than we have given them credit for. They are controlling the airwaves with some kind of device not yet detected. But they will be found out, make no mistake about it."

Reporters fought for a chance to ask questions. Barbara Lamb raised her voice. "Mr. press secretary, they have proclaimed that it would not rain and it didn't rain. The people of the world are worried; crops have failed. The drought is oppressive to men, land, and animals. What is the world president doing to convince them to call off the drought?"

The press secretary shifted slightly. "They have no real power. It is simply a coincidence that the rain stopped after they predicted it. The world president has no intention of being emotionally blackmailed by lunatics. That is all for today." He gathered his notes and left the pressroom quickly.

The witnesses captivated the attention of all who listened to them with an open heart. They were converting Jews to Jesus daily. Many of these young men and women were going out and continuing to speak and preach in the name of the Lord!

An army of 144,000 young men received Christ (Revelation 7:1–9 and 14). They preached daily the gospel of Jesus Christ. What had started out with two tattered, homeless old men had escalated into an awakening to the Messiah all over the world.

The Antichrist sat back, leaning his head against the plush leather of his chair. His eyes were covered by the cold compress his aid had brought him. He was the target of these antiquated people who hadn't the sense to come in out of the rain. Literally they had stood, even in the rain, preaching against him; that is, until they proclaimed there would be no rain and the rain mysteriously stopped. His fist hit his desk. "Why can't one of you imbeciles stop them?"

Three men sat rather uncomfortably. The Antichrist loomed over them on the other side of his desk. Their chairs were huge, overstuffed things that sank down as they sat in them, giving them the feeling of diminished size.

The Antichrist glared at the man seated directly below and in front of him. The poor man licked his lips nervously. His slightly balding head held only a few stray hairs in the front that stood at attention and seemed to wave at the Antichrist. His beautifully tailored gray suit rumpled slightly at the waist, pulling at its button. His eyes swerved in the direction of his companions. "Well, sir, it's like this."

"Shut up, you blabbering fool. Did I ask you to speak? I don't want excuses, I want results!" The Antichrist looked resplendent in his royal-blue silk suit. His tie, perfectly knotted, was extraordinarily beautiful. His crisp white shirt gleamed against his tanned skin. But for all his outward good looks, he was still the Antichrist. His true character emerged in his private office.

"Find out who is helping them stay on the air and destroy him." He barely controlled his temper, finishing through clenched teeth. "Now, get out, and while you are out, see to it they are killed, or I will take your lives for theirs!"

A flash of the guillotine shot through their minds—splattered blood everywhere, their heads rolling... Oh no! The scene was too awful to consider!

The terrified little man looked pale. He raised his hand to his throat and swallowed hard. Unconsciously, he loosened his necktie. He stood to his feet and started to bow profusely. "Yes. Sir. Yes, whatever you want we will do it." He was still bowing when he exited the room. "Don't worry, sir, we are on it."

The three men left the Antichrist's office in a state of panic. They were dead men! If they tried to kill these men they would be incinerated. And if they didn't try, they would be killed by the Antichrist. "What can we do?" they asked each other.

They decided to send in a suicide bomber with just enough explosives to blow him and those two old fools away. Even if nearby onlookers were killed, at least they would be rid of those two pests.

They set the plan in motion. They took a seat in the very back row. They were anxious for the show to start. They wanted to see firsthand the two witnesses blown to smithereens.

Midsentence, one of the witnesses lifted his long pointy finger toward the three men. Even in the back they were not hidden. His eyes were as sharp as arrows. His strong angled face reflected his resolve. An eerie chill ran down their spines. "You are weighed in the balances of God. He has found that you are wanting" (Daniel 5:27). The ominous words rang through the air and deposited themselves on the three onlookers.

Out of the crowd below ran a man. He was almost to the witnesses. "Stop!" rang the command from one of the witnesses. As was expected, the suicide bomber burst into flames. But why didn't he blow up? He was loaded with enough explosives to take out the two witnesses and all those nearby. They looked at each other; then they saw that long finger pointing at them again.

The witness' strong voice rang through the air. His dark eyes looked directly into their ashen, fear-covered faces. "God has judged you and you are found wanting." *Poof!* The fire shot through the air like a bolt of lightning at the three assassins. They exploded into flames; their flesh melted off their bodies as they looked in agony at the two witnesses. "No!" they screamed. There was gnawing and gnashing of teeth; as they burned, their bodies fell unrecognizable to the ground.

The crowd watched in horrified silence as the three assassins died. The witness called out to the guards who patrolled the place where they preached. These men were given orders to watch and wait for an opportunity to kill the two witnesses. "Remove them!" the command roared through the air. The nearby guards ran quickly to obey the men who seemed to breathe fire at anyone who displeased them. Their hearts raced as they realized, once again, they had better not try to stop these two preachers.

The two witnesses continued, "You are the seed of Abraham. God has not forgotten you. He has not turned from being your God. He says to you return to the God of your fathers. Remember the faithfulness of Abraham, Isaac, and Jacob. You are their seed. You are a peculiar people of the Lord (Deuteronomy 14:2). You are not here by accident. He has remembered you. He is calling you to him to be his own once again. He will return to fight for you. He sent his Son, Jesus, to die for your sins. He was the last sacrifice. You are not left off to be forgotten and destroyed. You are the original branches. He calls to you, "Come unto me, all ye that labour and are heavy laden, and I will give you rest. Take my yoke upon you, and learn of me; for I am meek and lowly in heart: and ye shall find rest unto your souls. For my yoke is easy, and my burden is light" (Matthew 11:28–30).

Their words expounded Jesus from Abraham all the way to Isaiah the prophet. "But he was wounded for our transgressions, he was bruised for our iniquities: the chastisement of our peace was upon him; and with his stripes we are healed" (Isaiah 53:5). "He was oppressed, and he was afflicted, yet he opened not his mouth: he is brought as a lamb to the slaughter, and as a sheep before her shearers is dumb, so he openeth not his mouth (Isaiah 53:7). He calls to you now, receive the gift of salvation from Jesus your kinsman redeemer. He is your next of kin. He is your older brother who has come to redeem you by clearing your debt. Come they beckoned come" (Ruth 4).

Many brave and weary souls rose from their place of listening, their hearts watered by the words of redemption that brought hope. They rushed to the prophets for prayer, thankful to God for the two witnesses, and gave their souls to Jesus. The Scriptures lined up forming the answers they had waited for all of their lives. Jesus is the son of the Living God—their Messiah!

The Antichrist sat plagued by the latest report of the loss of his three assistants. It wasn't that he would miss them or even that he felt any compassion for them. It was just that he simply could not rid himself of those two pests. They reminded him of the rat problem he had once experienced—only these two were much more annoying. He decided to speak to them personally.

He ventured toward his destination late that evening. Darkness had fallen, cloaking him as he slipped through the gates of the temple. He watched until the two witnesses were resting. Then he quickly slipped through the shadows toward his purpose. A dark, hideously disgusting voice spoke. Its sound, one of endless torment, echoed its path through the mouth of the Antichrist. "Why have you chosen to perplex me at this time?" he asked as though he did not know the Scriptures. "You know I have been given power to rule (Revelation 13:1–9). Why are you intruding?" The fork of his tongue slipped out as he spoke, revealing his true identity, his good looks changing to the vile individual he really was. The body he inhabited barely masked the ugliness of the being living in it. He could not hide from these mighty men of God.

The two witnesses faced Satan. They were familiar with his twisted way. "You know we are here for a specific purpose. Our coming has been foretold. You are not to interfere until the time is fulfilled. Then you will have your way for a very short season" (Revelation 11:3–12).

"God himself will destroy you, serpent." The prophet spoke the words with anger. His words jumped out like arrows striking the man of sin. You will be bound in chains" (Revelation 20).

A shiver went through the host body of Satan. A snarl marred the perfect mouth of his host as the ugly being inside looked with hatred on the two mighty men of God. The pungent stench of sulfur wafted through the air as he fought to attack them.

Their robes of sackcloth changed to garments of pure white as their humble dwelling lit up with the glow of the heavens. Satan raised his arm to cover his eyes, shielding them from the brightness of God's love. "He that is Faithful and True will judge you. You will be cast into the lake of fire (Revelation 19 and 20:10). You have lost the battle. Your destiny is sealed. You cannot change that. You are unforgiven!"

Unforgiven, unforgiven, unforgiven. The words echoed, repeating themselves over and over in the ears of Satan. The words of the witnesses rang through the air. They were carried by an unseen wind that started with his fall from heaven where Satan and his companions were first banished (Isaiah 14:12–17, Luke 10:18). They rang from the garden of Eden and whirled through the history of time into eternity. The being in front of them completely unmasked was a helpless, faltering demon who had thrown away eternity with God for the purpose of sin. The scales on his back rippled as he fought angrily to harm them but could not. They watched his display with detached disgust. "This is the man men fear?" (Isaiah 14:16–17) they asked themselves. Then with a nod they walked away from him, leaving him writhing in anger. How dare they dismiss him as though he were nothing? He slithered back toward his palace, a plan forming in his twisted mind as he oozed away. He would have his way. They would be killed. It was written (Revelation 11:3–12).

The two witnesses turned and watched him slip out of sight. They knew their destiny. For now he could not touch them. The time was short. They must spend it wisely. As they looked at each other, words were unnecessary. Each of them understood what the other was thinking. For now they would pray and rest: soon the people would return. They would preach again tomorrow.

The sun brought followers of the two witnesses to the temple. Their ancient garments billowed around them, flapping in the wind as they began once again to preach Jesus Christ and him crucified. Their long beards, white from age, reached down to their waists as they stood calmly expounding the Word of God. Their brown eyes glowed with fire as they spoke of the love of

God. "Only he can change you: only he can take away your sin."
The audience listened, captivated by the words of God's unending love. "Peace can fill your souls. This is not the peace of this
world. We speak of the peace of God. His peace passes understanding. His peace can keep you even in the face of death. The
peace God gives is supernatural. It is the only real peace men can
ever know. If you want this peace, God is willing to give it to you.
All you need to do is ask" (John 3:16, 14:27).

The tender hearts of the broken, persecuted people were
touched by their words. Reuben sat quietly listening. He leaned
in wanting to hear everything. All of his life had been filled with
turmoil. Violence had shaken and threatened his country. His
people had endured generations of hatred. But they had continued. They were still here. But peace had eluded them. His hungry
soul longed for that precious hope. Could a man really have peace
even in a time of war? Even when faced with death? Could it be
that the very thing he had longed for all of his life was Christ?
Would he actually come and live inside of him? Was there truly a
peace man could not rob him of? His eyes shimmered with tears
as he thought of true peace. He caught the eyes of the old man
and smiled (Psalm 85:8; John 14:27, 16:33; and Romans 5:1).

The speaker looked at him kindly with the compassion of a
grandfather counseling his only grandson. The man of God continued, "God has a purpose for your life. You are not here by
accident. You are part of his plan. He has been waiting for you to
hear his voice. He wants you to know that you are very valuable to
him. You are the apple of his eye (See Deuteronomy 32:10). He
pities you as a father pities his children (See Psalm 103:13). You
are not abandoned. You are priceless beyond measure."

The young man smiled as the words of love took root in his
weary heart. The many years of trouble seemed a far and distant sorrow. He felt the warmth of God's love penetrate his soul.
It filled all of the empty, tired, war-ravaged places with joy he
could not express. The peace of God was more than man's peace.

It was confidence in God. It was true understanding of God's love for him. This understanding took away the grief. It displaced the love of sin with a new love. This love surpassed the love of a woman. It was completeness with God. The years of separation from the Lord melted away as Reuben and many others received the promise of the Messiah. The years of waiting for the Christ ended when he asked Jesus to come into his heart.

Reuben felt revitalized. His days without hope were ended. For the first time in his life he was completely at peace. He released his breath. The air felt cleaner. He felt cleaner. He felt free! Free from the cares of life and the sorrows that had so weighed him down only moments ago. They were taken away. He was as light as a feather. He rejoiced from the depth of his soul. *I am free.* The words beat their path from his heart to his head. *I am free at last!*

The day ended with many salvations. Now, of course, Reuben and others like him were in even more danger. There was only one thing worse than being a Christian or a Jew to the new regime—that was being a Christian Jew; but for now, he was content to just know Christ as his Savior.

WORLD DOMINATION

The Antichrist glanced at the map on his office wall. Each pin was placed strategically to indicate his most recent endeavors. He had maneuvered cunningly to achieve his current position. For some time now he had control of the Israelis. He had convinced them to work with him. He smiled as he remembered it was his work with Israel that shot him to world recognition. *Now I have achieved peace where no one has succeeded before.*

Since the disappearances the world had continued to go to war. It was a time of turmoil. Many nations, who had always disagreed, fought with each other. He moved his mammoth military might into position and demanded they surrender. One by one he had taken authority over the obstinate countries. No one questioned anything about his policing the world. He was, after all, the world president. It was his duty to keep order.

He had plundered and prospered everywhere; in his wake he left fear and trembling. The people of every nation he challenged were given no options. They were forced into submission. His military strength was superior to any other.

It was now three years since he was given the assignment by the United Community to bring stability to the Middle East, by finding a way to bring Israel on board with the world plans. His heart beat faster as he considered the ruse. Israel had posed a problem for him. They did not suffer the afflictions of the rest of the world. Even in the face of insurmountable difficulties, they maintained their military strength. They were unwilling to give up control of their land. They remained strong in the face of the world economy. He knew what it would take to keep his backers happy: he had to show himself to be a true statesman. He had studied out this problem; he knew how to reach them.

They were a gentle people who desired peace more than anything else. He laughed as he thought on their Achilles heel. His mouth curved into a full smile. He had put his plans into motion. He sent ambassadors to meet with the leaders of the most envied people on earth. "My brothers," he spoke words of comfort to the people of the land. "I come to you in the name of peace. We desire to protect you from your enemies." His words softened the hearts of the people. His magnetic personality had enchanted them. He was careful to appear kind. He encouraged them. "Peace, peace, I say peace be upon you." Bowing low he lovingly humbled himself.

Oh, the promise of peace, not since the days of the great King Solomon had Israel been completely at rest. Behind closed doors the Israelis discussed his offer. The politicians weighed in. "He is not being unreasonable. He is asking us to be allies. We have an opportunity to live without the daily threat of attack. He has powerful backing from the United Community. These countries promise us their friendship."

The general fired back, anger evident in his voice. "He wants us to lay down our weapons! We will be as vulnerable as the rest of the world." His face glowed crimson red as his blood pressure raced up. "We cannot allow Israel to be overrun by strangers!"

The prime minister listened to his friends. Finally he spoke up. "We are not giving away our freedom to this man. We are simply agreeing to be at peace. If we go to war, we cannot sustain ourselves in our present position. We are surrounded by enemies. These are countries he influences. They will listen to him. He offers us the branch of friendship."

The general stood to his feet. "The branch of friendship at what price? What you are proposing is treason against the sovereignty of our state! I will not be a part of destroying my country."

He turned his back to the politicians, storming away from those who would not listen.

Turning to the messengers, the prime minister of Israel said, "Please tell the president we will be happy to discuss his proposal."

The messenger smiled and bowed politely, "My pleasure, prime minister."

The president arrived the next day. Walking over to the prime minister, he kissed him on both cheeks. "My brother," he smiled as they shook hands.

Reporters clicked pictures. "This is a monumental accomplishment for the president and the prime minister." Barbara Lamb, reporter for WNCB, announced. "The president and the prime minister are planning to spend the day working on the details. The prime minister has graciously offered Israeli assistance with the world challenges. There are rumors that Israel is willing to implement programs that will help alleviate hunger around the world. With all of the natural disasters that have taken place, the economic crash and the disappearances, the people have been left hanging in limbo. They have agreed to sit down and work out a plan that will benefit both the Israeli people and the world. I understand, Bob, that part of the discussion will include the president agreeing to protect Israel from her enemies."

"That's right, Barbara. Israel has been in constant danger. The president has the means and the strength to protect Israel from imminent current threats."

Israel made a covenant with the president. They agreed to sign a Peace Treaty. "We will do our part to help feed the world." They said, "It is a small price to pay for peace."

"And you agree that for our protection, you, as a nation, will be subordinate to the desires of the United Community as one of our greatest allies?"

"Yes, Mr. President, with the understanding that we are still our own nation. We do not want to be absorbed into the one-world union. Israel has to remain intact as a sovereign nation."

He nodded. "I have no problem with that. I believe we have reached an agreement."

The men and women who had already voted to allow the president to be their voice to the world started to clap. One by one they stood to their feet, cheering, "Long live the president. Long live Israel. Long live the president, our friend!"

At last Israel sat in safety. For the first time in many years they were at peace. It had come at a price. But hadn't everyone given up something in order to bring about this time of hope? The world had been turned upside down; unbelievable plagues ravaged the earth. Famine was in virtually every country but theirs. The Israeli officials worked around the clock offering food, water, and medical supplies to their friends and allies. They had agreed to help their neighbors as well. True to his word, the president extended his protection. He would guard their nation. They would supply food.

The tiny nation of Israel was surrounded by enemies who longed to swallow them up. And to the north lay the great land of Russia. Russia, for a long while, had supported their enemies. Asia presented a problem too. They formed a massive army. They had formed an alliance with the world president. He would not permit them to come against Israel. Finally, peace was possible.

The politics of the world president was simple. He who has plenty shares with others. No one does without.

ASSASSINATION

The Antichrist grew more powerful with every passing day. The years that had passed since the disappearances had left the people of the world in need. He promised hope. They followed him as though he were God.

But there were those who hated him. Many of them were his former allies. In a far room of the palace, late at night, they plotted secretly. Each man was a force to be reckoned with, a power in his own right. "He is too full of himself. He should know without being told that we are not his subjects."

One of the men sat listening to his friends. He was in his middle sixties and slim. His suit was tailored to perfection. The salt and pepper in his hair added an air of dignity. He spoke clearly; his tone thoughtful. "He has become a liability. He has forgotten his promises. Perhaps he needs to be reminded. Notify our people in the field. They are to move in and wait for our orders."

The plot was set. All they needed was a scapegoat. They worked out a contingency plan, just in case, developing the necessary strategy. They had a man in the field. He was no longer stable. Years of work no person should be expected to do had unhinged him. "It's true. The world president is nothing more than a devil. He is the Antichrist. What is wrong with everybody? Why can't they see that he is pure evil?" His eyes held a hint of insanity as he spoke.

His fellow agent listened as he ranted and raved about the world president. "I have orders for you." He handed the man a packet. "I think you're going to enjoy this assignment. Remember, no one moves until we receive the final go on this."

The Antichrist had commissioned the building of a statue in his image. They started work on it almost as soon as he took office. The Medium of Most Excellent Service swooned with anticipation. "It will be the greatest monument in history. He will speak. I promise you." The medium had been working with the designer to install a few interesting features into the statue. "He will have your voice. We have even found a way to reflect your expressions on his face."

"How will you manage that?" the president asked.

"We have a chip that can control the statue. It will be totally lifelike. The crews are working night and day. It will be ready soon."

"Are the workers aware of the modifications?"

"No, Mr. President, only the engineer and I. Of course, the laborers have helped with the movable parts, but no one knows why."

"I don't want this engineer talking to anyone; is that understood?"

The medium spoke in a calm, pleasing voice. "I have already explained the need for discretion. He assures me he has shared his designs with no one."

"Good." The Antichrist thought for a moment as the medium waited. "Once the monument is completed, see to it that this engineer has an accident."

"Yes, sir, I have already made plans."

His meeting ended with the medium. The president welcomed his longtime friend and confidant. "Welcome, welcome, my dear friend." Affectionately he shook his old friend's hand and kissed both cheeks. They sat, ate, drank, and talked as friends.

The visitor was not easily deceived; after their conversation he was satisfied. The president was interested only in himself. Anything he believed would advance his position was the only concern of this power-thirsty leader. He did not apologize for his behavior. He did not find it necessary to consult with his allies. It was obvious the president would not fulfill his original agreement. The visitor focused his attention to the map on the wall behind the president. He made a mental note. He didn't realize it when they first voted the president into power, but the president was far too ambitious. He would not stop until he had control of every nation, including the very countries who had given him authority.

The president sat comfortably, explaining, "I know many do not approve of the alliance with Israel. This is a temporary thing. Remind our mutual friends that I am the one they chose to lead at this time. I must be given the freedom to lead according to what I feel is best for everyone."

The president had forgotten all too soon what their objectives were. As this visitor listened to the polite talk of this man of sin, he knew there was no love in him for anyone or any cause but his own. This man lacked faithfulness. The sly visitor said what he had come to say. He confirmed what he needed to know. They could not expect any loyalty from this man they had so recently trusted. He stood up, shook his friend's hand, and smiling, he said, "Good-bye, my friend," as he left the meeting with the president.

They would not tolerate insubordination from this man. The United Community, once ten, had risen to thirteen. He and his friends represented three of them. They had helped put the president into his position. They would take him out. They still had some loyalty to mankind. A new leader would be elected, someone more docile; his old friend was no longer useful. He left the meeting with the president, walking through the oversize doors. He looked at his man in place, then with a slight, barely detectible nod from him to the president's bodyguard he left. The plan was now set in motion.

The next day the president was to speak to his people. He had planned a mercy mission that would bring him in contact with his adoring public. The day was warm, the weather perfect. He was escorted down the long city streets by his own police. They had every available squad car.

Men and women reached out to the Antichrist as his car drove slowly past them. The streets were lined with armed guards. Shouts of adoration rang through the air. The limousine stopped near the steps of the building. He jumped out of the car, full of life. His long, slim body moved easily up the steps. His beautiful blue silk suit caught the sun, shimmering as he moved. His stark-white shirt glistened against his beautiful tanned skin. The shirt was accented by a tie of cobalt blue, cranberry, and gold. He stopped on the steps, turned, and waved at his adoring fans. They worshipped him. He was handsome, articulate, a man of purpose. The crowd cheered as he turned to wave. Turning back toward the door, he took the rest of the steps two at a time, his youthful strength propelling him up the beautiful stone steps. Ornately carved pillars stood ascending toward heaven, their broad white forms resplendent against the blue sky.

Out from the side of the building a man emerged. His hand held a weapon. His face seemed to reflect the anguish of a troubled man. He raised his hand intending to shoot. Before he could fire, the two men nearest him rushed him; pushing him to the ground they disarmed him.

In the midst of the chaos, a distant shot whistled through the air. It drew the attention of the crowd. People ducked and ran for cover: one lone shot, then nothing. The people watched helplessly, their beloved leader lying in a pool of blood.

"He's been shot!" someone shouted. "The president, they've shot the president. Somebody help, the president has been hit!"

His bodyguard was near him. He had seen the glistening of the sniper's rifle barrel in the appointed place. The bodyguard did not throw himself in front of the president. He watched as the president of the world took the deadly shot. A small, almost indiscernible smile touched his lips. They had succeeded. They couldn't have planned it better. That nutcase had supplied a distraction at the perfect time. Quickly he rushed into cover-up mode. "Stay back, stay back," he said, pushing away the onlookers as though he was interested in the well-being of his boss. Blood was everywhere. The screams of the people were thunderous as they rushed to save their President. Immediately the world president was ushered off to the hospital where a doctor pronounced him dead on arrival. The lost soul of the man of sin was pulled by a dark force into the abyss of hell.

The statue was now finished. The Antichrist had made plans for the celebration to take place in three days. The medium made the arrangements. Tears welled up in his eyes as he tried to speak. "We will bury him near the monument."

Three days passed; the nations mourned. The Antichrist lay in a casket, on a platform built at the base of the monument, for all to see. The ugly scar had been covered by the best make-up artist in the business. They had filled in the wound as much as possible. The people wanted to look at him one last time. They held a prayer vigil led by the Medium of Most Excellent Service. The news of his death was broadcast everywhere. All the channels carried the same report. The wound to his head had instantly killed him. The nations mourned as men and women tried to understand why anyone would want to hurt him.

"He was the best of us," one man said, grief overwhelming him to the point of being unable to say anything else.

The trauma of the last three days left people shaken. They could not see how the world could go on without his insight, his talent, and his own brand of politics, which left the whole world feeling loved and appreciated.

Deloris, an older lady in her sixties, said with her hanky over her nose, "It's just senseless. We are all—every nation among us—less because of his death." She bent down, placing a wreath of roses near his casket.

As the world mourned and wrote songs about their beloved leader, Satan watched his gullible worshippers. The testimonies and eulogies continued.

John, Carly, Paul, and Shelby sat glued to the television. They watched it together, unable to grasp the grief these individuals felt. A strange sense of foreboding settled in on them. They were unable to take their eyes off the spectacle. They knew, of course—they understood—he would rise again. Prophesy foretold it. The Bible explains that the Antichrist is the beast.

> And I saw one of his heads as it were wounded to death; and his deadly wound was healed: and all the world wondered after the beast. And they worshipped the dragon which gave power unto the beast: and they worshipped the beast, saying, Who is like unto the beast? who is able to make war with him? And there was given unto him a mouth speaking great things and blasphemies; and power was given unto him to continue forty and two months.
>
> Revelation 13:3–5

He would be raised from the dead, as is plainly stated in the Scriptures. Things were really going to get ugly now. Look out, the man of sin—the beast—is going to come back to life, completely and fully possessed by Satan himself. The world is in terrible trouble!

Satan is still up to the same evil that got him thrown out of heaven. He yearns to be worshipped. In heaven he had everything. He was an angel loved by everyone. He was beautiful in appearance, but he became haughty. Pride was his real sin.

The Bible records, "For thou hast said in thine heart, I will ascend into heaven, I will exalt my throne above the stars of God: I will sit also upon the mount of the congregation, in the sides of the north: I will ascend above the heights of the clouds; I will be like the most High" (Isaiah 14:13–14).

What was he thinking? The creature equal to the creator—this is preposterous! But still he tried. He was thrown out of heaven. The Bible records Jesus as witness, "And he said unto them, 'I beheld Satan as lightning fall from heaven'" (Luke 10:18).

He is the one who rides on the four horses of the apocalypse. He loves no one. His only existence is to steal, kill, and to destroy (John 10:10). His goal is to drag the soul of every living person into hell.

The wind blew furiously as the world mourned for their leader. Barbara Lamb covered the burial service. Her voice broke, the only evidence of just how shaken she was. "We are here today, Bob, waiting for the medium to conduct the service. He, along with many other handpicked speakers, will be giving the eulogy. They have had several concerts, along with many magnificent displays of diverse cultures. The medium planned it to pay homage to his lifetime of achievements; he worked so hard to bring unity to the world. He would have delighted in the many nations who are represented here today. It is a true reflection of his life's endeavors. The medium is just now walking up to the podium. He is greeting the leaders of the churches as well as those of many other faiths." The camera followed the medium's trek to the front. A gasp sounded in the crowd.

Bob said, "Barbara, we just heard a stirring from the crowd the camera isn't catching..." His voice trailed off as another camera zoomed in on the world president.

On the third day of the death of the Antichrist, the world watched as he lay sleeping forever. Why was this great leader cut down in the prime of his life? All at once he moved. He gasped, taking in a deep breath. The entire world watched as the dead body of the man of sin became completely inhabited by Satan. He sat up. His entourage rushed to his side to help him out of the casket. He walked directly to the podium. "My beloved friends," he said to the cheers and screams of the crowd. "I am not dead; behold, I live. I am the one you have waited for. I am your king. I am the Messiah, the Son of God."

The medium ran to his friend. He bowed humbly at his feet. It took a moment for the medium to raise himself from his position of adoration, to speak to the crowd. After quieting their cheers, he said, "Who is like our king? Who can be compared to him? Isn't he the messiah? Worship him—he has proven he is God!" The world bowed and worshipped their king.

Sorrow swept over Christians as an impostor declared he was Christ. John, Carly, Paul, and Shelby fell on their knees. Paul prayed. "The time is short. The Antichrist has risen. Daily we are seeing the word of God fulfilled. Give us the courage to face the temptation that is coming. Help us, Father, to fight the good fight, to finish the course." Time stood still as they, along with Christians from all over the world, prayed for strength to endure to the end.

Israel watched in awe as a dead man stood to his feet! The resurrection was something out of a science fiction movie. Was this the Messiah they had waited for? Now free of death's chains, the man of sin smiled. Oh dear God, the land of Israel and the world did not know it, but true sorrow was on its way.

The two witnesses discerned the spectacle. They knew they only had a few short minutes left to preach. From the Wailing Wall, where many had gathered for the burial, they interrupted the airways carrying the resurrection and consequential worship of the Antichrist. They were appalled. They railed against the Antichrist. "He is a blasphemer!" All the major networks throughout the world carried them live as they began to rage at sin, injustice, and abomination in the earth. They pointed toward the temple, calling the world president the beast, declaring in no uncertain terms that he was an impostor. Their words were scathing. They had no mercy. "You are all breaking the law of God! He will judge you for your idolatry. This man is nothing more than

Satan calling himself God." Their eyes blazed with fire as they pointed at the Antichrist and shouted, "You are defeated, Satan! God has sentenced you!" They continued to reprimand the worshippers, condemning them for their sins!

The crowd that had gathered near the Wailing Wall grew angry. They would not allow their accusations to continue. One of the listeners started to run, furiously pulling out his hair. He screamed unintelligibly, running toward the two men.

"Stop!" was the command that came from one of the prophets as he pointed at the man. Immediately fire left his mouth and consumed the man, burning him alive in front of everyone.

"My husband!" the scream came from a woman who reached for the burning man. She was grabbed and held back by a man in the crowd. "They are demons!" she declared.

Another mad man tried to do what the first had failed to do. He lifted his gun. Once again one of the prophets yelled, "Stop!" Fire shot from his mouth, consuming the man as they watched.

These prophets continued to preach. The crowd did not move. The fire of their sermons burned deep in the hearts of the listeners. It was the kind of fire that consumes everyone in its path. But this was not a literal fire; it was a fire of the soul. Their words spoke of repentance, change, eternity, hell. When they spoke of hell, the listeners could literally smell the sulfur as they talked.

The troubled crowd couldn't stand it any longer. They cried out, "Kill them! Kill them!" The police rushed them to take them away for disturbing the peace. They too were consumed by flames so hot that those closest to them were also burned. Many ambulances came and went as these two witnesses continued to list, one by one, the sins of the world.

Their eyes held captive anyone who looked on them. They were men without substance, yet they lacked nothing. They had preached for hours every day for the last three and a half years, never changing their opinions. Who could stand before them? Who could answer them? The people of the world were weighed in the balances of God and found wanting. These men held court: the world was tried and convicted of their sins. Guilty! Guilty! The verdict was heard in the hearts of all those who worshipped the beast. They covered their ears refusing to listen. But still, they could not ignore the words that had been burned into their hearts.

Their accusations tormented the Antichrist. He began to sweat profusely. His heart raced. He was unable to catch his breath. His staff escorted him to a quiet place to rest.

"What are your symptoms?" his doctor asked as he checked his heartbeat.

"Leave me alone!" he pushed the doctor away. He looked at the general. "I want them dead, do you hear me? How dare they speak against me?" He loosened the tie at his throat. He could smell the suffocating odor of sulfur as their ranting continued to ring in his ears. The heat of hell warmed him as he remembered the flames that had surrounded him. The Antichrist screamed furiously, "Kill them! I don't want them here tomorrow!"

"But, sire, we cannot..." His words stopped short as the general faced the king.

The world king quoted from the Word of God.

> And I will give power unto my two witnesses, and they shall prophesy a thousand two hundred and threescore days, clothed in sackcloth. And when they shall have finished their testimony, the beast that ascendeth out of the bottomless pit shall make war against them, and shall overcome them, and kill them. And their dead bodies shall lie in the street of the great city, which spiritually is called Sodom and Egypt, where also our Lord was crucified.
>
> Revelation 11:3, 7–8

"You see, General, it is written. I am declaring war against them." His fist hit the desk as he bellowed the words. "Kill them! Kill them now!" His face glowed crimson as he fought to regain control.

The general bowed. "We will do all that is in our power to put an end to them, sire." Then he left.

The general called in his troop. The air was disturbed by the sound of a tank moving slowly toward the two witnesses. As it crawled down the streets, the people began to turn and watch as they guessed its destination. It moved into position in front of the witnesses. "Fire at will," the general commanded. The soldier held his breath. He had watched his friends die for trying to kill these two. The thought made his mouth feel dry as cotton. Sweat poured off him. He wiped the moisture from his brow, took aim, and fired. The first witness fell to the ground. Quickly, he fired again; the second body lay next to his friend.

They were dead.

At last the men who tormented the people day and night were silenced. The onlookers began to cheer, laugh, and dance in the streets.

The general ordered the burial of the witnesses, but the crowd wouldn't allow it. "Leave them there!" they protested. "Let the world see they are finally dead." He sent word to the king.

The servant went directly to the king to tell him the news. "The two witnesses are dead, sire. But the people are insisting their bodies remain in the streets."

The Antichrist smiled his cruel smile and said, "Tell the general to leave them there. Let the people enjoy our victory."

"Yes, sire." He bowed and left the king.

The people of the world rejoiced over the news of the two witnesses. They declared it a holiday and lavished each other with gifts. Three and a half days passed. The two witnesses' bodies lay undisturbed in the streets of Jerusalem. The heavens opened up. The voice of the Lord spoke to them, "Arise and come up!" They woke to resurrected bodies! The people watching them looked on helplessly as the two witness stood to their feet, alive. They were taken up to God in a cloud in front of those who hated them! (Revelation 11:7–13).

The earth began to shake. Buildings toppled, and men and women fought for their lives. They ran for cover. After the shaking stopped, Barbara Lamb spoke to her affiliate. "It has been terrible, Bob. The bodies of the two witnesses are missing; many are saying they were raised from the dead! The city has taken quite a hit. They are still looking for survivors. The number is expected to be in the thousands. Standing here beside me is an eyewitness. "Sir, you witnessed the earthquake; can you tell us about it?"

"First the clouds split. It was incredible. Then a great voice from heaven blasted the earth. I mean, it felt as though it shook it. The voice commanded the two witnesses to come up. I tell you they were raised from the dead! They stood to their feet and I watched them go up to God. Immediately the earth began to shake and buildings everywhere began to fall. I don't know how I escaped; I ran for my life. God raised them from the dead! This earthquake is a demonstration of his power. I heard the voice of God with my own ears. And I saw them raised from the dead with my own eyes! This is the hand of God himself."

Barbara seemed discombobulated as the man finished his testimony. "Well, Bob, that is pretty much what everyone here who witnessed the event has been saying. They are all saying the same thing—they heard the voice of God and that God raised the two witnesses from the dead! It is really remarkable. I simply have nothing more to add to that. This is Barbara Lamb. I'm reporting from location in Jerusalem. Back to you, Bob."

Bob closed the program with, "Keep it here, folks, for moment-to-moment reporting. Thank you and good-bye."

The first three and a half years were past. The second three and a half had begun. The world was in trouble. Sorrow such as has never been lay ahead of mankind.

An angel placed the mark of God on 144,000 of the Jews, 12,000 from each tribe. They were anointed. They were the firstborn who had kept themselves from women. They spent their days serving the Lord (Revelation 7:2–9).

THE DAY THE EARTH QUAKED

Carly heard something fall. "John!" she screamed. "What's happening?" Even as she asked the question, her mind filled in the blank.

"It's an earthquake," John confirmed. The house was shaking hard. He threw himself over Carly, rolling them both off the bed, then pulled at the mattress, forcing it over them. They felt the thud of something heavy hit the bed beside them. "Oh God!" Carly screamed. She felt panic rising; her heart raced with fear. She buried her face in her hands, waiting for it to stop.

John pulled her closer to him. "It's okay, honey." The rumbling continued. She could hear items falling off the shelves and glass breaking everywhere. It should have stopped, but it didn't. The rumble beneath them shook the house. Carly could barely breathe; she panicked. Her heart was in her throat. Finally it stopped.

John crawled out from under the mattress. As he did, his hand was sliced by a sharp object. "Don't move, Carly; there's glass everywhere." He looked for something to protect his feet from being cut. His shoes were nowhere in sight. He grabbed the comforter, shook it out, then threw it over the bed. He climbed onto it for protection. Then he moved to the other side of the bed where he had left his slippers. After a moment he located them and put them on. His hand was bleeding, so he grabbed a handkerchief and wrapped it around his hand. He pulled the mattress back onto the box springs.

Carly emerged from her cocoon. As she did, she took a look around. Her slippers were covered by debris that had fallen from the nightstand. She worked to get to them. "Oh, John," she said as she stood up, looking around at the damage.

"Just a minute, Carly; I have to cut off the gas to the house." He ran out the door to the location of the gas pipe valve. There was debris everywhere. Trees were down and cars were moved out of their locations. He worked to finish his task.

He knew he should check on his neighbors. He ran next door to Mrs. Lawson's; she was walking around, looking as baffled as he felt, but she seemed to be okay. "I just wanted to know if you were all right."

"I'm fine, Johnny, how's Carly?" She was one of the few people who still called him Johnny. Somehow he never minded hearing it from her. She was a good neighbor who had always offered her friendship. His mother had spent many hours talking to her about the Lord, but she was angry with God. She could never get past her son's death. "Why would God allow my son to die?" she would ask.

Mary Jenkins would always tell her, "God loved Doyle." She would try to explain that accidents happen even to good people. "I don't know why he died, but you have to understand that God loved Doyle and he loves you. He didn't allow him to die to hurt you. We don't always know the why of things. Sometimes we just have to believe that God does what is best for us and the people we love, even when it feels so wrong." Mary Jenkins would plead with her, "Please don't let this stand between you and the Lord. I'm going to keep praying for you, honey. You know I love you."

After Mary disappeared, Mrs. Lawson came to church. She was quick to give her heart to the Lord. John was touched that his mother's prayers had not been forgotten by God. Mrs. Lawson was a sweetheart who spent most of her time helping at the church.

"Carly's a little shook up, but she'll be fine. You let us know if you need anything." She nodded. He excused himself then ran to the next house, and the next.

He talked with Rick Jordan down the street. "We've been checking with everyone on our block too. Harry has Third Street covered. Karen Wallace was trapped under some debris at her place. Man, you should see the mess. Harry and some guys got her right out. Harry's son is taking her to the hospital. Thanks, man, for asking. I guess we'll all be cleaning up for a while." He shook his head, unable to absorb the destruction.

John said, "Well, I better get back to Carly."

"Sure, John. I understand. I'll see you later." Rick waved good-bye as John ran back up the road toward home.

Carly met him on his way back. She was dressed but still looked a little pale. "I have been checking with the neighbors. They are all okay." He stopped at an empty home to turn off another gas valve. He ran across the street to the vacant house. The owners were gone since the rapture. "There." He shut off the gas as well.

Carly breathed a sigh of relief. "John, I wasn't even thinking about all of that, and you've already taken care of the block." She shook her head. "You're amazing. No wonder I love you so much."

The earth began to tremble again; she grabbed his arm. "It's an aftershock," he said, helping her back to the house. The rumble stopped.

"John, your hand." She studied him, alarmed, noticing blood oozing from the handkerchief.

He looked at it as if it were nothing. "Oh, don't worry about that. Let's go inside, I'll put something on it." He went into the bathroom. Everything, from the medicine cabinet, was on the floor. He rummaged through the debris and located the hydrogen peroxide. He poured some of the fluid over his hand and let it bubble for a few seconds, repeating this a few times.

Carly was at his side. She found the bandages and some anti-bacterial salve. She placed them on the injury then looked up at him. "That should do it."

John began to assess the damage to their home. He walked through each room, picking up items that had been turned over. John had moved into his parent's home after the rapture. Once they were married, she joined him. John believed it was safer and more structurally sound than their old apartment. Since they knew earthquakes were coming, he was concerned for their safety.

The house was built solidly and dependably, like his father. The structure had withstood the quake. He noticed some cracks in the Sheetrock but no real damage had occurred. His mind raced to his dad. They had spent time working on it, building it together. His dad was a good carpenter; he had taught John how to work with his hands. Some of the guys from church had even shown up to help with the construction.

His dad had wanted him to follow in his footsteps, but John had set that side of his life experiences aside for rock and roll. That was something he deeply regretted now. A pain of remembrance shot through his mind. The night before Jesus came he had played all night long at a local hot spot with his band. He had not given one thought to God as he drank. Now, thinking about it, he felt ashamed. How did he ever get to the point of turning his back on his background? He knew God loved him from the day he was born. Oh sure, he had continued to go to church. But that was mostly to make his mom and dad happy. He wanted them to be proud of him. He tried to help his dad out with services by stepping in where needed. Shame filled his heart. All he could do was ask, "What was I thinking?"

Carly said something to him. He turned to look at her. "I'm sorry, honey, I didn't hear you."

"I was just wondering if we still have plenty of bottled water in the garage."

"Yes, we do. As long as none of the bottles was damaged, we should be fine."

John grabbed a broom and started to sweep up the glass. Carly began to pick up some of her things that had fallen then went into the closet to locate the vacuum. She turned it on. Nothing. "I guess we don't have electricity," she said.

John moved the mattress where he could reach the box springs. He swept the glass out from between the box springs and the mattress into the pan. "Don't worry about it, honey. I'll get what I can with the broom. We'll just have to be sure we wear our shoes for the time being."

Another aftershock shook the house. Carly was standing near an open cabinet, replacing the items when it hit. "Ouch," she said, covering her head, as one of the items came whirling out of the cabinet onto her. She moved away from the cabinet. John grabbed her, pulling her out of the line of fire and covering her head with his arms. Carly didn't feel so good. She sat down, feeling lightheaded; the room was spinning.

"Carly," she heard him say from somewhere far away. "Carly," he said her name again. "Carly, wake up. Are you all right, honey?"

"Yea, I guess that bump on the head was worse than I thought." She rubbed her head. "Wow, do I have a headache!"

John did a quick examination. "I'm taking you to the hospital."

"Oh, don't be silly. I'll be fine. We have too much to do to worry about me."

John looked at her. She was pale. He started to insist. "You're going to the doctor."

"No, John, really I'm okay. Look, the hospitals are going to be full of people who are badly injured. And even if I do have a concussion, I can take care of myself. I promise I won't overdo. But honey, we won't be able to see anyone for hours. I can't go down there and just wait around. I'll be much more comfortable here."

John weighed her argument. "All right, under two conditions: I'll fix the bed so you can relax. I don't want you running around trying to clean up. I can take care of that." Carly started to object but John was adamant. "I mean it, Carly, I want you to rest. And if you become sick, we are taking you to the hospital immediately."

She gave in. The whole thing was a terrible inconvenience. She wanted to help John but knew he was not taking no for an answer. It was difficult, but she finally agreed, with the understanding that if she felt better later on he would not continue to treat her like a sick person.

John grabbed a bag of ice from the freezer. He wrapped it in a towel then handed it to her. "Try this, it should help." She placed it on the bump.

The cell phones began to ring. John answered them several times then changed the greetings to say, "Hello this is Pastor John and Carly. We are fine. We are unable to answer the phone now, but leave a message. We will get back to you as soon as possible." After setting them to vibrate mode, he began to straighten up the house so they could at least get around in it. He replaced the furniture and smaller items that had tipped over.

She joined him in the living room and decided, while he was putting the furniture back, she might as well have him place it to her liking. She loved Mom Jenkins, but there was an enormous difference in their opinions on decor. She winced as she leaned back, not wanting John to notice she was in pain. She bit her lip. Her head was really beginning to throb.

She finally had to give in. "John, could you please bring me a couple of aspirin?"

"Is your head still hurting?" he asked, coming over to place his hand on her forehead to check her temperature.

"Yeah, but I'm fine," she assured him. "A couple of aspirin should fix me up."

He disappeared into the bathroom. After a few minutes he returned with aspirin and a glass of water. "Thank God we have the bottled water," he said.

She sipped at the water and then lay back against the cushions. John assessed the damage. He should have done more than just move them here. He should have removed the dangerous items. He looked at the broken glass from the closet doors. Carly had asked him more than once to remove them, complaining they looked out of date. He had become so busy with church he just hadn't taken time to do the chores around home.

"Don't worry about it, honey," she said, reading his mind. "It's nothing we can't fix. As soon as you let me off medical leave, I'll get everything back to normal. Come, sit with me," she invited, patting the cushion beside her.

John sat down, pulling her next to him. "What a mess," he said.

"We're blessed, John; God took care of us. I can manage with the mess. I would be devastated without you." He smiled and held her. They comforted each other just by being together.

After a while, John said, "I have to start calling people." She agreed and let him go. He handed her a book to read, cautioning her not to fall asleep. "I think I'll call Rebecca. I want to know how she is doing anyway; and she'll know what to do for you."

Aftershocks shook the house several times that day. Some of them were almost as frightening as the earthquake. John set up a safe place for them to be comfortable and protected from debris. He pulled an overstuffed couch away from the windows. When the room would start to shake, he would cover them with the mattress he had hauled in from the bedroom. It was a long day, but the shaking finally ended.

Darkness began to fill the room. "It can't be night," she said. "Honey," Carly asked, "shouldn't it still be daytime?" (Revelation 6:12).

"Yeah," he answered. "Just a minute." John grabbed the coal oil lamp he had retrieved from the garage earlier. He lit the lamp, but it did nothing to rid the room of the night. He turned on his flashlight. There was a beam, but like the lamp it did no good. He turned the lamp and the flashlight off. "They're not helping, so we might as well save them for later. I'll have to check them during the daylight," he said, placing them aside.

John and Carly waited for the daylight hoping the sun would return. It did not come. The darkness grew more profound. As it settled in, John said, "Carly, I think it is the plague of darkness. The electricity is down from the earthquake and now this thick blackness." He shook as a little tremor went through him. This day was not like any other. The darkness was eerie.

The night grew deeper. Carly looked around trying to see something; fear began to make her shake. "John," she spoke his name through trembling lips. "I'm scared." She couldn't see him even though he was right next to her.

He reached out, pulling her into his arms. He said, "I'm here, babe, don't worry. I'm not going anywhere." He held her for several hours, waiting for the darkness to pass. They prayed, asking God to take care of their friends.

Then they began to talk. Even though it was the darkest night of their lives, they were safe, at least for now. They were together. God had kept them from harm. "Do you think we are being selfish?" she asked John. "I mean, here we are, comfortable; and we don't even know if our friends are okay. Were you able to reach anyone by phone?"

"No, the home phone isn't working and the cells are down also."

"Both of them," she asked?

"They need charging, and since we don't have any electric…" he let his words drop off. "Anyway, Carly, what could we do if we knew there was a problem? We can't see anything. Even when we use the lamp or the flashlight it's still too dark. We might as well relax and wait for the plague to be over. We can pray for our friends. Right now that's about all we can do."

They had been sustaining themselves with the water that he brought in from the garage. He had prepared for the earthquake and plagues by storing several-gallon jugs. He reached over, feeling for the jug they were drinking from. It was beginning to feel empty. "Honey, I'm going to get some more water. I also think I should get us something to eat. Will you be all right?"

"No," she panicked. "Don't leave me. What if something happens to you?"

He held her tight. "It's okay, Carly. I'll be right back. I promise."

She agreed to let him go if he hurried. John moved into the kitchen. He felt his way around, fishing through the cabinet for the peanut butter and jelly. He grabbed the bread; feeling his way along, he made a couple of sandwiches.

Carly was beginning to become chilled; she started to shiver. When John came back he found her clinging to the blanket. "Your hands are as cold as ice."

She stammered out, "It's freezing in here."

John said, "I'll be right back." He felt his way down the hall to the closet and retrieved a couple of blankets. After making sure Carly was warmer, he ventured out to the garage. "Here they are," he said to himself as he found another jug of water. Grabbing one, he felt around for his emergency radio. He decided to see if they could get any reception. Slowly he felt his way back to Carly. He turned on the radio, tuning it to a local station. There was no reception, only silence. "The transmitters must be down." He turned it off and settled down next to Carly.

He did not know how long it had been since Carly was first injured, but he kept her awake for several hours. She seemed scared but fine. After a while they both fell asleep.

Everywhere, Christians handled the plague of darkness just about the same. Those who had heeded the warning were prepared for this time. They waited for the day to shine again; while they did, they knew this was just the beginning.

John's sleep was disturbed by something. He opened his eyes; it was the sun. "Carly," he shook her. "Carly, wake up, it's daylight."

She opened her eyes, turning them quickly away from the light. "It's over!" she said, "Thank God."

He grabbed his Bible remembering a passage in Revelation; he read it carefully. Somberly he said, "It's not over, Carly. It's just begun."

She got up and went into the kitchen; grabbing a slice of bread she smothered it with peanut butter and jelly. She made one for John as well. "Okay, so it's not over. At least we get a break." She gave him his sandwich. "Now, eat. We can talk about the end of the world later." He grinned. His beard had grown out and he looked disheveled. She couldn't, for the life of her, figure out where he got that shirt, but he was the cutest thing she had seen in days.

～～

Rebecca had spent her time hanging out at the hospital. The past few days and nights had been a series of horrifying nightmares for her. She spent most of her time trying to comfort patients she could not see.

As daylight returned she was awakened by a light that hurt her eyes. "Daylight," she said to herself. She looked over to see that the patient she was comforting had died. She pushed aside the blanket she had been using. Her hand reached over to check the pulse of Mrs. Randolph. Nothing. Tears swam in the rims of her eyes. She recalled her patient's fear of being alone. She had spent the night in the chair next to her telling her about God. Mrs. Randolph had listened to every Bible story she could remember. Finally the woman fell asleep. "I'm sorry, Mrs. Randolph, I wish I could have done more," she said to the lovely lady.

She walked out of the room. In the hall the place was a mess. The structural damage was minimal, but patients had suffered. The earthquake had taken out the electricity. For some reason the generators had also failed. When the darkness set in, it was so black that light seemed to get lost in it. She shivered as she remembered the eerie feeling that took over the hospital. Patients could not be operated on. Machines were of no use. The staff couldn't see to disperse medication properly. The computers were down. They knew where some meds were, so, even in the dark, they did what they could to help ease their patients' suffering. But that was very little.

The hospital was full of patients who had passed. Many were too weak to endure the hardship of the last few days. She held her emotions in check as she and other staff members began to deal with the devastation from loss of life. One by one they were taken downstairs to the morgue. Finally she was sent home. "I mean it, Rebecca, go home and get some rest. We need you back here tomorrow."

After the earthquake, she stayed at the hospital. She thought about the damage and assumed driving would be a problem, so she decided to walk to her apartment. The sliding doors of the hospital slid open in front of her. *The generators must be working again,* she thought. Outside she could see the damage: the streets were rumpled, homes were flattened, trees were down. She stuffed her hands deep into her pockets and walked home hoping her apartment was still there.

She didn't realize she had been holding her breath until she rounded the corner to see her apartment building still standing. "Oh, thank you, God!" she shouted. "Thank you," she repeated a little quieter this time, not wanting to alert her neighbors to her faith. It was just easier to not say anything. People were hostile these days. She ran up the front steps of the building, pulled open the entry door and began climbing the steps to the third floor. To her relief, they seemed sturdy enough. She walked to her apartment and inserted the key. The door swung open. Her apartment was still in one piece. All of her pictures were on the floor. Her smaller appliances were shaken out of their spots; but, all in all, she felt blessed.

She turned on the kitchen faucet; to her delight, water rushed out just as always. "Thank you, God," she repeated again as she started to pick up the pieces of her home. By 10:00 p.m. she was done for the day. She went into the bathroom, drew a bath and soaked, trying to wash away the sorrow she had witnessed.

The pounding at her door persisted; finally she managed to cover herself with a robe. "Who is it?" she questioned.

"It's Mom," she heard her mother's voice.

"Mom!" she answered back. Opening the door to her apartment she flew into her mother's embrace.

"We've been so worried about you, dear. We called the hospital. They told us you were there for the whole ordeal. Dad and I decided to come and see you tonight."

She invited them into her apartment. Suddenly she felt chilled, self-conscious of her robe; she excused herself to dress. Her mother was making tea when she returned to the kitchen. "Dad and I have been talking; we want you to come home with us. It makes no sense, you being all the way across town from us in an emergency like this."

"Mom, I have to be near my work. I couldn't possibly move. I'm sorry, but I believe this is where I belong."

Rebecca's stepdad looked bored. "She has always had a mind of her own, dear. Rebecca does things her way."

"Then we have to convince her to listen to us." Her mother seemed desperate.

"Mom, it's okay, really. I was fine the whole time."

"There is more to think about than you know. Some dangers can't be predicted," Dennis added.

Rebecca looked directly into Dennis's eyes. They were stone cold. She was used to that expression. She had seen it many times. He was without compassion. He had no remorse. She could not believe how evil he was. *Why couldn't Mother see it?* she thought, asking herself for the thousandth time. Her mother continued to plead with her, offering every reason she could think of to entice Rebecca into a visit.

Dennis finally looked interested in the conversation. "I think your mother is right. If not for yourself, do it for her. Can't you see how worried she has been?"

Rebecca put her arms around her mother. "Mom, I'm so sorry. What if I spend a few days with you? I don't know how I'm going to get back and forth to work with the roads the way they are, but I'll come for a few days if you like."

"Yes, please, darling. That would be wonderful. Dennis can arrange transportation for you, I'm sure. And that will give me time to convince you to stay."

Rebecca wanted to run away; but she knew instinctively her mother needed her. Something in her wondered just how much. She looked over at Dennis. He had always been good to her mother. But as she watched her mom, at this moment, she wondered if his feelings had changed toward her. Something was wrong. Her mom looked different. *Oh God, I should have known,* she thought to herself.

REBECCA ON THE RUN

It was well past midnight when Rebecca walked with her mother into the oversize home. The furnishings were expensive. Their extravagance was so out of place in this new-world order. They seemed to scream at Rebecca. Sharon excused herself and left the room.

Dennis said calmly, "Your mother hasn't been well lately. I believe your being here will be good for her."

"What's wrong with her?" Rebecca asked in her most controlled tone.

Dennis shrugged dismissively. "She seems to be suffering from a guilty conscience. She is convinced God has turned away from her."

"Why didn't you call me? If I had known, I would have come sooner."

"And done what?" he asked, challenging her. "Would you have told her Jesus still saves? That your God can ease her pain? That I am going to hell but there is still hope for her soul?" He laughed at her, mocking her faith. "I know all about you and your holier-than-thou friends." The look on his face was pure evil.

Rebecca decided to ignore his comments. "Father, I am tired. I will deal with Mother tomorrow. I am here now; perhaps I can help her." She stood to her feet, picked up her suitcase, and moved toward the guest room. Stopping, she looked back at Dennis. "I am here for my mother. I don't know what is going on, but I plan to do whatever I can to help her."

"I would expect nothing less." He said in his most gracious manner. She caught the flicker of self-satisfaction in his eyes. He thought he had her trapped. Her heart sank as she realized she was helpless to fight him as long as her mother's life was in his hands. She felt the invisible strings of a puppeteer threatening to strangle her. *Oh no, you don't,* she thought. *You can't control me, not ever again.* She went to bed but did not sleep. Instead, she prayed for deliverance for her mother from the stronghold that gave Dennis this power over her.

She heard his footsteps as he came down the hall. He stopped just outside her room. She held her breath. He tried the door but it was locked. After a moment he went on. She ran to the door and shoved a chair under the knob. He was playing his old game of cat and mouse. He thought he had her trapped. He would take his time tormenting her until he was ready to make his move. "Dear God, what can I do? I have to get my mother away from this monster." The dream came flooding back to her. She remembered him clearly lurking in the shadows. The hair on the back of her neck stood up.

When the quake rumbled, DC became anxious for Miss Millie's neighbors. As soon as the shaking stopped he began checking. He worked his way through the neighborhood. This time, however, he was not robbing anyone; instead he was checking on people. Many of Miss Millie's neighbors were older. They were upset by the quake. When the darkness invaded the world he was concerned Miss Orlando would fall in the dark. He remembered the walking stick he had seen in Miss Millie's hall closet. It took him a minute; but after feeling for it he found it. He used it to tap his way across the street to check on Miss Orlando. He knew she would be frantic. "Miss Orlando, it's me, DC. How are you doing?"

"DC, thank God you are here. I'm so frightened. What is happening?"

"Everything's going to be fine. You just stay calm, ma'am. Are you all right? Have you been injured?"

"No, DC, but I'm afraid." The tremble in her voice was an indication of just how much.

DC wanted to reassure her. "I've heard about this. Apparently it's some kind of blackout. Everything will be fine. You just have to stay calm. My pastor told us this would happen."

"He did? How did he know?" Her voice held a tone of curiosity.

"It's in the Bible. The Bible predicts the earthquake and even the darkness. I'll stay with you for a while if you like" (Revelation 6:12).

"Please do, I'm so afraid."

While the darkness settled in around them, he told her about Miss Millie's book. "She left a note about the Lord coming back for his church, explaining the whole thing. She even invited me to stay here and enjoy her home." The darkness brought the cold. He convinced her to go to bed to stay warm. It will pass, ma'am. I promise. I'll check on you again soon. You go ahead and get some rest. I'll let myself out."

Outside, the world was cold and inhospitable. He worked his way back across the street to Miss Millie's. He was unusually cold. Shaking, he climbed into bed. And much like his friends, he waited for God to turn the lights back on. Vaguely he remembered more than just the earthquake and the darkness. The Bible also foretells the moon turning to blood. He didn't want to upset Miss Orlando anymore by going into details, so he had not mentioned it.

~~

Ron Barton was taking his early morning walk with King. This was his favorite time of the day. He enjoyed watching the world wake up. A squirrel nearby chattered incoherently, fussing at him.

He smiled as he watched its antics. The birds in the trees were singing sweetly. From here he could hear the water flow from the mountain. It splashed and danced along.

He noticed the buck he was hunting stop at the creek to drink. He leaned down lapping at the cool refreshing water. Ron raised his rifle, placing the beautiful beast in the crosshairs. Without warning, the buck straightened up as if he had heard something then began running. There was an unusual rustling in the trees overhead. He looked up to see all of the birds flying away as if something had startled them. The squirrel he had watched was chirping wildly and also running for cover.

King barked and turned circles as if he wanted Ron to follow him. "What is it, boy?" he asked. The dog looked worried. Ron stepped back from the cliff at the edge of the ravine; as he did the earth where he had just been standing fell. The rumbling rolling of the earth shook beneath them. Rocks began to fall from over their heads. He and King took refuge under a ledge near the mountain of rock. They stayed there until the shaking stopped.

"We have to check on the neighbors," he said to King. They ran down the trail racing toward their friends. He stopped at the cabin; they weren't there. King was in front of him; he raced to the opening of the cave. When he arrived there King was already digging.

Sarah and Brad had held their breath as the mountain above their heads shook. Rocks tumbled down all around them. Sarah screamed with fear. Bounder barked steadily. Finally the shaking stopped. She ran to Justin. He and his friends were all okay. She heard the girls crying and hurried to check on them. Miraculously they were also fine.

Brad was talking excitedly about something. She ran to see what he was carrying on about. The cave opening was covered by debris. They were trapped! He already had an iron bar and was moving the rocks and debris from the entrance. The boys formed an army around him. They worked hard and fast. The tremors slowed and even caused their efforts to seem endless. Brad was concerned that a tremor almost the magnitude of the quake would hit. "We have to dig out of here before another tremor covers us for good." They finally managed to uncover a small opening. Justin shimmied through it. A hand reached out and steadied him.

Ron grabbed his hand, helping him out. "Easy, son," he cautioned. "The trails and slopes of the mountain have changed."

"What's wrong?" Brad asked.

Justin seemed confused. "I didn't realize it was night. I thought it was day.

"What do you mean?" Brad questioned.

"It's dark out here."

As quickly as possible, with Ron and Justin's help, they all eased through the small opening. "It can't be past noon," Justin commented. "We've only been working a few hours."

"Then why is it so dark?" Karen asked.

"I was working to remove the rocks, trying to dig you out, when the sun started to grow dim. I think God decided to turn the lights off." King stood close to Ron. He leaned into his master for reassurance.

Brad looked around thoughtfully. "That seems to be the situation. Thanks for coming to help us, Ron. Can you stay for a while? It might be better for all of us if we stick together."

Ron agreed. "I think that's a good idea. King and I will help you all back to the cabin."

Brad's biggest concern was getting everyone to safety. "Cole, can you find your way back to the cabin in the dark? We have to get to shelter."

"Yeah," Cole said. "The only thing is I don't know how much the quake has affected the terrain. There may be slides or crevices we can't see."

Brad had a rope. "Look, you and Ron take the lead. We will all follow you. Walk slowly and check the ground before you step.

We're right behind you. Don't rush, take your time." They walked slowly down the path. The debris changed the lay of the land. Tree limbs lay in the way of the otherwise clear trail. When necessary the others would help move the debris out of the way so they could keep going. Justin kept a tight grip on Bounder's leash. It was several minutes later when Cole felt the banister to the cabin. He used his foot to feel the steps. They were still intact.

Ron excused himself. "I think I better get back and check things out on the other side."

"Thanks for your help. You're a good friend, Ron. Let us know if we can return the favor." They shook hands, and Ron and King disappeared into the darkness.

They all breathed a sigh of relief as they entered the little cabin. Cole felt for the lantern, lit the wick, and waited for the light. The light burned but the room was still pitch dark. "It's the plague of darkness," Cole said.

Mackenzie rubbed her arms with her hands. "I'm so cold," she said through chattering teeth. Cole moved to the fireplace. He had left the fire ready to go. He lit the match. The little cabin began to warm.

Karen stared at the flames. "It's so odd; even the fire doesn't light the room."

"I know it's eerie, but God is taking care of us." Sarah wanted to comfort them. "We could all have been killed from falling rocks. But look, no one was even injured. God's angels were protecting us."

"We're going to be all right," Brad said. "When this is all over, we'll dig out the opening to the cave. Right now I'm hungry." They all agreed.

Sarah moved to the supply cupboard. Their supplies were unmoved, sitting comfortably in their covey. After reading prophesies about the coming earthquakes, Cole had insisted the jars of food always be placed where they were protected.

"This calls for a celebration," Sarah announced. They ate the dried venison Cole and the others had put up. Then Sarah opened some jars of canned peaches. The fire warmed them, the food satisfied them, and the water sustained them. Exhausted, they fell asleep scattered around the cabin. Sarah pulled out blankets and placed them over her young charges. Brad stayed awake and fed the fire.

Bounder slept faithfully next to Justin. After a while Justin woke up. "Dad?" he asked into the darkness.

"I'm here, son," Brad answered.

"What if we hadn't gotten out of there? I mean what if we don't make it? Next time we might die." Justin's voice penetrated the silence; one by one the young people began to listen to the conversation between Justin and Brad.

"Yeah, you're right. We could have died. But we didn't. It seems to me that God has a purpose for all of us. I think your escape from military camp was a miracle, but you all did. And you all made it here. This cabin was waiting for you. I'm proud of all of you. You worked together to accomplish something for others. I can't say we won't be in danger or that we couldn't all die tomorrow. But I believe God has chosen all of you and this place to help others. Why didn't the rocks land on any of us? God was watching out for all of us. He protected us then, and I believe he will continue to protect us in the future. His angels are posted around us, guarding us right at this moment." Mackenzie moved toward the sound of Brad's voice. She snuggled up close to him, wrapping her arms around one of his.

"You're right," she said. "God is taking care of us." She reached up and kissed his cheek, then lay her head against his arm and went back to sleep. Brad knew he couldn't allow anything to happen to any of them. They were counting on him. He had to do whatever it took to protect them. "God," he said. "Thank you for sparing our lives. Please continue to help us."

The darkness continued. Brad lost track of time. He didn't know how long they had stayed tucked away in the safety of the cabin. Several times they ran low on wood. He and the boys had placed a wood pile close to the side of the cabin. In the dark they all formed a line passing each piece to the next person until they had replenished their stash near the fireplace. When they became too tired to stay awake they slept.

Finally, the day began to break. They woke to a new world. The birds chirped outside the cabin. The smell of dew was fresh everywhere. They cleared away the opening to the cave. But just in case of another tremor, they stayed at the cabin again that night. Brad lay awake praying. He felt the weight of his responsibility to these amazing young men and women. Something had stayed with him since the shake, a sense of foreboding he did not understand, so he prayed. His eyes were shut, his heart's focus was on heaven. There in the warmth of the cabin he did not see. Brad did not notice the red glow of the moon or the appearing of yet another plague.

Rebecca heard screams coming from her mother's room. She ran down the hall, turned the doorknob, and flew into her mother's bedroom. "What is it?" she asked, alarmed.

Her mother was cowering on the bed. She raised the covers to shield her eyes from the sight. "The moon, it's turned to blood!" she cried. Rebecca walked to the window and looked out curiously; the blood-red color filled the sky.

Her stepfather handed her mother a tablet and some water. "You have to calm down. Here, take your medication."

Rebecca stepped quickly to her mother's side. "What are you giving her?" she asked suspiciously.

"The doctor has prescribed a sedative to calm her nerves."

"Thank you, Dennis; but now that I am here, I will be happy to give Mother any medication she needs. Please show me what she has been taking." She stood her ground with her arms folded, watching him.

Dennis looked at her, mocking her with his eyes. "Of course, I am more than happy to give you the job."

"Darling, Rebecca is here; she will be caring for you now. If you'll both excuse me, I need to make a call."

Her mother was agitated. Rebecca sat down. Taking her hand, she sought to reassure her. "Mom, it's all right, really. The moon is just red, that's all."

Her mother looked haunted. A barely sane expression flickered across her face. "It is blood. The moon has turned into blood. God's wrath is being poured out on the entire world. I'm afraid I'm lost, Rebecca. God has turned his back on me."

"No, Mother, you must not think that. He hasn't turned away from you. He is just waiting for you to ask Jesus to forgive you and deliver you from the evil of this world."

Her mother's anguish marred her beautiful features. "God can't forgive me. I've gone too far." A look of hopeless depression crossed over her face. "Thank God, Rebecca, you got out. I thank God you have found peace with him. I have taken another path. My path is one of destruction."

"It doesn't have to be, Mother. He is still God. There is nothing you can do to cause him to turn away from you. We are the ones who forsake him. He will never leave you or forsake you (Isaiah 55:6–7, Hebrews 13:5). You have to talk to him, Mother. Tell him you love him. Ask Jesus to forgive you. It's not too late."

The medication was starting to take effect, but Sharon repeated her daughter's words. "Forgive me Jesus. I need your help. God, I love you." A cross appeared on her forehead.

"It's going to be all right, Mother, you just need to get some rest."

Rebecca looked at Dennis. His face seemed to reflect compassion. For the first time in a long time, she saw the face of the man her mother had originally married. He moved to his wife. Taking her hand he spoke gently, "You must listen to Rebecca, darling. She loves you. She will help you to pull out of this slump you've been in. You have to stop thinking this way. Remember you were so happy when I first took on my new position."

Sharon spoke softly. "That was before, dear. Don't you see now I understand? I see what you've become. I am sorry. I was too weak to help you break away from this path you've taken. It's just that I love you so much. I just didn't see what was happening until it was too late." She turned to her daughter. "Oh, Rebecca, I've messed up everything. How can you ever forgive me?"

"Mother, I don't know what you are talking about. Please, just get some rest." Thankfully, her mother slipped into a deep sleep.

"What is she talking about, Dennis? Why is she so distraught?"

"She believes she is lost. I've tried to explain to her that her father's religion has caused her to be riddled by guilt, but she won't listen to me. She is convinced that God has turned his back on her and she has no hope."

In her mind Rebecca thought, *God help me.* She took a deep breath then said, "Dennis, I want to take her away from here. I want to help her. I want your permission. She won't come with me if we don't have your blessing. No matter what has happened between us, I know deep down you love her. You can't possibly be so cruel as to be willing to allow her to lose her sanity just so you can maintain your spotless reputation."

Dennis looked over at his wife. "I can't allow you to take her away from me. She's mine."

Rebecca stood her ground. "She's your wife, but she is God's child. She gave him her life a long time ago. You can't change that. She still has a chance to reconcile her relationship with him. I know you loved her deeply at one time. Can't you find it in your heart to allow her to make peace with him?"

Dennis looked at Sharon in a sick, possessive way. "Why does she have to leave me?"

"Because you have given Satan your life and if she stays with you she will follow you into hell. You and I both know you have sold your soul. You can't have her. God has his mark on her. See, look at her. I can see it. Can't you?"

He looked at Sharon as though he were seeing her for the first time. Her bangs fell away from her forehead. There in the red glow of the moonlight was a cross. Dennis turned away from it. His chest rose and fell. In panic he asked, "Why didn't I see it before?"

"She hasn't seen it either." Rebecca watched Dennis cower away from the cross on Sharon. "She thought she was lost. I just prayed with her and God has forgiven her. God claims her. Dennis, I want to know what is wrong with her. Why is she taking this medication?"

"You heard her yourself. Sharon knows what I am. She has awakened to the truth." His admission surprised Rebecca. Reading her thoughts, he smiled in a self-loathing way. "It's ironic, isn't it? I've worked all these years just to become a monster she can't stand. You look surprised, Rebecca. Don't you understand? I know exactly who and what I am. Your mother finally sees the truth, and she can't live with it, as long as she could pretend she was happy."

"You could ask Jesus to forgive you," she said softly.

"No, Rebecca, I can't. I have gone too far. It is too late for me. As you said, I have sold my soul to Satan. He owns me, free and clear now."

Rebecca felt compassion for Dennis, but it was her mother she worried about. "Dennis, she won't survive under your roof. She has to be free or she will die."

He looked at Sharon. The cross on her forehead pierced his conscience. "You have tonight to get her out of here. Tomorrow I will come looking for you both. If I find either of you, I'll punish you the same as any other criminals. Don't let me catch you. I will not care who you were in the past. You are both my enemies now."

Rebecca shook her mother, but she couldn't wake her. She looked at Dennis. "Help me carry her out to the car. Please," she begged. He picked up her mother as though he were carrying a child. He carried her to the garage. Rebecca held the car door open. He placed her in the passenger's seat. Rebecca lowered the seat to the sleeping position. "Dennis, the roads are a mess. You have to give me more time to get her away from here. Please, I know you love her. You have to."

A shutter dropped down over Dennis's eyes. "You have tonight." His words held the coldness of a statue. He turned and walked away.

The roads were a mess. She drove around a tree that was still in the roadway. Slowly she pulled the car over and onto the sidewalk. She drove the little car to John and Carly's house, praying all the way. She rang the doorbell. John asked, "Who is it?"

"John, it's me, Rebecca. I have my mother with me. Dennis gave her something. I can't wake her up." John hurried to check on her mother. He looked down to see the cross on the forehead of Rebecca's mom. Is she alive?"

"Yes, but we're in danger. I have to get her somewhere safe."

"Carly, I'll be back."

Carly had overheard the conversation. "I'm coming with you," she said, grabbing her sweater and purse.

John nodded, "Follow me to DC's. I'll need a ride back."

She agreed. "Go on. I'll lock up."

Some of the roads were damaged but many were still okay. He drove Rebecca and her mother to Miss Millie's, parking in the back. Rebecca knocked on the kitchen door. She looked around anxiously. John lifted Sharon out of the passenger seat. She was thin. He couldn't believe how light she was. DC opened the door. He carried her into Miss Millie's.

"In here." DC pointed. "Just go ahead and lay her on the bed."

"We have to get rid of the car," John said.

"I'm on it." DC stated. Leaving the house, he drove the car a couple of blocks over, parking it near the mall. It was beautiful. You didn't see many cars like this one around here. It was the perfect little temptation for a thief. He parked it leaving the keys in the ignition. On his way back to the house he dodged the lights, staying in the darkness. He made his way quickly back to Miss Millie's.

"How is she?" he asked as he walked through the front door.

"She's fine, thank you. She just needs to rest. I have to get her away from this place as soon as possible," Rebecca said.

John looked at her. "That's why we're here. DC can take you to a safe house as soon as she is able to travel. He'll get you two out of the city. You're safe for now. When she's able to travel he can help.

THE REFUGEE

Her box was large and heavy; she shifted it trying to get a better hold. Sweat poured down her brow. "What now?" she asked herself, looking for answers she really didn't want to hear. Her mind replayed the past. "How could I have been so wrong?"

Forcing herself back to the present, she adjusted the weight in her arms. Where was she actually going, anyway? She looked around longingly. The earthquake had left her homeless. All of her worldly possessions were contained in this box. She looked down at the thing, wishing for her beautiful luggage. She had spent so much money on it, wanting only the best. Never in her wildest dreams had she anticipated this loss. She wouldn't even have these things if she hadn't been clearing out her desk at work.

Still heartbroken, she let herself think back. Paul hadn't spoken to her since their breakup. He sent Shelby over to her place to pick up his things with not so much as a note.

She set her box down, studying the devastation. Looking off into the distance she scanned the horizon. She had heard rumors about an underground railroad of sorts. Supposedly there was a safe house. Maybe she could ask around and see if they would take her in. Christians were hated more and more. It seemed to Deseraie this was as good a time as any to make a move. She took a deep breath, let it out, and picked up the box. "I might as well get started again," she mumbled to herself. She decided to go by the church. If anyone knew about a hideout, Pastor John would.

The roadways were blocked in all directions. She had to get out of town, but how? After they released Pastor John and Paul, claiming it was an act of love by the regime, she thought perhaps people would be more tolerant of Christians. But that had not been the case. Her boss fired her for causing turmoil in the office. All she had done was just pray for a coworker, and she was out. "I know you have a plan, God. It's just that this is really not good." She talked to God as she walked down the road.

Things had been horrible since the Antichrist had come back to life. Immediately after his so-called resurrection, he ordered a crackdown on anyone who did not have the mark. She touched the place above her forehead. Somehow it comforted her just knowing God had placed his mark on her. She pulled her bangs down over her forehead with her fingers. She knew it was not obvious, but she felt it was there so strong. Sometimes she was sure anyone looking at her would notice it. Her boss had gotten really jerky about having a Christian working for him. Deep down she knew he only hired her because of her looks. She hated having to put up with him watching her, but she needed the job. Lately he was just hoping for an excuse to fire her.

Deseraie felt sticky. She could feel the sweat trickling down her back. She sobbed then choked back the tears. "You are the one who brought this on yourself. You knew better than to mess around with a married man, especially a preacher. I must have been crazy!" She moaned to herself. "Well, there is no need worrying about that now." She stiffened her spine, and with purpose set out for the church.

John was in the office when she reached her destination. She knocked, waited for his usual, "Come in," and then walked in with everything she owned in her arms.

"Pastor John," she began. John looked up from his studies to see Deseraie walking through his office door. Her hair was dirty. Her once-beautiful outfit was torn. She was scraped up in various places. Dirt and blood stained her skin and her clothes. She looked like she had just crawled out from under a building.

"Deseraie, are you all right?" He rushed over to her, taking the box from her arms. "Please, have a seat." He set the box down and motioned toward a seat. The church was intact. John had been straightening up, but it was relatively untouched by the earthquake.

She couldn't believe her eyes as she walked up the street. It was the only building standing. She nervously licked her lips. "Physically I'm fine, but"—she started to cry—"I lost everything in that earthquake. When the darkness set in I was petrified. Honestly, Pastor, I have never been so scared in my life. I was able to get to shelter when the quake started; but my apartment is gone." He handed her a hanky. She wiped her nose, then absent-mindedly she began to ring it, twisting it in her hands.

"I don't know how much more I can take. I mean, I know you were left behind, too, when Jesus came; but Paul just dropped me like the plague. I have no job and no prospects. My life is in shambles. I know God has a plan for me. I know his love for me is unending. But I'm not feeling very loved right now. I'm tired, hungry, and I haven't showered in days!"

John's heart broke for her. "How did you survive? How long has it been since you've eaten?"

She blew her nose. "I was packing up my desk when the earthquake hit. I went in early, before my boss showed up. The night crew was still there. I had just finished cleaning out my desk when I felt it. People started shouting, 'We have to get out of here!' It was chaos. I don't even remember thinking about it. I just knew I had to get to safety. I ran with the others down the steps." She started to cry harder. "Oh, Pastor, it was terrible. Some of the people were crushed by the building. I just made it down the steps when the walls collapsed behind me. I'll never forget the sounds of the many screams as people were being injured and killed."

She looked heartbroken. She raised her eyes to look directly into John's. "I don't know how I survived. I just keep thinking

God must have a plan for my life. I should be dead." She searched
for words to describe the ordeal. "After the quake, I set down my
box and went looking for survivors. My friend, Amy, didn't make
it. Peter, a coworker, helped me. We searched for hours. No one
above the stairs survived.

During the aftershocks, somehow we made it to the parking
garage across the street. Peter went back to take another look,
just in case we had missed someone. We were separated when the
darkness started to fall." She sobbed. "Peter managed to get back
to the garage. We were there with five others while the darkness lasted."

"Did you have any food?" He asked, concerned.

"Yes," she shook her head. "Ever since you told us to be prepared, I've kept some emergency supplies at work. It wasn't much,
just some crackers, a couple of candy bars, and a few bottles of
water in my desk. We ate that; then Peter and some of the other
guys started checking the cars in the garage for food and water.
They found a car with groceries. We slept in the cars. Some of
them even had blankets and coats, so we kept warm. We couldn't
believe we had survived. When the sun came back out we all
started walking home."

"Deseraie, you are so incredibly brave. I'm so very proud of the
way you took care of yourself and then helped others." Looking
at her possessions, he asked, "What's in the box?"

She looked down at her treasures. "My memories," she said,
reaching in. She took out a picture of her mom and dad. "My
other pictures were at the apartment. Thank God I still have this
one. They're both dead. Oh, and I have my favorite pair of shoes."
She held them up for him to admire. "Aren't they adorable?" She
pulled out an empty box of tissue. "I guess I used them all during the ordeal." Reaching back in, her hand touched a soft blue
sweater. "I kept it at work for when I was cold." Pulling it out, she
carefully removed another picture, one of her and a friend. "We
were in Hawaii." She fumbled past some miscellaneous items

until she felt it. At the very bottom of the box was a picture of Paul. She pulled it out. "I guess I shouldn't have kept this. I just couldn't let go of it." She wiped a hand across the frame, dusting it, then handed it to John. "Maybe you could see that he gets this."

John looked at the remaining contents: an empty package of crackers, some empty water bottles, a used package of gum, and some stationery. There was a purse that he assumed she was using when the quake hit.

"I have to make a new life for myself. I don't think I can go on like this. Even before the earthquake flattened my apartment building, I knew the manager was going to throw me out soon. I have nowhere to go." She began to rock herself. "I feel like an outcast."

John spoke softly. "I'm really sorry to hear that, Deseraie. I know Paul would be too. You are welcome to stay here at the church. It's not much, but we are letting people sleep here at night."

She looked at him with resolve. "I want to go to the safe house I've been hearing about. Can you arrange it for me?" She suddenly looked cold. The fear in her eyes was evident. "I don't think I can do this alone. I need to start over, where people don't know who I am and that I almost brought down the pastor of Redeeming Hope Church by ruining his marriage. Even now, after all of us were left behind, people are still judging me. It's like they don't understand that they weren't ready for Jesus to come either. I have a couple of friends, and that's it." She stopped talking. She looked John in the eyes. Her tears had stopped, the expression on her face was filled with strength, not self-pity. "Maybe a change is just what I need."

John walked over to the door; opening it, he looked around suspiciously. Placing a finger over his lips, he motioned to Deseraie as he spoke. "I am sorry, but I don't know what you're talking about. I do believe a change of scenery may do you good. If you like, Carly and I could give you a lift to the bus stop. Perhaps a vacation is just what you need." Taking her by the hand, he lifted her out of the chair. Then he ushered her out the back door of his office. Outside, he pulled her toward the other end of the yard, stopping under the shade of a large oak tree. "It should be safe to talk here. I'm sorry for pulling you out of the office, but we never know who might be listening to our conversations."

Deseraie felt terrible. "Of course, I should have thought about that. I'm so sorry."

"Don't worry about it." John said, brushing her apology aside. "What have you heard?" he asked her. John tried to picture the girl he knew with her perfect looks, fabulous wardrobe, and designer shoes hunting, fishing, and living off the land. The image just didn't compute. But neither did her story of escaping death, looking for survivors, and hiding out in a garage for days until daylight. Obviously there was more to her than he knew.

For the first time since she had walked through his door, Deseraie really looked at John. She stopped talking long enough to study him. She noticed the thinness around his jaw. He was paler than before, with dark circles under his eyes. John looked older and she was sure he had lost weight. A pang of pity for John went through her. Here she was, thinking she couldn't take anymore, while John had been to jail and beaten—all because he loved Jesus. She felt a smidgen of guilt but knew he wouldn't want her to comment on it. Instead she answered his question. "I've heard that Brad and Sarah know someone who is inviting Christian refugees to stay at a hideout with them."

John tried to warn her. "It's not the kind of place you would choose to go under normal circumstances. But it would be an opportunity for you to rest. And I think you could help the young women there. Everybody works, helping with food and shelter. You could visit for a while and see if it's something you can continue. I can arrange for someone to slip you out of the area tonight. They have moved up the travel time to accommodate people who are homeless from the quake." He studied her. "I'm not sure you will like it there."

"Why do you say that?" she asked.

"You'll see when you get there. You're a city girl. The lifestyle is rough. They are in the mountains. I understand it is in the middle of nowhere. They hunt, fish, and trap their food. I personally would love it; Carly not so much.

They also have a rule. You have to be blindfolded to go there. That is an absolute rule. That way if you want to leave you can. It is also a way of protecting the others. If you are ever caught, you don't know where it is so you can't be forced to give away the location."

Deseraie nodded her head. "I have nowhere else."

"Okay then. I'll make the arrangements." He walked her back to his office and through the back door. Turning to look at her, John studied the young beauty. She had once caught the eye of every man she passed. Her beautiful hair hung in tangled loops. The thought of her struggling to survive when the quake hit touched him. He studied her with compassion. "You poor girl, you must have been so scared."

He walked to the front door of his office. "Carly, can you come in here please?" Carly walked through the office door to find her husband with Deseraie. In the past that would have bothered her, but she had changed. She smiled warmly and greeted Deseraie with a hug. "How are you?" she asked.

For the first time since she had walked through the church she smiled. "I'm alive. I guess God has a plan for me."

John spoke up. "Deseraie will be joining us for dinner." He showed her a note he had quickly scribbled that said she would be leaving for the safe house. Carly nodded her understanding. As she did, he said, "She is tired and hungry; do you think we can get her something to eat?"

"Of course," Carly agreed.

"Is there anywhere I can clean up?" Deseraie pulled on her clothes self-consciously.

Carly guided Deseraie to a guest room they had set up for people needing help. "We're blessed; we have these showers from when the school was operating. The only thing is the hot water isn't working. But you can clean up. Here's some soap. I'll get you something to wear; then, how about a bowl of soup?"

"That all sounds wonderful."

Deseraie could not believe how much she enjoyed the cold shower. She pulled on the clean blouse Carly had left for her. There was also a pair of pants that looked as though they had once belonged to someone much older, but they fit. She pulled on the soft blue sweater from her box. Taking her comb from her purse she combed her hair out and left it to air dry. She looked at her reflection, no makeup, just her. She really missed makeup. She missed her own clothes. Oh well, she was alive; that had to count for something.

Carly was waiting for her in the kitchen. She had warmed some soup. She placed a rare piece of bread next to the bowl. When Deseraie showed up, she took her outside to eat. Carly had set a place for her using an old stump for a table. Deseraie was hungry; she devoured the soup. Her heart sank as she realized the church pantry was running very low on supplies.

She understood Carly had brought her outside so they could talk freely. "Carly, how are you managing? I mean, I know food is in short supply. How are you and John doing?"

"We are fine for now. But we have begun to run low on food and clothing."

"Why are you two staying here? I think you should come with me."

"I can't leave John, and he can't leave the church."

"Carly, you have to talk to him and somehow convince him to leave this place before they kill you both."

"I know we are in danger, but we could be in danger anywhere. The other day any of us could have died in that earthquake. They are still digging people out of some places. We know there will be more devastating times. We can do more good here."

"You can do more good if you both live. Please come with me."

"Thank you for your concern, but we can't."

Deseraie wanted to plead with her friend, but she knew Carly's mind was made up.

"I'll miss you. Besides April and David, you and John are the only friends I have."

"We'll miss you too." Carly looked at Deseraie with love. "You've become very special to me. I know that what happened between you and Paul devastated you. And, at first I was just trying to help you stay out of Paul and Shelby's lives. But you and I are so alike. We are two sides of the same coin. I love Shelby and I don't want to betray her in any way, but I also understand you. I know why you did what you did. In some ways you seem like the sister I never had. I know you still feel guilty, even though you know God has forgiven you. I can see it in your eyes. But you have to forgive yourself. Deseraie. You are so much more than you think. I know how special you really are. You're right. God does have a plan for you."

"Before you continue to look down on yourself, remember, I was the one who insisted my boyfriend not respond to the call of God that I knew was on his life. I was so incredibly materialistic. We are both guilty of distracting men, who love God, from their mission. It hasn't been easy, but I have forgiven myself. Please promise me, when the guilt threatens to strangle you, that you will remember God's mercy is everlasting, and let it go."

Tears came into Deseraie's eyes. She reached out and hugged her friend. "I promise," she said softly. "I don't know how to thank you. You and John have been true friends. Honestly, Carly, I don't know what I would have done if you hadn't been there for me."

Deseraie waited at the church until almost 1:00 in the morning. Her escort was late. Carly had taken one look at her beautiful shoes and declared them unfit. "You have to have something more suitable. You don't know this guy; he will expect you to be dressed for escape." She whispered. "He has a bit of a temper; but he's really nice, once you get to know him."

"What's his name?" Deseraie asked innocently.

"We never give names; someone could be listening."

So here she was, long after her friends had left, waiting outside the church for someone she did not know. And what was worse, she didn't even have a description of this mystery man. She checked her watch, once again, in the moonlight—1:05 a.m. "Great," she said to herself.

That's when she was approached by a very large shadow. "Are you Deseraie?" the man asked. His deep voice was barely above a whisper.

A chill ran down her spine. What if it was a setup? What if the real guy had been killed on his way to see her? She swallowed back the panic. "Yes, it's me," she whispered.

"We better be going then." He guided her out the back using the darkness as their cover.

"I thought there would be others. Where are all of the other refugees?"

"You're the only one; didn't PJ tell you?"

"Actually, no one has told me anything."

He shushed her. Slowly he guided her along in the dark as though he were a bat depending on his radar for directions. She hiked along behind him, working hard to keep up. The moonlight gave some light but not enough to keep her from tripping. He turned just in time to steady her from falling. "Be careful," he said through clenched teeth. "I don't want to have to carry you to safety."

She felt insulted. "The least you can do is slow down. I'm doing my best to keep up. But you are practically running in the dark. I can't see out here."

"I'm sorry for hurrying you, but aside from saving your life, I don't want PJ and Carly to get in trouble because someone catches us out here leaving the church under suspicious circumstances. By the way, if someone does spot us, you and I are on a date."

"Marvelous." she said with sarcasm. *As if I would be caught dead dating this overgrown egomaniac,* she thought to herself. The moon went behind the clouds. Deseraie could barely see. *Oh great,* she thought. *Dear God, don't let it be another plague of darkness.* As it emerged from the shadows, she stopped and gasped. It was blood red. She couldn't take her eyes off it. "The moon," she said pointing.

A hand came up and clamped down over her arm. "Don't just stand there. We have to keep moving." He continued his marathon pace. She worked hard trying to keep up with him. "Just you wait, Buster, when it's daylight and I can see where I'm going, I'll give you a run for your money." Deseraie ran three miles every day and when she had time, easily five. "So what are you, some kind of special forces guy or something? How did you end up with this job?"

"I promised someone I would do them a favor. You're the favor."

"Whom did you promise?"

"Pastor Paul; he wanted you safe. He said he owed you that much."

"Well, he needn't worry. I'm getting by fine on my own."

"Yeah, right. The way I understand it, you're homeless, jobless, and you've lost all of your possessions. Sounds like you're doing great."

"Well, I'm not sitting around crying over that jerk. Did he tell you he promised to marry me? Then in one day went back to his

wife and cut me out of his life over the phone. I don't know what
I ever saw in him."

"I don't either. He was, after all, married."The tone of his voice
was hateful, emphasizing the word "married." "What were you
doing, chasing after a married man?"

"Oh, you think you have all the answers, running ahead of me
like you are so superior. I didn't chase after him. He was more
than willing."

At that moment the man swung around and grabbed her by
the shoulders. Through clenched teeth he spoke menacingly. "I
know what you're like. I've met your type in every town I've been
in. You think only of yourself. If you hadn't shown up flaunting
yourself, he would have been in the rapture. He would be gone
right now. They both would. Shelby was devastated by your interference in their marriage."

"So you're just going to blame me for the whole thing? You
don't even know me." She couldn't wait to get out of this town
and away from people like this creep.

"I know you. Just because Paul and Shelby have forgiven you,
it doesn't mean I have."

"Who cares if you forgive me? I sure don't. All that matters is
that I get away from this place."

"That's right, so now we can stop talking." They walked
through the side streets and back alleys without speaking another
word. Finally they arrived at an abandoned home. They sneaked
into the garage where there was a motorcycle. He started it up.
"Get on," he said, handing her a helmet. She swung onto the back
of the bike, resenting having to depend on him for help.

They rode out of town just as the sun was rising. They traveled
with caution. The roads were congested with traffic from the
earthquake; in some areas the road was buckled. It was dangerous, but, to her relief, they quickly left the city behind. When
she thought about it, this was the best way to travel under the

circumstances. At times people tried to wave them down, but her hero kept going, refusing to stop for anyone.

Finally they stopped to stretch. The guy went into the gas station and came out with something to eat. "Here," he said, handing her a sandwich. She stared at it with her mouth open. "Did you steal it?" she asked.

"No, I bought it," he responded.

She swallowed hard. Who was he? None of the people she knew could buy anything. For the first time since they met, she became really afraid of him.

Noticing the look on her face, he tried to reassure her. "I'm not an enemy." He looked around for a place to talk to her in private. "Come with me." He started the bike. She hesitated a minute then got on. He drove to a nearby shady spot, away from listeners. He watched her as if he was expecting her to bolt. "Okay, so I'm one of them. You know, one of the bad guys." Her eyes reflected a deer caught in headlights. "Look, I'm not going to hurt you. I'm trying to help. I can go and come where others can't. Don't you see, they had to find someone like me to do this job? Pastor John and Paul both trust me. Isn't that good enough for you?"

"Who are you?" she asked. This time she wasn't going to be put off.

"I'm Paul's brother."

Her mouth dropped open in surprise. "Maxwell?" she asked.

"That's right. Can you believe that in the middle of all this crazy confusion, we finally found each other? I'm in the military. Most of us took the mark before we even knew what was going on. In the military you are expected to do what you're told."

"Oh." She wet her lips, trying to think of something to say. "I guess I understand." Maxwell handed her the sandwich. She began to chew quietly.

After a moment of silence, she added, "You must hate me." Her voice was barely more than a whisper.

She sounded defeated. Somehow hearing her give up made Max feel sorry for her. "No, I'm just glad to be getting you as far away from Paul as possible. He and Shelby have been through enough."

"I wasn't going to hurt them. When Paul said it was over, I accepted it. I've left them both totally alone."

"I know; Paul told me. At the same time, he asked me to take care of you."

"Who is he to decide I need to be cared for?" Deseraie was getting angry again.

"You talked to PJ. He talked to Paul, and Paul talked to me. You asked Pastor John for help. Paul asked me. I can get you through areas others can't. Since the earthquake, we have had some recent travel challenges. And there are new laws that are going to be enforced. Traveling anywhere without the right paperwork will be nearly impossible. My help is your best option under the circumstances."

"How do you know they aren't following you?"

"I know they are. They have followed me since we left the abandoned house. I know how and when they are tracking me. As I told you before, if anyone asks, we are a couple." Studying the worried look on her face, he added, "If I tried to avoid them, they would be suspicious. After a while they will get tired of tracking me and move on to someone else. I know how they operate. It won't take long for them to become bored."

"What if you're wrong? What if they don't get tired of tracking you? What then?"

"Don't worry about it. I know how to move them in another direction. They trust me; remember, I'm one of them."

She finished her sandwich. The taste in her mouth was bitter. She didn't like the guy and was more than a little concerned. She tilted her head in a defiant manner. "I don't want to lead the wrong people to the hideout. I can't risk hurting the ones who are there."

"I'm only taking you to meet someone who will take you the rest of the way to the camp. All I am is your escort out of the city. I promise I won't let anyone get hurt. Now, can we get started? We're on a schedule."

She thought over her options. She knew Paul had been looking for his brother. He had often told her, "It was just me and Maxwell against the world." She decided to trust him a little longer; if things later seemed wrong she could always ditch him. "Okay," she nodded her acceptance.

SAFE

Back on the road, he seemed to be even more determined to get rid of her as soon as possible. They took back trails and from time to time he referred to a map. "Don't you know where you're going?" she asked.

He turned to look at her as though she was an imbecile. "You're the first person I've ever taken there from this direction. One of the bridges collapsed during the earthquake. They are making repairs on the roads. Do you really want people stopping us and asking questions? I mapped out this route before picking you up. It avoids most of the main highways and offers an alternative route across the river."

They finally came to a stop in a tired little town in the middle of nowhere. She couldn't believe it when he removed his helmet and announced, "We'll stop here for now. We'll wait just a little ways down the road for your guide. He should be meeting us sometime after dark." Taking her by the elbow, he directed her toward a burger joint. "Let's get something to eat."

"So how many times have you slipped people out?" she asked, trying to make conversation. He looked around the room, focusing his attention on the television. There was no sound, so she was annoyed at the way he was ignoring her. Then she realized he was reading the reporters lips. Her mouth dropped open. *Who is this guy?*

After a minute he turned around. "They've started gathering up Christians. They plan to force them to take the mark."

"You read lips?" she asked.

"It comes in handy," he said, shrugging nonchalantly.

"Are you some special ops guy?"

"Let's just say I'm not Paul. We should get started. I don't want to draw attention to us."

She was confused. "I thought we were going to meet someone."

"We are, just not right here." He stood to his feet, tossing his napkin onto his plate.

"Well, shall we go, princess?" he asked, smirking at her.

They boarded the bike, rode through town, crossed a country bridge. Then they took the first right, stopping at a campground. "We'll wait here. The guy should be along in a few hours." He lay down on the grass; pillowing his head with his hand he closed his eyes.

"That's it? You're just going to go to sleep?" Her voice sounded strained as she stuttered from frustration.

"What do you want from me, lady? I was awake all night and spent the day bringing you out here. I still have to go back. I'd like to get some rest, if you think you could shut up." He yawned; then, almost instantly, he was snoring.

Deseraie was frustrated. She was tired, dirty, and had no idea where she was going. She waited, listening to him snore. The sun began to set. She was just beginning to calm down when she heard the sound of a pickup truck. It came from a distance, finally turning into the campground. Before she knew it, the pickup pulled in next to them. Max stretched, yawned, then stood up. After a moment she could see Brad getting out of the pickup

"Brad," she said, thrilled to see a face she knew.

"Hello, Deseraie," he smiled, giving her a hug, then reached over to shake Maxwell's hand. "Thanks for bringing her this far, Max. You have no idea how much we appreciate it. I was expecting more than just Deseraie. Was there a problem?"

Max nodded. "The bridge is out and some of the roads are being watched. The couple I was bringing decided not to leave until they know how their mom is. Also, DC stayed behind to help a friend; but I believe they will be coming next trip. I'll see you then." He got on the bike, gave her a nod, and left.

Brad turned to her. "Don't worry, Deseraie, you're safe now. Sarah will be happy to see you. She'll get a kick out of introducing you to the gang." He escorted her to the pickup; opening the door, he helped her in. "I'm sorry, it's just better for you and everyone else if you don't know where we're going."

"I know," she said. "John explained it to me."

He took out a bandana and secured it around her head. "That should do," he said.

She hadn't realized how tired she was until now. The sound of the engine lulled her; she finally relaxed enough to rest. They must have been traveling for hours. The sun was just coming up when he announced, "We're here."

She reached up and removed the blindfold. "Where is it?" she asked, expecting to see a house or something. He was out of the pickup. He worked quickly, covering it with limbs. "We'll walk from here."

"How much farther," she asked?

"Oh, it's not far. We just can't drive all the way to the cabin from here."

They walked along, discussing the most current events. Brad had lots of questions. "We're pretty isolated out here," he said.

Deseraie heard her name being called. She looked up. "Sarah," she answered. "I'm so glad to see you."

Sarah made the introductions. "You must be exhausted," Sarah said with compassion.

"I'm filthy." Deseraie longed for a shower. Looking around, she understood what John had meant when he tried to explain the place. This was really the middle of nowhere. "Do you have a shower?" she asked, praying.

"Oh sure, Brad and the guys fixed it up for us." The cave opening had been cleared of most of the debris. Sarah escorted her to the cave, showed her around, then pointed to the tub. "You can take a bath if you prefer." Deseraie was so happy she wanted to cry.

Sarah pointed to some extra clothing. "I know these are way too big for you, but at least they're clean. After you are refreshed, we'll get something for you to eat. Oh, and I have a place ready for you to sleep. I thought you would like a nap."

"That sounds like heaven!" Deseraie declared.

Sarah had steamed fish ready for Deseraie. It was absolutely delicious. She was escorted to a cot where she lay down. Her body ached everywhere. She was tired beyond comprehension. Sleep came quickly. An hour later Deseraie turned over, rubbed her eyes, and yawned. She decided to familiarize herself with her new surroundings.

"I can't believe you've done all of this," Deseraie said, speaking to the girls as they showed her around the camp. "You should be proud of yourselves. How many refugees are here now?"

"There are forty-three counting you. We are working to enlarge the camp, but food is a problem. However, we are learning how to dry meat and keep it without it being stolen by bears. We have a small garden and we are canning everything for the winter."

After dinner, the girls changed the subject, bombarding her with questions about the outside world. The guys stopped talking. Everyone looked at her as if she were a reporter for the evening news. The campfire lit the cave as she began to answer their questions.

"The earthquake was terrible," she said. Deseraie's voice caught as she tried to speak. "They still don't know how many lives were lost. It took out so many buildings; some parts of the city were unrecognizable. After the quake, when the darkness fell, I was trapped in a downtown parking garage with some others. They had also escaped death by making it to the garage. I don't know why it took the quake better than the other buildings. I guess it was stronger than the offices. The darkness settled in. We were unable to leave, so we took shelter in some of the cars. Many of them had blankets, coats, food, and even bottled water. We broke into them and used the supplies. Thank God we survived." Deseraie started to cry. "So many didn't."

"After it was all over I walked to my apartment building. It was gone. I don't even know if any of my neighbors made it out. I tried looking but there was too much debris. Some emergency workers showed up. They were busy searching for survivors. They told me I had to leave. I went on to the church. I talked to Pastor John. He arranged for me to come here. Thank you for taking me in."

"What about the Antichrist. What has he been up to?" Cole was curious.

Deseraie asked, "How much do you know? Have you heard about his so-called"—she raised her hands to make parentheses—"resurrection?"

"Just bits and pieces," Cole responded.

"He was on his way to another mercy mission when someone shot him. He, of course, died. It was all the news talked about for days. Then on the third day, he came back to life. The medium instructed everyone to worship him. He actually got up in the temple mound and declared he was Christ. It made me sick to watch it. Oh, and that monument he built of himself, it has been talking."

"The second half has started," Cole said. "What about the witnesses?"

A sad expression swept over Deseraie's face. "They stood up to him and everyone who was worshipping him. They said it was blasphemy. They said the wrath of God was here. It was really intense. Their time was ended, so he had them killed. It was so sad. The news showed them lying dead in the streets, and just like the Bible says, people would not let them be buried. They were partying and sending gifts to each other. Her expression changed to joy. "Oh, you've got to hear about this. This was so cool. The third day they just stood up. The news actually had footage of the clouds parting. We could actually hear a rumbling roar as if the sky was speaking. The Lord said to them, "Come up!" Then they went up into heaven on a cloud! I think that's the neatest thing I've ever seen! It was amazing! After that people were saying things like, "God resurrected them," and how they had heard the voice of God saying, "Come up!" It was actually pretty ironic. Here everyone was rejoicing, praising the Antichrist for his resurrection. And in front of everyone God himself parts the clouds, raises them from the dead, and commands them to come up on a cloud! The Antichrist's resurrection was definitely upstaged."

Her mind went to the suffering people. Somberly, she added, "We need to really be praying for Israel. They're in the line of fire. Since the resurrection you can watch the Antichrist and at times actually see Satan looking out of his eyes. It's disgusting." Deseraie trembled. "He's moving in on the Christians. I guess I got out just in time. The news was on in this place where Max and I stopped to eat. The sound was down but Max read the reporter's lips. He said, 'The Christians were being forced to either take the mark of the beast or go to jail.'"

"It's getting worse," Brad said.

She nodded. "Everything the Bible predicted is happening. It is the most frightening thing you could ever imagine."

The cave gave a beautiful amber glow as the group of refugees discussed the plight of the world. "Jesus is coming soon!" Cole proclaimed, leading them into their nightly Bible study. His understanding of the Word grew daily as he continued to immerse himself in God's description of the world events. "Jesus will soon return to rescue his people. We wait for his glorious appearing!" (Zechariah 14:4, Revelation 19:11–21).

After everyone had gone to bed, Deseraie and Sarah continued to talk. "Sarah, I don't want to just come here and not contribute. I've been thinking. I would like to be a guide for other refugees. I want to help people escape. I don't think those who can't get away from the arm of the regime will survive much longer. I think, maybe, someone who looks like me would not be as suspicious as Brad or one of the guys."

"Well, you don't look like an enemy of the state, that's for sure," Sarah said, laughing.

"I just want to help, Sarah."

"I know, Deseraie. Thank you."

The next day Deseraie went fishing. Justin pulled out a nice, fat worm from his can of dirt. Taking the hook from her line in his hands, he placed the worm on the hook for her. Then, smiling in his charming way, he said, "Now this is the fun part," as he showed her how to cast.

She sat quietly, listening to him talk about their plans. She asked about their escape. As he described running from the regime, she held her side, laughing. "Stop," she giggled. "I can't believe I'm actually laughing," she said. "You're good for me, Justin. Thank you."

He smiled. "You're welcome." At that moment something tugged hard on her fishing line. "You've got one!" Justin exclaimed. "Easy now, reel him in." She jerked on her pole. The fish came out flopping around on the bank. Justin placed it with his. "You're going to be good at this," he said, smiling at her.

"Beginner's luck," she said, denying any talent.

"No," Justin said. "I can see this is where you belong, right here fishing with me." He looked at her, his eyes twinkled mischievously, as he announced, "Tomorrow you bait your own hook."

"No, thank you!" she answered.

Back at Miss Millie's house, Rebecca watched her mom and was confused by the illness. For days her mother had been feverish and unable to speak coherently. "I don't understand, DC. Why isn't she improving?"

DC wanted to help. "Maybe she's too heartbroken. She seems to have given up." You have to keep talking to her. Tell her she is safe, that God hasn't abandoned her. Keep saying it until she believes you."

"Mother, please listen to me. God hasn't abandoned you. You have a mark in your forehead just like mine. He claims you. Mother, you have to try to fight this thing. Whatever Dennis has done to you, God is greater. You don't have to die. You can live. Trust the Lord; he's caring for us. Mother, I can't lose you, not like this. I can't bear to see you give up. Please, Mother, fight this thing. God is bigger than Dennis and everyone else!" She leaned over her mother, crying.

Rebecca was exhausted. DC insisted she get some sleep. "You have to rest. You can't help her if you get sick. I'll stay with her. Don't worry." DC smiled and added, "Mom and I will be fine."

Rebecca nodded her acceptance. She walked into the living room. The sofa looked welcoming. She lay down; as soon as her head hit the pillow, she was out.

DC sat in the chair near Sharon's bed. She was asleep, but he talked to her anyway. "You just lay there and rest, ma'am. I'll read to you." He picked up Miss Millie's Bible. "This is Miss Millie's Bible. It's too bad you never got to meet her. I think you would have liked her. She and I met on the bus. The next day was when the rapture happened. I needed a place to hide, and guess what—I ended up here, where Miss Millie lived. She was already missing, of course. But I didn't know what had happened to her. When I started asking around, I inquired at Miss Millie's church. That's where I met John, Carly, and Rebecca. By the way, she's a wonderful young woman. I admire the way she helps everybody. She really is a sweetheart. You did a good job raising her."

"Anyway, Miss Millie left this place for me and anyone who needed a place to hide. She invited us personally. As you can see, I've made myself at home. What do you say we start in Psalms? My grandma Grace used to love the Psalms. Here we go. This is the Ninety-first Psalm. You're going to like this one. It talks about God's protection. 'He that dwelleth in the secret place of

the most High shall abide under the shadow of the Almighty'"
(Psalm 91:1).

DC stopped to comment. "Now isn't that beautiful. It's just
like poetry. I'll bet a fine lady like you loves poetry.

> I will say of the LORD, He is my refuge and my fortress: my
> God; in him will I trust. Surely he shall deliver thee from
> the snare of the fowler, and from the noisome pestilence.
> He shall cover thee with his feathers, and under his wings
> shalt thou trust: his truth shall be thy shield and buckler.
> Thou shalt not be afraid for the terror by night; nor for
> the arrow that flieth by day; Nor for the pestilence that
> walketh in darkness; nor for the destruction that wasteth
> at noonday. A thousand shall fall at thy side, and ten thou-
> sand at thy right hand; but it shall not come nigh thee.
> Only with thine eyes shalt thou behold and see the reward
> of the wicked. Because thou hast made the LORD, which is
> my refuge, even the most High, thy habitation; There shall
> no evil befall thee, neither shall any plague come nigh thy
> dwelling. For he shall give his angels charge over thee, to
> keep thee in all thy ways. They shall bear thee up in their
> hands, lest thou dash thy foot against a stone.
>
> Psalm 91:2–12

DC looked up from his reading.

Sharon was watching him, smiling. "That is very beautiful,
isn't it?" she asked, as though she had heard the whole thing.

"Praise the Lord! It's a pleasure to see you awake. Ma'am, I'm
going to fetch Rebecca. She'll want to know your better." DC
started to leave but she stopped him.

"No, please don't. Let her sleep. We'll both tell her together in
the morning."

The next day her mom was awake. She was also well enough
to travel. Rebecca insisted she drinks a cup of coffee and eat.
"Mom, please, we have a long journey ahead of us. You need
your strength."

DC disappeared for a couple of hours. When he returned he announced, "It's all set."

At midnight there was a knock at the door. DC answered; it was Maxwell. He nodded to DC, looked at Rebecca, and asked, "Are you two ladies ready?" Rebecca grabbed their things. Maxwell almost carried Sharon. They walked several blocks to an abandoned warehouse. A beautiful SUV sat waiting for them. They loaded up and started out of town, leaving their past lives behind them.

Many miles later they stopped for a break. Lunch was simple: sandwiches and water. They moved on, eventually meeting up with Brad. His face reflected his concern when he saw Sharon. He blindfolded Rebecca and Sharon. They rode the rest of the way unable to see the road. Her mother slept the last part of the journey.

Rebecca and Sarah took turns caring for Sharon. Traveling had taken a lot out of her. It was a full week before she was back on her feet. Rebecca handed her a mirror and showed her the mark. "See, you are not abandoned by God. He accepted your cry for help."

Sharon started to improve, though it was slow. The camp agreed with her. Before long she was helping Rebecca with the nursing jobs. A steady stream of refugees had started to arrive after the earthquake. Sarah was happy to have help with the sick.

Sharon was finally at peace, but the more she thought about it the more concerned she became. "Dennis isn't going to stop looking for me, Rebecca. He will find me and then all of these people will be in danger."

"What do you want to do, Mother?" Rebecca asked.

"I think I have to go away from here." Sharon said, her eyes expressing emotion she could not explain. "I can't let these innocent people be harmed because of me."

Rebecca understood her mother's concern. "I think we should pray about it."

Brad often left without telling anyone what he was doing. Today he and Justin got up early. He kissed Sarah good-bye and left. Most of the day went by before they returned; this time with an army truck. At first, when Deseraie saw it coming up the hill, she was terrified. Then she recognized Brad driving it. They opened the back, and under a tarp was a group of people. They were tired, dirty, and seemed afraid. She walked over to them; Sarah and the girls were already welcoming the newcomers.

"You must be hungry," Mackenzie said. "Come with me." The young girl, now barely seventeen, escorted them to an outdoor sink where they could wash up. Then she showed them to a table. The others prepared food and started to serve the newcomers.

Sarah greeted Brad with a hug. The young heroes gathered around their newest refugees. Cole spoke, "Welcome to our safe camp. We are all refugees from the regime. You will eat and then we will show you around. The camp is divided into two locations. The men and the women are separate with the exception of husbands and wives. Families are housed together. We hunt, fish, and grow our own food. You will be asked to do the same. We have Bible and prayer time every evening. This is not a requirement, but we hope you will attend. If anyone has any special talents, please tell us. We are interested in continuing to improve. You are welcome."

After everyone had eaten, they were asked to give their names, occupations, and special abilities.

Deseraie was asked to help with the process. The line formed in front of her. One at a time the people approached her to give her their names.

"I am a teacher," Mr. Collins said as he walked up to Deseraie.

"What do you teach, Mr. Collins?" Deseraie asked.

"I teach math."

"Wonderful. We will keep that in mind." Deseraie finally looked up from her paperwork long enough to notice the man with his wife.

The middle-aged woman held his hand. She looked at Deseraie with such fear in her eyes that Deseraie almost backed up. "My name is Eleanor Collins. This is my husband. We have been running for our lives for days. Thank you for allowing us to come here. I am a good cook. You'll see."

Deseraie's heart went out to them. She got up from her makeshift desk and walked around it to the couple. "I am sorry I didn't think; I should have greeted you sooner." Reaching out, she gave them both a hug. "You are more than welcome. But don't thank me. I am like you. I came here to escape. Your help will be greatly appreciated. But for now you must rest. You are safe here." Mr. Collins held his wife tightly as she started to weep from relief. He rested his head on hers; a river of tears fell as they thanked God for the safe house. The prayer of praise rose from the man and deposited itself on all those who were watching. Worship sprang from the group as the others started to join them in thanks to the God of mercy. Their hearts were full as they took refuge in the most comforting safety of all—the Lord's presence.

Karen watched the scene. She walked up to Mr. and Mrs. Collins, waiting for them to regain their composure. "If you'll follow me, we have a room where you can rest." She led them to a private room in the cave. "This is for husbands and wives." There in the corner of the little room lit only by candlelight was a makeshift bed. Sarah had lovingly placed a collection of pillows and quilts she brought back from one of their trips home. Beside the bed was a small table that held a candle. It wasn't much, but here it was—the honeymoon suite.

Feeling the chill, Karen said, "It can get cold in here. There is wood for a fire." She bent down and lit a small fire. "This will break the chill. Get some rest; I'll see you in the morning."

The next day word spread through camp that one of the gentlemen who had just arrived was going to be installing a computer that would allow them to get the news. "It's completely undetectable." He had brought it to camp hoping to keep in touch with the outside world. "We can track the Antichrist and he won't know it. This opens up the outside world to us."

Cole looked skeptical. "I don't know about this. What if you're wrong?"

The young man, David, stood up facing Cole. "I'm not. Listen, I do this kind of thing. I know it's not particularly modest of me, but I'm more than just a geek. I'm the guy those guys would come to if they had a problem. I promise you. I wouldn't do this if I believed it was dangerous."

Cole knew he had to trust those who came to the camp, but his naturally suspicious nature made him cautious. "Since everyone here is taking a chance if you're wrong, I believe you should explain it tonight at the Bible study. We'll take a vote; if everyone in the camp is okay with it, we'll allow it." Disappointment flushed David's face, but he did understand. He nodded his agreement.

Mr. and Mrs. Collins turned out to be more than a math teacher and a cook. Mr. Collins was a man of many talents. He teamed up with Simon and the others, helping them make their solar system more effective.

Mrs. Collins began cooking. Her food was delicious. She seemed most content in the kitchen. Sarah and the girls were more than happy to help her. She took their venison and turned it into the best meal they had eaten since their arrival on the mountain. Her trout dish was succulent and like nothing they had previously made. Even with their limited supplies, she turned dinner into a dining experience.

Mackenzie piped up excitedly. "We gathered wild herbs today. And I picked the berries."

Mrs. Collins flushed with pride as the group began to flood her with compliments.

She was thrilled to be able to do something for those who had been so kind. The boys took their turn doing the dishes while the girls relaxed after helping Mrs. Collins cook.

After dinner Cole began the business of explaining David's desire to connect them with the outside world. Everyone was intrigued but some needed to understand how he was doing this. After about an hour of questions and answers, David had talked them through the whole process.

Justin was all for it. "We have to know what is really happening. We've missed so much."

Finally, everyone decided to go along with their refugee genius. He hooked it up. Quickly they were listening to the world news. David hit a couple of buttons, and reruns of the Antichrist's resurrection came up for them to see and hear. Even after the fact, the event still brought chills to the listeners.

"He is pure evil," Mr. Collins announced. "He declared war on the witnesses and had them killed as soon as he came back to life. God help us."

Cole wanted to see the footage of the witnesses. "Can you go back and show the witnesses?"

"Sure." David pushed a few buttons and the witnesses came into their cave. He let it play. The testimonies of the men rang out through the rock walls. That night they did not have their usual Bible study; instead, they listened as the witnesses preached to them. The sound of their ancient dialects warmed the hearts of those who were hungry for the precious word of God.

Deseraie couldn't shake the feeling that she should help others escape. She told Brad she wanted to go along. "There should be a halfway point that is more sheltered. We were out in the middle of nowhere in plain sight. There must be an abandoned house or something where we can meet Maxwell without being overexposed. Even under a bridge is better than out in the open."

"She's right," Simon agreed. "We need to find a shelter even if it is just to protect us from the weather."

THE WORLD OUT OF CONTROL

The world continued to spin out of control. Men and women were taken by force into rehabilitation encampments. These were the ones who dared to think independently of the Antichrist and his army.

The natural disasters that had come upon the earth were a mystery to everyone. There appeared thunder and lightning, storms so severe that fire mingled with blood in the form of a hailstorm fell from the sky. It sizzled along the ground, continued to the trees, blazing paths of destruction to everything in its way. Forest fires were reported everywhere.

The sun became dark, the moon took on a hideous bloody glow, and stars cast themselves to the earth. Nothing quite like the star shower had ever been seen. Spheres of fire rained down on the earth leaving the sky darker than normal for the loss of them. Whereas they ran a normal twenty-four-hour course, the world was dark a third of the day and a third of the night longer. The heavens appeared to roll away. Earthquakes continued to shake the planet, displacing mountains. The ocean reached up and covered the islands. Men, moved by terror, ran to the mountains seeking refuge. They were so frightened by the many plagues that they preferred to be buried by the mountains than to face more of the coming judgment of the Lord.

The ocean was hit with such a catastrophic event that many of the fish died. The water was turned into blood. Something unknown had fallen from the sky. The earth took on a foul odor as the blood curdled from the heat. The beaches were littered by dead fish and sea creatures.

As if that wasn't enough, the fresh water was also contaminated. A star fell to the earth. It damaged the freshwater source. It poisoned the creeks and rivers. Those who drank from them died. Christians, who remembered the story of the plagues of Egypt, dug near water for fresh, uncontaminated sources (Revelation 8, Exodus 7:17–25).

Most recently, locust-like monsters came up out of the ground to sting and torment people of the earth. At the same time as their arrival, the air became contaminated by sulfur. The smell was unbearable. The cloud of smoke darkened the world as it choked people, causing them to have trouble breathing.

Scientists attributed the invasion of these beasts to the freakish happenings. Apparently something had disturbed their natural habitat, leaving them no choice but to invade mankind's domain. They were hideous-looking creatures that flew. Other people claimed they were an invading army of aliens who had already kidnapped many of the earth's citizens. And that it was just a matter of time before they killed everyone on planet Earth. They attacked with speed. Anyone they stung suffered excruciating pain for months. There were reports of people who were stung, wanting to die because of the pain, but they could not. Whatever they were, whether animal or alien, their poison was meant to torment their victims. Only the children of God were safe from their vicious attacks (Revelation 9:1–11).

Justin and the others received word that churches were being burned. Pastor John and Carly were among those who were expected to change their faith in Christ for what the world dictated. They steadfastly refused. The soldiers arrested them and many others of the faith. Paul and Shelby were among the offenders.

"They plan to make examples of Paul and John," DC said sadly.

Sarah knew her husband. He would not just allow their friends to be murdered. He would try to help. She readied herself for what was coming.

Brad asked, "Have you heard from Max?"

DC nodded. "He was arrested yesterday for treason. They know he's been helping us."

Brad had to help his friends, even if it meant he wouldn't make it back. "Brad, you can't," Sarah pleaded. "It's too dangerous. You have a responsibility to all of us."

Brad held her in his arms. "I love you; you know that. But I have to do what I can to help the others."

Justin stood up. He was taller. In the past few years he had changed. His lean frame was muscled from hard work. The look on his face said "I'm not a child anymore." "I'm coming with you," he announced. "They're my friends too."

"You can't. It's too dangerous." Brad stared back, determined.

"I am," Justin argued.

"We all are," the guys stepped up next to Justin.

"What about the camp; a lot of people are counting on you. They need you here to keep things running."

Karen chimed in. "There are enough of us who can stay behind to work. We'll post guards around the camp. We'll be on high alert until you come back. We can protect the camp as good as any of you."

Simon said, "We are coming with you. You aren't going to run into a burning building without backup." Cole and the others stood their ground. "We may be young, but we aren't kids."

Brad nodded. "Okay, but you do what I say. Is that understood?" They agreed.

Justin turned to Sarah. "Mom, I love you. I know you're not my birth mom, but I want you to know I couldn't love you more if you were. I'll take care of him and bring him back. I promise. Don't worry. Everything will be fine. We'll go and help as many as we can. Then we're coming back, even if we all have to drag him back kicking and screaming. We won't let him throw his life away."

Sharon said, "I have to go back too, Rebecca. You know your father. He will not stop looking for me until he finds me. We both knew this was just a temporary stop until I got my health back. If I go to him maybe I can convince Dennis to stop this madness."

"Mom, you can't. It's suicide. Dennis warned me. He told me if he saw either of us again he would treat us like common criminals.'"

"I'm sorry, honey. I have to try. Rebecca, if I can help save just one of the Christians, it will be worth it."

A flash shot through Rebecca's memory. She remembered the dream as if it had just taken place. "You're right, Mother. I almost forgot. I dreamed I was caught. I didn't tell you before, because it was Dennis who had turned me in. I thought that when we escaped, we would be out of danger. I had forgotten until just now. These people, Mom, they were in the dream." She looked around, her mind connecting the faces of the people in the camp to strangers she had seen in her dream. "If we stay, we'll put everyone here in danger. We have to go. God will go with us."

Her mother smiled and stroked her face. "My beautiful Rebecca. You are and always have been my greatest joy. I'm so proud of you."

Deseraie knew she had to return as well. She looked at Mackenzie and whispered, "I'm going too." Mac nodded. She knew Deseraie had to try to help.

They piled into the army truck. Cole moved into the driver's seat. "We'll be back as soon as possible. We're just going to see if we can get to them and bring them back." Sarah and the others waved good-bye. Then they all began to pray.

Brad asked around. He managed to locate most of his Christian friends. They, along with John, Paul, Carly, and Shelby were in jail. He also learned they had tortured Max. He, of course, told the authorities nothing. Brad went by Max's home to check for a message. He and Max worked it out so that they could leave each other a message in a panel behind the wall. He felt around for anything Max might have left for him. His hand rested on a manila envelope. Inside he found copies of reports on Dennis, Harry, and others Brad did not know. No doubt, this was what Max had used to blackmail Dennis into letting the pastors out of jail in the first place. He noticed a handwritten note: *If anything happens to me, see to it the authorities get this.*

Brad waited to present his file of information. While he did, he arranged to see John and Paul.

"Brad." Their faces lit up as they greeted their friend.

"I'm going to get you guys out of here," he said.

"No, Brad, don't try. It's too dangerous. You'll just get yourself into trouble. How's Max?" Paul asked.

"You haven't heard?" Brad was sick; he hated to tell Paul that his brother had been caught and tortured. "They arrested him."

The look on Paul's face said he understood. "He knew what he was risking and he did it anyway." Paul looked sad, then he added, "God bless him."

Brad was flustered; he had something on Dennis, he just didn't know exactly how to use it.

John knew Brad was planning something. "Look, it's too late for us. You have to focus on your family and the others. We are scheduled to be put to death tomorrow morning."

"What?" Brad exclaimed. "Why, for what crime?"

"For serving Jesus," Paul answered. "You're a good friend. That's why you have to leave now." They stood to their feet. Looking at Brad, they both smiled.

John added, "It's okay. We're not sad, Brad. As Paul the apostle said, 'I have fought a good fight, I have finished my course, I have kept the faith'" (2 Timothy 4:7).

Brad managed to visit Max as well. Max looked at him with fire in his eyes. "You know what to do, now just do it."

"This stuff also incriminates you."

Max seemed resolved. "That doesn't matter."

They faced each other, both men reading the other's expression. "Okay, then we use it."

Max nodded. He made a fist and bumped the window between them. Brad did the same. Max stood up, looked at Brad and said, "Do it."

Brad prayed for wisdom. Then he remembered the judge who had first heard Paul and John's case. He did some checking. He was right. The guy was one of the names listed on Max's list of dirt. He watched until the judge emerged from the courthouse. He noted which car was his. Deseraie provided a distraction. She managed to get the judge's attention while Justin slipped a few choice pieces of the file into the car.

"It was easy, Dad." Brad had to admit even now Justin's talent for slipping in and out of situations was still paying off.

They made their way through all of the names on the list with a little note that simply stated, "We know what you've been doing and so will everyone else if the Christians aren't released."

Deseraie was about to slip back to the group when one of her ex-coworkers started pointing and demanding they arrest her. "She is a Christian. She was the girlfriend of that Pastor Paul. Someone arrest her."

Brad stepped forward. Simon grabbed him. "We can't help her, boss. There are too many police nearby. They'll just get all of us. We'll talk to the judge. We can still use Max's information. Let's see what the judge thinks." Brad held his temper.

Sharon and Rebecca walked into Dennis's office. "Hello, darling." Sharon greeted Dennis with a smile.

"Dear, how are you feeling? I trust your time with Rebecca has been good for you." Dennis stood up, walked over to them, and greeted them both with a kiss.

"I am much better. I understand you have some friends of ours in your jail. I would like for you to let them go."

Dennis smiled his evil smile. "I'm sorry, that is simply impossible. They are Christians, you see. I have to make an example of them."

"And what about me, darling? Are you going to make an example out of me too? I am, after all, a Christian as well. Are you going to hunt down and kill all of us? I love you, Dennis, but what you are doing is wrong. God will punish you if you continue. But if you change, he will forgive you. You just have to change, Dennis; and everything can go back to the way it was."

Dennis looked into Sharon's eyes. He watched her flinch as he drew her closer to him. "I have made my decision. I won't let them go. But you can still come home. I miss you. I will also take care of Rebecca. She doesn't have to die like the others. I'll protect you both."

Rebecca's mom looked at her daughter. "No, Mother. I'll never sit by while my friends die."

Sharon kissed her husband. "I will go to my grave loving you. But I won't come home unless you agree to help those people. Dennis, what are they to you? They're just chess pieces in this game of success you play. They haven't really even committed a crime. Let them go, darling. I love you. I'll come home."

For a moment she could see he was thinking it over, considering her offer. Dennis actually looked sad. Then the shutters closed over his eyes as he hid his emotions. "I'm afraid that would be impossible."

"Then we are at an impasse." She and Rebecca started to leave. She reached the door, turned the handle, and looked back at him. "I forgive you, Dennis." Then they walked out. In the hall guards were waiting to arrest them for practicing Christianity.

Willy looked at Dennis, questioning his decision. "Are you positive, sir?" he asked, confused by Dennis's cold demeanor toward his wife and stepdaughter.

"They are guilty of refusing to recant their Christian faith. Arrest them at once." Rebecca noticed a look of madness entered his eyes as he said the words. *He's insane,* she thought.

In his office, Dennis mentally rehearsed their conversation. *How dare they think I am so easily persuaded? Having them both arrested is the most difficult decision I've made so far. There is no doubt this move will prove to everyone I am totally committed to the regime. No one will dare question my loyalty now. Rebecca proved to be very useful. Sharon's faith was an unfortunate turn of events. I will miss her.*

"Rebecca." Carly ran to her and hugged her. "I thought you were safe. What are you doing here?"

Rebecca looked over at John. "Do you remember my telling you about the dream I had?"

"Yes. Why do you ask?" He studied her face, listening.

"Well, I remembered more about it. The people at the camp were here with us. I didn't think much about them in my dream because I didn't know them at the time; but everything came flooding back to me in a second. We decided to leave before we endangered them."

Looking across the room, she saw Deseraie. "What happened?"

"One of my ex-coworkers recognized me. They demanded I be arrested."

The next morning John spoke to the overcrowded room of believers. All of them awaited their execution for following Christ. They all listened quietly as he said good-bye. "God has always had a remnant; the chosen few. They are the believers who followed him even when it was unpopular, even when there was danger. How many times did he save Israel? How many times did he save, for himself, a small group of people who would not bend, who would not bow? They would not betray God even in the face of the most dire situations. They were God's chosen men and women, who could not be bought or persuaded to turn from their own personal convictions, no matter what the consequences were" (Hebrews 11:32–40).

"He will always call men and women to serve him. And they will: they will serve him even when death is their final destination! Stephen was stoned to death for daring to speak of and for Christ. Peter was crucified upside down. Peter's wife was also crucified. Many were fed to lions, burned at the stake and beaten mercilessly. What was their sin? What was their crime? They dared to love God to the death! Christ, our beloved Savior—the One we all look to for eternal life—is worth the sacrifice."

"Before the apostle Paul was put to death for following Christ, he wrote about his steadfast dedication and God's promises to us for our future with him in 2 Timothy 4:6–8. He said,"

> For I am now ready to be offered, and the time of my departure is at hand. I have fought a good fight, I have finished my course, I have kept the faith: Henceforth there is laid up for me a crown of righteousness, which the Lord, the righteous judge, shall give me at that day: and not to me only, but unto all them also that love his appearing.

Paul nodded, agreeing with John. He added, "He did not waver in the face of death but placed his faith in God, declaring, 'We are confident, I say, and willing rather to be absent from the body, and to be present with the Lord' (2 Corinthians 5:8). The most wonderful and amazing thing is that the moment we leave this earth, we will step into the presence of Christ, from death to life. It's as simple as that. Our last breath here is our beginning in the kingdom of our God. Nothing this world holds can keep us from the presence of God. The very moment we leave these frail bodies, we are in the glorious company of our Great and Holy King!"

John's enthusiasm got the best of him. He piped in with, "We are unbelievably blessed! There is no greater honor I can think of than to spend my life serving Christ with every fiber of my being, knowing one day I will walk into his kingdom as his own child. We are the sons and daughters of Father God. Christ has redeemed us, making a way for all of us to know him personally" (John 1:12).

Paul agreed. "That's right. We have the opportunity and great honor to worship him this final time on earth with the dedication of our lives for his glory. We are privileged to be here to give back to him the only thing we have left: our lives. They can torture us, they can kill us, but they can't separate us from the love of God. The apostle Paul writes,"

> Who shall separate us from the love of Christ? shall tribulation, or distress, or persecution, or famine, or nakedness, or peril, or sword? As it is written, For thy sake we are killed all the day long; we are accounted as sheep for the slaughter. Nay, in all these things we are more than conquerors through him that loved us. For I am persuaded, that neither death, nor life, nor angels, nor principalities, nor powers, nor things present, nor things to come, Nor height, nor depth, nor any other creature, shall be able to separate us from the love of God, which is in Christ Jesus our Lord.
>
> Romans 8:35–39

"We will not deny him. They don't understand that, 'For to me to live is Christ, and to die is gain' (Philippians 1:21). I am ready to meet the Lord. I long for his presence. I want to join him in his kingdom."

John noticed the tears in the eyes of their friends. His smile was bright. The joy on his face lit up the jail. "Don't cry for us. Don't waste your time mourning. We are rejoicing, for soon our feet will touch the streets of gold. We will be with our Lord. We will be praising him in the very presence of angels." John smiled at his friends. Shaking his head he added, "I have waited all of my life to join that choir. I intend to sing his praises in his kingdom."

"Please don't cry for me; I'm going home. I am finally going home to be with those I love. I'll see my mom and dad and all the others who have gone on before me. This is the happiest day of my life." John stopped speaking. Tears of joy ran freely down his face.

Carly studied him. Her face held the expression of a child. She was the only reason he had to stay, but soon she would join him. They would not be separated for long. Soon he would see her sweet face again. He opened his arms. She walked into his embrace. "We'll be together soon," he comforted her.

"Yes," she agreed. He kissed her.

The guard, Willy, pulled gently on his arm. "It's time, Pastor," he said, barely containing his grief. He watched as his coworker moved toward Paul. He had learned to love these two preachers. *What had they done to deserve death?* he asked himself.

Carly would not let go. She wrapped her arms around John, saying, "No, not yet. I love you," she whispered.

"I'll see you soon," he answered back. "I love you, Carly."

Rebecca stepped forward. Taking Carly in her arms, she tried to comfort her friend. "You have to let go now, Carly." Tears popped into Willy's eyes as he fought with his conscience to do his job.

"No, please." Carly cried pitifully as Willy led John away to be killed.

Paul was escorted, away from the little group of believers, behind John. Shelby sank to the floor of the jail as the strength of her body completely abandoned her.

Deseraie stepped forward. "Shelby," she said, with her voice barely above a whisper. "Shelby," she repeated. Her heart went out to the woman who had once been her rival.

Shelby turned to her; the look of despair in her eyes shook Deseraie to her soul. "I can't go on without him," she said softly to Deseraie.

"I know," the other girl whispered. "I know," she said, reaching out to hold Shelby. She wanted to protect her from the pain she knew Shelby was suffering, but she couldn't. The tears started to fall. Deseraie just held her and prayed for God to give her the strength to face the future without Paul.

One by one the little group of believers slipped to the floor of the jail. Their hearts broke as they sought the Lord. He was their only source of comfort. There, time melted away. The room was no longer a jail. It became their altar.

John and Paul walked up to the place of killing. They looked at each other; smiles crossed both of their faces. "I'll see you in his kingdom," Paul said to John.

John's smile of hope broadened. "We're going home, brother!" They were told to place their heads into position; they did. Both of them began to worship the Lord. John began to sing, "What can wash away my sin? Nothing but the blood of Jesus" (Robert Lowry). Two men stood nearby waiting for them. They wore hoods. They were there to make an impression on all who watched the executions. They raised their swords. John continued to sing, "What can make me whole again?" The one on the right nodded to the other, signaling he was ready. John's voice rang clear. "Nothing but the blood—" The music stopped. Simultaneously, the two men who had lived as brothers in Christ died as brothers in Christ. They went home. "O death, where is thy sting? O grave, where is thy victory?" (1 Corinthians 15:55).

John and Paul looked at each other. They were dressed in robes of purest white. The atmosphere seemed to support them as though they were standing on ground. They looked up, and in front of them were two enormous white pearls. They recognized them as the gates of heaven. The pearls glided open, revealing to them the streets of gold beckoning them to enter. They walked forward; as they did, they saw a great host of people surrounding them, standing, clapping as they walked through the gates. They looked around in awe as the great cloud of witnesses continued to cry out, welcoming them into their eternal home with words of encouragement (Hebrews 12:1). One man stood near the front and shouted, "I knew you could do it. Welcome home, boys, welcome home!" Their warm smiles and cheers of congratulations seemed to continue for several minutes.

John's father stepped out of the crowd. "Dad," he said.

"It's so good to see you, boys," Dad Jentson welcomed them. John's mom ran to them, hugging them both enthusiastically.

Paul's son and daughter ran to Paul. He held them as tightly as he could; tears of joy ran down his face as he was reunited with them. "I'm so glad to see you; praise God!"

John's father ushered them along. There, near the crystal sea (Revelation 4:6) was a throne with a rainbow hovering over it. Jesus stepped forward, greeting them. John and Paul bowed, worshipping him. Jesus wiped the tears from their eyes and led them down the streets of gold, stopping in front of their mansions.

Suddenly, they were with a multitude of those who had been killed for the name of Christ. In unison, they all began to cry out, "How long, Lord Holy and true, before you avenge our enemies of our blood?" (Revelation 6:10).

BLACKMAIL

Dennis had watched the scene from the back of the room. He stayed in the shadows near the guards. He heard the touching good-bye the two preachers shared with their friends and wives. A smirk came over his face. It was all so predictable. Those two were Bible thumpers to the end.

He paid particular attention to Rebecca and Sharon, testing them, watching their reactions to their friends' executions. At one point Rebecca had turned, staring at him. Their eyes locked. He watched her facial expression turn to disgust. Then she looked away, her head held high. He watched, amused, as even in her present situation she snubbed him. She was a hateful girl, always challenging him. She never allowed him to get close to her. She was constantly suspicious of him. It was that trait that he had enjoyed most about her. He enjoyed sparring with her mentally. She never bored him. He admired her spirit. She had been a worthy adversary.

The show was over. The pastors were led away to be executed. He turned to his assistant, Roger, who quickly read him his day's agenda. He listed all of the most important meetings and calls as they walked back to the office. They rounded the corner. Roger stopped at his desk. Dennis continued on through the door, closing it behind him. A quick knock and Roger walked through it, "I almost forgot. Late last evening I received this package for you. A young man delivered it. He said it was for your eyes only. You had already left for your 6:00 meeting and I was on my way out so I set it aside."

"Thank you." Dennis picked up the packet; opening it he looked inside. "Roger," he bellowed. "Who left this?"

Roger peeped back through the door. "It was a young man, sir. I didn't ask him who he was. Why? Is it important?"

Dennis picked up the phone. "Get me the number for Carl Massey!"

Roger rushed to assist. He dialed the number and then said, "Please hold for Dennis Billings."

"Stop the executions!" Dennis ordered. Roger's mouth flew open; he couldn't believe what he was hearing. He glanced down at the photos on Dennis' desk. There, Dennis was with the governor's wife. *Oh, this wasn't good at all. Dennis would blame him for any backlash.* He stepped out of the office and tried to disappear.

Carl Massey was confused by the demand. "I'm sorry, Dennis, but they have already been executed."

Dennis fumed. He was in trouble. He had to find out who was blackmailing him and stop them by any means necessary. "Postpone the other executions until you hear from me directly. Is that understood?"

"Yes, sir," Carl Massey agreed. *Hummmmmm.* The line went dead. Dennis had hung up. This wasn't the job-well-done call he had expected to receive from his superior. He hung up the phone, wondering what had caused Dennis Billings to change his mind. He made a mental note to look into it.

The judge was also in a quandary of his own. After returning to his car the night before and finding the packet, he looked around trying to identify anyone who looked suspicious. He had talked briefly with a lovely young woman. Now he wondered if she was there to divert his attention.

Alone in his office he laid the evidence out on his desk. Once again he studied its contents. He was ruined. Anyone exposing him would be condemning him to prison or worse. Judges can't go to prison and live. Who was this person? All the note said was, "Release the Christians or this goes public."

He studied the photos, remembering his early years as a young enthusiastic prosecutor. These were pictures of the payoff he had received for losing the case against Joey Maldoni. The guy was a thug. The charges against him were numerous. Judge Willibie thought he had destroyed all of the evidence; but there, in black and white, was evidence of Willibie's mishandling of the case. *Where did they get this?* he wondered.

He recalled the warning Joey's father had given him. "Take the money," the old man said. "Buy your wife something nice. Why should she be a widow at such a young age?" He took the money. It was the biggest mistake of his life. From then on he was theirs. He had not been able to shake the connection. They had placed him in his position as judge. They told him who to convict and who to let go. Their enemies were many. He had to talk to Joey's dad. They owed him. Maybe they could make this whole mess go away. He began to tremble. He hated his association with the mob. He wasn't in good health. His nerves were shot, and talking with them was not good for a man in his condition.

Brad had watched the execution. He became even more determined to get his friends out. His mind shot back to his conversation with Maxwell; he would not watch another one of his friends die!

Harry had also been in the crowd when the preachers were murdered. He liked those guys. He had tried more than once to get Dennis to leave them alone. It galled him to see the depths of Dennis's thirst for power.

He noticed Brad in the crowd. Brad hadn't been around much lately. He might have known he would show up for this. Harry had been willing to follow Brad to keep Dennis happy. He had hoped Brad would keep Dennis from focusing on John and Paul. It hadn't worked. The spectacle had been disgusting. He was sickened by the whole thing. There was no way he was going to help Dennis kill anyone else. He was curious though. Harry decided he might as well follow Brad for old time's sake.

Dennis decided to have Max brought to his office. Max walked up to the door. His large frame enveloping the doorway, he stopped. "Come in, Maxwell," Dennis invited. "Sit down."

Walking through the door, Max held up his hands, showing, without words, he was handcuffed. Dennis motioned to Willy. "Go ahead, take those things off. You may leave us now, Willy." He looked at Maxwell. "So you have decided to blackmail me?"

"So you received my package." Maxwell smiled arrogantly.

It annoyed Dennis, but he did not let on. "How can we work this thing out?"

"Let the Christians go."

"Unfortunately the preachers are already dead," Dennis stated as a matter of fact.

Max absorbed the information without flinching. "That makes me very unhappy." His manner was unreadable.

Dennis shifted in his seat. "I didn't get the package until after their executions."

"I'm sorry to hear that." Maxwell looked at Dennis coldly. "That is not good for you."

"I will release the Christians. I have already given orders to not kill the others."

"Why haven't you already released them?" Maxwell's patience was growing slim.

"I want a guarantee that this will never fall into the wrong hands."

"I'm sorry, Dennis, but I can't make that promise. As I told you before, if anything happens to me, I have left instructions concerning this information. My man in the field is probably calling the governor as we speak."

"Stop him!" Dennis's usual suave control slipped. "I want all of the copies or there's no deal!"

In the blink of an eye, Maxwell grabbed Dennis by the collar, pulling him close. "Listen, you slimeball, there's no way you're getting every copy. The day you went after these people, you sealed your fate! I would like nothing more than to see you twisting like a worm on a hook! My brother was my only family. His wife is all I have left of him. If anything happens to her or her friends, I'm coming after you! And what happened to Paul is exactly what will happen to you! My copy is insurance for both of us. They stay alive, and I don't kill you. That's the deal. The moment you cross the line, every reporter in the country gets a copy of you and the governor's wife!" Max smiled. "Oh, and I saved the best for last. I also have pictures of you with Helen Maldoni, Joey's wife. They will go directly to Joey if anything happens to me."

Dennis swallowed nervously. Perspiration formed over the top of his lip. His face reflected his fear.

Max pulled him closer; his voice was low and menacing. "Now, get my sister-in-law and her friends out of this despicable place before I lose my temper and remember just how much I hate you for killing Paul."

Dennis reached for the phone. He pushed the redial button. Carl Massey picked up. Dennis barked at him. "Release the Christians. Don't argue with me, just do it!" His usual control was gone. Bulldog had made his point.

Carl Massey hung up the phone, ordered the release of the prisoners, then decided to check things out for himself. "Willy, did the preachers have any guests in the last few days?"

"Yeah, they had a guy stop by yesterday."

"Bring me the tape on that visit. I want to look at any and all visitors who have been here to see them."

Soon, he was watching Brad; but what intrigued him most was the phrase. "I'm going to get you guys out of here." He considered the statement, taking into account Dennis's call demanding he stop the execution of the preachers. This was interesting. He walked to the door, opened it, and said, "Willy, bring me this Brad Holden. I want to talk to him."

Willy was sick. Things were way out of hand. He couldn't understand how so many decent people were being punished for just being themselves. Bringing this guy Brad in for a talk just made him more concerned. He didn't want to see any more innocent people hurt. He had to break free someway; he wanted out. "He's an okay guy, sir. He's just a friend, that's all."

"Bring him to me anyway. I'll decide if he's okay or not."

Brad wasn't surprised when his friends were suddenly released. He also wasn't surprised when he was unceremoniously picked up by the police. "Stay here," he told Justin and the others. We have to move these people to safety. I'll be back soon. Be ready to move.

Willy called Max as soon as he got the orders telling him he was going to have to bring Brad in for questioning. Max had a friend slip a note under Massey's door. It simply said, "Don't push your luck."

Carl Massey looked at the note, then asked, "Why would I receive a note like this?"

Brad looked it over. "I guess one of your friends is getting worried about you."

He showed Brad the tape of his conversation with the pastors, "What did you mean, you were going to get them out?"

"Just what I said, but I failed, didn't I?" Brad watched Massey as though he were sizing up his prey.

"Tell me more." Massey wanted the details.

"I have information on your boss and other key people. Let's just say they aren't happy about it. I don't believe they will be happy with you if you continue to hold me. It will be dangerous for them. And knowing some of your friends, that means it will be dangerous for you also. I believe that is what the note is inferring, don't you?"

"So you are blackmailing Dennis Billings. Who else?"

"I believe it's better for you and me if I don't elaborate. I also think that the least time I spend in your office, the better it is for both of us. Let's face it; the least you know about me, the safer. Why should you place yourself in harm's way by asking so many questions?"

He drew in a breath and released it. "So I'm supposed to just let you walk away?"

"Why not? Why should you have to pay for the sins of so many others? They're the ones in the hot seat. The longer I stay here, the more suspicious you become. After all, they don't know whether or not I'm telling you everything. If I disappear, my friends will see to it that these various people suffer for it. Your frienemies are going to know they're in trouble. It is better for them to simply kill you than to let me be harmed. I'm sure you understand."

Massey received the information, nodded, then added. "For now, but you are making enemies of some pretty dangerous people."

"You think we're not already in danger? You had two of my best friends murdered today!" Brad's face was red with anger. He stood to his feet. His fist came down, pounding Massey's desk. A look, far from Christian, covered his face. "They were men I thought of as brothers. What can your friends threaten us with that we aren't already living through?" He pointed at the door behind him. "Now, I'm walking out that door. And you're going to let me; because if you don't, the wrong people are going to know you were the one who placed them in harm's way and they are going to come after you." Brad walked out.

"Willy!" Massey bellowed.

Willy came to the door. "Yes, sir."

"I want him followed."

"Yes, sir." Willy fell in behind Brad, staying a safe distance from the target. He knew Brad would identify him. He didn't care. He just had to make it look official. His goal was to get Brad alone. He wanted out of everything. Massey had just given him the perfect alibi.

He followed Brad to the church. He walked through the door of Faith Fellowship. It was one of the few churches still standing.

This was also the first time in his entire life he had stepped inside a church. He followed the sound of people talking. The room got quiet, and everyone shut up as he walked into the room. He walked up to Maxwell. "You've got to get out of here. This is the first place they'll look. What are all of you people doing here in this church? You have to hide."

DC stepped forward, angry at the sight of Willy. "What do you care, man? Aren't you one of the guys whose been doing all of this stuff. You're the guy who delivered Paul and John to the executioner. Why are you here?"

Max quieted the commotion. "I'll vouch for Willy. No matter what you think he's done, he's a good guy."

"Oh yeah," DC challenged. "Then why is my pastor dead?"

Willy looked stricken. "I'm sorry, I shouldn't have come here. You better get these people out of here."

"Wait, Willy, why did you come here?" Max asked.

"I wanted to make sure everyone was safe." He looked around the room. "You may not believe me, but what happened this morning is one of the worst things I've ever witnessed. And I'm not the only one who feels that way. Bulldog knows, he understands how it is."

Brad stepped forward. "Listen, you don't have to leave. We are all hurting from what has just happened. If Max trusts you, I trust you. And any help you want to offer will be appreciated."

"I was ordered to follow you here." Willy looked at Brad. "There'll be more. The safest thing you and Max can do is be anywhere except where all of these people are. You have to separate. They know you and Max are behind all of this. If they catch you all in a room together, they will assume killing everyone will take out whoever is blackmailing them, as well as the Christians. For them, that's a win-win."

"He's right," Max agreed. "Brad, we have to let DC and the others evacuate everyone out of here. That's what I came here to tell you. Simon, you and Cole, get going. Justin, you have to go with them. Don't stop for anything, no matter what you hear. Brad and I will be fine. They may try to trick you into thinking we're in their custody. Don't believe it. Brad, let's go."

"I'm coming with you," Willy said.

Harry was intrigued. It was interesting to see Brad, Bulldog, and Willy leave the church together. He decided to find out what they were up to.

They had to take shifts evacuating their friends. Transportation was limited. They could only haul twelve people at once. They packed them into the back of the army truck that Max had confiscated for them. Large crates stood in front of them and the opening to camouflage the refugees. The crates were placed to block the view of anything else, then tied down. The space was tight. It was risky. They were virtually trapped if anything happened to the guys up front.

The others hid in the basement of Miss Millie's house, waiting for the return trip out. Rebecca and Sharon decided they would not be going. They knew Dennis would search the far regions of the country looking for them. They decided to behave as normally as possible. They went to Rebecca's apartment and acted as if they had no idea their lives were in danger. It was crazy, but this was better than hiding in someone's basement for the rest of their lives. "If we die, we die," they agreed.

Halfway to the camp they were stopped by a road patrol. Cole and Simon were dressed head to toe in army uniforms. Cole presented the papers Max had gotten for them. They looked in the back; nothing but crates. "We're delivering some supplies to the guys over in Fort Myers; they're expecting us this afternoon." After a few minutes they were allowed to proceed.

It was sweltering in the back. Cole was concerned for his passengers; he stopped in the country long enough to move one of the crates out of the way. The refugees filed out one at a time to cool off, stretch, and relax for a few minutes. "I know this is miserable for all of you, but it's just a couple more hours and we'll be at the camp. Don't worry, we're almost there."

The break was short. They had to quickly load back up. Simon helped him replace the crate. They drove from there directly to the camp. Their passengers were tired. Some of them were sick from the heat they had endured. They were given care and allowed to rest.

"We have to go back," DC told their friends. "This time Justin and I drive. You guys have driven all day. Stay here and rest up. Tomorrow you take the next shift." They agreed. DC and Justin dressed in the uniforms and headed down the mountain to the waiting Christians. DC didn't want to alert Miss Millie's neighbors so they parked the truck down the street from Miss Millie's. Justin stayed with the truck. DC crept down the street to the house for the others. "We can't take all of you; there's still too many." Some volunteered to stay behind, others were scared and wanted to leave immediately. They drew straws. The short straws stayed behind.

They slipped down the street, guided by DC. When they reached the truck Justin was waiting to help them into place. "Back here," he said.

April was terrified. "I can't, I'm claustrophobic."

"Listen, April," Justin took her hand. "You have to. This is better than being beheaded. You can do this."

Her husband, David, helped her, "We're alone together, honey. It's just you and me out for a romantic drive. Don't think about the space; just sit here next to me. You'll be fine." She nodded, slowly lowering herself into the place next to her husband. He wrapped his arms around her protectively. "You're with me. Nothing bad is going to happen as long as we're together. Just focus on God's presence and his love and protection."

The crate slipped in front of them; April felt panic rising. She started to scream, everything went black. She woke up to the sound of the truck engine. He was holding her, cuddling her. "It's okay, April. You fainted but you're fine now." As odd as it was, she had stopped feeling panicky; their place behind the crates seemed roomier than she had imagined. She leaned against her husband and fell asleep. It was early morning when they arrived at the camp. They drove directly to the cabin, moved the crate, and helped their friends out.

Cole and Simon were ready to make another pickup. They jumped into the truck. Unfortunately, on the main road they encountered a roadblock. They waited with the other traffic. Everyone on the road was being questioned and asked to show the proper papers. They looked overhead; helicopters were buzzing the outlying areas. They were searching for someone? The guys became more nervous as they got closer to the authorities. "What's going on?" Cole asked as the guard examined his paperwork.

"We're looking for a couple of criminals. They're wanted for terrorism. They blew up a military facility last night. They won't get far. One of them is injured. He won't be able to run for long in that condition."

"Do you have a picture? What do they look like?"

The guy held up a picture of Max and Brad; there, in bold letters, were their names and descriptions. "Have you seen them?"

"No, I can't say that I have. You say they blew up a military facility?"

The officer nodded. "We'll catch them, don't you worry."

"Where'd you last see them?" Simon asked.

"We last spotted them about twenty miles from here." The officer stopped to speak into his walkie-talkie. "You two guys can go." Cole put the truck into low gear, slowly driving away.

"We have to help them," Simon said.

"Do you think they would head for the pickup point near the river?" Cole asked, trying to anticipate what Brad would do.

"It's possible. They might head that way, hoping we would think to look there," Simon suggested.

"Let's try it." Cole turned right, taking the country road.

~

Max and Brad hid in the tall grass in the shade of the grove of oaks, waiting for help. Max applied pressure to Brad's wounded leg. "This will stop the bleeding. But you can't go any further."

Brad winced from the pain. "What if the boys don't think to come looking for us?"

"Don't worry about that. Dennis has the roads blocked. And he's combing the rocks for us. He might as well be sending out an SOS. There's no way the boys won't know we need help. This is the most logical place for them to look for us."

ESCAPE

The sun was just getting hot when Brad and Max heard the unmistakable sound of an army truck rolling toward them. Max whispered to Brad, "Wait here, I'll make sure it's them." To his relief, the truck drove right up and parked just twenty feet from him. "It's them, Brad," he said, waving to Cole and Simon as they drove up. They jumped out of the truck. "Brad's hurt." Max said, "Help me with him." The guys followed Max to Brad.

"Boy, I'm glad to see you guys." Brad beamed.

"We ran into a roadblock. This was the only place we could think to look." They lifted Brad, carrying him to the back of the truck; Max jumped in next to him. "We'll have you back at camp in no time."

"What about the road block?" Brad asked. "I'll take you around the back way. Hold on, it's going to be bumpy."

Harry watched them through his binoculars. Since he had been following them, he knew for a fact that they had not blown up a military facility. "It looks like Dennis is up to his old tricks," he said to himself.

He began to chuckle. Watching Brad with his friends, he mused, *This guy is more fun than a barrel of monkeys.* The truck pulled out. He followed the guys, keeping a safe distance from them. He didn't want to arouse suspicion.

Cole turned onto a gravel road just short of the roadblock. Every bump hurt, causing Brad more pain. But they rocked back and forth until they reached the camp.

Ron watched the army truck return early. He didn't like seeing that they were being followed. He studied Harry through the scope of his rifle. King lay beside him. His ears perked up. He raised his head and began to growl quietly. Ron looked over at his companion. King looked up, listening to Ron. "I think this guy is going to have to have an accident."

Sarah was relieved to have Brad back in the safety of the camp, bum, leg, and all. Once she was able to take care of him, she knew he would improve. He was resting. She heard a disturbance outside and decided to investigate the problem.

"He has to leave now. This guy is going to get all of us killed! He's one of them. They can track us down just by following that device in him. He has to leave."

Cole's face was flushed. He was angry. He objected. "Max is our friend. He has risked his life for us time and time again. If it wasn't for him, half of the people here would be dead by now."

"It's the rules of the camp," Mr. Haskell insisted.

Cole looked over at Maxwell; his heart was in his eyes. "I'm sorry, Max."

"Don't bother saying it. I know I'm leaving." Max's pride was hurt. "Justin, would you please show me how to get off this mountain?" Justin followed Max, heart sick. They walked down the trail to the pickup.

Justin was angry. "It's not fair, Max. Those guys had no right to talk to you that way. None of us would ask you to leave."

"I know, Justin."

Sarah returned to Brad's side to care for him. He was restless. Halfway awake, he asked, "Where's Max?"

"He left, Brad. He didn't want to put anyone in danger." She avoided mentioning that Max was driven away.

"That doesn't make any sense. Why would he leave? The device has been scrambled."

"What do you mean?" She wasn't sure of what Brad was trying to tell her.

"You know Max's partner, Willy. He's kind of a whiz kid with computers. He's figured out how to scramble the device so badly no one can get a fix on the wearer's position. He fixed it for Max before we left town." Brad began to laugh. "He even set it so that every time they tried to zero in on Max, the signal would lead them back to Dennis Billings. Max called it his going-away gift."

"Do you mean there is no way they can trace him here?"

"That's right. Why do you think they couldn't find us hiding in the brush? The helicopters were out looking for us because it was malfunctioning. That Willy is sharp."

"Oh, Brad, we just made a terrible mistake."

"What are you talking about?" It was his turn to be confused.

"Max didn't just leave. He was run off. Justin is showing him the way down the mountain right now."

"We have to stop them. Max has nowhere else to go. They'll kill him if they catch him."

Brad tried to get up. "Help me up," he barked. She let him rest his weight on her as he hopped out.

"What have you done?" he asked the camp of refugees. "He would never put any of us in danger. Cole, you and the boys go after him. You find him and bring him back now!" Brad pointed at the spot in front of him.

Mr. Haskell began to give a detailed report of the dangers of helping a disgraced member of the regime. "They'll come looking for him."

"You miserable coward. That man is worth five men just like you. If anyone leaves here it isn't going to be him. If you had asked him, I'm sure he would have told you he still has the device; but it has been scrambled. He can buy and sell like any of the others; but he is virtually untraceable. As far as the regime is concerned, the man's a ghost."

Cole looked stricken. "Brad, I'm sorry. He didn't say anything about that. He just left."

"Then you better go after him and bring him back before he thinks we have thrown him away like all the other people he has trusted. He saved my life and everyone who was released instead of being killed. They all owe him their lives as well."

Cole and Simon decided to run. They had to catch up before Justin took off with the pickup. Justin had just finished uncovering the old Ford when he heard someone running toward them fast. "Max, Justin, wait up. Hold on, don't leave," Simon and Cole were calling out to them.

The guys stopped in front of Max. "Man, you should have told us," Cole bent over trying to catch his breath.

Max looked at them. "You boys aren't in very good shape. You really should go for a run now and then."

"Very funny, okay, we're sorry. We want you to come back."

"What about the device?" Max asked.

"What device? You could have saved a lot of drama just by telling us about that."

Max sniffed. "I have no desire to be where I'm not wanted."

"None of us does, man. Do you think you're the only one of us who has been unwanted? Justin here was a thief. He can tell you stories about how he stole just to eat when his mom was high. No one wanted him. He had grandparents but they left him there. And the system, man, he learned all about that. Didn't you, Justin?"

Cole looked deeply saddened. He began to confess something he had never told anyone. "Do you know why I never mention my mom? I mean, a kid is supposed to have a mother who loves him. That's what you're supposed to have. Well, I didn't. My dad raised me because my mother didn't want me. She told me to my face. Most of us have a story. We've moved on. Maybe it has been easier for us since we're still young. But I think it's time for you to let go of your past and stop waiting for people to reject you. You have a family. We're your family. You became one of us the day you agreed to help. You belong, Max. We all love you."

Max was physically moved. He looked away trying to control his emotions. "You're right. I should have spoken up." The guys covered the pickup and walked back to camp.

"What about that guy, Haskell?"

"Don't worry about him. Brad told Haskell that if anybody had to leave, he would be leaving first." Simon laughed. "You guys should have seen Brad. I thought he was going to throw that guy off the mountain, right then and there. What can I say? The guy loves you, Max."

Back at the camp apologies were made. Haskell agreed that he should have given Max the chance to speak before demanding he leave. Max agreed he should have explained.

Harry had been watching the comings and goings of the camp through his binoculars. He was intrigued by what he saw. There was a garden, some animals, a cabin and a cave that were obviously being used for shelter. "Brad, you sly dog." He laughed. Something touched his back.

"Friend, I suggest you don't move. Why are you here?" Harry started to turn around.

"Not a good idea, pal. Stay where you are. King, guard him." A German shepherd dog stepped up beside him. The low, menacing growl convinced Harry he should remain still. From behind him he could hear someone walking. "Now, I'm only going to ask you these questions once, so you better convince me you aren't lying, or you're going to have yourself a very bad day. Who are you and why are you here?"

"I'm Harry. Brad and Max know me. I'm something of a friend of theirs. Max and I used to work together. You can ask them yourself. I'm sure they wouldn't want you to kill me."

"Well now, this is the thing. You see, whether or not you live isn't actually their decision to make right now. I'm the one who says who comes and goes on this mountain. And I haven't agreed that you should be here. If they're your friends, why are you sneaking around following them? I'd be careful how I answer that, if I were you." Ron sat comfortably on a rock, gauging Harry's response.

"Well, we aren't exactly friends."

"I didn't think so."

"But I'm not here to hurt anyone. You see, I'm something of an investigator. And Brad has been a challenge for me. I knew he was up to something, but I could never figure out what it was. I just wanted to see where he was going."

"Well, friend, you know what curiosity did for the cat. It seems to me you're on real shaky ground."

Harry was getting concerned. "Look, buddy, I promise you I just wanted to see where he was going."

"But by coming here you have endangered my friends. Now, how can I let you leave knowing that all you have to do is talk to the wrong person and everyone of those fine people is in danger of losing their lives? I'm sorry, buddy, but it's you or them."

"No, wait. Just ask them. Ask them if they want you to kill me." Harry was sweating, "Man, what kind of a Christian are you?"

Ron answered, "Well, Harry, I'm not a Christian. Not everyone who is running from the Antichrist is. You see, I'm probably more like you than any of them. And I don't think you are trustworthy." King growled as he heard someone coming their way.

Mac emerged through the trees. When she realized a stranger was on the mountain she looked terrified. Ron motioned for her to come close to him. Harry turned around to look at his enemy. Ron stood in front of the girl. "Who is he?" she asked.

"He says his name is Harry; does that sound familiar?"

"Harry, yeah. He's the guy who has been following Brad."

Ron smiled. "Well, Mackenzie, it looks like he's found him. Harry, you wanted to talk to Brad and Max; it looks like you're going to get your chance."

Maxwell watched Ron approaching the camp with Harry walking obediently in front of him. "What are you doing here, Harry?" he asked in a very unwelcoming tone.

Brad was sitting just inside the cave. Max brought Harry in to talk. "How'd you find us?" Brad asked.

"I saw you at the execution yesterday. I liked those guys. Dennis had no right to kill them. I have to admit I was curious, so I decided to follow you. I know you guys didn't blow up the military facility. I can testify to that."

Max didn't trust him. "So you liked the preachers; we all did. That doesn't mean you wouldn't turn us all over to the authorities as soon as you leave here."

Ron was aggravated with himself. "I should have just taken care of you while we were alone on that mountain."

"This guy's crazy! He's been threatening me from the moment we met."

"Because he caught you following his friend," Max said with emphasis.

"Look, guys, I don't want to hurt anyone. I've made up my mind. I'm finished with Dennis. I just wanted to know where it was you were going. I promise I won't tell anyone I was here."

Brad was decisive. The rules were set. "It's like this, Harry. Anyone coming here has to be chip-free and blindfolded. No one is allowed to actually know where this place is. By coming here uninvited you have violated the rules. We can't allow you to leave. But you can't stay with the chip either; so, we have a problem."

Harry looked at Max. "He has a chip. Why is he here?"

"Max is one of us. We trust him."

"Pastor Paul and Pastor John would have given me the benefit of the doubt."

"Give him to me," Ron said, "Let me have him; when I'm done with him, I promise you he won't be a problem for you."

"Thanks for the offer, Ron, but I believe we can work out a compromise. Harry, when Willy gets here he can deactivate the device. If you leave this mountain, your friends will think you're one of us. If you stay here you will be treated fairly. But you can never leave; however, that leaves us in danger until Willy arrives."

"I'll take him to my side of the mountain. At least he'll be away from the group. I'll tie him up. He won't be leaving," Ron said menacingly.

Max nodded. "I think that's reasonable."

Brad wasn't sure. "Look, Ron, I believe in self-defense and defending your own against present danger, but I don't want this guy killed. We have to be different from the world."

Ron was still regretting his decision to talk to Harry instead of having taken immediate action. "Brad, it's your call. But I have to tell you there's something about this guy I don't trust. I think he's capable of just about anything if he thought it would benefit him."

Harry knew his life was in danger. "Listen Brad, I'm going to come clean. I never intended to harm you or your wife. I just needed a diversion from the preachers. Dennis was focusing on them. He put me in the slammer just so I could get close to them. When you came along with your wild story about a safe house, I knew Dennis would take to following you around. I'm not proud of it, but I wanted to change his direction. I liked those guys a lot. I haven't met anyone quite like them. And then it got personal; you were an interesting challenge. You stayed ahead of me. After a while it became something of a game."

Brad nodded his understanding. "Can you live without leaving the camp?"

Harry agreed. "I don't like it, but if that's the only option, I guess I'll have to do it."

One by one, all—with the exception of Ron—who glared at Harry said yes. "It was agreed."

"Then, for now you go with Ron." Brad watched Harry for his compliance.

Harry looked at Ron with some obvious distrust then turned back to Brad. "Sure."

Once again, Cole and Simon began the trip back to Miss Millie's. Deseraie joined them. She couldn't stand the idea that

Rebecca and Sharon were alone, unprotected. Max hadn't exactly taken her into his confidence, but he assured her that Dennis was no longer a threat to anyone. She had the guys drop her off at the apartment. "You get the ladies and be ready. We'll be back for you as soon as we collect the others."

The day's events had delayed them. They knew the people waiting would be concerned and frightened. They slipped into the house and down the stairs. Way in the back of the basement was a small group of believers huddled together shivering. "Come on, let's go. I'm sorry we're late; we were held up. Everything is fine; we'll tell you about it later. The important thing is that we get you out of here now."

One by one they loaded into the truck. The crate was placed in front of them and secured. Simon drove this time. They circled by Rebecca's apartment. Deseraie had succeeded in persuading them. He stopped the truck. Cole jumped out to help them load up and then tied down the crate.

They drove all night, avoiding known check points, taking the extra time needed to bypass the traps. They used the same-side road they had used the previous day. They bumped and rumbled up the mountain until they reached the cabin. Slowly the newcomers emerged from the truck. Their faces wore the pain of their circumstances. Deseraie worked through the early morning, comforting and welcoming them to the camp. "You're safe now."

Willy had made plans to join them as soon as possible. Max and he had talked it over. Dennis would never give up. They had no choice but to stop him. He dropped a packet off at the offices of Joey Maldoni. He stepped onto his Harley. Brad had given him directions to the camp. He should be there soon. For the first time in years he felt free.

It was still early in the morning. The sun had not yet come out. "What do we do here, Deseraie?" one of the ladies asked.

"We work to stay alive and we wait for Jesus to return in the great appearing. If we work together, the wait will soon end. And we will be here when Jesus returns. This is our hope. This is our hearts' desire."

The little cave was lit by the fire. The warm embers reached up to comfort the battle-weary souls. "Jesus will appear in his Glory." Tears of joy and hope sprang from deep inside of them. "Soon," they said one to another. "He will return soon to set up his kingdom!"

After their meeting, Harry reluctantly followed Ron to the other side of the mountain. It was getting late. The sun was going down. Ron handed him a piece of dried venison. After dinner, Harry made a pretense of going to sleep. Ron knew he was up to something but played along to see what Harry would do. After an hour of pretending to sleep, Harry quietly slipped out from under his blanket. He tiptoed to the mouth of the cave. Ron watched him in the moonlight. He smiled to himself. He laid a cautioning hand on King. The dog watched concerned as his master allowed their captive to escape.

Swoosh. "Aah!" They heard the sound of Harry's mistake.

"Well, King, he's not going anywhere." He settled back down. This time, convinced Harry was otherwise occupied, he ignored the cries for help and allowed himself to sleep.

The next morning, Ron walked to the front of the cave. Looking up he saw Harry hanging snared, as pretty as you please, in his net.

"Get me down from here!" Harry demanded.

Ron walked past him as if he couldn't hear him. He moved to his woodpile, placed the wood, and started a campfire without looking up. Completely ignoring Harry, he quietly filled his coffeepot with water and grounds. Harry waited a good part of the morning before he tried again to convince Ron he would not run off.

"I don't believe you, Harry. I think you would slice my throat and take off in a heartbeat. I just don't feel up to guarding you today."

"Okay, so you and I don't get along. That doesn't mean you can just leave me here."

Ron bent down next to the fire and poured a cup of coffee. Sipping it slowly, he said, "I think I'm going to have to kill you one day, Harry." His voice was soft and thoughtful. "I know I promised the guys I wouldn't; but you know I don't believe a word that comes out of your mouth. You're going to have to convince me I'm wrong, or your days on this earth are numbered."

"What makes you think you can?" Harry challenged.

"I'm good at it," Ron said just as a matter of fact. "It's just something I do well."

"Me too," Harry confessed. "Don't you think we can change?"

Ron shook his head. "No, I think guys like us never change."

"Maybe you're right," Harry said with a sad, haunting sound in his voice. That was the first time Ron believed the guy was remorseful. He looked up at Harry. "Let me down; I won't try to escape again. I promise."

Ron cut the rope holding Harry in the trap. "Ouch!" Harry yelled as he hit the ground. "You could really hurt a guy doing something like that."

"I told you, no one comes on this mountain without my say-so. Oh, and by the way, there are traps everywhere. If I were you, I'd watch my step."

Harry stretched himself. "Do you mind if I have a cup of coffee?"

"Help yourself," Ron invited

"How is it you have coffee all the way up here? I know you can't buy it."

"Max has been buying it for us. He sees to it we have a lot of the comforts of home."

"Including the ammunition for that rifle?" Harry pointed to the gun resting beside Ron.

"I notice you have quite a lot of it in the back of the cave."

Ron nodded. "And plenty of guns, if I need them," he looked at Harry, a threat still looming in his features. "I brought that stuff in when the regime came to power. Since then I've continued to replenish it at every opportunity."

Ron stood up, stretched, and walked to the mouth of the cave. Harry followed him. Mackenzie emerged onto the distant trail. From here they could both see her coming. "Watch what you say. I don't want her upset," Ron warned.

Harry smiled. "Well, maybe. I'll just walk back with her now. You won't kill me in front of her."

Ron agreed. "I won't, but he will." Ron pointed to King, who stood up and growled, watching him.

She walked up to them, smiling. "Hi, I thought I would come to visit. How are you two doing?"

They smiled, pretending to be friendly. Ron said, "Harry here seems to be settling in."

Her eyes caught a glimpse of the trap still lying on the ground. She looked at Ron a little apprehensively. "I'm glad you didn't kill him. I want you two to get along.

We're having a party today to celebrate the deliverance of our friends and to welcome them to the mountain. We want you to come"—she looked at Harry—"both of you. Willy got in late last night. He's still sleeping, but you can come over and get Harry's device deactivated anytime. Please promise you'll stay to visit." Ron and Harry looked at each other. Ron agreed.

"It will be so great; Mrs. Collins has been cooking all morning. We're going to have music and everything, so bring your guitar." She hurried back down the trail. Turning back toward them, she waved. "I'll see you later."

Willy worked quickly, "There it goes," he said as the device became useless.

Harry rubbed the spot where it still protruded. "Thanks, Willy." It was strange how instantly free he felt. He had forgotten what it was like to move around freely without a rat like Dennis being able to track you down.

Ron watched Harry from a distance. "I don't like it," Ron said quietly to Max. "He hasn't had a change of heart like you and Willy. He was just here sneaking around and got caught. Who's to say he won't take off down the mountain as soon as he gets a chance?"

Max mulled it over. "It's been bothering me too, but we can't just kill him, not without hurting Brad and the others. Come with me." They moved toward Harry. He was sitting near the campfire drinking a cup of coffee. Max poured himself a cup then knelt down resting himself in a squatting position in front of the fire. He spoke softly. Only Harry, Willy, and Ron could hear. "I need to tell you something, Harry. I had Willy take care of some business before he left town. I had pictures of Dennis with Joey Maldoni's wife. I also had some pretty incriminating evidence of you skimming off Joey's receipts when he had you out collecting for him. Willy dropped them off at Maldoni's office before coming here. I'm sure Dennis is dead by now. And chances are pretty good; Joey's men are out looking for you. This place is your one and only chance to be safe. Back home trouble is waiting for you. And you need to know we love these people; if you try to harm them, any of the three of us will stop you. It's just that simple."

Harry's countenance changed to one of fear. "So I'm trapped," he said.

Max nodded. "That's one way to look at it. You could also see it as a second chance. Brad believes we can change. I'm sure going to try. I hope you will too."

The joyful sound of music filled the air. Cole was strumming a
banjo while Mac and Simon pulled their bows across their fid-
dles. Ron heard Mac call his name. He picked up his guitar and
began to play. David joined them. The crowd of refugees began
to congregate near the music. Harry and Willy moved closer.
Music filled the mountain. Soon they were singing songs of hope:
"Let Go, Let God" by Linda McAbee, "Amazing Grace" by John
Newton, "Rock of Ages" by Augustus M. Toplady, and "Tell Me
the Story of Jesus" by Frances J. Crosby. Willy pulled out his harmonica and joined them. Sarah and Shelby picked out the har-
monies. Cole added his tenor to the mix. One of the newcomers
sang base. There, on the mountain, away from the terror of the
world, they all worshipped God.

"Play a song, Mac," Karen requested. "Play us one of yours."

Mackenzie nodded to Simon. They silently counted off the
music in their heads; in unison they slid their bows over the
strings. The heavenly sound of the twin violins sweetly pierced the
air, denying the struggling of life. Even in the darkest moments
there is music. The notes stroked the souls of the battle-weary
Christians. Carly closed her eyes, allowing the music to wash
away the hardship of the past days. God had delivered them. This
was not a time of sorrow. God was restoring them to hope. The
notes, sweet and soft, wafted through the air. Worship began to
permeate the group. In the middle of it all, one lone voice rang
out gentle and clear,

> I have decided to follow Jesus;
> I have decided to follow Jesus;
> I have decided to follow Jesus;
> No turning back, no turning back.
> The world behind me, the cross before me;

The world behind me, the cross before me;
The world behind me, the cross before me;
No turning back, no turning back.

—S. Sundar Singh

Harry had never heard anything like it. Tears filled his eyes; at this moment he could almost believe.

Cole called them all to order. "We are privileged to have new to our camp Pastor Shelby and Pastor Carly. Ladies, do either of you have a word from the Lord? We would love for you to share with us what God has laid on your hearts."

The group relaxed, preparing to listen. "Go ahead, Shelby," Carly encouraged.

Shelby stood to her feet. "We all want to thank you for welcoming us to this beautiful place of refuge. Carly and I are overwhelmed by the love we have seen poured out to us and all of our friends. We are deeply touched by your generosity."

"As we traveled here, I couldn't help but think of our husbands, who have gone on to be with the Lord. They have also been welcomed by the residents of heaven. They have walked through the gates of pearl and now they are walking the golden streets of glory. Just think. They have seen the face of our precious Savior! They've hugged our loved ones and are rejoicing with angels!" She smiled as she continued, "Heaven, no tongue can do justice to its rare beauty. It is indescribable. And we will one day soon join them! Hallelujah! But not yet, God has kept us through times of great tribulation for his glorious purpose."

"Soon Jesus will come in great glory! He will split the eastern sky. There, standing on the Mount of Olives, he will cause an earthquake. It will divide the land, forming a gorge. The children of Israel will run into it for safety" (Zechariah 14).

"The Bible tells us in Philippians 2:10–11, 'That at the name of Jesus every knee should bow, of things in heaven, and things in earth, and things under the earth; And that every tongue should confess that Jesus Christ is Lord, to the glory of God the Father.'"

"I can't wait to see him coming! I believe the whole world will witness his arrival. I'm thankful I still have the opportunity to witness him set up his earthly Kingdom." Tears filled her eyes. "You see, we still have a great hope! And we are close to seeing his return!"

Praise rang through the mountain as men and women of God glorified him!

THE BATTLE OF ARMAGEDDON

While the refugees waited for Jesus to return, the world heated up. Countries all over the earth were suffering. Plagues, hunger, and financial devastation were the norm. The men who attended this meeting did so in secret. They were no longer content to wait. They needed to act. Their countrymen expected it of them. They had to come up with a plan that would solve the world's economic needs.

They had for many years considered the wealth of the country to the south. As they sat in counsel, they knew they were no longer content to allow such wealth to remain unexploited. The Jews were an affront to the world. How could they allow such a people to continue to exist? The thought of them made the men at the meeting fume. They hated the very existence of these people. Finally, they would accomplish what generations before them had failed to do. They would wipe them from the face of the earth!

The general laughed, low and calculating. "They hide in the mountains like rats in caves. We have taken their land. Jerusalem is now in the hands of our beloved leader. We have to draw them out. We must make them leave their holes so we can finish them off. They are small in number but clever. They have used our own weapons against us. Their last attack took out our computers. This has crippled us. If we allow them to continue, they will push us back into the stone age." The general continued his analysis. "I don't trust them. I know their general. He is very shrewd. He will move to destroy us."

Something in the general's voice fell short of courage. "You sound as if you are afraid of him," The prime minister of the north was annoyed.

The general didn't care what his so-called friends thought of him. He had fought with these people before, "There is something unearthly about them. They know what we are planning even when we are in our bedrooms. They stay one step ahead of us. And if that isn't enough, every time we plan to bomb them the winds change. It is as if God really does protect them."

"Foolishness!" the Antichrist bellowed. "I am surrounded by foolishness. You are like the old women who tell wives' tales. So you think they are protected by God. Then why do they cower in the mountains? Why are they hiding in caves? I don't care what it takes. We will infiltrate them. We will get someone on the inside if we have to. I want them out in the open, facing me. This thing is going to end. They are not going to stay 'the chosen people' forever. God has forgotten them. Has he protected them from me? Do you see them here now? Where are they? As soon as I raised my hand against them, they ran away!" His face changed as he scoffed. "Their God has left them and they know it. Now is the time to fight. They will face us or we will blow them off their mountain."

The northern prime minister spoke. "It would be a worthwhile undertaking. They have caused the whole region to be in turmoil. Who are these Jews to determine who may or may not live in their country? They hoard these natural resources with no thought for the rest of the world."

One consultant spoke up. "They continue to try to claim title to an area that is rightfully their neighbor's. Also the value of the minerals in the Dead Sea is estimated to be somewhere in the trillions of dollars."

The northern prime minister made a noise as though he were growling. He nodded his agreement with the Antichrist. "Then we fight," he said. Each man at the table gave his consent.

The Antichrist smiled condescendingly. "Then we are agreed," he said. "How long do you estimate the battle will be, General?"

"Israel is in dire straits. None of the other nations will raise a finger to help them. All of the others will follow your decision. They are alone and vulnerable. We have them on the run. Left alone to plot and plan, they will mount another surprise attack. If we meet them in the open, they cannot defend themselves against all of us. Now is the time to strike." The general finished his assessment with considerably less enthusiasm than his friends.

They looked at the map, enchanted by the idea they would soon rule the world. He was not so convinced. He had studied the Jews. He knew their military strategist. It would be a bloody, gruesome war.

Looking around the room, the northern prime minister observed, "Why does it take so many to conquer these people?"

The demonic spirit that possessed the Antichrist did not tell them that he had been fighting this fight for thousands of years. Satan did not want to disturb their euphoria concerning their chances. They were blind to his past failures. He couldn't risk their waking up to reality just before this momentous challenge. He had to keep them on the hook. They must continue to believe it was in the bag. This time he wasn't taking any chances. He would pull together the largest military force of all time. There was no way he could lose.

The past months had been unbearable for the world; the many plagues left it scared and polluted. The locust-like creatures tormented men daily. These men protected themselves from the stings by wearing protective clothing and staying inside.

The Antichrist listened as they all agreed. "We will move in first. Our friends from the east will join us in the valley. We will be ready to move as quickly as possible." They all knew it would take time to assemble a military force of this size. They would start immediately.

The Antichrist had broken his treaty with Israel almost forty two months ago. He stiffened as he remembered the end of the seven years was upon him. During that time he had also pursued the Christians, killing them mercilessly. Of the Christians, only small cells were left. They were insignificant to him now. His main objective was to grind Israel into the ground. Satan, who now inhabited him fulltime, was gleeful. At last he had Israel in a choke hold. They would not escape. He would exterminate them!

Israel was backed into a corner. "What will we do?" they asked themselves.

The Israeli general was once again talking to the same politicians whom he had walked out on before. "We have no choice but to defend ourselves. They are moving in to annihilate us."

He watched helplessly as every army came together at Armageddon. He moved his military force to the front, placing his best trained men in strategic positions. He worked to quickly arm every man and woman. "We must fight!" he said.

The other army was innumerable. They gathered before his people like lice covering the ground. The general bowed himself. There, in the presence of his people, he looked up to heaven and called on the God of Abraham, Isaac, and Jacob, "You, oh God, are mighty!" He remembered the stories of Moses, Joshua, and David. "You have protected Israel from their enemies throughout history. It is by your Word that our nation was established. I now plead with you to fight for us once again." His people began to pray with him. There, in the face of their most difficult circumstances, they sought the God of their fathers.

The prayers of the general, his soldiers, the hundred and forty-four thousand, the people of that nation, and the Christians who had survived ascended into heaven. The seven years have passed!

TRIUMPHANT!

"He's coming! He's coming!"

John and Paul watched in stunned silence as all of heaven began to bow. Neither one was certain how it happened, but they both found themselves on their faces prostrate before the King of kings! The pomp and splendor of the KING OF KINGS AND LORD OF LORDS (Revelation 19:11–16) was beyond comprehension. There, before them, rode the King of all the heavens! His mighty white stallion pranced with the majesty of a horse carrying the most magnificent King of all times.

In unison they opened their eyes to steal a peak at the majestic scene. They did not want to miss the arrival of the Lord Jesus on this momentous, holy occasion. Raising his head, John glanced at the most spectacular sight he had yet witnessed in heaven—there, in royal splendor, rode Jesus, the Great! The King that all mankind had waited for! People all around them were praising Jesus with shouts of joy. Their cheers rang out throughout the heavens. He was the mighty, victorious, God of all the ages. On his head were crowns of great splendor. His royal vesture, dipped in blood, glistened with the light of a thousand diamonds. His name is called the Word of God (Revelation 19:13). His holy countenance lit up the heavens with a light brighter than the sun. On his garment and his thigh, a name was written: KING OF KINGS AND LORD OF LORDS! (Revelation 19:16).

Behind him were the armies which were in heaven. They followed him, also riding on white horses. Their garments were of fine linen, white and clean (Revelation 19:14).

"Jesus! Jesus! Jesus! The Great!" Cheers rang through the Holy City.

Their minds quoted John the revelator as they watched, "And I saw an angel standing in the sun; and he cried with a loud voice, saying to all the fowls that fly in the midst of heaven, "Come and gather yourselves together unto the supper of the Great God" (Revelation 19:17).

"That ye may eat the flesh of kings, and the flesh of captains, and the flesh of mighty men, and the flesh of horses, and of them that sit on them, and the flesh of all men, both free and bond, both small and great" (Revelation 19:18).

Looking down at their own garments, they realized they also were dressed for the battle. Two angels handed them the reigns of two beautiful white stallions. Their magnificent manes fell long and flowing. Their beautiful white tails, also long, were touching the streets of gold. The two men jumped onto the stallions with ease and expertise, as though they rode daily. In their hands were swords that glistened bright in the light of the King.

The Great King held his sword high in the air. His stallion, waiting for the nudge of his master, reared up in anticipation of the fight. His beautiful white coat glistened in the light of heaven. The long mane swept down the side of the magnificent beast. His tail, long and beautiful, dusted the streets of gold. His mighty hoofs raked the sky, ready for action. The King and his stallion worked as one. A shout from the King of kings shook the atmosphere. "Charge!" rang through the skies of eternity as the Mighty Warrior of Glory descended upon his enemies.

⸺

The armies of the earth had been gathering for days. They had planned this event to the last detail. Satan had been actively working with signs and wonders of his own. He would win this time. They were innumerable. They had arrived from the north, south, east, and west. These were the peoples of the earth who rejected Almighty God and persecuted his people. They were enemies of God and his army, the foolish, haughty men of the earth who dared to rise up against the King of kings, who actually believed they could stand before so mighty a King! They were clueless gnats, who foolishly thought themselves a match for the "Creator of all the earth."

The generals of the vast army sat comfortably, waiting to attack. Their men watched and waited also. A loud screech rang through the air; another, then another bird called out. Soon they were accompanied by the sounds of thousands of birds. The commanding officer and his men looked up. Vultures began to circle while birds of all varieties watched. They darkened the sky. Some of them continued to circle, while others landed in places high above, in trees and on distant rocks. They stayed close to the military force. They lined up as though they were preparing to watch the war.

The officers trembled as they studied them. Fear filled their hearts as they looked at them. Something was wrong. They sensed it. The commander's heart pounded in his throat. His eyes widened as he continued to watch the gathering.

One colonel paled at the sight. "Sir, they're waiting for the battle." Some of his companions stopped to watch. All of them were bewildered by the strange behavior of the birds.

The commander stated. "They're here for a feast."

Jesus arrived at the battle. His sword was in his right hand. Out of heaven came the Lord of Glory! He split the eastern sky, taking his place between Israel and his enemies. His army was one so vast the men of the earth looked with stunned amazement as the army of the Living God filled the atmosphere as well as the stratosphere. A voice of thunder roared from him. "Who are you to come against the children of the Living God?" He placed his foot on the Mount of Olives. The earth rumbled, then quaked, forming a canyon wide and deep. His people, the nation of Israel, ran into it for safety.

The men of the earth began to shake. The strength of their bodies failed them and they fell to the ground. The God of Glory stood between them and eternity. They were destroyed by the awesome, all-consuming word of God! Jesus raised his voice. "You are conquered, Satan; remember the cross! My blood has bought the victory! You are unable to stand!"

Unearthly screams pierced the atmosphere as demons cried out in pain. They shook uncontrollably as they coward before the presence of Jesus. They were powerless at the blast of his nostrils. His army, those who filled the heavens, worshiped the King of kings with shouts of praise and adoration, saying, "Holy, Holy, Holy, Lord God Almighty!"

The men of this world stumbled with fear, trying to escape the God of all. "Hide us!" they cried out to the rocks, trembling as they looked everywhere for shelter. "Hide us from him who sits on the throne!" Abandoned by the devils that had driven them to this place of doom, they bowed powerlessly before the Great God and King. They ground their teeth in despair. "Hide us from him who sits on the throne." But there was nowhere to hide. They were in the presence of his royal majesty, King Jesus! They could not run. All they could do in that moment of indescribable despair was to bow to him as they shouted, "YOU ARE THE KING OF KINGS AND THE LORD OF LORDS!" (Philippians 2:9–11). Their words ripped from their mouths as they faced the majestic deity of Almighty God! His magnificence overwhelmed them. They could not breathe. They could not move. They were without hope. They were unforgiven!

The beast and the false prophet, who had deceived many with his enchantments working demonic miracles, looked around panic-stricken. "Where can we hide?" They screamed! Fleeing, they tried desperately to escape the Lord Jesus! From out of nowhere appeared a hand. It picked them up and flung them into hell; the fire blazed as torment reached up to catch them! (Revelation 19:20).

They heard a loud cry. From Satan rang a bloodcurdling scream! The voice of hopelessness, dread, and fear, "No!" was the resounding scream. It sliced through the air, reeling with terror. "No! No! Ahhh!" he screamed as the dragon, Satan himself, was bound for a thousand years by an angel who carried the key to the bottomless pit and a great chain in his hand. The angel worked quickly, securing Satan with the chain. He dragged his struggling captive to the gates of the bottomless pit then hurled him into the abyss. He shut the door to the cell. The sound filled the earth as the monstrous door clanged loudly and closed, shaking the ground around it. The angel locked the door and sealed it for a thousand years (Revelation 20).

Satan's folly started long ago, in the far regions of heaven. Then he was known as Lucifer. The lights of the city are gold, white, and silver. There is a rainbow that is always visible. Its colors of red, blue, purple, yellow, green, and some unknown to mankind are vivid and cannot be described by mere words. It shines continually over the throne of God. At the bottom of this magnificent rainbow is a street of gold. There really is a place where gold and rainbows meet each other.

The music of that city is one of tremendous beauty; it is the best of all the music ever heard. When it is performed it drifts through the city. Its melodies take the breath of every soul listening and catches the heart of the battle-weary men and women who have the privilege of hearing it. This music is without flaw, played by the best musicians with the best instruments. The singers sing the songs of the heavens. Their hearts pour out over every note, bringing the listener and singer to perfect worship. God himself stops to listen to the majestic sound made by his very own servants. The angels join in perfect harmony as they joyfully raise their voices to the King of kings.

There in the back of the chambers of glory sat the most regal, magnificent angel of them all. He was living perfection. His outward beauty was something to behold. He was the chosen angel. He was loved by all. He had been created by God to hold an eternal position of grace. His magnificent wings carried music in them; as he walked, the shuffle of his wings caused music to chime. His voice shook the heavens as he sang praises to the God of all creation. Yes, he was the one chosen to sing praises to God. He was created to acknowledge God's perfect deity. He was the worship leader in heaven. He was not like the other angels. The calling on his life to minister praise to God was greater. He had been given a gift so beautiful the angels in glory longed to be like him. But he was not happy. He was not pleased with the gift or the calling God had so graciously bestowed on him. He had too much.

Like many of us who grow up thinking we are entitled to every gift our parents give to us, he is selfish, self-centered, and has no concept of the magnitude of the blessings God has endowed him with. Sin changed his wisdom to foolishness. His pride grew daily. It diminished his common sense. Ultimately, it changed his perfection to flawed beauty. He knows no boundaries. He believes himself to be equal with God. The creature equal with God? He's delusional. Jealousy and pride have taken over his soul. The once happy worshiper, who poured out his heart with love to the God of all, has turned from him. As time passed by, his love became eroded with sin. Pride, jealousy, selfishness became his character. He spoke to his friends. Some of them agreed with him. God expected too much, wanting to be the only one who was worshipped. They were the ones who spent their days working for God. Where was their recognition for all of their days of service? As they continued to be disgruntled, heaven took on an unfamiliar atmosphere.

The great angels, Michael and Gabriel, watched these troublemakers with contempt. The brothers they once admired were now no more than enemies. The beauty of heaven was disturbed by the hateful spirits of these angels. Lucifer's influence over them and others grew daily. They were constantly bombarded with the ongoing politics of those rebellious angels. What had started as mere envy had changed their hearts to something detestable. Those angels wanted to do the unthinkable. They were not content to serve God; they wanted more.

The Bible quotes Satan, then known as Lucifer, son of the morning, "For thou hast said in thine heart, I will ascend into heaven, I will exalt my throne above the stars of God: I will sit also upon the mount of the congregation, in the sides of the north: I will ascend above the heights of the clouds; I will be like the most High" (Isaiah 14:13–14).

Even as he rallied the foolish angels, he could not help acknowledging God was "the Most High."

We often want more. Don't we? We find it hard to be satisfied with what we have, thinking the grass is greener somewhere else. They were angels, but they made a calculated mistake. They failed to see that the God of love they knew is also the God of justice. He is holy. Nothing unclean can live where he is (Revelation 21:27). That is why we have to be born again. If we do not accept the gift of salvation, we will lose our souls. Romans tell us, "For all have sinned, and come short of the glory of God" (Romans 3:23). We have to understand what the rebellious angels did not: that God is just. He is holy. And nothing unclean can come into his presence. His eyes are too pure to look on evil (Habakkuk 1:13).

We have no choice. We are flawed human beings. We can't live a life of perfection. Our only hope is Jesus, the one who came from God. He is the son of the Most High. He mercifully took our place. He paid the price for our sin (John 3:16–17). He is the only mediator between God and man (1 Timothy 2:5). When he died in our place on the cross, he took the hand of man and placed it in the hand of God. We are his property. He is the sin-less son of the Living God, yet he gave his life for us!

Satan's rebellion brought one-third of the angels of heaven down to his level. They gave up the love of God and heaven for Satan's lies. He could not exalt himself to be equal with the Most High. He had not created the heavens and the earth. He was banished from the kingdom of God forever. The Bible quotes Jesus, "And he said unto them, I beheld Satan as lightning fall from heaven" (Luke 10:18). Another scripture says, "Therefore rejoice, ye heavens, and ye that dwell in them. Woe to the inhab-iters of the earth and of the sea! for the devil is come down unto you, having great wrath, because he knoweth that he hath but a short time" (Revelation 12:12).

His goal is to take every person he can to hell with him. And that is where he is going. Hell was prepared for Satan and his angels (Isaiah 5:14). It was never intended for mankind. But we, as the foolish, rebellious angels, have followed him away from the throne of God. We have chosen the pleasure of sin, for a day, over eternity with God. We have sold our souls cheap; our souls, the part of us that God values so much. He gave his only son to die in our place so we could be rescued from destruction with Satan (John 3:16).

After, Satan sinned; he went to work in the garden on Eve. He told her the tree of the knowledge of good and evil, the one of which God said, "You will not eat of this tree," would make her like the gods (Genesis 3:1–5). She may have resisted his entice-ment for a long time until one day he got the best of her. And mankind has been paying ever since. Until she and Adam had partaken of the fruit of that tree they did not understand sin. They were naked in the garden. The Bible tells us God visited them in the garden. He walked and talked with them. They had a right relationship with God until they sinned (Genesis 2:19, 3:8–9).

After they disobeyed God, they saw their sin. They tried to dress themselves by covering themselves with leaves. God made them clothes from skins; he sacrificed the lives of innocent animals for them. It was more than physical nakedness they saw. They were ashamed. They recognized they were not able to be in the presence of God. They recognized his holiness. They saw themselves as unclean.

They were cast out of the garden. God could no longer trust them. Their disobedience had cost them everything. The most unthinkable thing of all was it cost them their relationship with God. That is the void we search to fill, even to this day. There is a deep cavern in the soul of man longing to be filled; and only God can fill it. But God did not cast them away forever, as he did Satan. He promised them Jesus would come to the earth and die in their place, that Jesus would reconcile them back to him. They started sacrificing those precious little lambs. It was a way of reminding themselves of God's promise and acknowledging they needed the blood of Jesus applied to their souls to cover their sin (Genesis 3 and 4).

We have the privilege of asking Jesus to come into our hearts and forgive us of our sins. It's that simple. He says, "Behold, I stand at the door, and knock: if any man hear my voice, and open the door, I will come in to him, and will sup with him, and he with me" (Revelation 3:20). Once we admit we are sinners and ask Jesus to reconcile us to Father God we are forgiven. All of our past sin is forgotten. He removes it from us as far as the east is from the west (Psalm 103:12). We are no longer servants to sin. We are new creatures in Christ Jesus. The Bible tells us, "Therefore if any man be in Christ, he is a new creature: old things are passed away; behold, all things are become new" (2 Corinthians 5:17). We are no longer separated from God. Jesus comes into our hearts. He lives through us. We are forgiven. Our eternity is changed because of Jesus!

Today, Satan plots and works, trying to fool us into believing he is higher than God. He is a liar. He longs to be worshipped. He is still the creature trying to be something he is not. For all of his scheming he is still going to hell. God has foretold it in the Bible (Revelation 20:10). He will be bound. But for now the Bible warns us, "Be sober, be vigilant; because your adversary the devil, as a roaring lion, walketh about, seeking whom he may devour" (1 Peter 5:8).

He is not our friend, not even to those individuals who are foolish enough to follow him. He wants to destroy us and keep us from the presence of God. He is jealous of the relationship we can have with Father God. He threw his relationship with God away for sin. He wants to keep us from the joy of God's presence and love, because he knows he can never again experience it. He is cast out. He is cast from the presence of the Lord… forever! The word echoes through the abyss of hell falling, falling, falling, deeper into the cavernous darkness of unending separation from God. He can never again experience God's grace! He is bound and condemned!

The armies of the enemies of Christ mourn as he defeats Satan with the sword of his Word. They watch, devastated, as Satan is bound by the angel and helplessly thrown into the pit. Men's hearts fail them for fear. The army of evil, rebellious souls, cannot face Jesus. They as Satan are doomed. They cannot stand before the Lord of Glory. His glory fills the heavens and the earth! His splendor cannot be contained by the mere size of this earth or even all the planets. He is glorious and his glory fills the earth; it ascends into the heavens filling the corridors of the entire universe establishing his throne on earth.

Those who are left to fight face overwhelming fear. The King of Glory speaks; his undisputable Word captures their rebellious hearts. Doomed, they die, slain with the sword of his Word; as they do, the birds descend upon them. Great and small, all of God's enemies die in the valley of Armageddon.

Cheers ring out as the people of God, the vast army that fills the sky, move aside. That beautiful city, the New Jerusalem, descends from heaven. It rests in its place destined from the beginning of time. It is splendid. The glory of Almighty God fills it. Nothing unclean can enter into it. It is the royal city of the Kingdom of Almighty God on earth, his habitation! Jesus, the Mighty, the Magnificent, Righteous King has won the victory!

EPILOGUE

Deliverance

On a distant mountain stood a group of young men and women, their friend and his dog, Carly, Shelby, and several other men and women who have turned to them for help. They saw in a sky vision the arrival of Christ with his great army, the battle, and the victory. They joined with the rest of the world, bowing and proclaiming that Jesus is the "KING OF KINGS AND THE LORD OF LORDS!" (Revelation 19:16). They watched in wonder as the New Jerusalem came to rest in the place of the city of David. Their hearts pounded wildly as they, one at a time, then in unison, began to say, "He's here! Jesus is here! It's over, we're free! Praise God, we're saved! No more sorrow, no more pain; Jesus our Lord has won the victory!" As they bow, humbled by his magnificent royalty, they proclaim, "He is the KING OF KINGS AND LORD OF LORDS!" (Revelation 19:16 and Revelation 21).